The Price Of Redemption

Gavin R Dobson

Librario

Published by
Librario Publishing Ltd.

ISBN : 978-1906775285

Copies can be ordered from retail
or via the internet at :

www.librario.com

or from :

Brough House
Milton Brodie
Kinloss
Morayshire
IV36 2UA

Tel / Fax : 01343 850178

Cover design and layout by Steven James
www.chimeracreations.co.uk

Printed and bound in Great Britain

© 2011 Gavin R Dobson

The Author has asserted his moral right to be
identified as the Author of this Work. No part of this book
may be reproduced, stored in a retrieval system, or transmitted
by any means, electronic, mechanical, photocopying, recording,
or otherwise, without permission from the author.

The Price Of Redemption

To : Billy Underhill, my Texan Mentor
and
my Father, for his comments

Chapter 1

The Boeing hit the tarmac and decelerated with a roar as its thrust reversers deployed and a hundred tons of hurtling metal slowed to walking pace. Mark exhaled, relaxed his grip on the arm rest and considered the day ahead. A nearby flight attendant sat with her legs crossed, her shoe perched provocatively on one toe, and babbled,

"Welcome to Newark Liberty International Airport. Local time is 10.25 and the temperature is 82 degrees. Thank you for flying with us today. We know you have a choice and we look forward to serving you again in the near future. Enjoy the rest of your day and have a safe trip to your final destination."

A slender African chauffeur stood in the International Arrivals hall displaying a placard marked *Mark Telford.* When Mark emerged from Customs the man took his bag and led him silently to the deep blue limousine parked in a bay across the road.

They sped along the Pulaski Skyway over railroad yards, container terminals, old landfills and miles of polluted tidal flats before burrowing under the Hudson River through the Holland Tunnel. Mark hated tunnels. One deluded fanatic bent on martyrdom could fry a thousand people here at the right time of day. But inward traffic was light that afternoon. It wasn't their style to explode themselves for one limo and a few random passenger cars.

Mark checked into an executive suite on the south west corner of the 26th floor of the Centennial Hotel. To the west it commanded sweeping views of the derelict World Trade Center site. Beyond that site stood a complex of bluish mid-scrapers known curiously as The World Financial Center. To the south Mark singled out the sleek black skyscraper at the head of Wall Street where shortly he was due to meet the gentlemen from Central States Financial.

He stripped and stood under a cold, sharp shower for ten minutes. He washed his black hair and scrubbed the grime of travel off his wiry body. Trailing water, he wrapped a towel around his waist, slumped onto the king size bed and pressed a button on his cell phone. It rang twice.

"Yeah- Blazerman here."

"Yeah – Blazerman, Telford here." Mark mimicked the New York abruptness of his friend.

"Mark, my man! I'll be damned. Been a long time. What are you up to? Where the hell are you?"

"I'm in New York. Short notice, Frank, but are you free this evening for dinner or a drink? I'm here on a quick assignment and it would be great to catch up."

"Sure- I'm working on a deal but should be done by dinner. Get yourself to Au Château on East 58th at nine o'clock. You alone?"

"Nine sounds good, yes, I'm alone."

"I may have a lady friend with me. Depends what she's doing tonight."

"The same lady friend?"

"Laura, from Texas?"

"No. Last time it was Claire from somewhere in the Midwest."

"Oh yea, Dubuque. She was a real pistol. I fired her. Look Mark, gotta go. Au Château at nine? It'll be great to catch up."

Mark grinned and clicked off. He hadn't seen Frank for a year. One pleasure of being on the road was catching up with old friends around the world. Nothing was bleaker than a day of business meetings followed by a solitary hotel suite, room service and soulless surfing around TV channels.

He buttoned his white cotton shirt and slipped into a silk-lined pinstripe jacket. He always wore Savile Row for important meetings. It gave him a confidence that only English bespoke tailoring can offer.

Twenty minutes later he stood before a wide marble reception desk in the airy glass atrium of one of the most powerful financial conglomerates in the United States. Central States Financial was the child of the marriage of multiple insurance companies, investment firms and regional banks from Ohio to Kansas. They'd moved headquarters from St Louis to New York City ten years earlier to take their place in the World Financial Capital. The move was intended to be their springboard to global financial domination.

A uniformed Hispanic commissionaire greeted him,

"Good afternoon, sir, can I help you?"

"Mark Telford, from Appletree Capital Management. I have a meeting with Steve Shilson, Chief Executive of CSF, at 2.30."

"You need a building pass. Got photo i/d?"

Mark handed over his dog-eared British passport. The commissionaire leafed through it and told him to look at the bulbous miniature camera mounted on the reception desk. A minute later, Mark was handed a plastic pass card with an elongated black and white photo of himself on it.

"Swipe it at the turnstile and take the elevator to the forty fifth floor. Someone will meet you in the lobby of the Executive Suite."

The elevator door slid open to reveal an expanse of dark hardwood flooring and Chinese rugs. The letters *CSF* were inlaid in light wood in front of the reception desk. A circular oak table surmounted by a sculptured Lalique vase filled with lilies and bamboo stems dominated the lobby. English colonial and sporting prints were spaced along the panelled walls. The decor was typical of the faux baronial style with which American financial companies liked to gentrify themselves.

A slim woman was standing by the elevator as Mark emerged into this hushed world. She wore a black silk trouser suit and a finely embroidered white blouse. Short auburn hair showed her *gamine* features to full effect. A string of pearls around her slender neck completed the impression of businesslike style and femininity.

"Hi, I'm Nancy Lindstrom, Compliance Officer of CSF. I'll be joining you in the meeting this afternoon."

"Good to meet you. I'm Mark Telford." Her handshake was firm and confident.

She smiled, "Follow me, please." She led him into a boardroom situated on the southwest corner of the floor. A highly-polished ebony table spanned the room, the padded beige back walls were hung with full size prints of The Quorn Meet and an indeterminate Hunt Breakfast. On the outer wall, floor-to-ceiling windows gave an Olympian view of river traffic teeming on the Hudson. New Jersey shimmered in the distant haze.

"Help yourself to a coffee or other refreshments. I'll get Steve and be back in a few minutes."

Nancy gestured to a side table containing a stainless steel coffee container, china cups and a plate of assorted *petits fours.*

Mark poured a coffee and surveyed the boardroom. Black leather chairs were spaced around the table. He wondered what momentous scenes had been played out there. The door swung open. Three men entered briskly, followed by Nancy, who closed the door after them. They carried sheaves of papers. The leading man strode across the room to Mark.

"Mark? I'm Steve Shilson. We're real thrilled you took the time out of your busy schedule to cross the Pond and meet with us." He gripped Mark's hand enthusiastically. "This is Dick Cosway, our Chief Operating Officer and Bill Tuckwell, Director of Marketing. You already met Nancy, our Compliance Officer." They nodded to each other.

Steve Shilson was tall, lean and athletic. He was in his late forties with short reddish curly hair greying at the temples. He wore glasses, which lent him gravitas, but a suntan marked him as an outdoorsman. A golfer perhaps, or an ocean racer.

"I'm delighted to meet you all." Mark was struck by their direct manner, energetic enthusiasm and firm handshakes. Also by the way Cosway and Tuckwell imitated Shilson's immaculate grooming. Thick pepper-and-salt hair sat sculpturally on their heads. Their nails were manicured and hands unblemished. These were evidently not men who swung from the trees with their children.

"Please- sit down. Take your coat off."

Mark removed his jacket and fitted it over the back of a neighbouring chair. Shilson sat instinctively at the head of the table. Cosway and Tuckwell were on Shilson's right, opposite Mark. Nancy positioned herself discreetly three chairs to Mark's left.

"The reason I asked you to visit us in New York," Shilson began, "is to continue the conversation we began by conference call a month ago. We could have spoken on the phone or by email, but I like to see and touch my business partners before firming up deals. It's all about chemistry." Mark watched Shilson attentively.

"I'll get straight to the point. I want to propose to my board that we appoint Appletree Capital Management to manage a new mutual fund for CSF. We will seed it with $300 million dollars. Its objective will be to invest in equity markets outside the United States. The fee will be a flat 60 basis points to Appletree. We expect the fund to grow rapidly, because CSF believes that international markets represent a powerful strategic diversification for American investors. The Fund should reach a billion dollars within a year, assuming good performance. But of course, we need you to agree before I make my proposal to the board."

"That's fantastic news," Mark said, "I'm stunned that a decision's been made so quickly. I thought today was to be the next round of a beauty parade." A tide of euphoria welled up inside him. A quick mental calculation concluded that $300 million would generate an annual fee of $1.8 million. One billion dollars meant $6 million of fees a year.

"We researched twenty firms and short-listed three at the same time as you. They're all great firms but we decided on Appletree for four reasons. First, you have no other business in America, so we won't fall over each other on this side of the Atlantic. Second, you're small and our business will be real important to you. Third, you've got excellent performance. Four, small as you are, we feel good chemistry between your folks at Appletree and our folks at CSF. That counts for a lot."

How Shilson determined 'good chemistry' between CSF and Appletree after one phone conversation and a ten minute meeting was a mystery to Mark.

"So, if we've got a deal, I'll leave you all to nail down the details. I gotta take a conference call in five minutes." Shilson glanced at the elaborate Swiss chronometer on his wrist, pushed back his chair and leaned over to Mark.

"Deal?"

"I need to discuss it with my colleagues, but as far as I'm concerned, we should have a deal." Mark shook Shilson's hand. "I'd like to thank you for your confidence in us. I know we'll do a great job for you. I'll get back to you within 48 hours."

"Sure. Take your time. We look forward to welcoming you to the CSF Family of Funds. We'll enjoy working with Appletree and you in particular." Shilson breezed out of the room.

Dick Cosway filled the vacuum. He was in his early forties, preppy, slim, the same height as Mark and well-dressed. Pale blue eyes set in a ruddy complexion signalled a short fuse. There was something about this man which warned Mark not to joke around. Quite unreasonably Mark associated him with a senior boy from his school days, a bully with a high-pitched voice whom he'd avoided assiduously on the playground.

"Anticipating the approval of your colleagues, I wanna run you through the process." Cosway slid a single sheet across the surface of the table, headed *Timetable for launch of the CSF International Fund.* The first item was *Secure Agreement with Appletree.* He then passed over a thick document, entitled *Draft Investment Management Agreement between Central States Financial ('CSF') and Appletree Capital Management ('ACM').*

Mark was flattered that Appletree's name was already associated, in writing, with CSF's global strategy. "We should be able to tick that box shortly." he said.

"Take it back to your folks in London, show it to your lawyers, make whatever changes you want and get it back to me as soon as possible."

Mark flicked through the 80 page document.

"Once the Management Agreement's signed, we'll file this document with the SEC."

Another wad of paper skidded across the table, entitled *Prospectus : CSF International Fund.* "Read this through carefully for accuracy, particularly the pages on Appletree. Be sure it fits with your understanding of what we're trying to do here. The prospectus is 90% boilerplate so it's not as scary as it looks."

"Boilerplate?"

"Boilerplate's all the standard crap that's bolted on to documents to make them look impressive. In reality it's lifted straight from the wording of previous prospectus filings. Nobody knows who drafted the first bit of boilerplate. Moses, perhaps." Cosway gave a modest smile.

"I'll read it carefully. Anything else?"

"Yea. To expedite this documentation, CSF will pick up the tab for your legal and advisory expenses relevant to this transaction. That means our management contract, your registrations and even headhunting fees for new talent if you need it to make this work. If we do business together we expect you guys to ramp up." He paused, adding, "Vertically. We recognize that you're much smaller than us, which is why we'll cover your initiation costs." He passed over a third document outlining this offer. "CSF always works with the top attorneys on the Street. We expect you to do the same in London."

"We use Howe and Smithsen in The City of London."

"Yea?" Cosway had evidently not heard of the venerable City law firm. "So long as they understand we're in a hurry to bring this fund to market. My department will run the business side of our relationship with Appletree. We have a great team of lawyers and accountants. If you ever have questions, let me know and I'll point you in the right direction. My team will pay all expenses incurred for this deal, calculate your fees and make the required payments each month. You will liaise with me on all business matters that arise between our firms. Do you have any questions?"

Mark shook his head.

"No? Over to you, Bill."

Bill Tuckwell was about the same age as Cosway. He was over six feet tall with pale blue eyes. He was distinguished in a way but had a comic, paunchy face that quivered when he spoke. He wore round-lens spectacles hinting at Ivy League aspirations and which tried a little too hard to say "Trust me." He gave an engaging smile. "Referring to the *Timetable for launch of the CSF International Fund*, this kicks in once the prospectus has been filed." He held up a copy of the document for Mark's reference.

He continued, "The prospectus can cook with the SEC up to 90 days before a fund gets approval, so there's no great rush yet. Once it looks like approval is gonna happen we wanna move fast. As Steve said we'll seed this fund with three hundred million dollars, but what makes a fund fly is the amount of money it brings in from retail investors". Mark glanced at the timetable of thickly-packed meetings in cities across the United States, starting in mid-September.

"It's June 9th. Assuming you turn these documents round fast, followed by a smooth regulatory ride, we'll be positioned to launch this sucker in early October." Tuckwell looked at him with a triumphant expression.

"What does a launch look like?"

"Once we get SEC approval I need all Appletree's key investment staff for two weeks over here. CSF has 80 wholesalers around the country who will arrange meetings in 135 cities, addressing groups of financial planners, stockbrokers, consultants, pension funds and sophisticated investors. Breakfast in Milwaukee, lunch in Chicago, dinner in Memphis, that kinda thing. Each wholesaler will prepare a list of his local prospects and every single prospect will be covered during the initial marketing phase. We market to every population center in the United States. Your guys will visit places they didn't know existed."

"Sounds like a presidential election campaign."

"Yeah, but without the bullshit. It takes a lot of planning, so the sooner we move on this stuff the better." He gestured at the pile of papers in front of Mark. "I'd better get a move on, then. Is there anything else I need to deal with at this stage?" Mark leaned forward and looked around the table.

Nancy spoke. "Yes, there is. As Compliance Officer, I will need to assess the regulatory fitness of each key person at Appletree. I know you're regulated by the Financial Services Authority – the FSA – in the UK, but we may need to get you registered with the NASD and get you compliant over here too."

"NASD?"

"That's the National Association of Securities Dealers."

"How does the NASD fit with the SEC?"

"The SEC was set up in the Great Depression to protect investors and promote stability in markets. The NASD was set up to promote the *observance* of federal and state securities laws among market participants."

"So the government makes the laws, the NASD ensures that everyone understands and obeys them?"

"Exactly. The NASD designed a number of exams, called *Series* exams, which focus on different aspects of the industry. You may need to pass some before the launch. There's a strong element of ethics in the Series exams. The objective is to raise awareness of the best standards of commercial behavior among practitioners."

"O-Kay" Mark wished he hadn't asked the question. "Not that we doubt our professional behaviour, but it might involve a lot of work in a short time. How much time would we need to pass these exams?"

"I need to check. It's possible that your UK qualifications will cover you in the US. On the other hand you may need to take some NASD Series Exams to get you registered over here. They're not too difficult."

"I'll take your word for it."

"You can call me on any aspect of our relationship, as I work closely with Dick." She leaned across and handed Mark a card. He noticed her short red-polished nails.

"Just to recap my understanding of who does what, Dick takes care of legal documentation and the structural stuff leading up to the launch of the Fund, as well as our business relationship, Bill orchestrates the marketing and Nancy takes care of compliance and is another business resource. Have I missed anything?"

"You got it Mark." Bill replied. "Feel free to contact us any time and we'll put you straight. I look forward to working with you on this project." They shook hands.

Nancy walked back to the elevator with Mark. "I hope that wasn't too much to take in at one meeting."

"We have a lot of work in the next couple of weeks. But for the moment I'll focus on just one thing. We've won an enormous account with an established franchise and I'm going to celebrate." He paused, barely resisting the impulse to invite her out to dinner. "I look forward to working with you, Nancy."

"I look forward to working with you too." she replied. She gave a smile and a small wave as the doors of the elevator slid shut.

Chapter 2

Mark left the building and strolled down Rector Place towards the river. He cut through the World Financial Center, entering an atrium like a botanical greenhouse. Full-height palm trees stretched skywards in the vaulted glass space. He exited onto a promenade by the marina where two colossal Bermuda-registered yachts were moored. The glaring afternoon sun hurt his eyes. He walked a few hundred yards to a shaded avenue of linden trees and sat on a bench with a view of the river. Water taxis skittered back and forth to New Jersey.

The message light blinked on his mobile phone. "Hi, this is Graham, calling to wish you the best of luck at the CSF presentation. Call back when you can and let me know how it went." It was nine o'clock in London. Mark hit the recall button.

"Graham Birch speaking."

"Hey Graham, this is Mark. I've just come out of the CSF meeting. I hope you don't mind me calling you at home at this hour."

"Not at all. How did it go?"

"We got the business." Mark tried to sound deadpan.

"You're joking! I thought this was just a preliminary meeting."

"They said they'd researched twenty investment firms and chose us out of three on their shortlist. They like the fact that we have no other business in the USA and won't be competing with each other. Second, they like that we're small and hungry. Third, they're impressed by our performance thanks to you. Fourth, they think we have great chemistry. Quite how they figured that, after only meeting me for ten minutes, I'm not sure."

"Well I'll be damned! What happens now?"

"We have a ton of paperwork to review. I've got a draft management agreement, a draft prospectus, a timetable for the launch of the CSF International Fund and so on."

"Where did you leave it with them?"

"That I get back to Shilson with a decision within 48 hours."

"How much money are we talking about here?"

"They're seeding the Fund with $300 million, but we'll be doing a due diligence tour around the USA before the launch. The idea is to raise billions."

"Bloody hell! That multiplies our assets overnight. When are you back in London?"

"I'll be in the office at 8 the day after tomorrow. Can you organize a staff meeting first thing? In the meantime I'll read the paperwork and have a more informed view of what's happening by then. I'd appreciate if you kept quiet about this until we're all in the room together."

After the call, Mark sat immobile as the enormity of the meeting washed over him. He would have to move fast. The little company he founded was about to be catapulted into the big-time. He would need to hire more staff, upgrade software and computer systems, buy more research, find a bigger office. "But all that can wait," he thought. Jet lag rolled over him like mist, "I'll deal with it in the morning".

He unknotted his blue silk tie and folded it into his jacket pocket. A powerful tugboat ploughed proudly up the Hudson against the current, twin plumes of diesel exhaust boiling skywards from its smokestacks. Mark dreamed back to his early career as a young financial planner in Slough.

There had been no hint in those days that he was destined to be, or even wanted to be, a financial wunderkind. He had moved south to university in the time-honoured way of thousands of ambitious young Northerners. The resulting Cambridge law degree impressed a financial planning firm enough to offer him a job. His role was to structure life assurance deals to pay for their clients' retirement, inheritance tax liabilities, their grandchildren's school fees or ideally, all of the above.

He'd lived near Datchet in a damp house by the Thames shared with a group of local lads. The house was directly under Heathrow's flight path, so close to the airport that the wheels were down for their final approach as the planes thundered past. Every ninety seconds from 6 am to 10 pm, day in, day out, heavy jets screamed overhead.

Mark was head-hunted by a venerable brokerage firm in Fenchurch Street. It was the era in the City when the rules of the game were changing rapidly. The traditional qualities of privilege, restraint and good connections were being overrun by hard-driving, balls-to-the-wall, predatory young financial hooligans who used their wits to wring vast sums of money out of the system. Although he'd thought he belonged at the traditional end of the City's values, Mark flourished in the new environment. He'd bought a flat in West Kensington and soon traded up to a duplex on Prince of Wales Drive. He'd spent long stints abroad, setting up offices for the firm and growing their business in Hong Kong and New York.

When Mark's employer was acquired by a dull European bank it became clear that his entrepreneurial style would become mired in the glutinous internal politics of a vast metropolitan institution. Six months later Appletree Capital Management was born.

There was no tradition of chasing money in his family; his forbears were university teachers, solicitors, doctors, middle-ranking army officers, farmers, churchgoers – Church of England on his mother's side, the Kirk on his father's. They'd have been astounded by his rapid ascent up the financial food chain. Many would have disapproved. Excessive wealth had not been so much vulgar, as irrelevant to them. His grandmother often told him that the most important role of a human being was to serve others. Leave the planet a happier place than you find it. By all means establish a lucrative career, but use it as a platform for improving the world, not self-enrichment. *All else is vanity,* he heard her words from beyond the grave.

Mark wasn't married, but had recently admitted to himself that he might be open if the right person came along. He was a young forty two. He jogged prodigious distances, swam daily and took part in every sport he encountered on the way – in the previous six months, he had biked in Hawaii, surfed in Cornwall, skied in Verbier, climbed Lochnagar, sailed off the New Jersey shore and played village cricket in Kent. The appeal of a companion to share some of these activities was growing.

Enjoying the balmy June air he strolled southwards along the Hudson River Walkway, passing The Holocaust Museum through landscaped gardens. He cut across Battery Park, the Southern tip of Manhattan, and ambled north across Wall Street to Fulton. He browsed in a cavernous bookstore and bought a book on sale for $1. It looked entertaining. It was by an Italian journalist warned by a fortune teller not to fly for a whole year.

Frank Blazerman sat at a table facing the entrance of Au Château. He leaped to his feet and hugged Mark like a brother. "Hey Buddy, how the hell are ya? You look great. Hey, I want you to meet Laura. She's heard all about you and's dying to meet you."

Laura looked nonplussed. She was a large dark haired woman with smiling deep brown eyes. She rose to the occasion, hugging the Best Friend she had never heard of before entering the restaurant ten minutes earlier. Frank had gained weight around the middle; his face had become more rounded and puffy, like his Eastern European ancestors. Yet he still exuded the same unassailable masculinity, personality and humour that Mark remembered.

They'd first met fifteen years earlier as co-speakers at an economics conference in Chicago and became firm if unlikely friends. Frank, the burly financier from a blue collar family in Akron Ohio and Mark, the over-refined Brit, had shared a podium at the Palmer House, debating the topic of limiting Japanese imports. They'd disagreed on protectionism, but their common ground in finance and a taste for off-colour, raunchy jokes had cemented their relationship. Mark loved Frank's ebullience and, in the way of all firm friendships, they picked up the threads instantly after a long absence.

"What the heck are you doin' in New York? It's so great to see you, isn't it Laura?" She smiled. "Waiter! A bottle of chilled Veuve. So what *are* you doing here?"

"I came to make a presentation and came away with a deal."

"Sounds real literary. Who with?"

"We'll be sub-advising an international equity mutual fund for CSF, starting as soon as we get the paperwork done."

"CSF? You better watch out." Frank's expression clouded.

"What do you mean?"

"Known for being sharp operators on the Street. Excessive pay-offs to intermediaries, aggressive lobbying, that kinda thing. It's said that a lot of politicians are in their pocket. They've been investigated for insider trading, market manipulation and hot money flows but somehow they always manage to come out smelling of roses."

"I vaguely recall a scandal a few years ago but the people I met seemed professional, efficient and successful."

"Yeah, they fired their CEO a while back and they look and sound like nice guys, that's for sure. Just be careful, buddy. I don't want to see you come unstuck after a long and illustrious career. You've worked too hard." Frank wiped the corner of his eye.

The conversation ranged across more interesting topics. Laura was the business editor of a well-known East Coast fashion magazine and gave some revealing insights into the world of journalism in New York.

Mark tumbled into bed at one o'clock, exhausted with jetlag and slightly drunk. He picked up the book he'd bought earlier but only mustered the energy to read the first two sentences:

> *"Life is full of opportunities. The problem is to recognize them when they present themselves, and that isn't always easy."*

Chapter 3

Thirty six hours later Mark was sitting in his London conference room with Appletree Capital Management's nine staff. His partner, Graham Birch, had organized the meeting but not disclosed the topic for discussion. He had kept his word to Mark and stayed silent before the meeting.

Graham was tall, wiry, fair-haired and laconic, a Kentish man married to his university sweetheart and the proud father of three young sons. He was the seventh generation of Birches to live in the same house in Goudhurst and to have attended Tonbridge and Pembroke College, Oxford. Graham was responsible for designing, maintaining and implementing Appletree's investment models. Analytical, deliberate and thoughtful, he was unflappable in all market environments. He was temperamentally ideal to be a Chief Investment Officer.

"Good morning." Mark surveyed the expectant faces of his colleagues around the table. Sunshine streamed into the conference room with its oblique view of river craft plying the Thames. He was fond of his colleagues and felt protective of them. They had taken a leap of faith from safe jobs four years earlier to join his start-up at Appletree. Mark knew them socially. He had shared happy moments when children were born and commiserated when marriages turned sour. They were his family, in a very real sense. He did not have one of his own.

Mark and Graham were the controlling partners of Appletree and had authority to make all decisions affecting the firm. But they'd agreed at the outset that strategic matters should be open to discussion with staff. It was a courtesy and always useful to hear different views.

"I have some good news, and some bad news." Mark had decided to play this out. Graham kept a stern face.

"The good news is that Central States Financial in New York, otherwise known as CSF, the four hundred billion dollar behemoth, have appointed us to manage a three hundred million dollar, American-based international equity mutual fund."

"And the bad news?" Syreta Mehta, Appletree's Chief Operating Officer, fell for the bait.

"The bad news is that Central States Financial in New York, otherwise known as CSF, the four hundred billion dollar behemoth, have appointed us to manage a three hundred million dollar, American-based international equity mutual fund."

"What's bad about that?" Syreta looked puzzled.

Syreta was in charge of Appletree's investment administration and accounting. She was quietly efficient and always pleasant, a petite, impeccably-groomed young Indian mother with shoulder length brown hair and smiling hazel eyes. Her pale brown skin and slim figure sometimes excited Mark's fantasies. She was married, however, so his fancy stayed suppressed.

"Here's the picture. Right now we make a decent living managing two hundred million pounds for a broad range of clients. Our annual fee income provides a comfortable livelihood for everyone in this room. As long as we perform well, Appletree will continue to offer a career in congenial surroundings. The deal with CSF would multiply our revenues, but we would need to re-design our systems, hire new people, move into a bigger office and bend our whole culture to fit with American requirements. CSF assert that this account could rapidly run into billions, with massive financial implications for us, so we must accept that it could completely change our culture."

"Perhaps you could explain what that might mean, in practical terms." Syreta enquired.

"In practical terms," Mark replied, "Appletree will have to register as an investment advisor with the American regulators, the Securities and Exchange Commission, aka the SEC. You will need to visit Bismarck North Dakota to meet CSF's administration team. We will have to provide rotas of investment staff to support CSF's marketing and servicing efforts. Graham, Alix, Paul, Bob and I will need to spend time in the USA next autumn to cover every city across the country in a due diligence effort."

"What do you mean by 'due diligence effort'?" enquired Bob Berwick, a redoubtable stock-picker with twenty years of investment experience from Tokyo to Buenos Aires. Currently he was managing UK-based stocks for Appletree.

Bob tended to overdress for Appletree's informal culture, always wearing a dark suit, well-pressed shirt and silk tie, when the rest of the team would show up in jeans and tee shirts. He was one of those City professionals who was born forty. He came across as the office curmudgeon, but in truth had a lively sense of humour. He had a thick head of black hair flecked with grey and was overweight from two decades of lunches hosted by stockbrokers in expensive locations.

"What it means is that we will have to exercise due diligence in ensuring that the fund is professionally represented and distributed around the USA. CSF will take care of the logistics. We will travel with their regional reps – they're called wholesalers – responsible for making sure that potential investors have prospectuses and understand the risks of investing internationally through Appletree. Your job would be to give speeches and presentations on our investment strategy to their clients."

"What would we talk about?" Alix Newlin asked anxiously. She covered Continental Europe and some emerging markets for the firm.

There was something of the spinster about Alix. She had a fine bone structure but had lost her waistline to years of slumping before computer screens and long haul business trips. The absence of a boyfriend and a reputedly shambolic personal life made her the butt of jokes in the brokerage community. She was a solid colleague, however, and the experience she gained while working for an investment trust in Dundee often balanced the performance of her more flighty colleagues at tense moments in the markets.

"We'll put together a standard presentation that we're comfortable with, and fit it into CSF's marketing format. Obviously they'll be looking for a personal flavour too – for example you could talk about the economic conference in Poland you attended last month."

"What about the administrative role we'd be expected to provide?" Syreta enquired.

"We'll need to provide administrative support to CSF's back office. The Fund will be priced every day at 4pm New York time. That's 9pm our time. While we can organize automatic price feeds for most stocks in the portfolio through Reuters or Bloomberg, I guarantee there will be occasional glitches that need to be dealt with personally at unsocial hours. That could include public holidays : just because London is closed for a bank holiday doesn't mean it's not business as usual in New York. Does that answer your question?"

"When can I start hiring? It takes six months to find someone good and another six months to train them."

"As soon as we sign the agreement with CSF. They specifically offered to resource us to hire more staff. Dick Cosway said they'd expect us to 'ramp up vertically'. They mean business over there."

"What other changes do you see being foisted on us by these Yanks?" Paul McKay chimed in. He covered the Asia/Pacific equity markets for Appletree. He was the office moaner. Whatever the outlook, his glass was half empty. Graham had persuaded Mark to let him hire McKay six months earlier to fill out the team's coverage of the Pacific. Mark hadn't yet seen evidence of McKay's supposed investment acumen and was irritated by his lack of team spirit. But Mark had respected Graham too much to block the decision. He reasoned that McKay would report to Graham and that he, Mark, wouldn't have to deal with him.

"Our client response time will have to be faster at every level than it is right now. Some of us may need to take US Securities exams before marketing in the USA. Nancy Lindstrom, their compliance officer, is going to get back to me on that. On a lighter note we'll need to entertain visiting Americans in London. Investors like to visit their money managers on site."

"Particularly during the Golf Open." intoned Bob Berwick.

"I'll take care of them." Wendy, the young dark-haired receptionist, chipped in hopefully.

"Let's not get ahead of ourselves." Mark paused. "Now, I know we're all capable of handling the workload, but it's important to flag to everybody today that Appletree will change radically if we take this business. Things will never be the same again."

"What do you think, Mark? Is this something you want to do?" Alix enquired.

"Personally," he replied, "I think it would be fun. It will leapfrog us into the most dynamic financial market in the world with one of its biggest players. We're lucky because we have two good choices. If we stay as we are, we have an assured future. If we go with CSF we might all get rich, but Appletree's staff numbers could easily triple along the way."

"There are too many risks to taking this business. I've heard dubious things about CSF in the past. What if we hire the team, build up our overhead, and they fire us? Americans are notorious for pulling the trigger on people who don't perform in the short term." Paul McKay once worked in an American institution and was in no hurry to repeat the experience. He often regaled his colleagues at beer time about 'the fatuous nihilism of the American business culture.'

"The simple answer is, don't under-perform, isn't it Paul?" His colleagues laughed. "Appletree has always delivered good results," continued Mark, "and I don't see why that should change. If we take this business we should do so on the assumption that we'll keep it for five years. We can manage this contract to build out the business and diversify our client base. Nothing is certain. I was reading a draft prospectus for this fund on the flight back. It stipulates that either party can give thirty days notice to quit. But if we do a good job we should be assured of a long-term relationship."

"Thirty days!" exclaimed Alix. "It would be insane to make all these structural changes and be on thirty days notice at all times. We need more protection. It could bankrupt us."

"That's exactly why I called this meeting. I would feel better if everybody was comfortable before we took this decision. CSF has agreed to pay our transitional legal bills and I'm sure we could negotiate a year's expenses from them to ramp up. Remember, to a four hundred billion dollar company like CSF, spending ten million dollars on this kind of project is a rounding error. Our starting costs will be mitigated by the rapidly-growing fee income from the fund, so in effect we'd be building ourselves at CSF's expense."

"Why are they so keen to do business with us?" Bob Berwick looked puzzled. "If CSF is so massively successful why do they want to team up with our little . . . er . . . peanut firm in London? We'll be a big distraction for them, so why don't they simply hire the staff and build out the capability themselves?"

"I've already discussed why they like Appletree." Mark studied the faces of his colleagues. "CSF has no credibility in this field. We may be small, but we're well-known. They want to launch an international equity fund now, but it would take years to develop the capability themselves. It's more credible for them to hire Appletree now to get the job done. Other questions?"

"Yes, are there any differences between American and British mutual funds?" Graham enquired.

"Mutual funds are essentially the same on both sides of the Atlantic. If 10,000 shareholders each invest 1000 dollars in a fund, they are each entitled to 1/10,000th of the profits generated by the fund after tax, They own a mutual interest in the fund and can vote the percentage of their share ownership at investor meetings."

"I think we all understand what mutuality means, Mark. What about the regulatory, tax and legal differences?"

"There are tax differences for investors but CSF will keep you straight. You can study this prospectus, which should answer your questions." Mark waved the document in the air.

"Operationally we'll need to make changes, but I know we can make it work. I think this is very exciting and we should take the opportunity. CSF will contribute to our legal, accounting and administrative costs. If we're clever we could get them to finance a brand new Appletree and be independent of their revenue stream in five years. This project has my vote." Syreta admired Mark for his *chutzpah* and enjoyed being the technical enabler for his creative projects.

Graham weighed in, "CSF gives us the chance to expand dramatically and deals like this don't grow on trees. I'm confident we can make this work on the investment side. I definitely think we should grab the opportunity. I'm with you Mark."

"Thanks Graham. What about you, Alix?" He turned to the diffident bluestocking from Dundee.

"Well, I won't be obstructive because it wouldn't make a difference, would it?" she shrugged at her senior colleagues. "But I would like to express reservations, for the record, so that one day I may have the dubious pleasure of saying, 'I told you so!' Not that I want to, you understand."

"Point taken. Any other questions? No? Motion carried." Mark banged the table with an imaginary gavel. "Now, if you'll just stay for a few more minutes, I'd like to celebrate." He crossed the boardroom to the kitchenette, pulled a magnum of Bollinger from the fridge, scooped a handful of glasses from a shelf and placed them on the table. He unwired the cork and eased it off with a satisfying bang that left a silvery dent in the plaster on the ceiling.

"Cheers, everyone. Here's to a new dawn."

As his colleagues sipped the champagne, Mark announced, "This is excellent news. I'll phone New York this afternoon and get the ball rolling."

Chapter 4

"Can you please put me through to Steve Shilson? It's Mark Telford from Appletree Capital Management in London."

"Just a minute, I'll see if I can locate him."

Mark stared out of his office window, watching a pair of herring gulls squabbling over a morsel on a window sill in the building next door. The gulls lived off waste bins filled with dubious-smelling scraps from the remains of office lunches in the area. The disputed morsel looked like the dismembered part of a chicken.

Shilson's voice barked into the phone in New York.

"Hey Mark. How are ya? Sorry to keep you waiting, I was in a meeting that was difficult to break away from."

"No problem, Steve. Reason I'm calling is that I promised to get back to you within 48 hours with our response to your proposal."

"Excellent, Mark. Hope it's a positive one."

"We discussed it this morning and would be delighted to enter an agreement to manage an international mutual fund for CSF."

"Great news, Mark. Was the decision that hard?"

"Not for me. There was some healthy scepticism among the troops, but Graham and I convinced them. We're prepared to make the necessary changes to make this work."

"Fantastic news Mark. Look, I have to get back to my meeting but let me switch you over to Dick Cosway. He'll run you through the process from here. I sure look forward to working with you, Mark. I'll bring my clubs across the Pond next time and we can do a round at Saint Andrews. Get to know each other."

"I'm not much of a golfer but I certainly look forward to developing our relationship." Mark hated the way some Americans referred to the Atlantic as the Pond. It may have been funny eighty years ago, when first coined by Noel Coward, HL Mencken, a Marx brother or whoever. But today, the expression was dated.

"You Scotch are always humble about your golf. Last Scotchman I played said he was a lousy player and came in at six under par at Pebble Beach. Beat the hell out of me. Look, I'm going to transfer you across to Dick. Great news."

"Thanks Steve, we all appreciate your confidence in Appletree."

"Sure."

Mark switched his phone to the hands-free speaker as he reached for CSF's draft documents in his briefcase. He turned the chair away from his desk and stared out of the window again as he waited for Dick Cosway to come on line. The smaller herring gull had won the contest and was stripping meat off the bone. The other stood on an iron rail a few yards away, sulking with its back to the wind, feathers blowing over its head.

"Hey Mark. That's real good news." Cosway's voice cracked over the speaker.

"Yes, we're all pretty thrilled to develop this relationship with CSF."

"Did ya have a lot of persuading to do?"

"Not really, just a lot of questions. People want to know how it will affect them. We'll need to add resources to handle the new business. That means change, but overall we're very positive about the opportunity."

"That's great, Mark. Now we have a few things to nail down as soon as possible. First, there's the Management Agreement between Central States Financial and Appletree. I gave you a draft in New York two days ago. Perhaps you could take a look and pass it to your lawyers in London for their comments."

"I read it on the plane back to the UK. I have a few minor comments but will show it to Howe & Smithsen in the City for a more thorough response. I'll tell them to turn it round as quickly as possible."

"I'd appreciate that. Why do you keep talking about the city?"

"The City is the oldest part of London, dating back to Roman days. Traditionally it's where most of London's investment and banking transactions took place. Like Wall Street."

"Cool." Cosway observed vacuously before resuming, "OK Mark. You'll note in the letter accompanying the Agreement that CSF will cover all legal, accounting and start-up costs. We're doing that because we wanna set the pace for launching the Fund and minimize delays."

"That's very generous, Dick. Even if the lawyers are representing our interests rather than yours?"

"Yes – within reason. Just make it happen fast, and don't tell your lawyers that we're paying. Otherwise their fees'll go crazy on us."

"I assure you we'll be discreet, Dick."

"Sure. First, we're gonna need Appletree registered with the SEC. We'll email you a questionnaire which I would appreciate you filling out and returning to me this week. It can take months to get SEC registration but our legal guys can push it through so long as you respond to their questions and have no criminal record."

"Sounds straightforward."

"Then we need to get the International Fund Prospectus to the SEC for approval. Sooner we file the quicker we start selling. It can take up to 90 days. Did you get to read it on the plane?"

"I did, actually. There's a lot of verbiage, but I assume it's all necessary for filing."

"Yea, what I need you to do, Mark, is read through carefully and make changes where necessary. Take particular care over the description of Appletree, the CVs of its officers and the section entitled 'Special risks in International Investing'. You don't need to spend any time over the boilerplate sections. That's received wisdom."

"Good, so to recap, I get the Management Agreement and the International Fund prospectus back to you this week. You send me the SEC paperwork, which we'll turn round as quickly as possible. Anything else?"

"Yea. I'm gonna put you through to Nancy to discuss any compliance issues going into this project. She's my back-up business manager for this relationship. I approve the payments to Appletree every month, but you can direct any questions to her. Got anything else for me, Mark?"

"I've asked Syreta Mehta, our Head of Administration, to get involved at the outset. Once the formalities are in place she'll monitor every aspect of the relationship from our end."

"That's fine Mark. As long as we know who's responsible for what. Anything else before I switch you over?"

"Not that I can think of. Thanks for your time."

"Sure- bear with me while I transfer you."

Mark reflected on the insight to a company's culture provided by the recordings played while customers were kept on hold. Advertising companies played trendy, arty music. Gershwin or Satie, perhaps. National banks offered safe, traditional music like Vivaldi or the Brandenburg Concertos, while regional banks played popular current recordings like

Ricky Martin. In Florida they liked James Last and Texan oil drillers consoled their lonesome wildcats with Willie Nelson. There was no such frivolity at CSF.

CSF's recording was a You- Know-It-Makes-Sense, smiley female voice scrolling through the net asset value of CSF's mutual funds. If you were on hold long enough to hack through the thicket of prices, you were treated to the Featured Fund of the Week, and why you should invest in it. Financial planners were referred to a subscription-only website 'for your protection' that told them the commissions they could expect for putting clients' money into the Featured Fund of the Week.

The Featured Fund today was the CSF Commodity Option Income Fund. 'Do you know that an investment in this Fund has returned investors 88.6 per cent since the beginning of last year? Here's why we believe the dynamics are in place for a secular reappraisal of the asset class and we are only at the beginning of a megatrend that could last many years'.

This guff was followed by the earnest voice of Portfolio Manager Ellie Schwartzein – MBA Wharton, PhD Imperial College London – in a sound bite to convince listeners why there had never been a better time to invest in commodity options. Then smiley female voice came on again at speed: 'Past performance is no guide to future results. CSF is . . . '

"Hi, Mark. Are you there? Sorry to keep you waiting."

"Hello Nancy, I was completely absorbed by CSF's daily recording as I waited for you."

"What do you think? We used to have wallpaper music, but the PR department had this brilliant idea. They saw it as a great opportunity to sell our image to the twenty six thousand callers who call in every day."

"Twenty six thousand?"

"That was last year. It's certainly higher now."

Nancy got to the point. "Dick told me that Appletree is going to join our stable of managers. That's good news. As we discussed in New York, my job as Compliance Officer is to supervise and monitor Appletree's activities in the USA. Also, Dick asked me to help if you have questions about our business relationship."

"That sounds clear enough. Is there anything we need to do right now so we get no surprises later in the summer?"

"No, but to give you the heads up, Bill Tuckwell asked me to look into your regulatory position. I'm not sure yet, but that may involve taking exams."

"Just give us as much notice as possible."

Chapter 5

As Mark ended the call there was a knock. Graham stuck his head around the door, "Got a moment?"

"Sure-come on in." Mark gestured towards the circular glass-topped table in his office. Graham was a high conviction investor. He analysed investment opportunities meticulously, then stood by his decisions despite gut-wrenching volatility. He had the highest pain threshold of any investor Mark had known, never buckling under pressure. Appletree had a solid following among a group of elite and sophisticated investors around the world. They were prepared to wait because, as one of them put it eloquently, "Graham always makes us a shit load of money in the end."

Graham and Mark had worked together for ten years before founding Appletree Capital Management. They knew each other well, each respecting the qualities of the other without wishing to occupy his space. Graham admired the mercurial flair which Mark brought to the business; Mark relied on Graham's attention to detail and logic. They disagreed occasionally, but never clashed. The resulting rapport gave Appletree a solid culture, in contrast to many firms in the competitive, high ego world of asset management.

Graham stood fiddling with the plastic cord that controlled the Venetian blinds in Mark's office.

"What's up?" Mark asked.

"How did your call go?"

"We've dealt."

"Oh." He grimaced. "Paul McKay gave me this – " He handed two pages to Mark. "He was searching the internet to look up CSF and see who we're getting into bed with". The pages were from a US newspaper article headed '***C****riminal* ***S****ecurities* ***F****raud – How does* **CSF** *get away with it?*' Mark scanned the article. It referred to allegations of front-running, insider trades and market timing at CSF in New York.

Mark noted the date on the article. "This was written three years ago. Since then, they've had a new chief executive, new head of marketing and a new compliance officer. As far as I know nobody currently at CSF was indicted. I spoke to Frank Blazerman over dinner in New York the other day. He told me to watch out, as in any relationship, but didn't seem to think there was still a problem."

"Maybe so, Mark, but at Appletree we've worked too bloody hard to risk our reputation. Remember we also have a legal liability if we fail to do proper research on the people we deal with. The FSA will slaughter us if we can't demonstrate that we know our client, and all that. We need to know more about who we're hitching our wagon to in America."

"Fair enough. What do you suggest?" Mark's heart sank at the prospect of playing for more time with CSF. They were in a great hurry to get things done.

"We could ask some brokers who deal with CSF on a regular basis."

"That's fine, Graham, but we really need to put a time line on this process. We don't want to piss off CSF. Remember they have two other firms on their short list. Either of them would be thrilled to get the contract that we're dithering over." The pair fell silent.

Mark spoke first: "I have an idea. I need to email some documents to Nancy Lindstrom this afternoon. We'll then call to make sure she has the information she needs. I'll introduce you and you can bring up your concerns. That way it comes over as an innocent question rather than an investigation."

The call went more smoothly than Mark had feared. When Graham brought up the newspaper article Nancy seemed amused.

"We wondered how long you guys would take to pick up on this one. I'm glad you did the background check, it shows you're thorough. The situation you're referring to took place under our former CEO. He was indicted on a range of offences. He used to take portfolio managers out to lunch to find out what they were buying or selling. He then invested his own money, long or short, in those stocks. His secretary blew the whistle. He was investigated and fired, along with the compliance officer who approved his trades, and the director of marketing, who traded on the same information."

"Nancy, would you mind writing us a paragraph saying that we investigated the matter and that you gave us this response? It would be comforting to have a paper trail showing that we made thorough enquiries."

"Sure. No problem at all, I'll email it to you today."

After the call, Graham suggested phoning Frank Blazerman, just to square the circle. Mark tapped out the number in New York. It rang twice.

"Yeah – Blazerman here."

"Yeah Blazerman – Telford here."

"Mark, my man! I'll be damned. Twice in a week! How the hell are ya?"

"I'm on the line with Graham. Do you have a moment?"

"Hey guys. Absolutely. What can I do for you?"

"Frank, when we had dinner the other night you expressed forthright opinions about CSF. It looks like we're moving ahead with them and it would be useful if you could answer a few questions from Graham."

"I'm always up for an opinion, gentlemen. Whaddya want to know?"

"Hi Frank," Graham began, "I heard CSF had problems a couple of years ago and I would appreciate your perspective on them today."

"Sure – I remember the problems well. Their CEO was called O'Reilly. He was caught front-running CSF trades on a massive scale. Tens of millions of his own cash. In cahoots with another director, can't remember his name. There were also irregularities over using the company jet. He took his secretary on urgent business trips to Bermuda and Hawaii. When he dumped her she blew the whistle on him."

"Is CSF clear of these problems now?"

"These specific problems? Yea. But never forget the Wall Street adage – if you put an asshole in charge of a unit, everyone he trains will be an asshole. CSF is full of O'Reilly appointees. Shilson, all of them, are in the same club. They're bent as hell but they'll hang low for a while because they know the regulators are watching them like shithawks on a phone wire. There were two other guys who came out of the mess looking clean. The SEC tried to pin them down but found nothing. A guy called Bill Tuckwell in the marketing area and Dick Cosway in Operations."

Graham and Mark exchanged looks.

"Those are heavy allegations, Frank."

"Dark rumors, I would say, rather than allegations. As I say I'm always up for an opinion. Nobody in the saddle at CSF today was indicted and as far as I know there are no ongoing investigations. In this fair country you're innocent until proved guilty."

"Bottom line Frank," Graham wanted a black or white opinion, "would you be confident about going into business with CSF?"

"You'll certainly raise a lot of cash and get rich, but you need to always cover yourselves. If you get uncomfortable about anything they do, bail out. But you know, Graham, I would give the same advice about any relationship on Wall Street. CSF is no worse than any other financial institution on the Street today. They're all shysters, every goddam one of them. Go for it, but be sure your lawyers get you covered."

"CSF said they'll pay our legal bills for this deal."

"You gotta ask yourselves what their agenda is. Don't get yourselves compromised."

"Thanks Frank, you've given us useful information. Mind if we call from time to time for your perspective?"

"Hell, no. Thanks for calling . . . and congratulations for landing one of the biggest fish on the Street. You obviously impressed the shit outta them. See you in the Marina at Monte Carlo." He hung up.

Mark and Graham stared at each other across the speaker for a moment.

"What do you think, Graham?"

"Maybe we should get them to pay only for mutual fund-related legal work, and pay for our own advice on the Management Agreement. That way we keep control of our integrity."

"Up to a point."

Graham stood to leave the room, "I like the idea of that yacht in Monte Carlo, don't you?"

The partners did a high five.

In the following weeks Mark became embarrassed that he'd been so petty for questioning CSF's good faith. Dick Cosway and Nancy were always understanding and helpful, even when confronted by Mark's doubtful tone over some terms of the Agreement. CSF were exemplary. Legal bills submitted by Appletree were paid promptly and without question.

The famously nit-picking lawyers at Howe & Smithsen finally declared themselves satisfied with the terms of the Agreement, if surprised by the cooperation of CSF's lawyers, declaring, "We didn't expect to deal with any gentlemen in the American legal profession." Praise indeed.

Appletree were actively encouraged – and financed – by CSF to 'ramp up vertically'. A further six staff joined the firm, three on the investment team and three to bolster administration under Syreta Mehta. Dick Cosway kept urging them to expand. "You gotta have the slack to handle the surge when it comes."

Mark signed a lease for 5000 square feet of additional office space on Temple Avenue. Fortune favoured them: the unit adjoining Appletree on the third floor had recently been refurbished and became available.

The additional space gave Appletree a full view of the Thames and Blackfriars Bridge, which would be a selling point for visiting clients.

Mark picked up the lease on favourable terms, helped by CSF, who paid the first year of rent. Appletree, the erstwhile investment boutique, was now tooled up with thirty staff, metamorphosed by hard cash and the expectation of exponential growth.

Chapter 6

By late summer the ramped-up investment factory was ready for production. Steve Shilson visited in August with his young and decorative third wife, Skye. They landed at a private airport in Kent in CSF's corporate Gulfstream and were chauffeured across London to spend an hour viewing Appletree's expanded premises. Skye was impressed by the entertainment potential of the new conference room. She adored the view of the Thames and the 'cool bar' aboard HMS President moored at the Embankment nearby. Mark smiled as he pictured Skye in her designer denims, lizard skin cowboy boots and unbuttoned silk blouse wowing CSF's straight-laced European clients on deck in the sunset.

After an hour of simulated work the Shilson circus flew on to more pressing business on the golf course at Gleneagles. Mark wondered how Shilson differed from O'Reilly, his deposed predecessor.

Bill Tuckwell arrived in London the day after Shilson left. He was one of those you-never-get-a-second-chance-to-make-a-first-impression, all-American air-brushed motivational road warriors, found in bars at every sales convention in America. Impeccably groomed and as cheerful as red plastic, he arrived straight off the overnight from New York and insisted on meeting the entire staff. He shook everyone vigorously by the hand and set up his Powerpoint show in the conference room.

"I'm truly thrilled to be here in London Town." Alix and Paul squirmed. "I'd like to give you guys a quick presentation about Central States Financial, to give you a flavor of the fantastic company you all have hitched up with. If you have any questions as I speak, feel free to interrupt."

He began by showing an organizational chart depicting the pyramidal structure of the company. Steve Shilson dominated the apex above an unnamed Finance Director. Bill Tuckwell and Dick Cosway shared equal billing just under that, then the chart splayed out like a family tree all the way down to 'facilities management and building operations'. Mark was intrigued that Nancy Lindstrom reported to the unnamed Finance Director, theoretically sharing third place, equal to Tuckwell and Cosway in the CSF pecking order.

The second slide was a map of the United States showing CSF's regional representation. "At CSF we're real proud of our wholesalers. They're better paid and more experienced than any one else in the industry."

"Can you explain exactly what a wholesaler does?" Bob Berwick interjected.

"Sure. A wholesaler is one of our reps in the field. They're called *wholesalers* because they represent our mutual fund products at a wholesale level. They go into brokerage firms and financial planners and set out our stall. They don't sell to the public directly, but are responsible for making sure that those who do sell to the public are well-serviced."

Wholesalers were flagged by red pins on the map and the region covered by each was shaded. The biggest land area was Alaska, followed by Utah, Wyoming and Idaho—an area the size of Western Europe covered by one person. Mark fantasized about being responsible for that area. He recalled those old maps in the geography room at his prep school, showing The World coloured according to who owned each country. British possessions were red, French yellow, the Dutch were blue. No wonder the Germans went to war. Too little of the map was coloured German.

"We got 80 wholesalers in 24 cities covering every state in the Union. Each wholesaler has an assistant to plan their schedule and make follow up calls."

Bob Berwick asked, "How are the wholesalers rewarded?"

"Base salary and benefits, then a bonus based on numbers of calls and money flows. When the stock market is down and we don't want to penalize them for slow sales, we increase the reward for the number of calls they make. Our customers will always remember you for calling in bad times, and they'll give you business when the market picks up."

"Is it a constant formula, or does it change over time?" Bob persisted.

"It's a formula that shades this way or that depending how the market is doing. If the stock market is blazing, sales should be blazing too, so the wholesaler is rewarded according to market share in our peer group. Like you guys get paid more for beating your benchmark, so we compensate our sales force for outselling their peers."

"That sounds like a high pressure way of running a team." Syreta Mehta remarked.

"In this business you eat what you kill. When you eat, you eat real well. If you don't eat, you're in the wrong business." Tuckwell smiled and looked around. "Any more questions before we move on?"

"Two quick questions." Alix Newlin was intrigued by the topic, "What's the time period over which performance is measured and are wholesalers measured on net flows or just on new business that comes in?"

"I'll answer this one quickly, Alix, because we need to get on with the presentation." Bill Tuckwell's gloss began to wear thin. "We pay bonuses on gross new assets per month. The wholesaler is paid only for new sales on the books at the end of each month in his region.

We don't net off any business that's lost over the month. That's the job of the client service team to keep business on the books. I gotta keep my killers killing rather than worry about holding on to old business. CSF has an excellent client service team. Their bonuses are calculated on a different metric."

"Thanks, that's helpful." Mark interceded, "I think we should let Bill get on with his presentation."

They were shown a slide of CSF's asset growth in the past five years. Assets had grown from $96 billion to $415 billion.

"This is entirely organic growth. CSF made no acquisitions over the period. About half the increase was the stock market rising and lifting all stocks, and half was new money from our marketing efforts. As you can see, folks, CSF is one of the most successful investment firms in the world."

The next five slides were performance charts for CSF's key mutual funds, set out by product, peer group and ranking against their index.

"These numbers prove that CSF is the top-performing mutual fund group in the business, outstripping our rivals. You'll see that our US large equity fund was in the first decile over 1, 3 and 5 years. Our intermediate bond fund was in the first quartile over the same periods."

Tuckwell clicked onto the final slide. It read, simply, **C**onsistently **S**uperb **F**igures. "That, folks, pretty much concludes what I have to say this morning."

"Bill," Mark spoke up, "I'd like to thank you very much for giving us an excellent insight into Central States Financial. I must say we're all excited to be in partnership with such a dynamic organization." Turning to his colleagues, he concluded, "If any of you have further questions, you'll have the opportunity to spend time with Bill over lunch or this afternoon. Now, if Graham, Bob, Alix and Paul would stay behind, the rest of you can get back to your offices."

The room thinned out.

"Thanks Mark. Legal told me yesterday that we're only two weeks away from SEC registration of Appletree and the International Fund, barring unforeseen screw ups. We need to spend time today to discuss the Road Show before the Fund's launch."

"I thought we were being seeded with $300 million by CSF. Why should we have to travel to raise assets?" Paul McKay was forever the smart arse.

"Seed money is just to get a fund started, Paul. The real action is in the assets that flow in from our distribution network. CSF always seeds new funds with $300 million from its own balance sheet and repays it as new assets come in. We expect this Fund to be $10 billion within five years. Such growth will only come from marketing, and for that, we need your support."

Mark's head swam with the financial implications of this number. Ten billion dollars would generate Appletree a fee of *sixty million* dollars a year. After costs, retained earnings and taxes his partnership share would be close to fifteen million dollars a year. The others did similar mental arithmetic. It was not lost on Paul. "OK. Just tell me where and when you want me in the USA."

"Good." Bill Tuckwell returned to his Powerpoint.

"I need two weeks from Bob, Alix and Paul, three weeks from Graham and four weeks from Mark. Please clear your calendars from mid-September for the CSF International Fund Due Diligence Campaign."

He flicked to the next slide.

"We've split America into three zones. We've put provisional itineraries and schedules together. They will certainly get changed but I wanna give you a flavor of the intensity of the operation."

"Alix flies to Seattle on Thursday September 11th. You spend the weekend at the Four Seasons to get acclimated. Nothing is planned until 12noon on Sunday, when our wholesaler hosts an exclusive brunch for ten leading financial planners from Seattle. This will be over by 2pm, after which you have the rest of Sunday to yourself." He stared at Alix. "You may want to use the hotel's spa facilities, or if the weather's nice, rent a bike, ride a ferry or go jogging. Seattle's a beautiful place to spend a weekend in the Fall.

By Monday morning you will be over your jet lag. You are the featured speaker at a 7.30 breakfast for 80 financial planners and stockbrokers at the Four Seasons. At 10 am you fly to Portland, where you have a lunch meeting with a group of investment consultants. At 1 pm you fly to Oakland, then drive to Berkeley for an afternoon meeting with some of CSF's biggest hitters in California. A limo will take you to the Embarcadero in San Francisco, where at 6.30 you host cocktails for 30 intermediaries, followed by dinner for an elite group of brokers. You will be free to hit the hay after 10pm.

On Tuesday you are the featured speaker at a breakfast conference hosted by JP Shapiro in Sausalito at 7am. You then have two meetings downtown San Francisco in brokerage offices, lunch in Palo Alto at 12.30 and an office visit in San Jose at 3. From there you fly to Los Angeles, where you host a dinner in Beverley Hills at 7pm.

On Wednesday you attend cluster meetings of planners and consultants in Anaheim, Santa Monica, Glendale and Long Beach. You should be through by 8pm, and will stay at the same hotel in Beverley Hills for the second night.

On Thursday you host a breakfast and lunch in Newport Beach and do office visits in Santa Ana and San Juan Capistrano. You drive to San Diego, where you host dinner. On Friday you have six meetings around San Diego and you're done for the week by 4pm.

You're booked at a resort in Tucson for the weekend, with nothing scheduled. You host a breakfast meeting there at 7.30 on Monday 22nd, followed by a short flight to Phoenix. You spend the next two days around Phoenix/Scottsdale. Wednesday night you fly to Denver. You have 11 meetings around Denver, Fort Collins, Vail and Aspen on Thursday and Friday, and you're free to fly back to the UK any time after 6pm on Friday. A direct flight leaves Denver for London at 8.30 that evening."

Alix listened to her itinerary with mounting panic. "But what will I say? Who are all these people? I'll be shattered."

"It sounds worse than it is, Alix. You travel first class for two weeks, staying at premium hotels and chauffeured by limousines. Where scheduled flights are not available you will fly in a CSF corporate aircraft. You will travel with the wholesaler covering each part of your itinerary. They will be instructed to take the best care of you, fully responsible for all your logistics, hotels, meals, etc. CSF will pick up the tab for your entire trip. We believe in travelling first class. Other questions?"

Tuckwell surveyed his stunned audience. He flicked to the next slide.

"No? Then I wanna touch on Paul McKay's itinerary for the same week.

You fly into Chicago September 11th. You get the weekend in the Park Hyatt to rest up. Sunday evening you meet a group of Chicago financial planners, then from Monday breakfast through Friday you give presentations in Greater Chicago, Rockford, Milwaukee, Minneapolis, Omaha, Indianapolis, Kansas City, Louisville, Detroit, Columbus, Cleveland, Akron and Pittsburgh. I'll spare you the specifics right now – you can check the Powerpoint pages after I've gone."

"Can you confirm that I won't have to buy tickets or worry about how to get from meeting to meeting?" Paul's ginger hairline receded deeply. Mark often noticed that whenever Paul was agitated his face turned as red as a tomato. He was a hopeless negotiator.

"Sure, Paul. You will be met at each airport by CSF's local wholesaler and taken personally from location to location. We want you totally focused on giving your presentations. We don't want you to waste energy over logistics. That's our job. Always remember : CSF will build the opera house and you guys just hafta sing."

Paul nodded thoughtfully.

"Other questions? OK Bob, that leaves you. You get the easy zone because you only have five hours of jetlag. On the 11th, you fly and spend the weekend at the Langham Hotel in downtown Boston. Same as the others, you get an opportunity to practice your presentation at dinner on Sunday. Then after a day of meetings around Boston you hit the road for 2 weeks in Concord, Springfield, Providence, Hartford, Stamford, New York City, Philadelphia, Wilmington, Baltimore, DC, Richmond, Raleigh Durham, Chattanooga and Atlanta. You can check the specifics of your itinerary on Powerpoint.

"Now, over to Graham and Mark. I want three weeks of your time, Graham, because we need you Stateside for TV shows, press meetings, talking to our wholesalers, educating the sales force in New York and getting to know the administrators in our office in Bismarck, North Dakota. OK?"

"That's a lot of time to be out of the office, you know, Bill. We still have money to run and other clients apart from CSF." Graham sniped irritably.

"You'll get plenty of time to communicate over the Net and by conference call. We'll keep your schedule light in terms of firm appointments, though heavy when we put you in front of people. We'll make sure you can access Bloomberg, Reuters and all your client accounts 24/7. Happy?" Without waiting for an answer, he continued,

"We'll work over the next few weeks to develop the presentation so everyone's comfortable with what you're gonna say. I want everyone at CSF totally prepped up on your investment process. I don't want any surprises when we go live."

"Will you need me in the States at the same time as Graham, Paul, Alix and Bob are over there?" Mark asked hopefully.

"Absolutely. We need you all in the USA at the same time. It's CSF's mailed fist approach to marketing. Saturate the financial community from coast to coast. We wanna get the press, radio waves and financial TV programmes buzzing about the CSF International Fund. There will be local press coverage for every one of you as you travel around. We have relations with the major regional papers in Chicago, LA , Denver, Cleveland, Hartford and so on. Our PR team will invite financial journalists to your keynote speeches in every city. Those Press guys are always a sucker for a free lunch. This brings me to you, Mark."

Mark looked up.

"Your role is to pinch-hit the campaign. I want you for four weeks. We'll keep you uncommitted in advance, because we need to parachute you into hot situations. When Alix stirs up a storm in the Bay Area, you jet out as the CEO of Appletree and speak with the key players in the region. Top guy to top guy."

"Wouldn't it be more efficient to have me on call in London rather than hanging loose in New York?" Mark was concerned about the potential risk to Appletree by being absent for four weeks.

"You won't be hanging loose in New York. You may have noticed that I skipped Florida and Texas from the itineraries. We're gonna base you in Saint Pete and you'll circle round giving 4 presentations a day from Jacksonville to West Palm until we need you for more important stuff. CSF's got real strong representation in Miami, Orlando, Fort Myers and Tampa. Once you've covered Florida we fly you to Houston and you'll do DFW, Austin and San Antonio. Our Gulf States wholesaler, Zack Overwood, is a legend in the CSF system. The greatest rainmaker in the business. He can pull five million bucks out of Beaumont Texas in an afternoon. We designed your itinerary loosely, so you can break off and fly anywhere in the US to close business for the International Fund."

"Sounds fun. At least I'll pick up a suntan at weekends." The idea of touring the Gulf States in the Autumn wasn't all bad, although Mark was apprehensive about the impending stress of the road show, in particular the flights. He hated flying.

Chapter 7

"Mark, my man, I've been inside this goddam building too long." Bill Tuckwell stretched back in the chair, tapping his watch. The surface of the conference room table was scattered with half-drunk coffee cups, empty Perrier bottles, crumpled wads of paper, sandwiches in the early stages of rigor mortis, cell phones and papers outlining CSF's marketing strategy. "It's been a long day since I landed at Heathrow." he yawned loudly. "Time for fresh air and a drink, whaddya say?"

"We've covered everything we set out to do." Mark replied "A couple of the lads usually go to the pub around the corner after work. They may still be there. We can join them for a beer then I'll take you over to your hotel."

"Sounds good. Where's my hotel?" Bill tapped his papers into a tidy sheaf and slipped them into a yellow inter-office memo envelope.

"The Savoy? About ten minutes walk from here."

"Good, let's go." Bill closed his briefcase.

Mark cleared his confidential papers into a drawer, picked up an attaché case and exited with Bill onto Temple Avenue. They were encased by the sticky, soupy air of London in August. Exhaust fumes from the late afternoon traffic along the Embankment stung Mark's eyes. Tuckwell trundled his wheeled suitcase out of the building, loosening his tie as they hit the street. "Man, it's humid out here."

"Not far to go. Our local pub's just around the corner." They turned left and walked sixty yards to *The Witness Box.* Graham and Bob were still sitting at an outside table on Tudor Street.

Mark returned from the bar with four glasses of chilled lager. "Your good health, Gentlemen. Bill, we appreciate your visit today and look forward to a long and lucrative association."

Bill raised his glass. He looked grey and fatigued, but seemed to revive as the lager found its spot.

"This pub played a crucial role in the formation of Appletree." Mark explained. "Graham and I used to meet here after work to shoot the breeze. It put us in a conspiratorial mode. This is where we developed the idea that we should set up our own shop."

"Maybe they'll put up a blue plaque to Appletree on the pub wall one day, what do you think, Graham?" Bob asked with a wry smile.

"Maybe when we hit ten billion."

"This time next year, right?"

"You guys got the right idea." Tuckwell slurped down his beer and slammed the empty glass on the table.

Refreshed, Bill and Mark strolled through the Inner Temple garden. Couples dallied by the flower beds after a day's work at the Inns of Court. A young blonde woman came down the steps exiting from an office building and passed them on Crown Office Row, rapt in conversation with a professorial older man. She was dressed demurely in a plain, medium-length blue skirt with matching jacket, but her dowdy clothes did not disguise her long athletic legs and full breasts.

"You never get gals like that in New York." Bill commented.

"How so?" Mark stared furtively as she walked by.

"Every half pretty woman in New York thinks she's God's gift. That kid doesn't know how beautiful she is. I like that."

They turned left on Middle Temple Lane and walked under an arch leading to Victoria Embankment. A kilted schoolboy stood there with bagpipes, playing an excruciating rendition of *The Barren Rocks of Aden.* Bill winced.

"Holy shit, why don't they arrest that guy for wearing a skirt?"

"You're supposed to give him a pound and he might stop for five minutes."

"If I give him five, will he shuddup for an hour?" Tuckwell riposted with a chuckle.

Fifteen minutes later they sat in comfortable chairs in the Savoy in front of two frosted flutes of chilled lager. Mark raised his glass, "Your good health – again."

"Cheers – here's to raising a trainload of cash."

"Amen to that."

They each smacked down half a glass of lager.

"Tell me Bill, how does CSF normally launch funds? Is this a typical launch?"

"There are many ways to launch a mutual fund in the United States as there are mutual funds. In its crudest form a group of guys get together, they file a prospectus with the SEC and the State regulators, pay their fees and wait. It takes about 90 days for a prospectus to clear the SEC, then the fund goes live and they have a licence to pull cash from the public.

Some firms pump out funds like chickens lay eggs. New funds can sit on the shelf with minimal seed capital for years. They're normally given to young team members to manage. If they screw up nobody's hurt because the public's not at risk. The worst that happens is that the kid stays where he belongs – in obscurity.

If the kid performs well he's lionized and the fund is launched publicly. In the past we've promoted quite a lot of funds like this and raised billions in a short time."

"What does 'perform well' mean, exactly?"

"To the public" Tuckwell shovelled a fistful of peanuts into his face, "it means making a high percentage return- say, 30% in a year. That's the level where most people are happy, even if competing funds make 40% and the index makes 35%.

To marketers, 'performing well' has a different meaning. Some years the index is down 20% and a mutual fund is down 10%. In a year like that losing only 10% of someone's money is great performance and a marketer will go to town on it."

"You lose less than the index and you're a great manager?"

"Bingo. 'Well' also means beating your peer group. If one of our funds loses 10% and our competition loses 20%, we broadcast that fantastic performance to the world."

"Who selects your competition?"

"We do." Tuckwell flagged the waitress for two more beers.

"I assume that when CSF launches a fund it's more proactive than you described—a few guys filing with the SEC and waiting?"

"Hell, yes. Central States Financial markets its funds like a mailed fist, like I said before. There's no slow incubation shit at CSF. We gear up a powerful campaign of marketing energy and public relations before a fund goes live. Every wholesaler makes a list of hot prospects in his region, which gotta turn into sales on the day the fund goes live."

The potent European beer was filtering through Tuckwell's jetlagged brain.

"Lemme tell you something, Mark. I'm under real pressure to launch a fund that makes an impact on CSF's bottom line. In the past year we pumped out funds that grew fast, then peaked. Special-interest funds where CSF mopped up all investor demand, like the CSF Illinois Tax Free Fund. A great idea but it capped out at eight hundred million bucks."

Mark reflected that a mere eight hundred million bucks would be a handy sum for Appletree to manage.

"Also, I hafta say . . . " he hesitated, then shrugged, "Shilson's bonus keys off the profitability of CSF, so he's on my ass to come up with funds that reach $10 billion in a hurry. $10 billion generates fees of $60 million a year to CSF. $5 million of that goes into Shilson's pocket, based on a sweet formula he struck with CSF's board."

Intrigued by the resentment growing in Tuckwell, Mark ordered another beer-and a club soda for himself. Tuckwell didn't notice.

"Wow, that sounds like a sweet deal."

"Sure is. He sits in his 4000 square foot office creaming the company and flying around the world in the Gulfstream with that chick. Four miles high in Skye, so the co-pilot said."

Mark raised an eyebrow.

"How did CSF decide that international equities were the way to go?"

"As you know, Mark, in recent years international equities have exploded. They have the capitalization and liquidity to meet CSF's criteria for large, money-spinning new mutual funds. Everyone's doing it – every rinky dink investment outfit in the United States's got an International Fund now."

"Why not CSF?"

"Because Shilson is a 'be American, buy American' cave man. He thinks it's unpatriotic to invest American money overseas. He doesn't wanna know it's the income off of foreign portfolios that keeps the Dollar on life-support and pays for America's pensions and education bills."

"So there's not much commitment from the board to diversify outside the USA? " Mark probed.

"Correct. Except for one thing: Shilson's bonus is leveraged to asset growth at CSF. His target is $600 million profit next year and there's no way he's gonna reach that without large scale new products. International investment is the only direction we can go."

"So where did you go from there?"

"Two steps. First, we nailed down a great international equity firm". He lifted his glass and toasted Mark: "Ta daaa!"

Mark smiled.

"Second, I'm getting the fund underwritten by twenty regional stockbroking firms. Each broker's got to sell fifteen million bucks to their clients on the day it goes live. The underwriting guarantees at least $300 million of assets in the fund at the launch.

As Tuckwell spoke, Mark mused that, added to the $300 million of seed money from CSF, it would amount to $600 million to manage on Day 1. That would give Appletree an annual fee of $3.6 million, he calculated greedily.

"Getting small regional stockbrokers to underwrite the Fund was a stroke of genius. It was my idea. The volume of trading business that CSF gives these brokers means we're a mighty valuable client to them. Broking fees generated by CSF amounts to over $1billion a year. To a small brokerage in St Louis or San Diego, this business is major moolah."

"It would be a brave stockbroker to turn down a place in the underwriting syndicate of the CSF International Fund." Mark observed.

"Damn right. We avoid the big East Coast names – the Wire Houses – because CSF has no clout there. Guys like Lynch & Burnham might place $50, $70 or even $100 million into one of our funds, but a month later they blow it out and reinvest elsewhere to keep their commissions flowing. We let them invest in our funds if they want to, but our priority goes to smaller distributors. We mean more to them; they mean more to us."

"What does a broker get for underwriting the fund?"

"The underwriting fee is 1.6%, plus a front-end sales fee of 5% into the International Fund. That means $15 million of client money invested in the International Fund generates nearly $1million for the broker. That's a good deal for everyone."

"Including the clients?"

"The *clients*?" Bill looked piteously at Mark "Sorry to say, but who gives a shit? You gotta pay to play in this business. Clients are for the long term. If 5%'s taken off your money on Day 1 you won't know it was gone in 3 years."

"Mmm . . . "

Tuckwell was oblivious to Mark's reserved tone. As he drained his third beer he flagged the waitress for a fourth. Mark ordered another club soda.

"So we got underwriting agreements from 20 regional brokers. Excellent names, like HD Mason in Denver, Ray Hutton in Chicago, Weil, Bateman in Memphis and AG Stiphel in California. They're all established blue chip brokers in their regional markets. We also got distribution agreements with over 700 financial planners, smaller brokerages, even some wire houses.

So we're guaranteed $300 million from the underwriters and are sure to get a lot more from broader distribution channels. Everyone wants that 5% commission."

"So when Alix travels around the West Coast, she'll spend a lot of time with AG Stiphel brokers who are connected into the local investor scene?"

"Correct. Paul will do the same with First of Kentucky around the Midwest. The underwriters expect CSF's wholesalers and the Appletree investment team to make a big effort. It's a test case. They got a lot of international funds to sell. There are some well-established competitors in the international field out there, so CSF's gotta go the extra mile."

" . . . or the extra dollar."

"Or the extra dollar." Tuckwell nodded. Mark was beginning to notice that he had no sense of irony. "I need to go to the Men's room."

"So do I."

They stood in adjacent cubicles emptying their bladders.

"Hey Mark, you married?"

"No. Are you?"

"Divorced and dating a hot lady."

Chapter 8

The phone rang at 11 o'clock.

"Hi Mark, this is Nancy Lindstrom. How are you doing?"

"Nancy, great to hear from you. It's pretty early over there, isn't it? "

"Six in the morning. This is when I do my best work." Nancy was businesslike. "Mark, we have a problem. I've discussed the matter at length with our lawyers and was hoping not to bother you, but I'm afraid you've got to take an exam prior to going on the road in September."

"But Nancy, that's only a few weeks away. I can't run a company, invest money, launch a mutual fund and study for an exam all in the next few weeks. What exam are you talking about? "

"The lawyers said you could get away with just taking Series 63 before you come over, and follow up with Series 6 and 65 before Christmas."

"How generous."

"I know you're real busy, Mark. If it makes you feel better I persuaded them that you don't need to sit Series 7. That's the Mother of all Series exams. Also I never make anyone take an exam I haven't passed myself. It's one of the joys of being Compliance Officer. "

"Good lord, how many have you done?"

"Fourteen so far. If I can pass them all first time, you sure can. Series 63 is easy. It covers state securities regulation and the Uniform Securities Act."

"Quite so. But what's that got to do with launching a new mutual fund?"

"Everything, potentially. Our lawyers say that if you haven't passed it, state regulators may prevent you from selling in their states. It's a stretch but they say that CSF simply can't take the risk before a major launch."

"OK Nancy, so where do I go from here? It's clearly a waste of time to fight, so let's get on with it." Mark was more petulant than he meant to be—Nancy was only the messenger.

"I'll email the study papers and I've got a date and time for you to take the exam. It's Friday September 12th in New York, 8.30am. The Testing Center is at 201 East 42nd on the 10th floor. That's between 2nd and 3rd streets. You'll need to show them a driver's licence or a valid passport for ID purposes."

"8.30 am . . . New York . . . September 12 . . . That means I have to come over a day earlier than planned."

"Yes. Please can you tell Graham, Bob, Alix and Paul that they need to take Series 63? Bob and Graham can do it in New York at the same time as you: Alix in Seattle and Paul in Chicago. Tell them to expect my email today with their times, details and study materials."

"They'll love you for this, Nancy."

"Just doing my job, Mark. Nothing more."

He admired her coolness. Without thinking, he blurted:

"Since I'm going to be stranded in New York on the evening of September 12, would you care to join me for dinner?"

"Let me see . . . September 12 . . . sure. I can do that."

"If you find the place, the evening's on me."

"Whatever. Let's play it by ear on the night."

"Fair enough. You'd better send those study materials for Series 63 ASAP, because that's my only reason for being in New York, you know."

"Good luck with your studying, Mark. Bye."

"Bye."

Mark felt more elated than the need to take exams at this late stage in his career might suggest. He'd liked Nancy as soon as he met her. She radiated calm efficiency. He liked her hands, her profile, her clothes. Her voice softened when they crossed over from business to social on the phone. He liked that.

Chapter 9

Alix and Paul were furious when they were told about Series 63.

"Why the hell do I have to take this exam when I've got a university degree and I'm a CFA? I knew this deal would be more hassle than it was worth." Alix complained.

"I'm a qualified actuary. Why do I need to take this pissy little American Series test?" Paul whined.

Mark was firm. "If you're as bright as you think you are then you'll sail through this exam. My advice is to use your energy studying rather than fighting. We're all in it together."

Bob Berwick was more sanguine than his colleagues. "It's years since I last took an exam. It'll do me good to get up to date in a subject." adding mischievously, "Besides, it'll look good on my CV, won't it Mark?"

Predictably everyone on the team passed the Series 63 exam comfortably. The beauty of NASD exams was that they were taken on computers at testing centers. Results were known instantly. The Appletree team were now experts on the Uniform Securities Act and officially permitted to whisper the words *mutual fund* in every state across America.

Dick Cosway had invited Mark and Graham to lunch on September 12 after their exam in New York. They met at a German restaurant in Tribeca at 1 o'clock.

"So, gentlemen, how was it?"

"We passed. Glad it's over." Graham was relieved.

"Great news, because it might have held up the launch of the International Fund."

"That's a bit extreme, isn't it? Couldn't we have travelled under the wholesalers' registrations?"

"Sure-some of them. But they don't all have Series 63. Also you'll be doing some solo press and radio work so you have to be registered."

"You got us to do this exam when your own wholesalers are not even qualified?" Graham's hackles were rising.

"Put that way, yes. But you guys are so high profile that we needed to get you registered as a priority."

"Better not tell Bob and Paul. They'd go ballistic." Graham shook his head in disbelief.

"It does seem inconsistent, Dick. We came into this in good faith. CSF should at least ensure that its own sales people are qualified to sell the product. Now it looks like you guys are coming in under our umbrella, not vice versa." Mark's fuse spluttered.

"Gentlemen, keep calm. Please. Bill Tuckwell has committed that every person in the sales force must be qualified and registered by year end. If they're not, they're fired. You guys are part of the process. We asked Nancy Lindstrom to implement the program. She's a first rate compliance officer and I have no doubt she'll get the job done."

On hearing the words *Nancy Lindstrom*, a surge of excitement zapped through Mark's chest. In all the morning's craziness he'd forgotten about his date that evening. Series 63 suddenly seemed irrelevant and intensely boring.

"Hey Dick, that's no problem. Let's move on and have a good lunch."

Graham was astounded by the change of direction. Dick Cosway grabbed the chance to steer Mark's mercurial nature towards safer waters.

"One reason I wanted to take you guys to lunch was to thank you for the brilliant work you all, and in particular Syreta Mehta, are doing to help us set up our international settlement system. There's no way CSF would otherwise know about the differences in trading rules between the countries where the Fund's going to invest."

"She's the best in the business, Dick. Educating our clients is a key part of the service. If you're trading on twenty stock markets a day, and if your systems aren't in place, you can get into an administrative nightmare very quickly."

"So we're learning. Syreta's a great resource for this venture."

As they waded through plates of goulash and schnitzel the conversation ranged from golf to the United Nations and the direction of US interest rates. Over coffee, Dick made a proposition.

"Since you guys are based across the Pond" – he nearly lost Mark right there – "Bill and I thought you guys could use a point man in the US for Appletree's marketing and client servicing."

"What exactly would he do?"

"He'd organize your trips to the USA and make sure you were always fully utilized when you come over. You would coordinate with each other and fix dates in advance. We'd expect him to visit London to understand your thinking and escort parties of American clients over there."

"Do you have anyone in mind?"

"Yeah, we have a kid called Vernon Badore. We call him Vern. He's our wholesaler in Tennessee; lives in Chattanooga. Bill says he's a pain in the ass, but thinks it's because he needs a new challenge. If he operated on a bigger stage than Tennessee, we reckon Vern would do a great job."

"Who would he report to?" Mark asked.

"It would be a split report. Like with your new staff and the extra space you took in London we'd front the cost of a guy, so he would report to Bill. But obviously he'd be accountable to Appletree as well."

"How would he be budgeted for?" Graham needed to be clear on anything that might affect partnership overheads.

"Like I say, we propose that he'd be financed by us. He'd come in on Bill Tuckwell's budget. Going forward we'd expect him to be self-financing from the business he brings in, but we'd switch him to your budget after a year."

"I thought you guys were going to cover our US marketing costs under our agreement?"

"We agreed to cover all *mutual fund* marketing costs. But Vern can help you guys to turbo-charge Appletree's sales beyond the mutual fund area. He would open doors to the institutional market for you. We've crunched the numbers and they look sexy. We'd pay Vern a standard base and he would earn a commission on sales."

"So it would be a self-financing exercise?" Mark asked.

"Exactly. But before anybody gets too excited I wanna make two important points. First, this is just an idea and you're under no obligation to take Vern on board. We won't think worse of Appletree if you don't have him. Second, if you like the idea but don't like Vern, we can look for someone else. We're just trying to find a way of pushing Appletree into every corner of the US market."

"Put that way," Graham said, "I'd consider it, but I think we should meet Vern Badore as soon as possible."

"Good, I'll speak to Bill Tuckwell and arrange a meeting."

As they left the restaurant, Mark put his arm around Graham's shoulder.

"I hope you don't mind but I've made plans for dinner this evening."

"That's a relief. Frankly I'd prefer to crash out. I'm knackered, what with the travel and the stress over the exam."

They arranged a conference call at noon on the following Sunday with Alix, Bob and Paul 'to ensure that everyone's cool' with the week ahead. Graham would initiate the call from his hotel room and patch in the others.

Chapter 10

Mark arrived early and sat in a comfortable chair at a table in the Algonquin Bar, ordered a Kir Royale and flicked vaguely through the evening newspaper. It had the usual Tri State headlines about corrupt politicians, police shootings and college football scores.

He realized the full extent of his distraction when he reached the financial pages and skimmed over the day's Market Movers. Normally he studied the charts with fascination and calculated the impact of the day's stock market action on Appletree's net worth. Tonight, he couldn't even focus on a mass murder in The Bronx.

Nancy was thirty minutes late. Mark had left his mobile phone at the Morgans Hotel. He began to feel relieved that he'd been stood up. It would save the hassle of small talk and the risk that he might make a fool of himself. Intimacy was not his thing; he was too bloody British, or maybe just plain independent. He caught the barmaid's eye and scribbled in the air to mimic writing. She brought his check.

As he tapped his PIN onto the keyboard, Nancy entered the bar. She was radiant. Instinctively and without embarrassment Mark stood and kissed her on both cheeks.

"Mark, I'm so very sorry. Getting around New York tonight's like swimming in glue." Nancy was flushed.

"Couldn't matter less." Mark stepped back to look at her oval face, her short auburn hair tied back with a blue ribbon, her deep blue eyes, the porcelain complexion, her slightly flushed cheeks. She wore a light beige silk jacket over a diaphanous white blouse. A fine gold chain with a crucifix, a pleated pale green floral skirt. No stockings, long legs, Italian loafers . . . "You look wonderful. I'd have waited all night." He lied.

"That's a cute thing to say. Can I sit down now?"

"Oh . . . yes, of course. What would you like to drink?"

"I'll have what you have."

He ordered two glasses of Kir Royale.

"How did your exam go?"

"94 per cent. I hope they let me into Iowa now."

"Iowa? That's where I'm from. I was born and grew up in Muscatine, Iowa. What made you say Iowa?"

"It sounds exotic and impossibly distant."

The drinks arrived; they clinked glasses.

"Exotic and impossibly distant? My family would crack up if they heard that. Muscatine Iowa's about as down home and heartland USA as it gets. High school football, Thanksgiving, cheer leaders, barges on the Mississippi, Burlington Northern boxcars rattling across the plains, Iowa State tee shirts." She paused, "You got *what* in your Series 63?"

"94 per cent."

"94 per cent? That ties with the CSF record. You must be real smart."

"I could hardly go out for dinner with CSF's Compliance Officer with a low score in my Series 63 exam, could I?"

She touched his hand, "Please – I'm not Compliance Officer now. It's Friday evening. I'm just Nancy."

"You never know, just Nancy, I might just need to be regulated."

"Cute. Changing the subject, where shall we eat tonight?"

They dined in an overstuffed restaurant overlooking Central Park South. The clientele were old, rich, mainly Jewish; some quite famous. Mark and Nancy were given a table overlooking the park, where they talked and laughed until they were the last to leave the premises. It was nearly 2 in the morning.

"You know," Nancy said, "I've only had three glasses of wine all night, but I feel giddy."

"And I should be jetlagged and shattered after staying up last night studying for an exam that *someone* forced me to take. Yet I feel fresh as a spring lamb."

It was a muggy night and it rained lightly. They crossed the road and strolled northwards, arm in arm, through the park. The earth smelled of damp leaves.

"I love rain on a warm September night." Mark cooed.

"Yer quite a poet, mister." She teased.

When they reached her apartment building on East 63rd, they stood in the doorway. Nancy kissed Mark provocatively on the lips. "I'd invite you in, but my husband wouldn't like it."

"Fair enough. I guess my wife wouldn't be too thrilled either,"

"You're married?"

"Absolutely. Three children under 5. How about you?"

Nancy pouted, playing with Mark's collar. "Seriously, though, I think we should take our time. I'd like to get to know you. It looks like CSF and Appletree are going to be together for a while, so there's time to get to know each other."

"I'll be round at ten o'clock tomorrow morning. I'll take you to brunch, then I fly to St Petersburg from La Guardia at three."

"See you tomorrow, Mark. I've had a wonderful evening."

"Me too."

Mark seemed to skip the thirty-odd blocks along Madison Avenue to the Morgans Hotel. It had been a long time since he'd met someone whose company he really enjoyed. Someone to laugh with.

Chapter 11

A fax printout was stuck under Mark's door at the Morgans Hotel. It was timed 11.45pm Friday 12th September.

> From : Bill Tuckwell, CSF
> To : Mark Telford, Appletree
>
> I called but you were out on the town. Dick spoke with me after lunch today. I've rerouted your flight tomorrow. Flight 45 leaves La Guardia at 9.45am for Atlanta. You will be met by Vernon (Vern) Badore at your arrival gate at 11.30. I've told him you will be discussing the job opportunity. He will identify himself with a CSF tee shirt and golf cap. Your flight from Atlanta to St Petersburg leaves at 3pm. He'll buy you lunch and take you to the St Pete gate. This gives three hours to acquaint yourselves with each other and see if there's a fit. Let me know what you think on Monday.
>
> Bill

"Shit. I don't want to chew up this weekend with business." But it was too late to call anyone. Mark called the hotel operator for a 7am wakeup, stripped, splashed cold water on his face and crashed out.

In the morning he instructed the concierge to deliver flowers with a note to Nancy Lindstrom on E 63rd Street by 9.30am.

Mark was duly met at the gate in Atlanta, on time, by the young man called Vern Badore. He was short, square and earnest, oozing salesmanship. Mark hated the CSF golf cap wedged on Vern's head all the time they spent together. But since most other young men in the terminal at Atlanta Hartsfield wore similar hats, either back to front or straight on, it occurred to him that perhaps *he* was the oddball by having a bare head, not Vern.

"Tell me about yourself, Vern."

"I was born in Chattanooga and went to Clemson, where I got a sports scholarship."

"What sports did you play?"
"Football. I also did wrestling and weights. Today all I play is golf."
"Have you been to London?"
"No sir, but I'd love to go there. I always wanted to play Royal Lytham and Saint Andrews. My club in Tennessee is called Carnoosty."
"Tell me about your job."
"I'm the CSF wholesaler for Tennessee. I enjoy it and I make good bucks but I'm ready for a new challenge."
"How much business did you bring in last year?"
"A billion two."
"What was the product breakdown?"
" $400 million Municipal Bonds, $300 million US Treasuries and $500 million US Equities."
"What was the breakdown of the US equity sales?"
"Ninety per cent large cap S&P. Ten per cent small cap NASDAQ."
"What do you know about Appletree?"
"It's a leading London investment company specializing in international equity management. You have ten investment staff, up from five a few months ago. CSF is totally committed to this asset class and wants Appletree to grow fast."
Mark liked the ring of 'leading London investment company.' He smiled when he thought of their cramped offices on Temple Avenue with an oblique view of Blackfriars Bridge. Until they took the extra space, courtesy of CSF, they couldn't afford the rent that came with full river views.
"What do you know about international equity investing?"
"A lotta my friends drive a Mercedes. There's a Cemex plant near where I live. The US economy's gotten taken over by foreigners. International equity investment has to be the way forward."
"I see. Do you know how many stock markets there are outside the USA?"
"No sir, but I can find out real quick."
"Do you know what benchmark is used by international investors?"
"The EAFE Index, sir." Vern was relieved to answer a technical question correctly.
"Married?"
"I could sue you for asking that question."
"Are you married, yes or no?"
"Yea. One kid." Vern replied quietly.

"How much travel are you prepared to do?"

"Five workin' days a week."

"Vern, I'm sure you're a top wholesaler in Tennessee, but there's a huge difference between selling muni bonds in Memphis, and international equities through sophisticated intermediaries in metropolitan America. I'm not convinced that you're the man for this job. Is there anything you want to ask me – or tell me?"

"First of all, sir," Vern stuck out the thumb of his left hand, "selling muni bonds in Memphis is not dumb. It's a sophisticated sale. I wholesale them through financial planners to high net worth individuals. Second," Vern's index finger came out, "I doubled CSF's mutual fund sales in the State of Tennessee in three years. Third, I have more indications of interest for your International Fund in Tennessee than all our wholesalers combined in the State of California. Fourth, I may not know the answers to your questions right now, but I'm a quick study and I won't take long to get up to speed. Fifth,"

Finally – Vern's pinky – "Nobody can do this job better than I can. I'm the top wholesaler, adjusted for territory and head of population, in the CSF system. Therefore in the United States." After making his points, Vern held up his left hand with five outstretched fingers.

Mark was impressed by Vern's counterattack. He liked people who stood up for themselves. "All right." He put up his hands in a placating gesture. "Dick and Bill regard you highly. I'm not going to make a decision in a terminal at Atlanta airport on a Saturday morning at our first meeting. I want you to meet my colleagues in London and we'll make a team decision."

Vern grinned. He had got to *maybe*. Mark didn't know it yet, but Vern's particular genius was in turning maybes into yeses.

"I'm in America for four weeks, so I suggest you visit us in London in mid October. How does that sound?"

"It sounds great, sir. I won't let you down."

"And for God's sake, don't wear that bloody hat when you come to see us. You've no idea how stupid it looks."

"Don't say that, please."

"Say what?"

"Utter The Lord's name in vain."

The twenty minutes it took to reach the St Petersburg gate were filled with how Vern came to the decision to be Born Again. He was lying drunk on his bed in a hotel room in Nashville after a night out with "a bunch of financial planners". Trying to log onto a porn movie, he chanced upon "a TV evangelist who really spoke to me. I realized then and there how meaningless my life had become."

As the flight taxied towards takeoff Mark reflected on what the young man had said. He liked Vern's grit, and wondered what his colleagues might think of this rough, sanctimonious boy from Chattanooga. The least he could do was oblige Cosway and Tuckwell and take it as far as it would go. With this thought Mark dozed off and slept throughout the flight to St Pete.

Chapter 12

The limo picked Mark up at the airport just before five o'clock and drove him to the Don CeSar Beach Resort. The huge pink wedding cake of a hotel held affectionate memories for him. Six years earlier he had spent a stag weekend here with a group of Italian friends. He wondered what had become of Massimo and the delectable Serena.

Mark checked into a suite on the fourth floor overlooking a glorious swimming pool, a wide sandy beach and the Gulf of Mexico. The light was fading. He unpacked, hung up his suits, put on his swimming trunks and headed to the beach.

He crawled a hundred yards out into the warm waves and swam parallel to the shore, back and forth in front of the Don CeSar for a long time. He floated on his back and stared at the buildings as the lights came on along the shore, one by one. Flights of pelicans skirted the cresting waves a few feet from his head.

He was tired, but felt good about life. Recent events were about to change his financial position profoundly. Not that he'd ever been poor, exactly, but the CSF deal was going to push him into the financial stratosphere. He had met Nancy. He looked forward to getting to know her, even though, lying in the tepid waters of the Gulf, he simply couldn't conjure up her face. Best of all, he was young and fit enough to enjoy his turn of fortune.

At 12 noon East Coast time on Sunday, Mark's phone rang.

"Hi Mark, Graham here. How are things going? If you stay on the line I'll get the others." Paul answered from his room at the Park Hyatt in Chicago. A minute later Alix was patched in from the Four Seasons in Seattle and finally, Bob Berwick from the Langham in Boston.

"Hi everybody, First and foremost, congratulations to everyone for passing Series 63. Did you have a good journey? Hotels OK?"

"The limo was waiting at Seattle Airport to take me to the Four Seasons. The hotel's brilliant. CSF is picking up the tab for everything – beautiful room, spa, room service, the lot." Alix was intoxicated by the top flight treatment she was receiving. "And Seattle's a beautiful city. Yesterday I went down to the harbour and took a boat trip around Puget Sound. I saw sea otters. I got soaked on the way back. The weather reminds me of Scotland."

"I can't complain too much," Paul chipped in, "but Chicago's a bloody noisy city. My room overlooks Michigan Avenue. There was too much traffic coming in from the airport. It took over an hour."

"Graham?"

"Oh, I'm having a grand old time in New York. The hotel's comfortable and discreet. I went to the Metropolitan Museum yesterday. Saw Henry VIII's suit of armour and some fabulous paintings. Walked through Central Park, just chilled out, really."

The unexpected surge when Mark heard the words *Central Park . . . Must call her.*

"Bob?"

"Boston's fine, glorious Fall weather here in New England. I took the water taxi from the airport, which is a great way to enter Boston for the first time."

"I want to be sure that everyone's psyched for the road trip for the next two weeks. Has everyone got everything they need?"

"There was a pack waiting at the hotel, detailing my full itinerary, how long I have to speak, the slides I have to present. It's great because I don't need to add anything to what they've given me. The itinerary's changed a lot from the original plan, but that doesn't matter." Alix enthused.

"I've got the same pack. They don't give much opportunity for customizing what you want to say. It's completely canned. They could get a monkey to give this presentation. Why did they get us to fly over and spend two weeks of our lives on the road, just mouthing a pre-set text?"

"The reason, Paul, is that your illustrious presence adds credibility to the process. You've travelled round the world for years, you can inspire with anecdotes of life in Asia, talk about the companies you like, paint some local colour. And don't forget, mate, you helped to design the slide show. You signed off on it and have had every opportunity to customize it to your own style."

"I know, but . . . "

Paul was interrupted by Bob in Boston. "Well, mine's great. I practised in front of the mirror this morning. I strutted like Mussolini at a rally. Very inspiring, I thought. Changing the subject, I got a call yesterday afternoon from a guy called Vernon Badore. He said he'd just met Mark off a plane in Atlanta and that you were keen to hire him. What's the story, Mark?"

Pushy little shit. "Absolutely not. I got a message from Bill Tuckwell in New York that he'd set up a meeting with Vern Badore on my way through Atlanta. He met me between flights. He's CSF's wholesaler for Tennessee and wants to be our marketing guy in the USA. I told him to visit us in London in October so that everyone could meet him."

Paul added, "That's funny. He called me in my hotel here in Chicago. He said CSF wanted him to be Appletree's rep in the USA, and that he and Mark got on really well. He said he would be at my speech in Kansas City next week."

"He called me too, said he had to be in Palo Alto and would meet me for my lunch presentation. What's a wholesaler for Tennessee doing in California? He didn't mention anything about meeting you guys. It sounds like we're being set up." Alix was always ready to sniff out a conspiracy, "I thought CSF was supposed to do our marketing in the USA. Why do we need to hire our own man?"

"He said he had to be in Philadelphia and would meet me there. He was keen to join our 'due dilly in Philly', as he put it." Bob added. "I thought one of the main reasons CSF liked Appletree was that we wouldn't be tripping over each other in the USA. As a matter of interest," he asked, "who pays for this guy?"

"All we know is that Cosway and Tuckwell thought it was a good idea. Cosway said we have no obligation to hire Vernon or anyone else. He called me too. I just saw it as smart lobbying." Graham was more charitable than the others.

"Thanks Graham. I told Vern to come and visit us in London. That's all. No promises, nothing. I did not tell him to contact you in your hotels around the country. As far as payment's concerned, Cosway said that CSF would pay for a marketer for Appletree in the USA until he became self-financing."

"If we don't like Vern, would CSF pay for someone of our own choice?" Alix asked.

"I think so, but we'd need to clarify."

"If Vern's as good as Cosway thinks he is . . . " Graham began,

"Or as good as Vern thinks he is." Paul couldn't resist the swipe.

"If Vern's as good as Cosway thinks he is," Graham continued, "and shows the same doggedness in the marketplace as he's shown with us, and if CSF are paying the freight, we'd be stupid not to consider the offer."

"I'm not comfortable. The guy sounds underhand. If he behaves like this when he's looking for a job, what's he going to be like once he's working with us? In our office, this kind of behaviour could become pretty political." Paul commented.

Paul should know, Mark thought.

"I don't know; he's just a kid. He's pushy because he sees Appletree as a great opportunity. I don't think he's being political, as you put it, so much as trying to meet as many of us as possible while we're over here. He's lobbying aggressively, I admit, but as Graham said, that's no bad thing in a marketer. What do you think, Alix?"

"I want to meet him before making any judgements. I'm concerned about adding numbers, because the time will come when CSF will say "You're on your own." and we'll be left carrying the overhead. Admittedly we should have the supporting revenues by then, but I'd be careful."

"OK, let's leave it like this. We'll all meet Vern back in London. We'll interview him thoroughly and decide then." Mark concluded. "If we still have reservations we don't need to hire him. Any other questions?"

"No? All right, everybody, enjoy the road show. Work hard and raise a ton of bucks for the Fund. If you need me for any reason, I'm based at the DonCesar in St Petersburg. My number's on the itinerary, and you all know my mobile. Ciao."

Mark slid open the window. Humid, 85 degree air from the Gulf flowed in and eased the edge off the air-conditioned chill of his room. He sat in the sunshine and dialled Nancy in New York.

"Hey Marko. What's up? I really appreciated the flowers you sent yesterday."

"Oh – you're welcome. I'm sitting on a balcony in the sunshine overlooking the Gulf of Mexico, thinking about you. What are you up to?"

"Not much, the usual Sunday stuff. Church, tidying the apartment. It's a fine day so I'm going for a bike ride in Central Park this afternoon with my girl friend."

"Sounds fun."

"I like to get out as much as I can. You've gotta be careful or your job takes control of your life."

"True. But you know something? If it wasn't for our jobs we wouldn't have met."

"That's a cute thing to say, Marko." Only his sister and his closest friends from school called him Marko. He liked the way she instinctively used his familiar name. She seemed comfortable and confident with him. "I really enjoyed having dinner with you on Friday night. Thanks for thinking of me."

"It was a lovely evening for me too."

"Well, perhaps we could get together when I'm in New York again?"

"That would be fun. I've always wanted to visit London too."

"I'll be your tour guide."

Chapter 13

The road show began in earnest on Sunday. Alix addressed her group of underwriting brokers over brunch in Seattle. Paul, Bob and Graham hosted their dinners in Chicago, Boston and New York.

Mary Cohen, the CSF wholesaler for Florida, singled out Mark in the crowded lobby of the Don Cesar and introduced herself.

"You must be Mark?" They shook hands.

She was beautifully manicured; her slender fingers reminded him of a Florentine Madonna's hands. Her face was made up to look as pretty as the house of L'Oreal allowed. Mark admired her big hair in the way one might be struck by an amazing Viennese confection. But despite her valiant efforts, nothing disguised Mary's short legs, large backside, small breasts and plain face.

"Let me brief you on this evening. We're hosting dinner for ten of the biggest financial hitters in the Tampa Saint Pete area. Try to keep it conversational rather than presentational. Before dinner we'll have a few cocktails then sit down to a set meal. I'd like you to talk informally about your background, about Appletree, the Case for International Investing, the objectives of the new CSF International Fund and the outlook for international markets."

"That's all?"

"Yea- and if you could throw in a few stock tips I'm sure that would be appreciated."

"No problem. Let's roll."

They crossed over to the Maritana Grille where they met the elite group. They were heavy players, well-informed and receptive to new ideas. Mark enjoyed the bonhomie. They were obviously successful. A strong competitive undercurrent buzzed between them – particularly in the matter of golf handicaps. Like millions of Floridians they were nuts about the game which Mark had decided, years before, to postpone until old age. This had turned out to be a self-imposed handicap: he had since learned that golf was as much a prerequisite for American business success as an MBA.

To minimize disruption of the evening's discussion, dinner was a fixed menu of Maine lobster salad, filet mignon ('Rare, unless anyone objects') and the famous Maritana soufflé for dessert. Little alcohol was drunk in the course of the evening, although nobody was averse to a glass of chilled Chateau d'Yquem before heading home into the sticky night.

"That was perfect," Mary turned to Mark as the last broker slipped into his valeted Mercedes and glided back towards the freeway. "They enjoyed your comments. They really appreciate spending time with the CEO of Appletree. This International Fund is big news." Mary looked conspiratorially over her shoulder, adding, "Particularly the fat up-front fee."

"I hope it's more than that." Mark replied "I enjoyed meeting them too. They're a lively bunch."

"Let's have a drink at the bar before we turn in for the night. It would be useful to run through our schedule for the next week." Mary didn't give him the chance to say no.

"Sure, a quick drink would be fine. Something non-alcoholic; I need to turn in soon. Jet lag, you know." Mark noted the flash of disappointment in Mary's face. One certainty of being on the road with her was the zero chance of an indiscretion on his part.

After consuming a club soda in the minimum time consistent with politeness, Mark returned to his suite. He called New York.

"This is Nancy."

"Hi –you sound sleepy."

"What time is it?"

"Eleven o'clock. Sorry if I woke you up."

"That's OK. What's up?" she yawned.

"Late at night, back in my hotel room. I thought of you."

"That's nice. How was your day?"

"I just hosted my first meeting of the road show."

"Go well?"

"I think it went OK. I can tell you're really sleepy so I'll say goodnight. I just called to say I'm thinking of you."

"I'm thinking of you too."

Monday for Mark started with entertaining a room of reps from EF Lowi Nicolas, the Florida brokerage firm. A buffet breakfast was set up in a diner adjacent to their office building in Tampa. Mark watched the reps heap their plates with bacon, sausages, scrambled eggs, hash browns, maple syrup, pancakes and muffins. One or two fitness freaks ladled stewed prunes over bran flakes and drank decaffeinated coffee. The rest gorged themselves on enough calories to feed an African village for a week.

Mary Cohen started with a slide presentation introducing the CSF International Fund. One particular slide raised their attention above the trough for a few minutes.

"As you know, EF Lowi Nicolas have agreed to underwrite this fund. This entitles you to a special commission for all sales during the launch period. You will receive the introductory 5 per cent front end commission for sales, plus the special 1per cent underwriters' fee. So your commission on a $100,000 ticket will be $6000."

Several brokers stomped their feet and shouted "Yeah!"

"Most of you have high net worth clients in Tampa Saint Pete, as well as state or other public sector pension business. This fund is a perfect vehicle for large, sophisticated investors to diversify overseas. Recent studies from consultants show that up to 40 per cent of pension investments should be diversified into foreign investments. Any of your clients who have less are perfect candidates for investing in this fund. A million dollar slug into the Fund from a municipal pension fund will gross you sixty thousand dollars in commission. Think about it."

More stomping, thumping and catcalling.

"Now I'd like to introduce to you the Chief Executive Officer of Appletree Capital Management, Mark Telford. Mark has twenty years experience in global investing. He founded Appletree Capital Management in London after working as a highly successful investor in Hong Kong, Paris and New York. CSF chose Appletree after an exhaustive search in six countries for the perfect manager to sub-advise the CSF International Fund. It'll become clear why CSF chose Appletree as Mark describes in the next half hour how he manages money. He speaks three languages and has a degree in law from Cambridge University. Over to you, Mark."

"Thanks Mary. Before I start I would like to say how honoured I am to be here in Tampa. I've followed the Buccaneers for many years and look forward to their next Super Bowl win."

"Right on!" a broker to his left jabbed a fist in the air.

"Today, I'm going to talk about three things." Mark flicked up the first slide. "First, why you should invest in international markets. Second, Appletree's approach to investing and Third, the outlook for markets over the next five years."

Mark had been speaking for a few minutes when brokers, having consumed their stack of food, began to slip out of the room in twos and threes. Mary motioned to Mark to speed up.

"I can tell that some of you need to get back to the office, so I'll just focus on a few key points." Mark flicked through the slides, slowing down to show Appletree's stellar performance since inception, and a chart showing projected economic growth around the world.

"As you can see there are many reasons to invest overseas, Appletree has a robust process and we know how to deliver the goods. Any questions?" Mark had compressed half an hour's presentation into ten minutes.

"Yea," an older gentleman stuck up his hand. "What's with Appletree? Why the name?"

Mark was irritated, after his forcibly shortened presentation, that the first question was so trivial.

"It's because after working and travelling around the world for most of my professional life, I came to roost in London. The apple doesn't fall far from the tree. Hence Appletree."

"Nice." Was the gentleman's only response. He rose to leave the room.

"Any other questions?"

The remaining questions were of a more probing and technical nature. Mark was relieved that at least some brokers had paid attention to his talk. After twenty minutes, Mary stepped up to the podium,

"Well folks, this concludes breakfast. We really appreciate you taking the time out of your busy schedules to come and hear about the CSF International Fund." She stepped back and clapped, leading the remaining handful of attendees in a desultory round of applause for Mark.

They left the building and walked to the car park in the searing morning sunshine. Mark's eyes narrowed in the glare,

"So, Mary, what did you think? I'm amazed how those people stuff themselves at the trough then get up and leave without hearing what I have to say."

"Happens all the time, Mark. I wasn't too concerned, because they've already bought into your Fund. The commissions are too rich for them to ignore it. They've gone back to their desks and are calling their clients to say they just had breakfast with the manager."

"Shameless bastards."

Mary looked surprised.

He climbed into the white Eldorado with tinted windscreens. He closed his eyes, sinking deep into beige leather as the air conditioning blew on his shirt and cooled his face. Mary's seat was pulled close to the dashboard. She'd become one of those thousands of little Floridian dames on the road behind the wheel of her oversized Detroit monster.

"OK Mark, we got two meetings before lunch in satellite offices of EF Lowi Nicolas." Mary merged into the traffic stream and headed east past the Raymond James Stadium. "Our first meeting is with two big hitters in Brandon. The second's a walk through in the Seffner office. All mega-producers."

"What do you do when you walk through?"

"That's when you don't have a prior appointment, but the office manager says it's OK to walk through and see if anyone's interested to spend five minutes with the CEO of Appletree Capital Management. Sometimes they can be real productive. Other times, they're desperate. It depends on the time of day, what the market's doing and who's around."

"Sounds a bit unstructured."

"Sure. But you can get lucky and it gives you exposure." Mary paused. "By the way, I liked your touch about the Tampa Bay Buccaneers. It's not often a Brit comes to town and tells them how great their football team is."

"Thanks- I remember ages ago hearing how many Americans defined themselves by their sports teams."

"On the back seat you'll see a folder. Can you grab it for me?"

"Sure." He leaned back and grasped the green file, "What do you want out of it?"

"The top sheet's your schedule for the week. You're with me today and tomorrow, then Wednesday morning you fly to Dallas, where Zack Overwood will pick you up for three days around Texas."

"That's a lot for one week."

"Yea – we were hoping to do it sequentially. Florida first, then Texas, but it hasn't worked out like that. Instead, you've got Tampa, Saint Pete, Bradenton and Sarasota today and tomorrow. Depending what Zack has for you in Texas, you should get the weekend to yourself. Then I pick you up next week to cover Port Charlotte, Fort Myers and Naples. We then drive East and spend the rest of the week in Miami, Fort Lauderdale and West Palm."

"Sounds like a hell of a week. I thought I was supposed to hang loose and cover for my colleagues as opportunities arose."

"You are, but not yet. Your colleagues are still travelling around the country. If the wholesaler covering Milwaukee wants you to close a big account, you fly to Milwaukee. But not while your colleagues are still in the country."

"I see. So I tool around Florida and Texas in a holding pattern until I'm needed for the real work?"

Mary laughed, "Not exactly. What you're doing now is important. You're doing exactly what your colleagues are doing, only you have the additional responsibility of covering the whole country as a trouble shooter once they're gone, plus Florida and Texas."

"I'm hungry. I was so busy talking to the masses this morning that I missed breakfast. When's lunch?"

"After those two meetings I told you about, we have a lunch appointment at 12.30. If we arrive early I'll make sure you get something to eat before you're on."

"Before I'm on what?"

"You're the featured speaker at a lunchtime meeting of the FSDC – the Florida Securities Dealers' Convention. They're an influential group and we're real lucky to get in front of them. Your speech should be educational, not salesy, but I figured they'd like to hear your story. It helps our cred."

"Fair enough. As long as I eat something first. What have you arranged for me this afternoon after I address the FSDC?"

"We walk through two more EF Lowi offices, then drive back for an early dinner at the DonCesar. We're hosting thirty high net worth investors and their advisors. You can crash out after 10.30.

The rest of the day passed in a blur. As they drove back to the Don Cesar after a day of six meetings, Mark felt a curious bond of comradeship with his companion,

"You know, Mary, it makes a difference to travel with someone on days like this. I appreciate you taking care of the logistics, the timing, the meals, the map reading. All I had to do was come for the ride, be there and perform."

Mary looked surprised, "In our wholesalers' conference call last week, Bill Tuckwell said CSF was gonna build the opera house, and you guys were gonna sing. You're doing me a favor too when you come to Florida. The faster we get around, the more brokers we get to see, and the bigger my cred. The more commission we pay the brokers the more they sell. The more they sell, the richer I get. Simple." She laughed.

"That's a straightforward proposition." Mark reflected, "As a matter of interest, and you don't have to answer this if you don't want to, how are you paid? I mean, what's the structure of your comp?"

"Wholesalers' base pay is designed to put food on the table and pay the mortgage. Nothing else. We get a standard T&E allowance and benefits. All the action is in the commissions calculated from the type of business we sell. In a fund like the International Fund, with a 5% front end load, we get 1% of all sales. That may not sound much, but if EF Lowi Nicolas deliver their $15 million at the launch, I get $150,000 commission."

"On top of the 6% that the broker gets?"

"Sure. It's a service charge."

"Who are you servicing?"

"The intermediaries – the brokers and financial planners."

"Who pays?"

"CSF."

"Yes, but where does CSF get the money to pay these commissions?"

Mary looked incredulous: "The clients, of course."

Noting his scepticism, she added,

"In funds with a slimmer load we get slimmer commissions. So with Muni or Treasury bond funds, our commission is calculated on the fee paid to CSF, not on the dollars we bring in. The sums can be large, but the commissions are small, right down to zero with Money Market Funds."

"So CSF charges bigger fees and commissions for equity and high alpha funds?"

"Sure. The better the performance, the less the client notices his haircut from commissions."

"So, for example," Mark persisted, "if a fund is up 20 per cent and the market is up 12 per cent, the fund's alpha is 8 per cent."

"Correct."

"And if CSF pays out, say, 3 per cent in commissions to the wholesalers, the client still has an alpha of 5 per cent from the fund's performance?"

"Correct. The formula isn't as simple as that, but that's the basic idea. Commission payouts vary, depending on the fund's alpha. If the portfolio manager has a bang-up year everyone benefits. If he has a shitty year then our commission pool gets smaller."

"So the publicized performance of a fund may have nothing to do with its real performance?"

"Correct." She turned to him, "In case you haven't noticed we've arrived at your hotel." Mary's Eldorado glided up the DonCesar's driveway. "It's six o'clock and we're on at seven. I need to freshen up and make some phone calls. Why don't we meet in the lobby just before seven?"

Mark was glad to get back to his room. It had been a hell of a day. Breakfast, followed by two meetings; lunch, followed by two meetings. Now, dinner. He stripped, emptied the ice bucket into the sink, filled the sink with cold water and buried his face in the coolness. As he towelled himself he spotted the lilies in a tall vase on the credenza beside his bed. An envelope lay beside them. He ripped it open.

I thought you'd appreciate these after a heavy day on the road.
Take care.

Nancy xx

It was ten past six on the East Coast. She would be on her way home. Mark changed into his trunks and headed to the pool. He swam lengths for twenty minutes and returned to his room, showered and put on fresh clothes. He had ten minutes. He called New York.

"This is Nancy."

"The flowers smell wonderful. I really appreciate them."

"Oh – you're welcome, Marko. I thought you'd like something homey in your hotel room."

"You're very sweet to do that."

"You're welcome. What are you up to tonight?"

"Another dinner in a few minutes. What about you?"

"I just got home and was about to get in the shower when you called."

"What are you wearing?"

"A towel. How about you?"

"A towel."

"Cute."

Chapter 14

The morning wake up call was due at 6.30. He picked up and yelled at the automated message, "Thanks a hell of a lot for waking me up" and was about to slam the receiver down when he heard a male voice saying "Hey Mark, is that you?"

"Yes, it's Mark. Who's that?"

"I'm real sorry to wake you up. It's Bill Tuckwell. I'm in Bermuda and wanted to catch you before the day started."

It was 5.47 am, exactly 43 minutes before Mark needed to get out of bed.

"So what's up?" he asked drowsily.

"I wanted to ask how the trip's going so far in Florida, and if you have everything you need."

"The trip's going fine. I hosted three meals yesterday and six office presentations. They were mainly to brokers from EF Lowi, and they seemed quite keen on the fund." He yawned loudly, hating Tuckwell for intruding on his sleep.

"There were also some financial planners from other firms. Mary's keeping score on who turns up at the meetings. I guess we spoke to over a hundred brokers yesterday. If each one comes up with a quarter of a million, we got $25 million for a day's work."

Tuckwell laughed, "One reason I wanted to call was to tell ya that our broker liaison department contacts every 'hit' you make on the road. You saw 111 brokers and planners yesterday. The feedback is real good. They like you, they like the International Fund and they expect to smash through EF Lowi Nicolas's underwriting commitment of $15 million. Congratulations.

We're keeping score on each of you. Great feedback from Seattle and Boston. Not so good from Chicago. The word is that Paul McKay's too bitchy for the Midwest. Graham hasn't started yet. He spends this week with our marketing guys in New York. He goes to Bismarck, North Dakota to visit our admin team next week."

"What do you mean, too bitchy for the Midwest?"

"I guess they just don't appreciate his sense of humor in Peoria."

"Are you guys running a book on us?"

"That's exactly what we're doing, Mark. The warm and fuzzies you generate for the International Fund will fade before the launch date. But our broker liaison team calls to remind the reps daily by squawk box. In our experience the daily total we track tends to be pretty accurate."

"So how much are we in line for?"

"On the basis of yesterday's feedback, the Fund will be between $400 and $450 million at the launch."

"Added to your seed capital of $300 million, that's over $700 million. That's an excellent start to the Fund."

Tuckwell glazed over this comment. Mark's mental arithmetic came up with an annualized fee of $4.2 million from the first tranche of money in the Fund.

"How did your meeting go with Vern Badore?"

"We met in Atlanta airport. He's a determined young man and I want him to visit London before anyone makes a decision. I was amazed how he took it on himself to call Alix, Bob, Graham and Paul separately. He plans to visit them at various locations around the USA this week."

"Yea, he's got balls that boy." Bill didn't pursue the discussion beyond this admiring observation.

"OK Mark, gotta go." Tuckwell changed gear. "Just want you to know we're tracking your performance. Call if you need anything. You got my mobile number. Cheers, mate." Bill hung up. His attempt to be British and matey sounded hollow.

It was now six o'clock and too late to sleep more. Mark slid off the bed, drew back the curtains and shuffled blearily onto the balcony. It was humid and dark, with a streak of dawn widening in the East. Way below, maintenance boys vacuumed the pool and tested the water. Hotel staff straightened the poolside lounge chairs and replenished piles of white towels. Further out, a bare-footed jogger splashed along the beach. The sea was flat calm; the waves barely lapped the shore.

"OK – action time." Mark pulled on his trunks and took the elevator to the beach. He swam steadily in the glassy lukewarm Gulf water for twenty minutes and returned to his suite.

Tuesday was much the same as Monday – a crazy swirl of meetings and meals in South Saint Pete, Bradenton and Sarasota. The meetings were well-attended by EF Lowi brokers. Feedback from the previous day had filtered through the system and Mark was received with more enthusiasm. Most brokers didn't slink off after eating; they stayed behind to ask questions and satisfy themselves about CSF's commission structure. Some even wanted to know about the international markets and discuss the benefits of portfolio diversification for their clients.

The day ended as it had begun. After an early dinner presentation, Mark went for a long swim at dusk in front of the hotel. The water was deliciously warm, if not invigorating, and he crashed out early in his room, ready to rise and fly to Dallas before dawn.

He was met at the gate in DFW Airport by Zack Overwood.

Mark liked the wall-to-wall style of CSF. They understood the importance of spoiling their road warriors. Since the hook-up with CSF, Mark had been impressed by their culture of can-do and rapid implementation. CSF practised the Law of Comparative Advantage; everyone played the role they were best suited for, and were supported to do it to the limit of their capabilities.

Mark never had to fret about the minutiae of travelling. The limo was waiting at the DonCesar at exactly the appointed time that morning. It was paid for and the driver would not accept a tip. At the airport he was checked in before arrival; they let him take his oversize bag on board. The CSF name was a byword for prompt and generous payment. Service everywhere was immediate and efficient.

Mark's right hand was grabbed and crushed. "Good to meet you, son. I'm Zachary Overwood. Call me Zack. How was your trip?"

Zack was six foot four with a straight back and a barrel chest. His black cowboy boots sported a rattlesnake motif stitched on the sides and converging at the arch of each boot. A black lace tie was held together by an Indian turquoise brooch. His jacket was beige linen; his charcoal trousers were conventional enough, but for a bronze belt buckle stamped with the insignia of the Sparta Police Department. A black Stetson sat atop his head, adding six inches to his already impressive presence. He looked Mark up and down with a hard glint.

"You got some dressing to do, son. In Texas you don't do business lookin' like that." Mark wore his pinstripe London-tailored suit, black wing-tips, a white shirt and a red spotted silk tie.

"Maybe, but I don't keep a separate wardrobe for Texas."

"We're committed to meetings around Dallas today but tonight we drive to San Antone. In the morning I'm gonna take you to a place I know. I can't take you to the Hill Country lookin' like that." He caught Mark off guard, but slapped his shoulder in a paternal way.

"In the meantime, son, we got breakfast at the Crescent Court Hotel downtown. Fifty producers from Pierce & Foster, They're underwriters for the CSF International Fund in Texas, Louisiana and Oklahoma. Real big players."

Mark had been up four hours and the New York Stock Exchange was not yet open. He wanted to relax but the day was only just starting. The temperature in Dallas was about the same as in St Petersburg but less humid. Zack weaved his metallic blue Cadillac Seville through the four-lane traffic along the John W Carpenter Freeway towards downtown Dallas.

Zack's Seville had the same suspension and all-enveloping leather seats as Mary Cohen's Eldorado. His car was pristine and gave few clues. The only suggestion of a hard-driving salesman was the no-hands mobile phone plugged into a socket by the driver's seat.

Mary's car, by contrast, was like an office cubicle on wheels, with yellow stickers on the dash and back seats piled with brochures, folders and maps. A pair of shoes was stuck under one front seat, an umbrella under the other. The car carried the rancid odour of old clothes, cat litter and empty yoghurt pots. Zack's car had nothing on, or under, the seats and smelled of new leather.

Mark gave his presentation in a private dining room of the Crescent Court Hotel to a group of Type A, balls-to-the-wall East Texas stockbrokers from Pierce & Foster. He began,

"It's a privilege to be back in town. I've always been a huge fan of the Dallas Cowboys and look forward to watching them at the next Superbowl to prove that they're the greatest football team of all time."

The brokers expressed their appreciation by loud clapping and raucous cheering. The rest of the speech was icing on the cake. After questions, a Managing Director of Pierce & Foster took the podium.

"I don't know how the heck a limey with an accent like that gets away with it in Texas, but we'd all like to welcome you to the Lone Star state and thank you for your investment ahdeahs. Can we have a show of hands from those whose clients intend to put over $200,000 into the CSF International Fund?"

About thirty arms went in the air.

"How many of you will put over $500,000 in the Fund?"

About twenty arms stayed in the air. The Managing Director turned to Zack Overwood.

"There you go, Zack, Ah guess that takes care of our underwriting obligations. Thank you for your hospitality, gentlemen, and have a safe day."

The brokers applauded and filed out of the room. As they walked through the car park, Zack complimented Mark, "That was one heck of a rebel rousing speech, son. You sure know how to work a crowd."

The rest of the day was spent in much the same way as the previous two days in Florida: two office meetings, a lunch speech, two afternoon meetings, dinner. After dinner with more hitters from Pierce & Foster they drove to Waco and checked into a roadside motel. Mark declined Zack's offer of a bourbon nightcap and crashed out in his room. It was 11.30, 19 waking hours since he'd left the DonCesar that morning.

The following day Zack took Mark to Lucchese in San Antonio. Zack commanded the sales assistant to procure the very best boots in the store. As he unlaced his classic English black wing-tip brogues, Mark surveyed the row of multi-coloured, intricately tooled boots sculpted from the skins of various fauna, commenting,

"I don't know how anyone can wear stuff like this."

"Son, there are folks in Texas who'd say the same about those English bootees." Zack nodded in the direction of Jermyn Street's finest.

After trying on a wide array of footwear, Mark left Lucchese carrying a bulky box under his arm. On his feet was a surprisingly comfortable pair of black lizard boots, cowboy to the core. They were a bizarre contrast with the style of his London suit, but what the hell. This was Texas.

"Well, son, we gotta work on that suit of yours yet, but the boots are a start. I'm not a-shamed to be seen with you up-country now."

Two hours later they rolled up at the Faust Hotel in New Braunfels. It was early so Mark and Zack strolled around the pretty German town. They were celebrating a Wurstfest. The air was filled with the succulent aroma of cooking sausages.

As they strolled to the car after a speech to 31 brokers, Zack put a hand paternally on Mark's shoulder, observing, "Son, if bullshit was music, you would be a brass band."

The remainder of the week was a tangle of meetings and drives around San Antonio and Austin. There was massive interest in the fund from the satellite offices of Pierce & Foster. Mark agreed to stay the weekend and spend part of the following week in Texas. Zack called Mary Cohen to reschedule her meetings planned in Florida on the Monday and Tuesday.

Mark got to know Zack on these drives. He'd been born in Guthrie Oklahoma of Scottish missionary and Cherokee descent and moved to Sparta Texas when he was an infant. His father ran a beef ranch, found oil and became a player in East Texas politics.

"Son, you're staying on the Overwood Ranch this weekend, I've spoken to Sara and she's getting the kids round for a barbecue on Saturday. Youngest is 28. Penny Lane. She's married and is raising my two beautiful grandchildren. My oldest boy, Zack Junior, is the senior police officer in Sparta township. Middle one, John, is a pilot in the Navy. He's based on a carrier out of San Diego. You won't get to meet him this weekend."

They stopped in Austin for the last meeting on Friday afternoon. As they pulled off the I 35 on Martin Luther King Drive, Zack briefed Mark.

"The guy we're about to see's a piece of work. I've known him since college days. Name's Jesse Le Mesurier, he runs his own brokerage firm."

Le Mesurier & Associates were based in a restored brownstone within sight of the State Capitol. A cute young black girl greeted them at the reception.

"Hi Zack. Jesse's expecting you. If you'd like to take a seat in the conference room, he'll be along momentarily. Can I get you a coffee or a cold drink?"

"Just water, please, Miranda."

"The same, please." Mark was repeatedly struck by Zack's memory for peoples' names. He knew the name of every secretary and receptionist they'd met that week. And they knew him. He didn't need to announce himself. They saw Zack coming and the door opened; a precious quality for a mutual fund wholesaler.

Jesse LeMesurier was a black man in his fifties. He was immaculately tailored in a white linen suit, pink silk shirt and cream silk tie. His full head of close-cropped hair was graying at the temples, which gave him an air of distinction and authority. He had the slim build of an athlete and the smile of a politician.

"What can I do for you today, Zachary, my man?"

"I wanted you to meet my colleague, Mark Telford. He's the CEO of Appletree Capital Management in London. They were appointed to manage the new CSF International Fund we're launching in two weeks time."

"Great to meet you, Mark. What's your view of international markets? They've had a strong run-up in the past year and the Dollar's fallen nearly 20 per cent against the Euro and the Yen. Don't you think it's a little late to commit sums to international investing, when the next big move could be a Dollar recovery and better performance by US equities?"

This guy knows what he's talking about, Mark was immediately impressed by the man.

"Good observation, Jesse. Tactically, it's as you say. Markets are getting rich and you might get a better timing opportunity. Strategically, it's accepted wisdom that everyone should diversify their wealth into different assets.

One US consultant recently produced a paper arguing that US investors should have 60 per cent of their equity assets overseas. The average American investor has 10 per cent or less, so there's huge scope. My suggestion is to get your strategic allocation in place with 30 per cent of your equity assets, and wait for a suitable timing opportunity to put the second 30 per cent to work overseas."

This guy knows what he's talking about, thought Jesse.

"Have you ever thought about getting into marketing?" Jesse teased Mark. Before waiting for an answer he continued, "To tell the truth I don't need to be convinced. We're already committed to your fund at the launch. Now, what do you want to know about Le Mesurier & Associates?"

"I know very little. Why don't you fill me in?"

"Le Mesurier & Associates is the premier black-owned, black managed and black-staffed brokerage firm in the Confederacy. You might think that's not a big deal, but politics being what they are, we are beautifully positioned to benefit from the law that mandates a percentage of state business should go to minorities."

"That's a nice position to be in."

"Sure is, buddy. Le Mesurier & Associates manages a nice slug of all new Muni and Transportation bond offerings in the Confederacy. We consult to state pension fund boards and invest some of their assets. It's mighty useful being a token sometimes."

"Jesse, you're underplaying your hand." Zack interrupted. "You have an economics degree from Southern Methodist University, a PhD from Princeton, an MBA from the University of Chicago and you're a CFA. You left me way behind at SMU. There's no way you're successful just because you're black."

"No, but it's not a bad business model." Jesse's face crinkled with a broad smile. He lifted his water glass to his visitors.

"Well, gentlemen if there's nothing else, I need to get a few things done before we wrap up for the weekend. I appreciate you folks dropping by and wish you all the best with your fund launch. I'll watch it with great interest. Who knows, there may be an opportunity for us to steer some Texas State funds in your direction."

"Jesse my friend, I truly appreciate you taking the time out of your Friday schedule. I look forward to your investment in this fund. In the meantime, you know who to call if you need anything. By the way, Sara sends her best and asked me to ask when you're coming our way again? There's always a suite waiting for you and Diana in Sparta at the Ranch."

"I know that and appreciate it, Zachary. We'll get the girls to plan a weekend. Perhaps we could come down in a few weeks to hunt Texas quail?"

"Just get Diana to speak to my wife. Great to see you, buddy." The old college friends hugged in the lobby. Jesse turned to Mark "Before you go, I want to leave you with something." He reached into a closet behind the reception desk and brought out a small flat cardboard box.

"Compliments of the Lone Star State."

Mark opened the box. It contained a folded Texas state flag with a certificate attached, *This flag flew above the State Capitol, Austin Texas, on July 10th 19 –.*

"That's extremely kind of you. It will be flying in the skies of England before the month is out."

"You're welcome. Send me a photo of it flying above Bucking Ham Palace. Good luck my friend."

As they motored north along the I 35 towards Dallas, Zack asked, "What did you think of Le Mesurier & Associates?"

"As you said, he's a piece of work. It was kind of him to give me the Lone Star flag."

"Yea, he liked you. They say there's guy in the Capitol who raises and pulls down flags for a living. Hundreds every day. They go up and down like hookers' pannies."

The Overwood Ranch was a 6000 acre property on the western fringe of Sparta, East Texas. It was entered by a rough drive that crossed a cattle grid into open pasture fenced around the entire perimeter of the ranch. Steers grazed over lush, green prairie to the horizon. They drove past stands of oak trees and muddy ponds where cattle stood up to their haunches to cool off. The one storey ranch house was half a mile into the property, facing South West and nestled behind a roll in the landscape.

Sara Overwood embraced Mark as he entered the house,

"Welcome to the Overwood Ranch. Zack will show you your suite, then we can sit down and have some iced tea. You must be exhausted after the week you've had. Zack told me all about it."

Mark sank into the all-embracing hospitality of Sara and Zack Overwood. He occupied a quiet guest annex and slept ten hours on Friday night, finally overcoming the jet lag and fatigue from a punishing week. He met their kids at lunch on Saturday. It was a cordial and tipsy affair, with more beers sliding down than Mark was accustomed to at lunchtime.

The highlight of the weekend was visiting the Sparta Township Correctional Facility with Zack Jr. They drove down after lunch in the SPD police car, bristling with electronics and manly accessories like Winchester rifles, hand guns, belts of ammunition, handcuffs, a night stick, a stun gun and a laptop computer. The jail consisted of rectangular steel modules bolted together like cargo containers, fitted with indestructible toilets and devoid of anything that could be broken off and used as a weapon or suicide accessory. The steel boxes were packed with inmates. As he walked by, they implored him in Spanish for cigarettes, drugs, food, sex, freedom. *Señor, señor, señor.* Some were very young men.

"What are these guys in for?"

"Illegals. We pick 'em up on construction sites, farms, hotels, supermarkets, restaurants . . . We round them up and deport them to Mexico. They're usually back in a few days. One guy I've had twelve times. It's, like, "Hi Rodrigo, back again?" There's no point fining them, they're broke. These guys are so determined to work that America should let them in. We need to get the work ethic back in this country. They got it big time in Mexico."

He was interrupted by clamouring from a grille in a cell door.

"We want Justees, meester cop. When do we get Justees?"

"You get Justice when you go to heaven, buddy. What you get down in Texas is the Law."

"Que?

Late Tuesday afternoon Zack drove Mark to DFW International for the return flight to Tampa. Mary said she'd pick him up for an event in Clearwater that evening. He reclined his seat in the aircraft and reflected how much he'd enjoyed his stay with Zack and Sara.

Bill Tuckwell called as the plane was taxiing at a crawling pace towards the runway. "Hey, Mark. I understand you're number 32 for takeoff."

"You're joking."

"No – just checked with our source in the airline industry."

"That's spooky."

"Just good management, buddy. I'm calling to update you with the running score. It's still in the $400 to $450 million range, but the numbers are harder. They're no longer an indication of interest, but a real commitment to invest."

"Sounds good."

Bill gave feedback from Alix's tour, "She hit pay dirt with AG Stiphel in LA and Refnes Wheat in the North West. They like her up there. She's real smart and gets on well with the wholesalers she travels with.

"Bob's doing well in the East. Boston's a tough place to crack. Some of the world's best money managers are located there – and they know it. Launching a fund in Boston is hard, but Bob did good. We contacted First Boettcher Securities after his New England tour and it looks like they'll meet their underwriting commitment. He also made a mark with a coupla wire houses in New York. Looks like Lynch and Burnham are gonna put some business into the fund.

"Only problem is Paul McKay. He's a smart ass and makes disparaging comments about Graham and you."

"What the hell's he saying?"

"He attacks your lifestyle. Says you're never on time in the morning, says you leave important things undone, that you know diddlysquat about investment management."

"What's he saying about Graham?"

"That he doesn't give credit where credit's due, that the bonus system at Appletree is 'tilted against talent' is how he put it."

"Who's he talking to?"

"Whoever's listening."

"Leave it with me."

Mark immediately called Graham in Bismarck, North Dakota. "Hey Graham. Sorry to disturb you, but we've got a problem." The animated sounds of a restaurant could be heard in the background. Mark relayed the information which Tuckwell had just given him.

"What's the hell's he playing at? Let me find a quiet spot. Just a minute." Graham re-entered the conversation from a quieter location.

"We have two courses of action." Mark continued. "The compassionate one is for you to call him, as his employer and closest colleague, find out what he's saying and tell him to get a grip."

"And the second?"

"We call Bill Tuckwell, get him to freeze Paul out of the roadshow and fire him."

"What other feedback's Tuckwell giving you on the roadshows?"

"All positive. Everyone's wowing the crowds and sales look strong, except in the Midwest. Paul seems to be our only problem."

"Mark, if you don't mind, before we take extreme measures I'd like to hear his side of the story. I hired him and we've worked together for a while. It's possible he's so fatigued by the roadshow that he doesn't know which side is up. Maybe he's just not cut out for marketing. He's a useful resource for us, you know. Remember that call he made on the Asian markets?"

"The only meaningful investment call he ever made for Appletree." Mark responded sharply. "He's not a resource if we can't harness him without the constant fear of collateral damage on the way."

"Let me talk to him. I've got his mobile number and I'll get back to you shortly.

Twenty minutes later, Mark's flight had edged forward to Number 12 for takeoff. Graham called.

"Paul denies everything. He can't understand how these rumours started. He certainly isn't aware of saying anything that could cause offence. He wanted to know who reported him to Tuckwell."

"It's the wholesalers, Graham. He's been on the road with three and they all report the same thing. His indicated sales are far lower than the rest of us. Something's not going right."

"Paul did say one thing, Mark, which you should be aware of. When I confronted him with what you told me, he bitterly said, "I really can't understand why you ever got into partnership with Mark Telford, or why you stay in business with him."

"What did you say to that?"

"I said that I *was* in business with you, like it or not, and that it wasn't Paul's position to comment on it. I don't know what you've done but there's real animosity there, Mark."

"I wasn't aware of it. The only time I crossed him was during his annual review last year. He said that he could easily double his salary by moving across the City."

"I remember. You said that if he was unhappy at Appletree he would be foolish not to move across the City and double his salary."

"I would give the same advice to any ambitious person who saw a better opportunity."

"Maybe, Mark, but he took it the wrong way. He thinks you don't rate him."

"Well, the more I see him behaving like this, the more I come to exactly that conclusion. We have to move as a team, all the time. The only edge Appletree has over its competitors is that we're a happy group of professionals dedicated to superior performance. I don't trust Paul as a team member."

"OK Mark, so what do you want me to do?"

"Get him off the road. You or I may have to cover the cities he's missed or screwed up. Give him a severance package and kick him into the sunset. I didn't start Appletree to put up with this kind of crap. I really didn't, Graham."

"Fair enough. It needs to be procedurally impeccable, Mark, or we risk a real mess."

"I'll call Tuckwell to give him our decision. I'll also call Syreta in London to check with an employment lawyer over there."

Five aircraft before takeoff. Mark called Bill Tuckwell and passed on the decision.

"Smart call Mark. Guys like that steal more energy than they give out. I'll get Jack onto it."

"Jack?"

"Yea, Jack Bolt, our enforcer. Ex-Marine, Vietnam. He specializes in surgical strikes against, er, *unnecessary* employees. McKay won't know what hit him. He'll go out like a lamb, I promise."

This intriguing conversation was cut off by the announcement that his flight was next for takeoff and all mobile phones had to be switched off.

All the way to Tampa, Mark agonized over the professional assassination he'd just authorized. It was bound to cause huge waves at Appletree. Alix would hate him, Bob was more level headed, Paul had never truly bought into the Appletree story, but Graham had the freedom to hire a replacement immediately.

He stared helplessly as the lights of Baton Rouge passed thirty thousand feet below, then New Orleans, then blackness as he flew over the Gulf, punctuated by offshore rigs flaring gas into the night sky.

Chapter 15

Mary Cohen had left a message earlier on Mark's mobile phone to say he was to be the after-dinner speaker at an investment convention in Clearwater that night. She would meet him off the Dallas flight. The timing was tight, so he changed into a fresh shirt and suit in the aircraft toilet twenty minutes before landing at Tampa St Pete.

He wasn't prepared for the sight that met him at the gate. Mary was in a pink tee shirt without a bra, revealing . . . precisely nothing. She also wore a pink tracksuit bottom that highlighted her ample, wobbling backside. Pink flip flops completed the scene.

She spoke first.

"Welcome back to Florida. Bill Tuckwell called to say you had a tough day in Texas. He got me to cancel this evening's appointment. Said we should have some R&R instead."

He was speechless. They climbed into the Eldorado and she pointed her office-cubicle-on-wheels across the bridge to Clearwater.

"On the back seat's a cooler. I got OJ and Korbel champagne there. Pour yourself a drink. There's two glasses." *Korbel Champagne?*

"I'll wait, thanks."

Mark sat motionless, exhaustion filling the space just vacated by the last drop of adrenalin reserved for the evening's speech. He wanted to be at his hotel, take a swim, eat a light supper. Above all he did not feel like having R&R with Mary Cohen that evening. He desperately wanted to know what had happened to Paul McKay. However much he disliked Paul, he would never wish on him the devastation of being fired four thousand miles from home. How would he feel as he boarded the plane in Chicago for London tonight?

Act in haste, repent at leisure. Mark didn't have Jack Bolt's phone number and it was too late to call CSF. On the plane he'd reflected that the best course of action would have been to fly Paul back to London and get him out of the spotlight. He was disgusted by his own weakness in letting Jack Bolt, CSF's hatchet man, pull the trigger. Paul had always been the most sceptical voice about the CSF deal. Mark had let CSF eliminate Paul, thus fulfilling all his reservations about the deal.

The manly thing to have done would have been for him – Mark – to confront Paul and deal with it face to face.

Mary pulled up at a parking lot beside grassy dunes leading to the beach. "Come on my friend, lighten up. It's OK to play sometimes, you know." She lugged the cooler to a municipal picnic table where she set out smoked salmon, bread, cheese and fruit. Mark felt bizarre wearing a business suit on the beach. It was very humid and about 85 degrees with a steady breeze blowing along the shore. She poured two glasses of Korbel. "Cheers."

Mark tried to get his head around Bill Tuckwell. He knew he was being set up. He was being watched. But why? If he made a move on Mary – a zero probability – Tuckwell would find out immediately and store the information away for future use. If he did not make a move Mary might be pissed off. She might report a harassment incident anyway. It would be his word against hers. He'd heard of friends getting tangled in similar predicaments, and with far prettier women.

"Mary, please don't take this personally," a flock of sandpipers skittered peep-peeping along the shore, "but I feel absolutely shattered. I need to head back to my hotel and crash out."

She looked wounded.

"Oh . . . of course . . . I'm so sorry . . . I didn't think. Why don't you sit down for a few minutes? We may as well finish the champagne and eat the smoked salmon sandwiches. We'll go afterwards."

On their way to the DonCesar Mary diverted into a housing development along a creek. She stopped by a row house lit by dim solar lamps spaced along a concrete path. "Mark, I need to go potty. Why don't you come in for a few minutes?"

They were assaulted by hordes of insects along the pathway.

It was a sad little condominium reeking of old cigarette smoke, cat litter and humid fabrics. A sliding glass door opened onto a patio adjoining a crabgrass lawn leading down to the creek. A mangy old cat lay motionless on a tatty armchair. The place was filled with the clutter of a solitary life. Mary disappeared to the bathroom. When she returned, she asked,

"Can I get you a drink, or a coffee?"

"That's kind, but I'd really like to return to the DonCesar, if you don't mind."

Mark was relieved to be back at the hotel. After a lengthy swim in the pool, he returned to his suite and called New York. It was nearly midnight. Nancy was still awake. "Hi, Honey, how's everything going?"

"Today was crazy. Meetings around Texas followed by a weird encounter when I returned to Tampa." He described his evening. Nancy woke up as he spoke.

"Speaking as a friend, Mark, be real careful of that man. He likes to get something on everyone he deals with. This would have been a lulu. He'd get something on you and Mary both at the same time. Sounds like you handled it well."

"I handled it honestly. Told her I was exhausted after a long day and wanted to go back to the hotel. There's nothing to get a handle on there."

"Sure you weren't tempted to cosy up to her in that snug little condo of hers?"

"I had to battle my raging hormones and won the struggle in the end, but it was difficult. How about you? How was your day regulating CSF?"

"Same old same old. Nothing too serious. Changing the subject, where in Florida are you going to be at the end of this week?"

"Hang on," Mark shuffled his papers to find the itinerary for Week 2. "Let's see. On Friday I'll be in Jacksonville. There's a lunch and walk-through at EF Lowi's regional office. I'm free after that."

"Have you ever been to Jacksonville?" she asked.

"No I haven't and don't have the faintest clue what to expect there."

"Me neither. But I've always wanted to visit the Okefenokee Swamp. You fly into Jacksonville and rent a car. I was looking at the map earlier. It's less than an hour North of Jacksonville Airport."

"The Okefenokee Swamp? What on earth do you want to go to a swamp for?"

"It's an eco-paradise. Birds, snakes, alligators, plants, flowers, that kind of thing."

"I didn't know you were into eco-stuff." Mark pictured her porcelain complexion in the wilderness and her perfect nails as she swung off a vine. "Sure. I've been a member of the Sierra Club for years. I've hiked Yosemite and sections of the Appalachian Trail."

"OK, so how do you sign up for visiting a swamp?"

"So you're up for it?"

"Sure, I'll do anything once, for the hell of it."

"Leave it to me. I'll make the arrangements. Call me after work tomorrow."

"Nancy?"

"Yes?"

"What if I said I'd be finishing the week in Miami?"

"I would have planned a weekend in the Keys or the Everglades. Or even a quick jump over to the Turks and Caicos."

"Just wondered. Talk tomorrow. It'll be good to see you on Friday, wherever we end up."

The following morning Mark checked out. Mary picked him up at six thirty in the lobby of the DonCesar. She was back in her corporate dress-for-success mode. Mark thanked her for meeting him the previous evening, and no more was said. They drove south for a breakfast presentation at Fort Myers, followed by meetings and walk-throughs until lunchtime in Naples. Appropriately, the Naples presentation was hosted in an Italian restaurant, with plush wallpaper and *O Sole Mio-style* background music. Thirty two brokers and financial planners showed up to hear Mark talking about international investing. Afterwards Mary congratulated him as they walked to the car park.

"You did a great job, Mark. They love your accent."

"Sometimes I wonder if it's the content or the delivery that turns them on. Last week in Texas a blue rinse lady came up to me after a speech. She said, "I didn't understand a word of what you said, Honey, but it sure sounded great."

"Probably some of both." Mary unlocked the Eldorado and Mark slipped into the airless vehicle, baking in the Florida sun. She turned on the air conditioning.

"Where now, chauffeur?"

"We've done the West Coast of Florida." She replied. "We're now heading to Miami across a swamp. It's about 120 miles, so if you wanna close your eyes I don't mind."

"A swamp? I like swamps. I want to see what it looks like." His heart leaped at the thought of his adventure with Nancy the following weekend.

"Flat and boring. It's called Alligator Alley but I never once saw an alligator there. I hate swamps." She headed East along the I 75, setting the car's cruise control at exactly the speed limit. After twenty miles or so, with one hundred miles still ahead of them, Mark became restless as they were overtaken by most other vehicles on the road. Mary sat motionless at the wheel, staring into the middle distance and sticking resolutely to the centre lane of the highway.

"Aren't you ever tempted to nudge your speed up by 5 miles an hour? I'm sure the cops wouldn't notice." A Georgia-registered semi thundered past on the inside lane. "See? The cops are after trucks like that. It would absolutely fill their radar screen."

"Maybe, but I can't risk it. I live in my car. I plan my trips at this speed so I'm never late. Racing along faster wouldn't improve my life. I do all my thinking as I cruise along Florida's highways."

"What are you thinking and planning right now?"

"Oh, the weekend, seeing my parents."

"Don't you ever fall asleep? With cruise control you don't need to do anything." Mile upon mile of palmetto scrub sailed by on both sides of the highway.

"Sure. Once I drove twelve miles with my eyes shut. I last remember seeing my exit sign then I woke up twelve miles beyond it. I hit some kind of road works. The driver behind me said he flashed and honked as he saw me drifting steadily off the road. I hit a line of plastic cones. I was OK, the car was dented and scratched, but nobody was hurt."

"When was that?"

"Oh – about three weeks ago."

"Were you alone in the car?"

"No. I had one of CSF's portfolio managers with me. We had had a full day in Fort Lauderdale and he was asleep as we drove west along this road."

"Crikey, I'd better keep talking or we'll end up in a ditch full of alligators."

"Yea. Your job is to keep the chauffeur awake."

"If you don't mind I'd like to make a few calls as you drive."

"Go ahead, Mark."

Graham picked up the phone, "Hey, Mark, how's it going?" He sounded surprisingly light-hearted.

"I'm calling to see what happened to Paul. Do you have any insights?"

"Jack Bolt pulled him off the tour in Omaha. The wholesaler had to step in and do the presentation. Paul was bundled into a limo and taken to a CSF corporate jet at a US Airforce base in Nebraska. The plane flew directly to a private airfield in Kent. On board Bolt read him the Riot Act and explained why his services were no longer required. Then the *pièce de résistance* – he was given three years severance pay, full bennies and a hundred percent vesting of his pension plan. It's going to be paid in tranches over three years on condition that he never bad mouths you, me, Appletree, CSF or anyone else. One squeak, in public or private, that comes to CSF's attention, and Paul's in the poor house."

"Who's paying for this?"

"CSF. Jack Bolt reported that Paul went from shock to ecstasy. He knows he's not worth three years salary."

"He's not worth one year's salary. How do I get myself fired? What does the rest of the team think of this?"

"It's a condition that they mustn't know he was fired. Officially, Paul left Appletree for family reasons and the jet was sent over to help a friend in need. This fits quite well with the facts. His little son has health problems and it's entirely plausible that Paul would miss him terribly while on the road."

"Devious bastards. I'd like to meet Jack Bolt one of these days."

"Just don't accept his offer to ride on a CSF jet."

Over the following three days Mark gave speeches and presentations from Miami northwards along the Atlantic seaboard through Fort Lauderdale, Boca Raton, West Palm Beach, Vero Beach and St Augustine. Lunch on Friday found him addressing fifty brokers in Neptune Beach after which Mary left him at Jacksonville Airport at 4pm. She headed off to stay in Gainesville with her mother for the weekend. Her faithful Eldorado had driven over seven hundred miles that week.

Nancy's flight was due at 7 o'clock. Mark picked up the rental car and waited in the Arrivals Hall for the La Guardia plane to land. His phone rang. It was Bill Tuckwell.

"Hey, Mark. I hear you just finished a crazy week down there in Florida and Texas. The feedback we're getting is great. Looks like we're in line for $550 million at the launch . . . "

"Fantastic, that's $850 million including your seed money."

"Mark, if the sales figure is anything close to $550million, we won't be adding seed money into the fund. There's no point. Seed money is there to get a fund going, not to make the managers rich. Besides, seed money doesn't pay a fee, so there's no point computing it in any way."

"That's not what we were led to believe."

"As I say seed money won't be required if the Fund raises as much as our reports suggest. We're getting huge preliminary sales numbers coming through from the Atlantic Seaboard. Bob went down real well there. And California, Arizona, Washington State. Alix did a great job. Only disappointing region is the CTZ north of Texas."

"CTZ?" Mark repeated.

"Central Time Zone. Texas is coming up strong, but the region north of Texas covered by Paul didn't catch fire. Everyone's going home this weekend except Graham, who has one more week, and you, here for another two weeks. I may need you to travel the Mid West with the wholesalers next week to rustle up some interest."

"Just let me know where you want me Tuesday to Friday."

"Tuesday? We work Mondays too in America, you know."

"I'm taking a long weekend. Frankly Bill, I'm pooped and need a break."

"You limeys ain't got no stamina. What the heck are you doin' in Jacksonville Florida for three days?"

"Just rest and recreation." Mark refused to be drawn.

"Moving on, I got feedback from Vern Badore. He visited with Alix in California, Paul in Kansas City and Bob on the East Coast. He also met with Graham. He said everyone was enthusiastic about having him on board. He was invited across to London when this launch is over. I think you're making the right decision to hire him."

"Don't jump the gun, Bill. I haven't decided to hire him. We don't want to rush this decision."

"Sure, I hear ya Mark, keep your cell phone on over the weekend. You'll hear from us where you gotta be on Tuesday morning."

Chapter 16

Nancy was dressed in jeans, topsiders, a white tee shirt and the familiar gold chain around her neck. She carried a light tote bag over her shoulder. Mark gave her a passionate hug as she came off the arrival ramp. "It's so good to see you. Let's get your stuff from the baggage claim and we'll get on our way."

She was prettier than he remembered. Her eyes radiated a smiling glow; her hair was loose. The last time he saw her it was swept back and held with a blue ribbon.

"This is all I've got. We can leave right away." she replied.

"A weekend in the wilderness and this is all you've brought with you?"

"Absolutely. Everything else we need is provided by the Waycross Adventure Camping & Kit Yourself company. WACKY for short. They have canoes, tents, sleeping bags, waterproofs, cooking stuff, everything. They're meeting us in Folkston at 8.30 tomorrow morning at our hotel."

"So where are we staying?" his lips touched the nape of her neck as she bent to get into the car. He caught a faint floral scent.

"We're booked at The Woodsman Inn at Folkston. It's the best in town. A small Colonial place with great food and comfortable rooms." Nancy pulled a sheet of driving directions from her bag.

"When you leave the airport you want to find Route 301 North and keep going. Folkston's 24 miles north of Jacksonville airport, just across the Georgia state line."

"No problem."

He drove in silence until they cleared the airport.

"I've been looking forward a lot to seeing you this weekend. I appreciate the things you've done to make it happen. I could never organize a canoe trip down here." Mark squeezed her hand in the dark.

"It's something I've wanted to do for a long time. Not many guys in New York want to spend a weekend canoeing around a South Georgia swamp." She laughed, "They think of Georgia like it's the Congo, the Heart of Darkness."

"I never gave it much thought, but I'm always up for an adventure in the wilderness."

"That's why I like you."

The Woodsman at Folkston was a charming wooden Colonial-style bungalow surrounded by a veranda. Easy chairs were scattered on the stoop, candles flickering on low tables beside them. It was a windless, warm evening. Fireflies were dotted around the garden. An American flag hung limply above the shallow stairs leading to the main entrance of the inn.

They were welcomed and shown to their room by a prim hostess.

"Will y'all be wanting dinner tonight?"

"Yes, that would be great. Can we please have a table in half an hour?" Mark wanted to deflect attention from the Tracy Lou Honeymoon Suite they had been shown into. While previous signals suggested an intimate weekend together, the reality of that enormous, overstuffed bed brought it home to Mark. He'd hoped for this, he'd wanted this, but he'd never actually broached the subject. He would not have been fazed if Nancy had booked two separate rooms, nor would he push his luck over the weekend. But she'd taken the initiative, went for broke and cracked his infuriating reticence.

"I'm so glad you booked the accommodation. I wouldn't have dared to presume we would be sleeping together." He sat and bounced on the bed.

"I heard that Brit men need encouragement or nothing ever happens. We'll talk about that at dinner. Right now, I'm going to take a shower. It's been a long day." Nancy turned the lights down, leaving the room bathed in the soft light of honeymoon candles, threw her tee shirt and jeans on the bed and wandered into the bathroom in her underwear. Mark's senses were swimming.

The evening unfolded with ease and humour. Later, as they curled together in the deep bed, she confessed she'd found him attractive from the moment they met. "I love your easy humour and self-effacing manner. It's so different from the usual mindless in-your-face crap that women have to put up with all the time."

"It's there to match the usual mindless in-your-face crap that men have to put up with all the time."

She dug a claw into his leg.

"I like your quiet confidence, your sense of efficiency. Your blue eyes and auburn hair. And this fabulous bod." He squeezed her closer. "I thought you were unattainable, but it all seems so easy and natural now."

"That's because it *is* easy and natural, Honey."

The following morning they enjoyed a hearty breakfast. They checked out of the inn after confirming their reservation for the same room on the Sunday night when they returned from the swamp. A guy from WACKY met them at the Inn in a beaten-up Cherokee and drove them to the East entrance of the Okefenokee Swamp National Wildlife Preserve.

Their canoe was ready, together with all the camping gear and food they were likely to need for a weekend. Every object they intended to take into the swamp was laid out on a tarpaulin sheet. A ranger handed them an inventory and they had to sign for everything they took into the wilderness. The inventory would be checked on their return. If anything were missing – even an empty beer can – canoeists had two choices: go back and find it, or pay a fine for littering. Most people paid the fine, but it was not unknown for some canoeists to turn back and paddle seven miles to an old campsite to retrieve a forgotten beer can.

They were given a channel map and the location of their camp site for that evening. It was nine miles away, an easy journey of six hours of relaxed paddling. They had plenty of margin to arrive before sundown. Itineraries at the Okefenokee Swamp were organized for canoeists to paddle from site to site without meeting other people. Even though the swamp was quite full of tourists at any given time everybody had the solitude and peace needed to appreciate the beauty of the place.

Mark and Nancy positioned themselves in the canoe with much hilarity and pushed away from the jetty. They paddled to the middle of the Suwannee and made their way along the channel through groves of cypress trees festooned with Spanish moss. Morning sunshine filtered through the rising mist; herons perched motionless on tree roots, poised to spear a passing meal. Apart from the rhythmic lapping of their paddles the only sound in the swamp was the call of birds high in the trees and the buzz of insects.

"Sometimes I wonder who the smart ones are in this country." Nancy mused, "The ones busting themselves on Wall Street or the folks who live in places like this, communing with nature."

An alligator basking on a mud bank among the reeds slid silently into the water twenty yards away.

"It depends what kind of reptile you choose to spend your time with." Mark replied.

They turned off the main channel where indicated on the map and canoed through moss-covered swamp cypress trees into open water. Floating white markers every few hundred yards indicated their route across an expanse of lilies. They passed low-lying islands, some of which had muddy beaches cleared from the undergrowth and set up for camping. Alligators were scattered like logs along the beaches. They were not exactly inviting places to camp.

"Let's find a shady place to stop and eat something." Nancy suggested after they'd been canoeing for two hours. "I'm thirsty too." They paddled up a narrow creek on an island until they found solid ground. Mark wedged the canoe onto a bank and they got out to stretch their legs. They sat in the intense humidity in the shade to eat their sandwiches. Insects were attracted by their fair flesh and pestered them in swarms.

"The problem with this nice shady spot," Mark swatted a horsefly, "is that there's no breeze to keep the insects moving."

Nancy screamed. As she laid her water bottle on a pile of vegetation, the undergrowth stirred and a water moccasin emerged from the dry leaves. In the time it took Mark to yell "Don't move!" Nancy had leaped ten feet from the snake. "Let's get the hell out of here." Keeping a watchful eye on the serpent, they gathered up the picnic, jumped on board, pushed the canoe off the mud and paddled like hell away from the infested island.

They slowed down once they were back into the main channel. "So much for our shady picnic spot," Mark commented dryly. "Still want a sandwich?"

Dreading what their designated campsite might be like, they were relieved that it was not on an island, but consisted of a platform constructed six feet above a vast field of water lilies. They moored at the base of the platform. Nancy climbed up a wooden ladder and Mark handed her the camping gear. The platform was partially covered by an open-sided roof, where they would set out their camping gear.

"First things first," Nancy reached into the cooler and found a bottle of Moët & Chandon. She eased off the wire and popped the cork, which flew twenty feet and landed amongst the water lilies. She poured the champagne into two plastic mugs. "Here's to eternal love and friendship."

Mark raised his mug." . . . And to our great adventure. I have to say it's not quite what I expected."

She laughed, "Yea, it's more primeval than I expected, even with the champagne. But that's what I was hoping for."

Their evening passed in pleasant revelry. When the champagne was finished they worked through half a bottle of bourbon and shared life stories.

"What do you do in your weekends in London?"

"Depends. I usually try to get out to the country. I have an aunt in Wiltshire, a hundred miles west of London, my parents live a long way north. I have friends in Wales. Sometimes I take the train to Paris. What about you?"

"Nothing so exciting. I go biking around Central Park or jog in my neighbourhood. I go to movies and concerts. In the winter I go up to the Catskills and ski at weekends."

"I'd love to see you jogging."

She prodded him with her foot.

Mark cooked a meal on the small gas stove that came with their camping kit. The temperature and humidity stayed high, but a steady breeze across the water kept away the insects. It darkened rapidly after the sun set. There was no street lighting, nor even the slightest slip of a moon. They were alone in total darkness on a platform above the water in the wilderness.

The swamp came alive at night. Frogs croaked and plopped off the lily pads; occasionally there was a mighty splash and the sound of flailing in the water as one creature caught another. A frog catching a dragon fly, a snake catching a frog, a snapping turtle catching a fish, an alligator catching a snapping turtle . . . The ancient sounds of this primeval ecology enveloped Mark and Nancy in their dreams.

Chapter 17

They returned to the Woodsman Inn at dusk on Sunday evening. Knackered, sweaty and insect-bitten, they'd at least avoided being attacked by alligators, bears, snapping turtles, snakes or other lethal denizens of Okefenokee. But in terms of pure fun their canoe trip to the ancient swamp was ten out of ten.

As they climbed the steps to the inn they were met by the woman who'd showed them their room two nights earlier.

"Mr Telford, Sir, some people have been trying to find you urgently. I told them you were on the Swamp and wouldn't be back here until Sunday evening."

"Who knows I'm here? Were they here in person or are they trying to get me on the phone?"

"By phone, sir." She went behind a desk and handed Mark an envelope containing messages.

He tucked them into his back pocket. Turning to Nancy, he took her hand. "Come on, let's find the hot tub. We can read them there." They returned to their room, stripped and rested their aching limbs in the bubbling hot water. Mark opened the envelope.

The first message was from Bill Tuckwell at 9am on Saturday :

> *Call as soon as you get this message. Could not get through on your cell phone and tracked you down to Folkston Georgia. Trust you're having fun down there?*

The second was from Bill Tuckwell at 12 noon on Saturday :

> *We need you in Chicago for breakfast on Tuesday at the Drake Hotel. Please confirm.*

The third had the name Chuck Anderson on it. Saturday 2pm :

> *I'm the wholesaler for Chicago and the North Central States. You're giving the opening speech at an investment conference at the Drake Hotel. 8am Breakfast on Tuesday. Booked you*

into the Drake Monday night on my Amex card, Guaranteed Late Arrival (GLA).

The fourth was from Mary Cohen. Saturday 6pm :

Hi, I've closed you out at the DonCesar and sending your baggage by courier to the Drake in Chicago f.a. Monday noon.

The fifth was from Graham. Sunday 2pm :

The Paul matter is resolved amicably. No repercussions. Call when you can.

"How in heaven's name do they know I'm here?" Mark looked at Nancy.

"Don't look at me like that Mark. Nobody knows we're here together."

"How did they track me down to this love nest in rural Georgia? It's like a game to Tuckwell. He's a total control freak."

"I told Darnelle in the office I was going on an adventure to the Okefenokee Swamp this weekend, and that I was taking Monday off. She didn't ask, nor did I tell her, who I was going with or where I was staying."

"I mean – look at this message from Mary Cohen. What if I'd not received it and gone to the DonCesar tomorrow afternoon, as planned? Who gave her authority to check out my room?" He suddenly caught up with Nancy's comment,

"Who's Darnelle? "

"Dick Cosway's secretary."

"Is she the office gossip?"

"No more than anyone else. But I guess that a swamp adventure is unusual enough to a New Yorker that she might gossip about it casually at the coffee station."

"Tuckwell knew I was in Jacksonville for an R&R weekend. He knew I was taking Monday off. He tried to winkle out my intentions when we last spoke. I gave him the runaround."

"That would be enough to make him crazy to know what you were doing this weekend."

"Did you make our hotel or flight reservations using the office fax, or phone?"

"I made the reservation by email."

"The office email?"

"Yes."

"There's the answer. Tuckwell knew I was in Jacksonville this weekend. He heard that you were flying to Jacksonville. He ordered your email records from CSF's IT unit. He found your hotel reservation for two in Folkston. On a jealous man's hunch he called the hotel and Bingo! He hit pay dirt."

"I'm so sorry I gave the game away, Mark. I didn't mean to." Nancy kissed him.

"Let's not worry whose fault it is. Everyone's entitled to some privacy when you use the email system, even in the office."

"I've always known that nobody can rely on privacy when they use the office email system." Nancy replied quietly. "Everybody signs a disclaimer when they join CSF. It didn't occur to me that my weekend plans would be of any interest to Bill Tuckwell, Marko," she kissed him again. "I hope I haven't embarrassed you by coming on a weekend with you."

"Don't be ridiculous. I love being with you. It just makes me mad that Tuckwell is so bloody intrusive. He sees it as a challenge to know what I'm doing all the time."

"He's real interested in you. The other day we were talking about compliance issues that affected Appletree and he kept asking questions about you, your qualifications and your background."

"Is he gay?"

Nancy laughed, "Can't say I ever looked into that. But I hear that Jack Bolt has a few kinks. They say he's got a thing going with a guy in the CSF Legal Department. Why do you ask?"

"Just looking for an explanation. I'm trying to get a sense of the man."

"If he *is* gay, he's got exceptionally good taste." She kissed Mark's mouth as her hand found him in the bubbles. "Now, you need to chill out. You have all day tomorrow to call these guys and get to Chicago. Kick back and enjoy yourself."

Chapter 18

Mark arrived at O'Hare late on Monday afternoon. The cab driver was Middle Eastern but proudly announced he was a Chicagoan. More than in any city he knew, Mark was struck how everybody in Chicago had a view on politics and the city's sports heroes. As they bumper- to-bumpered along the Kennedy Expressway he heard about the latest shenanigans in City Hall and how the Chicago Bears were doing in the football season.

"Da Bears are Four and O. They gonna win the Superbowl. Tonight they play Minnesota at Soldier Field. They gonna kick ass."

"Great. I'll watch that on TV."

"I get you teeckets. A Kurdish friend get them."

So they bantered until he was delivered to the Drake Hotel on East Walton. As with the DonCesar in Saint Pete, long-buried memories flooded back as Mark entered the lobby. He was surprised how cast-off recollections came to life so intensely when he travelled around America.

Years earlier he'd accompanied an English friend around various blues bars on the South Side. They heard Otis Rush, Sugar Blue and Mighty Joe Young. They saw Detroit Junior play at Teresa's. They boogied at Kingston Mines and Buddy Guy's. They saw Johnny Winter jamming with Muddy Waters one steamy summer evening at Navy Pier. As for Koko Taylor belting her songs into the smoke-filled night, *You can have my husband, but leave my man alone . . .*

Chuck Anderson had left a note at the registration desk. *Welcome to Chi-town.. You're in front of 90 brokers from Ray Hutton at 8 tomorrow morning. Let's get together at 7.30 for coffee. I'll call your room if I don't see you in the lobby. Regards, Chuck.*

Mary Cohen had packed his stuff and couriered it to the Drake. It was waiting in his room when he checked in. Much as he disliked the thought of her going through his clothes and papers, he was getting accustomed to the intrusive culture of CSF. Besides, his effects harboured no secrets so Mary could riffle through his underclothes as much as it gave her pleasure.

Mark threw his bag on the bed. The evening was young. He left the hotel and sauntered down the east side of Michigan Avenue as far as the river. Chicago was an early town. The crowd on the street looked like late shoppers and out-of-state conventioneers looking for a good time. How the city had changed. The sharp, muscular, brisk, ambitious, dress-for-success Chicago he remembered had given way to obese, sloppily dressed people schlepping along the street sucking ice creams. The city had changed so much, he could barely relate.

He searched for the chunk of Westminster Abbey built into the wall of the Tribune Building. It was still there: yes, some things are permanent in America. He crossed Michigan Avenue to the Wrigley Building and strolled back to the Drake along the West side.

"It's a huge pleasure being back in Chicago to address this meeting." he began the following morning. "One of my most enjoyable memories of this great city is of a bitterly cold January night in 1985. Remember it?" A handful of older brokers smiled and nodded. "When the Bears thrashed New England at the Superbowl in New Orleans. Remember The Refrigerator thundering down the line to score a touchdown? Remember the Monsters of the Midway? Dan Hampton, Mike Singletary, Walter Payton?" Proud smiles and nods.

"I watched the game with friends in Sandburg Village and it took me two hours to fight the crowds through Division and Rush to get back to my hotel on Delaware. The streets went crazy when the final whistle blew. I've never seen a city like it." Mark paused as he relished having his audience eat out of his hand.

"But I haven't come to Chicago to reminisce about its football glories. I've come to talk to you about the new CSF International Fund."

He received heavy applause when he finished the speech half an hour later. A knot of brokers from Ray Hutton clustered around and congratulated him, asking for his views on markets and promising to invest in the Fund. Chuck Anderson muscled into the throng to extract him.

"Sorry, folks, I've got to take our star off to his next performance in Oakbrook. Thanks for having us to speak today." They left the hotel and Chuck Anderson drove west along the Eisenhower Expressway in his BMW. He had closely-cropped, thin fair hair. He was athletic in a weight-lifting kind of way and seemed to smile all the time. He was a down-to-earth, solid Midwestern kid.

"Man, that was some speech. And the Chicago Bears ! Were you really there at the time?"

"Sure. I was on my way through Chicago and stayed to watch it. What I remember most was the intense cold. It was about 60 below, with wind-chill. I remember guys walking around without shirts. Beer was frozen to their bodies. Even the cops were delirious."

"Moving on, Mark, let me fill you in with the week ahead." Chuck changed the subject.

"Today, we mainly have Ray Hutton meetings, but right now we're going to Oakbrook Terrace to visit Schleman, Weld. They're big producers for us, specially on the fixed income side. Tuckwell wants us to go in and convert their fixed income folks to international equities. Commissions are higher for the broker and fees are higher for us in equity products than fixed income. And they're *much* higher for selling this new International Fund. Schleman has a mega distribution pipeline."

"And after Schleman?"

"We have a Ray Hutton walk-through in Oakbrook, followed by lunch in Schaumburg, then more walk-throughs in Evanston and back to the Loop . We finish the day at the Cape Cod Room where we're hosting eight financial planners for dinner. That should be quite relaxed."

"Am I just filling in for Paul McKay in your territory?"

"To be honest with you, Mark, after Paul's first three meetings I didn't want him in front of my best brokers any more. He was always complaining, speaking ill of people behind their backs, as if it was of any interest to his audience. Nothing was ever right." Chuck was clearly bruised by the experience of escorting Paul McKay around his territory.

"Like what?"

"His hotel room, the passenger seat in my car, the food, the sound systems where he spoke, the projector, his colleagues. You name it, he bitched about it." Chuck recounted the litany of complaints from Paul. "I wouldn't mind so much if he had a reason, but CSF always travels premium class. Everything is done at concierge level here. The flights, hotels, restaurants . . . Paul had no reason to complain. None at all."

"Well, the problem's solved now. He's out of the picture, permanently. Does this mean that I now need to cover his territory in the next two weeks?"

"We'll revisit his cities in the aftermarket once the Fund's launched. In the meantime, after Chicago we're going to hit Detroit to work with Turbin

Elles. They're big in Michigan, Ohio and Indiana. We'll visit Cleveland, where they overlap with Ball & Edwards. If we have time we'll go to Louisville to see First of Kentucky."

"FOK?"

"Yea, FOK. Know them?" Chuck replied without the slightest irony.

"Only by repute."

After an evening of stimulating company and exquisite seafood at the Cape Cod Room, Mark was off duty. He changed into casual clothes upstairs in the hotel and walked through the underpass onto Oak Street Beach on Lake Michigan. By Lincoln Park he sat on a bench overlooking the beach curving back towards the lights of the Gold Coast. It was a perfectly still night. The John Hancock Center soared and shimmered majestically above the exclusive neighbourhood of Streeterville.

He reached into his pocket for the aluminium tube and book of matches a broker had given him after dinner. He unscrewed the red top and tapped out a Bolivar No 3. He sniffed the rich Havana, bit off the end and spat a small plug of tobacco into the darkness. He circled the cigar over a lighted match until the tip was glowing, sat back, closed his eyes and played with the fragrant smoke in his mouth and nostrils.

Where was he now?

Life was moving fast. He saw how CSF might dominate his life for years, but he would become a very rich man in the process. Would he lose himself on the way? Quite possibly. Maybe he was just shedding his old, limited self and finding his true destiny? A financial entrepreneur on a global stage was a major advance over a start-up money manager in London. Or was he just a high-level bullshitter, as Zack Overwood described him one night in Texas? He would need to rein himself in, remind himself of his origins and, above all, be careful never to believe his own publicity.

He blew a cloud of smoke into the air. It drifted into the low hanging branches of a cherry tree.

He had fallen for Nancy. She was beautiful, professional, bright, urbane and sexy. Her skin was as soft as a child's. She was as comfortable under canvas in the backwoods as in a classy restaurant on the Upper East Side. She was well-read, to be expected from a graduate of Wellesley, yet retained a warm sense of humour. Crazy thing was that she seemed to really like him too. He loved the way she took up the slack when his emotional diffidence held him back. They fitted like peas in a pod.

The routine was well-established. Mark rose at 6.30, showered, dressed, packed and checked out. Chuck Anderson picked him up at the Drake for a 7.45 breakfast meeting at the Metropolitan Club in the Sears Tower. It was not so much a presentation as a discourse about global markets with seven monster hitters from Lynch & Burnham. These guys knew their stuff and expressed it combatively. Mark always learned as much as he taught in meetings like that.

They took the elevator down from the Club on the 66th floor. Their first walk-through was nearby in South Wacker, the second at LaSalle and Monroe. During the second walk-through, Chuck excused himself from Mark's presentation to make calls. In the elevator after the meeting he announced a change of plan.

"There's heavy congestion around O'Hare, both on the Kennedy Expressway and at the airport. It's gonna be three hours to get there, park, check in and get through Security. We'd need to leave straight after lunch for our 4pm flight. Then there's the likelihood of weather-related delays. Flights are leaving O'Hare ninety minutes late. Add the one hour flight and Air Traffic Control around Detroit and we could be travelling for seven hours."

"So we skip Detroit?"

"No, we grab a sandwich at Lloyd's, get on the Chicago Skyway and drive to Detroit. There's two Turbin & Elles offices we can see on the way. If we leave now we'll be in Kalamazoo by two and Battle Creek by three thirty. I know a place in Ann Arbor to stay the night. It's where we have our breakfast meeting tomorrow."

"Sounds well thought out. Let's go for it."

"OK. Once we clear the steel mills and pollution around Gary, it's a pretty ride. We should see great Fall colours in Northern Indiana and Southern Michigan."

An hour and a half into the trip, the trucks thinned out; the I94 interstate highway was uncongested and moving well. The two travellers chattered openly and easily.

"You know, Chuck, one of the great pleasures of a job like ours is visiting unexpected places. I never imagined that I would be paid to drive across this beautiful farmland and see parts of America that people don't normally get to see."

"You gotta take it when you can or the job devours you. Nobody thanks you for the weeks you spend on the road all year. Wholesalers have a sixty per cent divorce rate. My wife left me for a carpenter in Naperville. He was always there and attentive. And you know what? She got my house." Chuck spilled out his demons.

"Amazing. That's like the victim reimbursing the criminal."

"You got it, pal. My lawyer said she got the gold mine and I got the shaft."

"Kids?"

"A five year old daughter, Amy. I get to see her at weekends."

They were silent for a few miles. "Point is, Mark, you gotta enjoy your work a heck of a lot because it puts heavy demands on your soul. So, yea, I love seeing the trees in Fall colours, but I don't see it as a privilege. It's a necessity if you do this job. Though it's great if you can find a lady to share your travels with you. You married?"

"Not yet." Mark surprised himself by the *yet*.

"Got someone in mind?"

"Not exactly, but I'm open to suggestion. Until recently I was a confirmed bachelor. Now if the right person came along…" the conversation tapered off as they approached the turn-off to downtown Kalamazoo. What a load of crap he was talking. He had found the right person. For some unexplored, deep-seated reason he kept it to himself.

"I always wanted to visit Kalamazoo." Mark ventured.

"There's nothin' to doo in Kalamazoo, as the song goes. It's the pits."

"What about Osh Kosh?"

"Pretty location, it's on Lake Winnebago. We do a lot of business up there through Ray Hutton. Fonnelack too." Mark figured he meant Fond du Lac.

"Battle Creek?"

"Battle Creek Michigan. World Headquarters of Kellogg. It's a well-endowed city. President Gerry Ford came from there."

"A cultural metropolis, in other words."

"Sure." Mark's irony missed its target once again.

The next day was the busiest yet. Breakfast in Ann Arbor at 7 o'clock. At 8.30 they were in Farmington Hills, then Southfield at 10, Birmingham at 11.15, Troy at 12.30. The event at Troy was a revelation to Mark. CSF's normal style was to host lunch in a private function suite at a local restaurant. In Troy they walked into the offices of Schleman, Weld. The pizza delivery man was waiting at Reception for CSF to arrive and pay for 20 full size pizzas, 40 containers of coleslaw,

40 bags of chips, 8 six packs of carbonated drinks and enough chocolate brownies to feed a platoon. The feast was set out on trestle tables at the rear of the conference room.

After Chuck paid, the branch manager announced over the office intercom that CSF was hosting lunch in the conference room. Dozens of employees converged on the food, cramming as much pizza, coleslaw and brownies as would fit on a disposable paper plate. About twenty brokers sat guzzling around the table, waiting for the presentation to begin. Others filled up at the trough and slunk sheepishly out of the room carrying plates piled high with pizza and brownies. Secretaries and mail room staff joined the food fest once the alpha producers were glutted.

"Haven't they got any pride?" Mark asked Chuck, as he witnessed the pig-out.

"Par for the course. Most brokerage office managers won't let mutual fund groups through the door unless you feed them. And that's a minimum. You should see some of the other stuff they expect. Pens, golf balls, paper weights, executive toys, tee shirts, trips for top producers."

"These are some of the best paid people in America. They're like refugees grovelling for scraps." Mark shook his head in disbelief.

Chuck opened the proceedings. "Folks, we really appreciate the time you've given us out of your busy schedule. We're here today to introduce you to the new CSF International Fund. Mark Telford . . . " Chuck read out Mark's CV by way of introduction.

"It's a great pleasure to be in the Detroit area again. I've always been a huge fan of the Detroit Tigers and it's great to see them get off to such a strong start this season . . . " The response from the crowd was more muted than he'd been accustomed to in other cities. Chuck pencilled a few words on the cover of a CSF brochure and passed it across to Mark. "*The Tigers are their goddam BASEBALL team. You mean the Detroit Lions.*"

They rushed from Schleman Weld's office to a meeting in Sterling Heights at 2pm with Turbin & Elles. Then St Clair Shores at 4 followed by an early dinner with ten unbelievably spoiled clients and their advisors in Grosse Pointe. By the time the last guest exited the restaurant, it was 9 pm. Mark was burned out.

"Eight meetings in fourteen hours. Is there anybody else we could possibly have seen in this town?" his voice was hoarse.

"One more thing tonight, buddy. We drive to Toledo to position ourselves for tomorrow morning. It's an hour. I don't mind if you want to stretch out and sleep in the car."

But as they barrelled down Route 75 Mark was wired.

"Sorry about the cock up between the Detroit Lions and the Detroit Tigers."

"You know, Mark, they expect Brits to know shit about their local sports teams. They were so charmed by your effort that I don't think you lost any brownie points. But your bullshit sure did catch up with you today."

"On a different subject, tell me about the set up in New York. How do you guys interface?"

"Whodya wanna know about?"

"Start at the top. Steve Shilson. What's his story?"

"Slippery Steve Shilson? Great politician. He brought down his predecessor on grounds of corruption and has lived an even more larcenous life on the company ever since. He's real charming but he's quick to assassinate anyone who gets too close."

"Too close to what?"

"Too close to the truth. You gotta accept him as he is, but never, ever, let it be known that you have a problem with his lifestyle at the company. His wife's a fox."

"Skye?"

"Howdya know that?"

"They visited us in London. What about Dick Cosway?"

"Same as Shilson. Real charming and helpful until he feels threatened. He comes across as an easygoing, helpful guy, but it's easy to miss the signal that his suggestions are really commands."

"What do you mean?"

"Oh, he might call and say something like, "I've noticed strong sales coming out of Detroit. Do we need to beef up our representation there?" In Cosway-speak, that means, "You better goddam get more reps into Detroit."

"Like he suggested we should take a look at Vern Badore."

"Vern? That's an interesting thought. Vern was Cosway's idea?"

"As far as I can tell, yes."

"If he said you should take a look at Vern that means you should hire him. That's if you want Cosway on your side, but also because Vern's one heck of a wholesaler. You could do a heck of a lot worse than hire Vern Badore."

"Good feedback. What about Bill Tuckwell?"

"Bill's the same. Helpful and commercially-minded but he's the most insecure man at CSF. Don't be fooled by his Mr Nice Guy manner. He's a shit and the most controlling man you could meet."

"As I'm discovering. He goes to the most extraordinary lengths to keep tabs on me. Why, I don't know, but it's creepy knowing that someone"s watching me 24/7."

"Sure is."

"What about Nancy Lindstrom?" Mark finally, circuitously, reached the person he wanted to discuss more than anything.

"Nancy's a sweetheart. But she's a tough Compliance Officer. Nothing slips by her. She even got Shilson to sit a coupla Series exams."

"That makes me feel better. I thought she'd singled out Appletree for special treatment."

"Not at all. Personally, I got all the exams I need, but a few wholesalers don't. They got till Christmas to pass everything they need. Or they're out."

"What's Nancy's story?" Mark asked casually. He felt sleazy for asking about her.

"She comes from the Midwest somewhere. Tuckwell's fox. He had her at the CSF wholesaler convention in Hawaii in May. She caused a real stir at the beach, but man, he got pissed when the guys spent too much time talking with her. That's what I mean by insecure."

"And Nancy? Is she crazy about him too?"

"She had eyes for him in Hawaii, that's for sure."

Chapter 19

After breakfast with thirty financial planners in the back room of a roadway diner outside Toledo they drove east along the I 80. The road took them through ripe vineyards and prosperous Ohio farmland in all its autumn glory. They passed a number of buggies driven by Amish farmers. It was like being in an 18th Century European landscape.

Their next commitment was a mid morning presentation to brokers at the Elyria branch of James & Dane. Mark enjoyed visiting out-of-the-way brokerage offices. He always felt welcome because they appreciated being visited by the CEO of a London investment firm. Office managers in small Midwestern towns rounded up their troops to ensure a full house. The questions were respectful and the hospitality was genuine.

Mark's mobile rang as they accelerated away from Elyria. "Bill Tuckwell here. How you doin?"

"Fine, thanks." Mark found it hard to be civil to the man. He pictured those jowls slobbering over Nancy. What on earth did she see in him? Was he wearing his Yale spectacles when he . . . "We're now on our way into Cleveland."

"Sure. I know. We got great feedback from Chicago plus the James & Dane offices in Detroit yesterday and Toledo this morning."

"That's good to know. Bet you don't know where we are right now." Mark challenged him.

"You're on 80 East, near the 480 interchange."

"How the hell do you know that?" The bastard must have had a tracker on Chuck's car. There was no other way he could follow them so accurately on the map.

"It's my job to know where my wholesalers are all the time. And it's their job to tell me." That sounded sinister. Was Mark travelling with a spy?

"Reason I'm calling is we hit $600 million of committed funds last night. There's been a change of plan. Once you finish your speeches in the Cleveland area, I want you back in New York tomorrow afternoon. We got four days to launch date and you need to come off the road to start putting the money to work."

"You should be reassured that I'm in daily touch with Graham in

London and we already know where to invest the money." Mark replied.

"If you say so." Bill added, "But you're booked at the Morgans tomorrow night. Guaranteed Late Arrival."

"Thanks Bill. "Bye."

"Tuckwell?" Chuck asked with a smirk.

"He wants me off the road after Cleveland and to return to New York tomorrow."

"We have a light day in Cleveland today. Lunch, then nothing this afternoon and a speech near Akron tonight. You can head out after breakfast at the Union League Club tomorrow morning."

They met four Lynch & Burnham brokers at One Walnut for lunch. The conversation was about emerging markets and oil service stocks. They were intrigued by the launch of the CSF International Fund and promised they would invest 'a few hundred grand' in it. Chuck picked up the tab.

"Mark, we're free now until six thirty. If it's all the same to you I need to check into the Marriott and make phone calls this afternoon. I gotta backlog of office admin to take care of."

"I'd be glad to play hooky." Mark was relieved. "It's been a cracking pace for three weeks. I hardly know Cleveland; I'll take this opportunity to wander about and see the place."

They checked into the Marriott. Mark changed into casual clothes and strolled into the sunny, still October day. Leaves were turning but not yet falling from the ornamental trees that landscaped the Soviet-scale plaza beside the hotel. He walked towards Lake Erie and dialled the familiar number in New York.

"Nancy Lindstrom speaking."

"Mark Telford here."

"Mark ! I thought . . . "

"I know we agreed not to contact each other at the office, but we need to talk. If they check our phone records we can say we discussed compliance matters, can't we?"

"So?" Nancy replied cautiously.

"So I'd like the scoop about you and Mr Tuckwell."

"This is absolutely not the time to talk about that. Can I call you after work?"

"We're travelling and I'm giving a speech tonight. I won't be back at the hotel until late. Can you leave the office for a few minutes and call me from your building lobby?"

"That's difficult. I'm right in the middle of something for Dick Cosway."

"When's a good time, then?"

"Bear with me," She spoke in a serious tone. "I'll call back in a few minutes."

Mark was standing in the plaza outside the Rock & Roll Hall of Fame in the sunshine when the phone rang.

"Mark, I'd appreciate if you never, ever throw a curved ball like that again. You have no idea how embarrassing it might have been. What if I'd been on the speaker? Besides, all calls to and from CSF are recorded."

"Nancy, I need some answers. Everyone knows CSF has a highly invasive culture. They have to know everything about everybody. I was told yesterday that you and Bill Tuckwell were an item. Why didn't you mention it? You know very well that he takes an unusual interest in me. Don't you think you should have told me?"

During their idyllic weekend together neither had broached the subject of former – or current – lovers. Mark knew too well that the early flush of a love affair was always the best time to talk openly and completely about everything. That's when ecstatic feelings overlooked minor inconveniences like marital status or prior commitments. The failure to be candid early in an affair invariably had a way of coming back to bite people on the backside.

"I broke off with him in August."

"How long did you go out with him?"

"Two years."

"Why did you break off with him?"

"You really want to know?"

"Yes."

"When you came into our office in June I liked you. You were so different. I realized that I couldn't commit to Bill if I was so easily intrigued by another man. Does that make sense?"

"Carry on."

"I joked with him afterwards that you were cute. He went ballistic, called you a fucking limey. I said it was nothing and that everyone fancies other people in a casual way all the time."

"I still don't understand why you didn't tell me. It would have explained everything. The man's pathologically obsessive."

"I had no plans to date you. It was pure fluff. I never gave it any more thought. But Bill kept needling me."

"About me?"

"Sure. He called at weird times of day and night, he showed up randomly at my apartment on East 63rd."

"Even though I was in London?"

"Yes. He spied on everything I was doing. I began to realize that he was stalking me. I broke off with him, not because of you, but because I saw a side of him that would have come out sooner or later anyway."

"When did you last go out with him, or spend . . . intimate time with him."

"You want to know about our sex life? It's over, Mark, absolutely over. We don't need to go into details."

"When, Nancy?"

"You sound like a jealous high school teenager."

"Just for my peace of mind."

"I wouldn't call it spending intimate time, exactly. He attacked me in August the night after he got back from seeing Appletree in London."

Mark was stunned.

"Hello? Mark? You still there?" Nancy sounded angry.

"Yes, I'm here. I'm sorry, but why didn't you tell me this stuff when we were away together?"

"I didn't tell you because I wanted to put everything behind me. I didn't want to get you involved in my problems. It's ancient history, Mark, I absolutely hate Bill Tuckwell."

"Did you tell the police?"

"You're kidding. They wouldn't believe me. Bill would get the entire board of CSF as character witnesses. They saw us together in Hawaii in May. That's when he got real jealous when guys talked to me at the pool. It's flattering in theory, but I hate male jealousy. He went wild as soon as we were alone in our room. He would be OK for a while, then it started over."

"Does that explain why Mary Cohen tried to seduce me in Tampa the other night? " Mark asked quietly. "And why he tracked us down in Folkston last weekend. He's stalking us. He knows every move we make." There was silence on the line. "Nancy? You still there?"

"Yes I'm here. I have another confession to make."

"OK – give it to me straight." It sounded ominous but he tried to make light with her on the phone. She was obviously angry and upset. But what was it this time – HIV? Pregnant?

"Remember those Series exams we talked about? You never needed to take them at all. Bill persuaded everyone to take his side at a board meeting, then I was ordered to orchestrate it with Appletree. I guess he hoped that forcing you to pass Series 63 at short notice before you got on the road might put you off the deal. I guess he kinda hoped you would see me as a corporate bitch for making you take the exams."

"Bloody hell, Nancy. This has got really messy."

"For what it's worth we were all amazed how you guys pulled together and passed the exam." Nancy said.

"A bit of straight talk earlier in the game would have been helpful. I've got sixteen families whose livelihoods depend on Appletree's success. I feel like I've led them into a minefield."

"I'm real sorry, Mark. I've got you into all sorts of trouble."

"Here's the deal, Nancy." He suggested, "I'm coming to New York tomorrow. I'm going to cancel my room at the Morgans and stay with Frank. I have to unhook from Tuckwell. Perhaps we can get together?"

"I'd like that, and Mark?"

"Yes?"

"Congratulations for getting the best score at Series 63."

"I love you too."

The Rock and Roll Hall of Fame was exactly what he needed. It was a shrine to his generation; he felt as happy as a biker at a Harley convention. All the shit and complications flew off him, his wannabe hippie persona flowered as he toured the building. Exhibits of Elvis, Buddy Holly and Tamla Motown recalled the incredible energy of the 1960s. They evoked the confusion of his youth, Vietnam, the Civil Rights movement and everything that culminated in the wackiness of Woodstock.

Mark was proud of the homage paid to British bands, how they turned American Blues on its head, turbocharged it and flung it back at the world. How did such a small island produce the range of talent and plain fury of bands like The Rolling Stones, Cream, The Who, Led Zeppelin, Pink Floyd, Queen, The Clash, Ten Years After, the Beatles? Could anyone name a French rock star who'd closed down an American airport? Where were the Italian stars who trashed hotel rooms in Los Angeles? How many Pakistani acts flew customized jet liners from gig to gig like Led Zeppelin? Even Hendrix went to London to pick up his band and conquer the world.

He absorbed the atmosphere of the Hall of Fame for an hour then strolled over to the Cleveland Union Terminal Tower, which housed the railroad station. The Tower was built in the late 1920s and for decades was the second highest building in the world, so the brochure said. In its day the building site was the biggest excavation on the planet after the Panama Canal. He explored the concourse and its warren of shops, which he found claustrophobic. The arches were so low he felt crushed by the deadweight of masonry stacked above.

He left the Terminal Tower, passed the Civil War monument and headed up Euclid, which was once the main business drag of Cleveland. It now consisted of building after empty building, sad monuments to faded hopes, pork politics and economic decline.

It seemed there had been an economic implosion in Cleveland. The city should have been as powerful as Chicago, but something had scared off the money. As he strolled back to the hotel, he passed the Federal Reserve Bank, a magnificent testament to Cleveland's former optimism. This was the first city in America where Mark felt rich.

His speech that evening was at a country club twenty miles out of town. It was a new and stunning building with timber beams exposed high above a sweeping staircase in the hallway. 275 attendees took their seats in an auditorium. Mark chatted with some as they entered. They were retirees, local businessmen, hard working professionals, school teachers, doctors, solid mid American folks. After Chuck's usual introduction, Mark began his customary address:

"It's a great pleasure to be back in the Cleveland area after such a long time. It's particularly exciting that the Browns have started the season so strongly. I'll really be pulling for them to win the Superbowl this year."

Cheers, claps, whistles and smiles. Chuck rolled his eyes.

Mark felt melancholy as he waited for the flight at Cleveland Hopkins. He was exhausted. The due diligence tour had been one hell of an experience. In three weeks he'd delivered eighty seven public presentations in Florida, Texas, Chicago, Michigan and Ohio. He had travelled thousands of miles to raise hundreds of millions of dollars for the CSF International Fund.

He reflected about the magical detour to the Okefenokee Swamp with Nancy, and the unwelcome complications he now faced. Life in London would never be the same. A sweet announcement hit the terminal: his flight was delayed by forty minutes. Time to make calls to New York.

"Yea, Blazerman here."

"Telford here."

"Hey ! Mark, my man, how are ya? Where are ya? "

"I'm in Cleveland, Frank, heading towards New York."

"Tonight?"

"My flight leaves in forty minutes."

"Fantastic – I'm a bachelor tonight .Where you staying?"

"That's why I was calling. I need a room which isn't in a hotel, for convoluted reasons." Mark had the uneasy feeling of crossing a line in the sand.

"Sure, Buddy. Come stay on Park Avenue, or in the New York Athletic Club. You choose."

"Would it be incredibly inconvenient if I were to stay with you?"

"Hell no. You sound so goddam British when you talk like that. We got plenny of space. I'll call our housekeeper to open up the guest apartments. Don't need to fit around me – just come and go as you please."

"Can I buy you dinner?"

"I'm working on a deal but should be out by 9pm. I could be up for partying tonight."

"We can talk about that. First I need to discuss an interesting turn of events."

"CSF?"

"Let me treat you to dinner tonight and we'll talk about it."

"You got my curiosity flying, man. Au Château at 9 sharp. Same table."

"One more thing – I'd like to invite a friend along. I'd like her to stay, too, if that's OK."

"Holy Cow, this gets more interesting by the minute. Wife of a good friend?"

"I'll fill you in when I see you."

"See you at nine sharp, my man. Don't be late."

Mark called to cancel his reservation at the Morgans Hotel. He dialled Bill Tuckwell's cell number to tell him. He knew Tuckwell was in the office and wouldn't pick up his mobile, so he left a message.

Mark was first to arrive at Le Château. Nancy entered five minutes later. She wore black slacks and a see-through silk blouse, her hair was meticulously tousled, lips glistening. Heads turned from the tables. She carried the small tote bag that she'd brought to Okefenokee. "My clothes for tomorrow." she smiled, tossing it on a spare chair.

"What time's Frank coming?"

"He said nine o'clock sharp."

"It's 9.05 now. Let's give him a few more minutes. If he doesn't show, let's just leave. I can't wait to be with you." Nancy squeezed his hand.

"At least have a drink. We need to be polite. We're staying at his apartment, after all."

"OK – I'll have a Kir Royale. That's our drink, isn't it?"

As providence would have it, at 9.20 a waiter came to their table to say that Monsieur Blazerman was unavoidably detained at work, so not to wait for him. His housekeeper would stay up and show them their rooms at his apartment on Park Avenue. The waiter looked hungrily at Nancy, adding, "Monsieur Blazerman said to have a wonderful time."

Chapter 20

It was a glorious, crisp, back-to-school, turn-over-a-new-leaf October morning. The girls walking through the Embankment gardens were lovelier than usual. They still carried the glow of summer fitness and were dressed prettily for the office. Sunshine slanted through the trees over the bronze statue of Sir Arthur Sullivan outside the Savoy. Mark began unconsciously whistling a tune from The Pirates of Penzance.

Whatever the weather, however busy he was, Mark always left the Underground at Westminster and walked the last half mile along the Thames to his office on Temple Avenue. On his way to work, it gave him the space to organize his thoughts for the day. After a long day at his desk, cutting through the Victoria Embankment gardens on the way home lightened his mood for the evening.

Every day he passed multiple monuments dedicated to forgotten worthies: Robert Raikes, the Founder of Sunday Schools; a fountain dedicated to Major General Lord Cheylesmore GBE, KCB, KCVO, Grenadier Guards, Born 1848 Died 1925, Soldier, Administrator, Philanthropist and Steadfast Friend. Presumably too old when the generals ordered up Passchendaele, but you never know. And who was this pretty boy, Henry Fawcett , a handsome profile erected in bronze By His Grateful Countrywomen? Was he some amazing Victorian stud? Was he the fellow who invented the tap? No clues offered.

At one with the world, the conquering hero entered the World Headquarters of Appletree Asset Management after an absence of four weeks. There was a buzz about the place. Syreta Mehta was the first to welcome him back with a warm smile.

"How was your trip?"

"An amazing experience. We should order sandwiches for the staff and have a debriefing session at lunchtime today in the conference room. What do you think?"

"Great idea. I'll get it organized."

Graham shot out of his chair as soon as he saw Mark. He couldn't contain his delight.

"Six hundred and seventy two million, four hundred and twenty seven thousand dollars."

"For immediate investment?"

"Yup. The money is on deposit, earning interest pending immediate investment. The CSF International Fund is now officially up and running." He handed Mark an email printout. It confirmed what Graham just told him,

> *Congratulations Gentlemen. You are now the managers of the CSF International Fund, launched today with $672,427,000 to invest. Good luck and Shoot the Lights Out. Best regards Dick Cosway.*

"Holy Moly, let me see, that gives us an annualized fee of . . . "

" . . . Just north of four million dollars." Graham had worked out the number earlier, within seconds of receiving Cosway's email.

"What are the practicalities, here and now?"

"The Fund is now closed to new money – and redemptions – for ten business days. That enables us to put the money to bed. I see no reason why we shouldn't have it all invested by then."

"What happens after ten days?"

"A daily Net Asset Value is calculated and the Fund is open for purchase or sale by investors."

Alix and Bob left their desks and joined Mark and Graham chatting in the reception area. A new manager covering Asian markets sat in Paul's chair. She was considerably more decorative than Paul – tall, backswept chestnut hair, smiling brown eyes, leggy and shapely, with an open, generous face. Mark was relieved that Paul had gone. He was always the dam to Appletree's flow, the cynical bugger with a negative comment for every occasion.

Mark spotted her and walked over to her desk. "You must be Clarissa. Welcome on board."

"Thank you. It's great to be here." A nice firm handshake. "Sorry, I didn't mean to eavesdrop. I was interested to hear what Graham was saying about calculating the Fund's NAV."

"The beauty of London is that we straddle the world." Graham pontificated. "We catch markets in Asia before they close, and we're still at our desks for three hours after New York opens. Our dealing price for every international stock is always fresh, unlike New York where prices can deviate from international prices because of time zone differences."

"I think I knew that" Clarissa said politely to her new boss.

"Well, at 4pm each day in London we get the closing price on Reuters of every European and Asian stock in the portfolio. I verify and email them to New York. At 4pm in New York CSF gets the closing prices of our Latin American and Canadian stocks, checks the currency rates and prices the entire portfolio in US Dollars. Any cash in the portfolio is added to the pot, which is then divided by the number of shares. That's how you get your Net Asset Value per share."

"So," Graham looked at Clarissa, "if the Fund is six hundred million dollars and there are sixty million shares, the Fund's NAV per share is . . . "

"Ten dollars . . . ?" Clarissa ventured.

"Exactly."

"What's the opening NAV of our Fund going to be?" Bob asked.

"When we were funded with the cash today, the NAV per share was ten dollars a share. Depending how we invest in the next ten days, the NAV will open up or down. It's up to us now, isn't it?" Graham smiled confidently.

Mark turned to Graham, "Got a minute?"

"Sure."

Mark's office had the same neglected feel as his flat in Battersea. His papers had been sorted neatly into *critical* and *non-critical* piles by Wendy, who spent much of her working day at the reception desk sorting voluminous mail for Appletree's investment staff. The non-critical pile consisted mainly of research reports from stockbrokers around the world, back copies of the Economist and old financial journals. The critical pile was smaller, comprising legal documents, audit reports, meeting schedules, compliance letters and invitations to functions in splendid locations around Europe.

"How's the office since you got back? Clarissa seems a bright spark."

"We were damned lucky. As you know it can take months to find the right person to fill an analyst's role. Providentially, her CV arrived here the same week as Paul was fired."

"She was on the Asian team at Kornfeld Neuhoffer, wasn't she?"

"Stupid buggers closed the team down and fired all their experienced Asian equity staff after buying Hang Mao in Taiwan. Still-their loss is our gain."

"Any repercussions from the Paul incident?"

"You know Mark, I'm amazed by everyone's silence. By way of illustration we had three dogs at home. They slept in a pile on an old sofa in the boot room. They played together, ate together, walked with us together, slept together. You'd think they would be as close friends as conceivably possible, wouldn't you?"

Mark wondered where Graham was going with his tale.

"Well, the other day, Sasha, our dachshund, was run over by a builder's van on the drive. Bang, end of story. Did the other two dogs mourn her? Hell, no. After I buried her mangled little corpse in the woods, the other two dogs came home and demanded their meal just as usual. They curled up together as usual and I swear they haven't noticed poor Sasha's not there. So with Alix and Bob. Paul may as well not have existed."

"I suppose they got wind of his deal from CSF, did they?"

"Rumour rather than fact. Apart from the assassins at CSF only you, Paul and I know what his deal was. He's forbidden under the terms of his severance package to say anything. Jack Bolt made it clear that he'll be watched closely. Any indiscretion by Paul and he's toast; he forfeits the lot. If I were Paul I would keep my trap shut. It's not often that you're offered three years salary and benefits to do nothing."

"Lucky bugger. I wouldn't mind the same package myself." Mark fantasized momentarily of disappearing to the Caribbean with Nancy.

"I think you would mind having Jack Bolt staring over your shoulder. He dropped into the office here for an hour while you were gone. It was weird but he seemed to be in London on a reconnaissance mission. He seemed exceedingly furtive. He looks normal enough but I've never seen such cold eyes in a man."

"Who exactly is he? What's his role at CSF?"

"He is officially some kind of security/human resources consultant at CSF, but as far as I can tell he is the personal henchman of Shilson, Tuckwell and Cosway. Their interests are paramount – over and above CSF's. He's off balance sheet, as it were, but attends board meetings and everyone seems afraid of him."

"It all sounds very cloak and dagger. You almost sound like you believe all this financial superpower bullshit stuff at CSF, Graham. Remember we are an independent firm. They don't own us and never will."

"No, but they have a big stake in the success of this venture. It was just like he was a CIA operative checking that an ally was on message."

"Hmm. Well, I'm delighted that Paul's demise worked out to everyone's advantage." Mark changed the subject. "Let's talk about the construction of the portfolio. What do you want me to do?"

"If you boot up your computer you'll see the country weights recommended by my model."

"Fine . . . " Mark tapped his keyboard and turned to the CountryAlloc site. "Let me see . . . UK 16%, Japan 10%, Germany 7%, France 7%, Australia 7% , Canada 6% ,Spain 5%, Switzerland 4%, Netherlands 4%, Sweden 3%, Norway 3%, Finland 2%, Denmark 2%, Singapore 2% Hong Kong 2%, Zero in Italy, Portugal, Austria, Belgium and New Zealand . . . Looks plausible. You've taken some big bets. You've still got 20% unaccounted for. Keeping it in cash?"

"Patience, my man. Scroll to the next page."

"OK-sorry, let's see." He tapped again to reveal the allocation of the remainder of the portfolio. "Excellent. 19% in emerging markets and 1% in cash. That's ballsy. Interesting emerging market allocation: Brazil 5%, India 5%, Mexico 5% and Israel 4%. Zero in Russia or China – why's that?"

"The Chinese and Russian markets are overvalued and they have corporate governance issues." Graham dismissed two of the world's fastest-growing economies out of hand.

"I can understand your temporary overvaluation analysis, but two billion people can't be wrong, surely?"

"My problem with China is that most major companies have a controlling stake owned by the government. The rhetoric to foreign investors is "come in, the water's fine". So far, it's been all right. But what if the economy cools down, or hardliners take over power again? You'd feel a bloody fool for investing there."

"Don't we risk missing one of the biggest economic booms in history by avoiding China?"

"Not really. We can invest in Hong Kong, Taiwan and Singapore, where you can play the China game more safely. There are fortunes to be made in Australia and Brazil right now on the back of the Chinese boom. Remember the Klondike principle?"

"Sure – when everyone's digging for gold, you want to be in the pick and shovel business."

"Exactly. The miners may or may not find gold, but they'll always need tools and supplies to prospect for gold. The richest people during any gold rush are the bartenders, brothel-keepers and supply store owners. A Chinese company may or may not be well-run but it will need constant supplies of raw materials, shipping and trade finance from overseas. You can make a fortune by supplying the Chinese boom without taking any of the risk of investing in the stock market."

"And Russia?"

"They may come right in the end, but the economy is controlled by an unholy mix of unscrupulous chancers and government officials. As soon as you're onto a good thing in Russia a government official steps in and expropriates your assets, or revalues them retrospectively and sues you for what they think you should have paid for them in the first place."

"So the BRICs are overhyped?"

"Totally. It's crass to boil the world of emerging markets down to four letters – Brazil, Russia, India, and China. They're not the only important markets in the developing world. I like India and Brazil. Both have dynamic economies growing at 5% to 10% a year; both have growing populations and high spermatic energy." Mark admired Graham's position against the consensus. That's how to make money over the years.

"Testosterone powers growth." Mark observed.

"Of course. Consider the difference between Brazil, with its dynamic, multi-racial, teeming population, half of whom are under 15, and Russia, where male life expectancy is 52 and the overall population is expected to decline by 40 million by 2050. That's why I can't take it seriously when Russian politicians threaten to "return to the Cold War". It's a joke. I can't think of a single example since the Rape of the Sabines of a country starting a war of aggression with a declining population. Can you?"

"Not off hand. But Russia does have natural resources which the world needs. You shouldn't dismiss Russia."

"Quite so. That's where stock market valuations come in. At the moment, equivalent natural resource companies in Norway, Canada and Australia are cheaper, but without the political and governance risk. Russian companies need to be cheaper than their global counterparts to justify the risk of buying them. In other sectors, why would you want to own Russian bank shares? I'd rather own a Swiss Bank or a boring European financial stock."

"Fair enough. So what do you want me to do in the fund?"

"Find me some good ideas in Brazil and Mexico. Shouldn't be too hard, after your Latin trip last year."

"Delighted." Mark enjoyed managing part of the portfolio. His role as Chief Executive Officer precluded a fuller investment role, but he brought many years of experience to the table, even when he only managed a small percentage of the Fund.

Chapter 21

Syreta unwrapped the plastic film which covered two trays of sandwiches and she placed a pile of plates and napkins on the conference table. Just after 12 noon, the staff of Appletree entered the room excitedly, helped themselves to food, popped open soda cans and sat around the table.

"It's great for the whole team to be together in one place after such a long time." Mark began. "We need to talk about a number of things. First, you may be wondering what happened to Paul." He hesitated, then continued in a measured way. "He had a family crisis while we were in America and CSF kindly flew him home. After much deliberation he decided to stop working, so he won't be coming back. You can rest assured that he's fine now with his family and that he's been well taken care of."

"We had the good fortune that Clarissa was available, so it's been a seamless transition." Graham added.

Mark didn't want to spend more time on the subject. In the absence of any immediate response, he continued,

"The four of us who went on the American road show want to share our experiences with you. Afterwards I'd like to discuss a proposal by CSF that we hire a marketer in the US. They've suggested a guy called Vern Badore, who introduced himself to us in America recently. Graham will then give a situation report on the Fund's investment allocation. Finally, we can discuss any other topic that you might want to talk about. Sound OK?"

Everyone nodded.

."Alix, why don't you start?"

"Yes, of course." Mark had never seen Alix so bright-eyed. "I was responsible for marketing on the West Coast. Starting in Seattle, I worked my way south, almost to the Mexican border. In Washington and Oregon the major underwriting firm is called Refsnes, Wheat & Co. They're an old brokerage firm that's been around since 1905. I spent three days in the Seattle/Tacoma area then we drove to Portland, going from office to office. I spoke to clusters of financial planners in places I'd never heard of like Centralia, Longview , Eugene and Salem. The country was gorgeous. We did a detour to Mount St Helens and I visited Crater Lake National Park on the way south."

Some younger team members looked wide eyed at the thought of the travel opportunities that Appletree might offer in due course.

"After Portland I flew to Sacramento, where I spoke to more brokers and financial planners, as well as visiting the offices of AG Stiphel in the area. We then drove to Oakland . . . "

Syreta interrupted, "Who's 'we'?"

Alix blushed, "Oh, 'We' was me and the local wholesaler responsible for each area. In Washington and Oregon, she was a girl called Maggie Lee; in Northern California a guy called Randy Marx and in Southern California, a guy called Babe Legge."

These colourful names caused a hearty laugh around the table. The pinstriped Bob Berwick added to the merriment, commenting,

"It's surely a matter of time before CSF hires someone called Randy Babe."

"Very funny." Alix retorted." They're serious and hard working people."

Bob smirked.

"To continue, I addressed a series of cluster meetings in Oakland and Berkeley, then crossed the Bay to San Francisco, where I attended six downtown meetings. Randy and I then drove to Menlo Park and Palo Alto."

"What's a cluster meeting?" Wendy asked.

"It's where the wholesaler gets together a group of brokers and financial planners into one place, usually over breakfast, lunch, cocktails or dinner, and kills a lot of birds with one stone. It's easier to see a group of people all in one place, than travel around twelve offices to see them separately."

It wasn't clear if Wendy had understood a word of what Alix had just said, but she smiled sweetly with a quiet "Thank you."

"At Palo Alto I met Vern Badore. He flew from Tennessee to introduce himself. To be honest I thought he was a pushy wee sod. He said he was the biggest producer at CSF and was looking for a change. I got the sense he was being set up and that there was a CSF agenda at work. I think that if we hire a person in this role he or she should be an Appletree hire, one hundred per cent. I don't like someone being foisted on us."

"I felt the same." Bob added, "Vern came to see me in Philadelphia. He's young and very green – particularly about International Investing – and tried to convince me that it was better to hire a top salesman who could learn about investments than a top investor who knows bugger-all about sales. I thought he was taking the piss. I totally agree with Alix that we should keep control of anyone in the marketplace representing us.

Vern's being paid by someone else, reporting to Bill Tuckwell. We mustn't be seduced by another freebie. It'll come back and haunt us. "I liked him," Graham joined in. "He came to see me on the road. He's thorough in the way he's canvassing for the job. Can you imagine how determined he would be if he got a state pension fund in his sights, or a Fortune 500 company? He'd never let go until he wrung the money out of them."

"I liked Vern, but I suspect he's too political." Mark was sceptical. "In a small firm, political behaviour saps everyone's energy. It's extremely corrosive. I agree with Alix that there's an agenda at work. Why else did they pay for him to travel around the USA to drop in and see us all? Dick Cosway's pushing him. We need to be careful not to make euphoric decisions resulting from our relationship with CSF."

"Yes, but remember we can write a contract setting out our expectations. If Vern behaves badly we simply call in Jack Bolt. He'll do a surgical strike and Vern's history." Graham said.

Reflecting on their earlier conversation, Mark thought Graham's assessment of Jack Bolt was naïve. If Vern was Cosway's placeman, it was unlikely that Bolt would be brought in to remove Vern. He kept this thought to himself, but enquired,

"Did Vern discuss money with anyone? I didn't get that far."

"I asked him point blank." Graham replied. "He said he gets 'a basic salary to cover the mortgage', then a commission based on assets he brings in. There's no cap to his commission. He said he'd expect a commission on all assets that Appletree generates in America."

"What, even assets in this new Fund? And what about the existing relationships we have in the USA? He can't possibly take a cut of those." Alix riposted.

"I told him we'd only pay for new business that he introduces, nothing else. He looked disappointed and said, "then we probably don't have a deal". I told him we should table it for further discussion and he brightened up."

"He emailed to say he can come and visit us next week. I'll speak to Cosway and Tuckwell so that we fully understand the deal they're proposing. Personally I'm sceptical but if Vern wants to come over and talk, I have no problem. Bob, can you add anything to Alix's adventures?"

"Sure. I found the travel stimulating and fun, but CSF seemed to lose sight of the fact that the brokers and planners we spoke to represented real people with real savings. It's easy to get caught up in the glamour of what we're doing, but underlying every sales meeting is the need to deliver investment performance to honest people. My wholesalers were far more concerned about the terms of the deal and their commission structure than the integrity of the product."

"Interesting – Graham, what do you think?"

"I didn't travel as much as the rest of you. I spent most of the time in CSF's offices in New York and Bismarck teaching them how to settle international trades. I also taught them about our investment process."

"I hope you didn't teach them too much or they'll dump us and take over the Fund." Bob chipped in cheerfully.

"They're a long way from that. Besides, I was talking mainly to CSF's administrative staff. Their investment guys in New York are far too opinionated to listen to a Brit's view on the markets.

Going back to Bob's comment about real peoples' savings, my instinct is that the market will always sort it out. If we don't perform, it shows in the industry rankings, brokers will dump us and the Fund won't grow. The US mutual fund market is highly efficient. Money gravitates to performance. So, while I'm always concerned for the savers of America, they'll dump us damned quickly if we don't perform."

Graham then outlined the country allocations for the Fund which he shared earlier with Mark.

"We have ten days to invest the money. The portfolio must not exceed 100 stocks. Alix, I've allocated seven per cent for Germany, which is $47 million for you to invest. I want you to find 7 stocks in the German market."

"No problem." Alix responded enthusiastically.

"Each manager must structure their portfolios by Friday this week. Before anybody invests one dollar, please discuss your ideas with me so we create a consistent portfolio. I don't want our Asian portfolio to be a play on rising global interest rates while our UK portfolio is geared to falling global interest rates. Any questions?"

Clarissa had paid close attention to Graham's comments.

"Could you clarify how the portfolio manager knows if she has money to invest in a particular market?"

"Good question. Bob, why don't you outline to Clarissa how it's done?"

"Turn your computer to Country Alloc and you'll see a spread sheet that sets our target percentage for each market. It shows how much is there and how much cash you have to invest. If Graham allocates 7% to Germany, Country Alloc flags it for you to invest. Everyone can see if it's been implemented, so you need to put it to work immediately."

Chapter 22

Vern Badore flew into London on Sunday night, checked into an upmarket hotel a few hundred yards from Temple Avenue and presented himself at the office at 8 sharp on Monday morning. From the start he tried to charm with a boyish enthusiasm and a determination to score points at Appletree.

Since meeting Mark in Atlanta a few weeks earlier he'd learned the constituents of the Morgan Stanley Europe, Australia and Far East Index. He'd checked the market capitalizations of the major stock markets, he could name the top three stocks in each country and had memorized recent cross-rates for the Dollar, Yen, Sterling and the Euro. He'd paid close attention to Bob's speech in Philadelphia and Alix's presentation in Palo Alto. He'd read their materials and made notes. Vern was proving to be a quick study worthy of representing Appletree in the USA. But still, even after three days, acceptance of the Vern proposition was far from unanimous.

Mark and Graham were doubtful about him and wanted to flush out Cosway's agenda. The proposed deal was for CSF to pay Vern's compensation, travel and entertainment for a year, after which Appletree would take over the costs. If Vern was unprofitable after a year, Appletree could choose not to continue.

"Two clouds hang over this proposal, Mark. First, I don't like Vern reporting to Tuckwell and second, he gets commission on all new future American business into Appletree ." Graham winced.

"I travelled in the Midwest with a wholesaler called Chuck Anderson. He said that Cosway had a particular way of making his opinions felt. If you didn't take the hint he'd go ballistic and you risked making an enemy for life."

"Look, CSF is only one bloody client. This is getting out of hand. The simple answer is that if we wouldn't hire Vern in London we shouldn't hire him in America. We have to keep our integrity in the US institutional market. It's an appalling idea to concede such a crucial market to a 28-year old salesman who, frankly, is a greedy little shit." Bob could always be relied on for a forthright view.

On Wednesday afternoon, Mark invited Vern into his office.

"You've been here three days. What do you think of Appletree?"

"Like shootin' fish in a barrel, Mark. Appletree's a great team, great performance, great location. It won't take long to position you guys and get to a coupla billion dollars. I know I could get y'all in front of a lotta big state funds in the South East."

"They would be separate accounts, rather than investing into the mutual fund, right?"

"Sure. They're too sophisticated for mutual fund investment. You get smaller percentage fees but much bigger sums to manage."

"What would your marketing strategy be for these accounts?"

"Real easy. I would spend all my time talking to the pension fund consultants. They control the gateways to success. If a consultant has twenny pension clients and you've impressed him, he'll recommend you to all clients. You can pick up twenny new accounts by making friends with one consultant."

"Which consultants do you know well?"

"There's Buckshire Consulting in Malibu, Fallon in Sausalito – they also have offices in Chicago and Atlanta. There's Mid West Associates in Chicago, Bock Consultants in New York, LOA in Atlanta, Fincke & Posselthwaite near Seattle and dozens of small guys from Kansas City to Columbus."

"These are names we're familiar with. What about the mutual fund? How do you intend to get assets flowing into the CSF International Fund?"

Vern gave a reply that hardened Mark's decision not to hire him. "The Fund has enough momentum to grow without my effort. CSF has a lot of great wholesalers who'll keep assets flowing without me."

"But you'll be picking up commissions on the Fund. Surely you need to contribute to sales if you're getting commissions on it?"

"Yeah." Vern brushed off this idea. "My role with the Fund will be more as sales manager. If I see sales flagging in Texas, I'll get on the road with Zack Overwood, or get one of you guys to come over. We'll do a roadshow through Texas and get sales movin' again."

"So you see your job as, first, to open up the institutional market to Appletree, and second, to keep momentum behind the Fund wholesalers. Isn't that Bill Tuckwell's job?

"Sure. But Tuckwell has to take care of all CSF's funds. My job would be as internal wholesaler for Appletree exclusively. My entire comp structure would hang on Appletree's success in America. Tuckwell has other fish to fry."

"OK, Vern. Here's what I suggest. It's Wednesday night. I want you to take tomorrow off, look around London, get to know the place. Go to the British Museum and the National Gallery, walk around Hyde Park, go to a matinee show. Come back for lunch on Friday and we'll give you our decision."

"Sounds cool, Mark. I'll see you at twelve thirty on Friday. Sound OK?"

After Vern departed, Mark felt uneasy. While he saw Vern's evident qualities as a hunter-killer in the US marketplace, he was being compromised. He could never adopt CSF's commission structure. He wandered across to Graham's office,

"I'm in a quandary over Vern Badore."

"So, he's a plausible young man, obviously a good salesman, but wrong for us. Where's the quandary?"

"How do we placate Cosway if we don't hire Vern? Remember that lunch in New York? He felt strongly that we should have our own marketing guy in the USA."

"To hell with Cosway. He's just the Chief Operating Officer of CSF. They're our clients, not our owners. We've been through this discussion about Jack Bolt. We've got to keep the CSF juggernaut in its place."

"We've already compromised ourselves by letting them pay our legal bills, contributing towards our new hires, moving into a bigger space." Mark added.

"All the more reason why they don't owe us any more. We simply accepted their financial contribution to tool up to meet their needs. Just tell him that we're not moving ahead with Vern because we don't want to add to our payroll in a year's time. Thank him profusely but make it clear that if we have anyone on the ground in the USA we'll make our own hire, at our own cost, in our own time." Graham was forthright. There was silence between the two partners, then he continued,

"Look, it's a no-brainer. If the fund grows by five hundred million next year, he'd pick up $250,000 commission just for being there, and that comes out of our fees. He'd have the right to that commission for three years even if we terminated him. Also, crucially, the money doesn't have to stick. He's measured only on new sales. So we could end up paying commissions to Vern for business we no longer managed. Not to mention that if we pick up any institutional business in North America, he'd get a cut."

"The decision is easy, but we need to tell Tuckwell and Cosway in a way that doesn't cause offence. Supposing they don't have an agenda, it would seem churlish to turn down such a generous offer."

"But they do have an agenda, Graham. We all know that. We just don't know what that agenda is. We'll have lunch with the kid on Friday, be totally honest with him. Nobody could possibly say we didn't give him a fair crack."

"Fair enough." Graham replied.

They took Vern to lunch at La Grande Marque in Middle Temple Lane. The restaurant was in the former Middle Temple library with an open view over sweeping formal gardens at the back. After they'd ordered their meal, Mark turned to Vern.

"What did you do on your day off? There's so much of London to see – did you manage to take in a few sights?"

Vern looked down at his hands. "Gentlemen. It would be easy for me to tell y'all that I went to the zoo or the British Museum. But I cannot tell a lie. I took my clubs and flew to Scotland on Wednesday night, stayed at the airport hotel in Edinboro, hired a car and made the first tee time at Saint Andrews on Thursday morning. This might be the only time in my life that I get to play Saint Andrews. God gave me the opportunity so I took it."

Graham caught Mark's eye. "That shows a certain initiative, don't you think, Mark?"

The bastard. He's making it hard. "I'm amazed. When did you get back to London?"

"I flew back this morning. I had the opportunity to play Carnoustie after Saint Andrews on a two o'clock tee time yesterday. I was back at the airport hotel by nine and took the seven o'clock shuttle this morning. I got back to my hotel in London at eleven, showered, changed and here I am."

"Well I'll be damned. How did you play?"

"Par at Saint Andrews, plus four at Carnoustie. I hit my ball into the burn on the 18th. I wanna go back there one day and take better control. Carnoustie's the most challenging course I ever played. The cool thing is that my club in Tennessee's called Carnoosty."

"That's cool indeed." Graham was caught up in the story.

"Vern, we're all impressed with your initiative and energy." Mark got to the point. Vern smiled knowingly. This was the moment he knew so well, when maybes turned to yeses.

"In a perfect world I'd like to shake hands and do a deal right now. But for the moment we've decided that it's premature for Appletree to have our own rep in the USA. We've decided to do a rain check on hiring you for this role. Please don't take it personally in any way. I can assure you that we're not actively searching for anyone. It's just that . . . "

"Gentlemen, before you continue with your artsy assed British explanation, lemme say I gotta flight to catch this afternoon. I need to pick up my stuff at the hotel and make some calls before the flight. Will you excuse me?"

Vern stood up and leaned across the table to shake hands with Graham and Mark. He strode out of the restaurant, leaving an astounded silence at the Appletree table.

Graham looked at Mark:

"Who gets to call Cosway?"

Chapter 23

The CSF International Fund opened three days later for trading. Its first share price was exactly ten dollars, quite a feat considering European markets had fallen two per cent since the money was invested. Brazil and Mexico saved the day. Mark's stocks had risen seven per cent and compensated for weakness elsewhere. In Brazil, he'd made a play in logistics and mining stocks. In Mexico he invested in the shares of home-builders. Mexicans were becoming affluent, billions of dollars were being repatriated from the United States. Everyone wanted a house; Mexican construction companies were soaring on the stock market.

Markets fell for a few days and the Fund fell with them. It was valued at $9.97, then $9.91. On the fourth day the NAV fell to $9.87. At noon on the fifth day Bill Tuckwell phoned. Mark was in Graham's office when the call came through.

"Hey Graham, how's it going?"

"Fine thanks Bill. I've got Mark here. I'm going to put you on the speaker." he announced.

"Hi Mark, how you doing? Graham, I see you got some movement on the share price." He paused, then added, "All you need now is to work on the direction."

"That's a good line, Bill. I'll have to remember that." Graham gave out an insincere laugh that sounded more like a hyena than his usual polite educated English chuckle. "At the risk of sounding defensive, Bill, the Fund's actually doing well relative to its peers and the Index. We may be down a little but we rank seventh out of 193 comparable funds in the industry in the one week we've been in business. That puts us close to the top of all managers."

"That may be the case, gennlemen, but we got some pissed-off clients and I want you on a nationwide conference call this afternoon. They wanna know what you're doing with their money. When you guys toured the US of A you preached diversification and how international investing had a low correlation with the US stock market."

"That's correct, Bill. Over time correlations have been low . . . "

"Hi Bill, this is Mark here. Sorry to interrupt. Of course we're available to do a conference call today. What time do you want to do it?" he gestured to Graham to wrap up the call.

"Four PM East Coast Time. I'll call the client and patch you in."

"That's nine PM in London. Is there any way we could do it earlier, say noon your time?" Mark was attending a black tie dinner at a friend"s house in St James that evening. 8.30 for 9.

"Sorry, gennlemen. It's gotta be later to catch the West Coast. There's some AG Stiphel guys in Honolulu who got cash in the Fund. I need half an hour of your time at four PM. OK?"

"This is Graham here. Could you call my home number?"

"Sure, email it to me. Mark, what number will you be on?"

"You can call my mobile. Before we hang up, is there anything we should prepare for specifically before this call?"

"You should be prepared to run through the portfolio, talk about the markets and answer any questions the brokers may have."

"OK, thanks Bill. Talk to you later." They hung up.

"What was that all about?" Graham looked puzzled. "The Fund's only been up for four days and we're getting Nervous Nellie phone calls from a guy who's supposed to be sophisticated? Now I have to organize my whole bloody evening around him."

"Sorry I interrupted you like that. I just didn't want the conversation to drift into you having to defend yourself. You're doing a damn good job with the portfolio. I'm busy tonight too; I'm going to a formal dinner. Butlers, black tie, the lot. I may have to slip into a dowager's powder room at nine to take this call."

"I've forgotten how complicated a bachelor's life can be. Dowager's powder room, my arse." Graham winced.

"Graham, talking about a complicated bachelor life there's something I need to tell you about. I didn't bring it up earlier because I thought it might resolve itself. But it could get a lot more messy before it's over."

Graham arched an eyebrow in anticipation.

"You know Nancy Lindstrom, CSF's Compliance Officer?"

"Yes, I met her when I was in New York a few weeks ago. I was impressed by her efficiency. Cute as a button."

"Well, I've become rather fond of her." Mark sketched out details of his budding romance. He talked of their night out in New York, the weekend in the Okefenokee Swamp, the messages left at the Woodsman Inn at

Folkston. On hearing the revelation that she'd been assaulted by Tuckwell, Graham whistled.

"Holy Shit, Mark. That's heavy stuff. I can see now why there's a . . . certain tension between Tuckwell and us. He seemed unusually abrupt on the phone just now. Like he's trying to pick a fight."

"That's charitable of you. The tension's between Tuckwell and *me*. I'm sure the conversation would have been more accommodating if you hadn't put me on the speaker."

"We're in this together, Mark. It's a partnership. So what else?"

"What else is that Tuckwell lobbied the CSF board to force us to sit Series 63 just before the road show. Nancy confided to me that we didn't need to take the exams at all, as long as we're accompanied by someone registered with the NASD when we make public presentations. We're not sales people. We're articulating investment policy – the wholesaler does the selling."

"The less said the better." Graham reacted. "Clarissa's already swatting for her Series 63 and Alix asked this morning about the other exams she needs to study for between now and Christmas."

"I'll get a special ruling that we don't need to take any more exams and quietly close the issue. I'd like to portray it as a piece of luck that the rules were reinterpreted in our favour, rather than that they needn't have sat 63 in the first place. I don't want anyone to get wind of the politics at CSF."

"Good thinking." Graham reverted to the more salacious possibilities of Mark and Nancy. "So is Nancy a passing fancy, or are you going to keep seeing her?"

"Actually I've grown rather fond of her. Nancy's the first woman I've known for a while who has brains, looks, education, strength, poise, humility and, er, downright sexiness. She even goes to church sometimes."

"So what on earth does she see in you?" Graham arched his eyebrow again.

"Good question. I know it's dangerous to speculate but I think she quite likes me too."

Graham stared out of the window for a long time before he broke the silence.

"Lucky bastard. That's all I can say. But why are your affairs always so bloody complicated? The last time . . . "

"Yeah, yeah, yeah. The drainpipe in Chelsea, my clothes in the street. Very funny."

"Just watch out for Tuckwell. The guy sounds deranged. If he was angry enough to attack Nancy physically, he could easily do something crazy to you."

"I'm trembling already."

"Back to Nancy for a moment, Mark. You portray her as The Perfect Woman. Get real, mate. *She* doesn't exist, any more than the perfect man."

"Present company excluded, of course."

"Hmm." Graham paused. "Changing the subject, did you call Cosway about Vern?"

"He wasn't there when I called yesterday. I didn't leave a message because I wanted to handle it in person."

"You have an exciting afternoon ahead of you."

Mark had a choice. Should he make a sweetheart call to Nancy first, or start a potentially explosive confrontation with Cosway? Being of a Presbyterian bent, he chose to call Cosway first. He would chat with Nancy at leisure afterwards.

"Dick, hi, it's Mark Telford in London."

"Mark, my friend, how's everything going? You'll be glad to know that we've got eighteen million bucks coming into the Fund overnight."

"Any particular source?"

"Lemme look at the printout. Let's see . . . some coming in from HD Mason in Denver, Weil Bateman in Memphis, Ray Hutton in Chicago, Ball and Edwards in Cinci . . . a coupla wire houses throwing cash at you . . . three million from Lynch and Burnham, nationwide. So, it's coming from a range of sources. It's the best marketing scenario. Also we're getting indications of cash flow from AG Stiphel on the Coast. So, Buddy, what can I do for you?"

"Dick, I wanted to talk to you in person about Vern. You were kind enough to set up our meeting in Atlanta, and introduce him to Alix, Bob and Graham when they were in the States. As you may know Vern came to see us last week in London. He's an impressive guy and clearly capable of putting a lot of business on the books, but we've decided to pass on this opportunity."

There was no response from the far end.

"Dick? Are you there?"

"Yeah, go on." The frost was palpable.

"There are various reasons for our decision. First, we're only just beginning to get involved in the US marketplace. Vern would plunge us in too quickly. We want the CSF International Fund to get established in the USA before hiring a marketer.

Second, we were nervous about the management protocols – With Vern reporting to Bill Tuckwell and me jointly, there was too much potential for misunderstanding.

Third, his commission structure was too rich for our culture. He had the potential to earn a multiple of the staff's compensation in London. We would be supporting a marketing effort on his terms and he would pick up all the commissions. It didn't feel like a team reward for a team effort. Bob described it well: Vern would be writing a check on Appletree's energy.

Above all, we really appreciated your offer of financial support but didn't feel it was appropriate in light of everything you've given us so far. Appletree existed before CSF and it's my job to ensure that Appletree exists after CSF – perish the thought." Mark's attempt at levity fell flat.

"Anything else?"

"Bottom line, Dick, we'll need someone in the USA at some point operating on our behalf, but it would have to be on our terms, and only when we're ready."

"Mark," Cosway began," I understand your position and you're right to be cautious. You're a shrewd businessman. What I can't credit is that you sound like you see us as the Enemy. You sound scared to take a risk – and it's not even a risk."

"I wouldn't put it that way. We're just not ready to plunge into the US institutional market on the scale which Vern outlined, particularly as we're so involved with the CSF retail marketing machine. Besides, we already have some existing institutional relationships in the USA but we're just not tooled up for the kind of marketing push that Vern would bring."

"When we had lunch in New York a few weeks ago I said if Vern didn't work out, it was no big deal. I'm disappointed but I'll keep my word. Let's leave it like that. We can revisit on another occasion."

"Thanks for your understanding."

"Sure. So long."

Mark recalled his conversation with Chuck Anderson in the car in Ohio. He described Dick Cosway as having a soft manner that disguised an iron will, or something along those lines. *Don't be deceived by his placid exterior.*

"Two out of two" he thought grimly, "Tuckwell and Cosway must now be seriously pissed off with me. I won't even need to work on Shilson: the other two will poison his mind. Oh well, that's what CEOs are paid to do – make difficult decisions and stand by them." He called New York again.

"Nancy Lindstrom."

"Mark Telford."

"Marko!"

"Can you talk?"

"Sure, my office door's shut and nobod's here with me. I've got a meeting in ten minutes, though. What's up?"

"Thinking a lot about you. You work in a complicated environment."

Nancy laughed.

"Welcome to our passive / aggressive organization. What complication have you encountered today?"

"Tuckwell is pissed off with our performance and wants us to do a conference call this evening, and Cosway was too quiet when I told him about Vern."

"Well, Mark, it's clear that Bill wants to pick a fight with you. He's extremely insecure and he'll stick you with a knife however he can. Dick's politically insecure and he'll make a mountain out of the Vern molehill. I'm not sure how it'll all come out, but be careful."

"And you? Still like me?"

"Crazy about you. When can we meet again?"

"Why don't you come across for a long weekend?"

"I didn't tell you yet because I wanted to wait until I was approved, but I need to visit Appletree to do a compliance audit. There are differences between your British FSA regulation and our SEC registration that need to be reconciled."

"When can you come over?"

"I need to arrange a time with Syreta, but I think I can come next week."

"Come and stay."

"It looks better if I stay in a hotel if I'm in London on business. I booked at the Savoy Hotel. They told me it was near your office."

"Very near. How long can you stay?"

"I can come over Tuesday, spend Wednesday and Thursday in your office and play hooky on Friday. You can show me around London. I've never been there. I need to be back in New York by Monday 10am – that's the Compliance Committee meeting at CSF."

The 9pm conference call went well. Mark excused himself from cocktails and paced Cleveland Row in his dinner jacket, mobile phone glued to his ear, speaking to brokers on the West Coast and Hawaii. Their concerns were not as acute as Tuckwell had implied. They simply wanted to know where the Fund's assets were deployed and were looking for stock ideas to discuss with their clients.

It felt odd to have Nancy at Appletree in London. Mark acted with detachment when she was around. Apart from Graham, nobody had the slightest idea that they were lovers.

He took her to La Bohème at Covent Garden; they toured the Victoria and Albert Museum and the Globe Theatre; walked for miles through parks and gardens and even spotted a jaded Royal at the gates of Buckingham Palace returning from a late night out.

On Sunday morning they strolled through Battersea Park and across Chelsea Bridge glistening in the rain. They found a brasserie off Kings Road where they huddled over brunch. In the early afternoon Mark flagged a taxi for Heathrow. They sat wordlessly, watching raindrops track across the windscreen as the cab headed west. Nancy slipped her arm around Mark's waist and laid her head on his chest.

"I wish I lived in London. It's so civilized here."

Chapter 24

The tensions which seemed likely to erupt into hostility in October had evaporated by December. The Fund was running like clockwork. Its NAV had risen to $10.78, it was comfortably ahead of the index and its performance was in the first quartile of competing funds in America. Sales flowed steadily into the Fund. Everyone was pulling strongly – the investment team in London, the administrative folks in Bismarck and the marketing team in New York.

At the close of the last trading day of the year, the entire staff of Appletree repaired to the pub around the corner, *The Witness Box*. Four bottles of champagne were popped in quick succession.

"Look at this," Syreta handed a printout to Mark amidst the happy din at the bar. It was the daily email from CSF. He read it and shouted,

"Hey everybody, we're getting seventeen million dollars into the Fund tonight. That brings our year-end assets to nine hundred and sixty five million, two hundred and twenty two thousand dollars. Any bets on when we hit a billion?"

"First week of the year." Alix predicted. "That's when cash flows hit the mutual funds. Stock markets look positive well into the first quarter of next year. The combination of new money and strong markets should get us there on the third working day of the year."

"A magnum of Bollinger for the date we hit a billion. Any advances on January 6th?"

It got silly. "January 12th," "January 14th," "January 17th" – "No, that's a Sunday," "February 2nd," "March 9th – that's my birthday," purred Clarissa, "I want to win a magnum of champagne on my birthday." "February 29th is a lucky day. I'll go for that."

They were all wide of the mark. There was a two percent surge in global equity markets on Monday 4th January and an email note from Cosway's office in New York that $36.6 million was coming into the Fund. The Fund hit a billion dollars on the first working day of the year.

Syreta worked with IT specialists over Christmas to refine Appletree's new proprietary investment system. Whenever new money arrived in the Fund it was automatically deployed into the model's allocated markets and the managers' chosen stocks. The model fed into a computer that implemented all trades, ensuring that the Fund was always optimally invested.

"Never leave a Fund open to unnecessary discretion" was Graham's mantra. Decide the course, set the compass and leave the rest to the markets."

This philosophy was simple, easily articulated and, often as not, dead right. When Graham adjusted the model and equities needed to be bought or sold, Appletree's stock transactions were put out to automated tender. This meant that the best deals in the market were identified and executed electronically. Clients demanded proof that every trade got 'Best Execution'. Every portfolio change had a transaction cost, so the careful choice of brokers to deal on behalf of the CSF fund was critical to its performance. Automated tender trading provided a clear audit path for clients to track.

One afternoon in early February Steve Shilson called,

"Hey Mark, I haven't called you for a while. Reason is I believe that my managers need to be left alone to strut their stuff. If the CEO'S in your face you're always looking over your shoulder for him to second-guess you."

"Not at all, Steve," Mark mustered all his diplomatic skills to avoid pointing out that Shilson was not actually his CEO. "You're always welcome to call. I'm not concerned about you second-guessing me."

"I know that Bill and Dick were all over you guys at the beginning. Maybe it's because you're Brits and they were looking for reasons to go to London. Maybe it's a control thing. Who knows? I told them to back off last November."

"They've been quiet for a while, Steve. I hope you're pleased with what we're doing at the Fund."

"Pleased? You guys are a dream. You present good, you support our marketing efforts real good, and your performance is up there with the best."

After a few minutes of banter, Shilson got to the point.

"Say, you need to mark your calendar for April 9th through 12th. The Fund's trustees are meeting at the Saguaro Canyon Resort in Tucson Arizona. It'll give you a chance to get to know them and present the Appletree story. It's smart to get on the right side of the trustees of a mutual fund when things are going good. When things turn ugly you'll have them on your side. At least for a while."

"Who are the trustees?"

"All friends of mine. I chair the board. There's a lawyer, an accountant, an actuary, a professor, a black guy, a Jewish broad and a well-known entrepreneur. They're all non-executive. Me, Dick Cosway and Bill Tuckwell are the executive directors of the Board."

"Will they be friendly?"

"The trustees do exactly what I tell them. So yea, they're friendly."

"Sounds interesting." Mark was uneasy but didn't feel it was the moment to discuss the fiduciary role of trustees.

"Yea. Most of my trustees don't have much going for themselves outside the CSF honeypot, and they know it. So bring your clubs and your wife. Skye's coming."

"I'm not a golfer and I'm not married."

"Everybody plays one round, Mark. We make allowances. If you don't have a wife, bring a lady friend. We like to play at CSF."

"Do other unmarried guys bring lady friends?"

"Sure. Bill brings Nancy to these events. She came to the Board meeting in Hawaii last year. I hear they're gonna announce an engagement on this year's trip. Skye's working on the celebrations. Last year we thought they'd get married on the beach on Maui."

"OK – Steve, my other line's blinking. I need to pick up." Mark lied, swimming in a stew of jealous incomprehension. He had to stop this conversation immediately or he would explode.

"Sure – Feel free to bring a cute English lady friend. She'll get on real well with Skye and Nancy. Lemme know. Talk soon."

"Thanks for calling."

Mark swivelled his chair, leaned back, rested his feet on the window sill, crossed his hands on his lap, took a deep breath, closed his eyes and murmured,

"Holy shit."

Syreta tapped on the door.

"Are you all right, Mark? You've not moved for at least fifteen minutes. You look terrible."

He opened his eyes. She was such a naturally beautiful woman; delicate, petite, chocolate brown with a gorgeous mouth and an iron will. He had always been attracted to her. Her husband Jayanthkumar spent most of his life working in Dubai, leaving her to juggle their daughter's schooling and daily family life. Mark liked Jay but reckoned he played a dangerous game by leaving Syreta to the tender mercies of London, month after lonely month.

One move, of course, and Mark would be open to a flood of lawsuits. But he never felt closer to touching Syreta's lithe body as she leaned over to see if he was all right. He badly needed the solace of a woman's touch. He could swear she would reciprocate, but it wasn't worth the risk. He had to keep his instincts firmly gated within the realms of fantasy. If only he weren't so bloody British.

"Oh, hi Syreta. Yes, I'm fine thanks. Just having a zen moment. I got really tired so sat back and closed my eyes."

"You should go home. The office can wait."

"No, I'll be fine. Absolutely OK. But thanks for your concern." He touched her hand in a gesture of gratitude. She gave him a knowing smile.

"Just checking on you. There's something I'd like to show you, though, if you're up to it." It sounded ominous.

"I'm up for anything. Give it to me straight Syreta . . . "

"Remember last Thursday when we had that huge inflow of cash into the Fund?"

"Sure, it was a bigger chunk than we're used to. Fifty million dollars or thereabouts, wasn't it?"

"That's right. Normally I don't pay attention to the provenance of the flows because the brokers' names don't mean anything to me. Whether it's Ray Hutton in Chicago or Weil Bateman in Memphis doesn't register with me. But I did notice that the money on Friday came from Schleman Weld's office in Hamilton Bermuda."

"They're a reputable shop. What's the issue?"

"Mark, the issue is that after three business days they've requested to sell their position."

"Syreta, investors are allowed to sell. There are many reasons for wanting to get out of a fund. It might have been a clerical error. Someone might have screwed up, meaning to send the money to the Prudelity International Fund instead of CSF. If they're an insurance company they might have had a big claim to pay out. I wouldn't read anything into it. Why are you so concerned?"

"I'm just being protective of our Fund. We invested the money in a programme trade last Thursday, incurring three hundred thousand dollars of brokerage costs. Now we have to meet this redemption on a day when there's no cash in the portfolio. So we now have to sell stocks, incurring more brokerage costs. The NAV of the Fund has risen 1.6% since they invested, so they're picking up eight hundred thousand dollars of profit in less than a week. That's a huge annualized profit."

"God bless them. I would too, if I could. Let's not read too much into this."

"Except for one other thing, Mark. The money being controlled from Bermuda bothers me. There could be a money laundering issue here."

"Give me a scenario."

"Well, it could be South American drug dealers with Bermuda connections. They open an account with Schleman Weld in Hamilton, instruct them to buy an onshore US mutual fund that's liquid enough to absorb fifty million dollars, keep it there for a few days and sell. The money becomes legitimate onshore US cleared funds. They've just laundered fifty million dollars, plus any profit that the trade generates."

"Maybe, but remember, it's CSF's job to screen all clients coming into their funds. I know we're obliged by the FSA to 'know our clients', but CSF assumes responsibility for business going into this fund. Can you imagine the difficulty of policing every dollar that comes into the Fund through CSF's sales network? I'm confident that knowing CSF is tantamount to knowing their clients.

Secondly, Schleman Weld's a highly reputable outfit, Syreta. The Bermuda authorities are known to be tough on financial hanky panky and Schleman are not so stupid as to test them. My guess is that they misplaced a trade on behalf of a Bermuda-registered reinsurance company last week and they're unwinding it in a hurry. They're damn lucky to have made a profit on the transaction – it could easily have gone the other way."

"All right. I just thought I'd bring it to your attention. You never know."

"Semper vigilans."

"What?"

"Nothing."

After Syreta left his room, Mark scooped papers into his briefcase, grabbed his umbrella and left the office for the day.

It was sleeting; people leaned into the bitter wind blowing through the Victoria Embankment gardens. The ground was slushy, the traffic on the Thames side of the hedge was heavy and obnoxious. Mark had a pulsing headache by the time he boarded the District Line at Westminster.

His flat in Prince of Wales Drive was usually warm and inviting. His maid had left the table light on in the hall and the atmosphere was welcoming. Yet Mark found the apartment jejune and grey. It smelled dead. A few weeks ago Nancy was here. It was a loving, uncomplicated weekend. They laughed a lot, it all seemed so fun.

"It's got so bloody complicated," he said out loud, "effing bloody complicated."

The phone broke his mood.

"Hello? Mark Telford here."

"Nancy Lindstrom. How are you, Marko?"

"To what do I owe the pleasure?" Mark sounded surly.

"That's a funny way to say hello."

"Look, Nancy. Things took a weird turn today and we need to be absolutely honest with each other. You agree?"

"Of course, why would I not be honest with you?"

"I got a call today from Steve Shilson. He invited me to the Trustee meeting at the Saguaro Canyon Resort in Tucson from April 9th through April 12th.

"Yea? That sounds fun."

"You would know."

"What's that supposed to mean?"

"He said you are accompanying Bill Tuckwell and that it was expected you would announce your engagement in Arizona."

"Pardon me?"

"He said they all expected you would get married on the beach in Maui last year."

"Total bullshit, Mark. We've already talked about that."

"He said you were close to Skye and working with her to make preparations for Arizona."

"Skye's a bimbo."

"Not what I heard, Nancy. Shilson said I should bring my own English lady friend and that you, she and Skye would get on really well."

"I can't believe you believe this crap, Mark. Why would I play games like this?"

"Why would anyone play games, Nancy?" He heard a sniff at the other end of the line. "So tell me, are you going to Arizona in April?"

" . . . Yes, I am." She replied quietly.

"Did you know I'd been invited?"

"No, I didn't."

"Are you going as Tuckwell's date?"

"Maybe he thinks so, but . . . "

"That's not a clear answer, Nancy. Let me ask the question in a different way. Were you invited to Arizona in your official capacity as Compliance Officer, or as Tuckwell's date?"

"They always need a Compliance Officer at Trustee meetings."

"I see. So you put it on your calendar as a normal business event, oblivious of the fact that half the board of CSF expects Tuckwell and you to announce your engagement in the desert?"

"This is unbelievable."

"What are the sleeping arrangements at the Saguaro Canyon?"

"You're taking this too far, Mark,"

"Answer me. What are the sleeping arrangements at Saguaro Canyon?"

"April is months away. I can't tell you. You've got the wrong end of this story, Big Time, mister."

"So if I come to the meeting in Arizona you'd be prepared to stay with me?"

"Maybe."

"Why then did Shilson tell me you were expected to get married on the beach in Maui last year, and that Skye was preparing a party for the event in Arizona this year? Shilson obviously thinks there's something going on between the two of you. Why would he think that? What the hell's going on, Nancy?"

"Maybe it's because I attend official functions with Bill hanging around in the background. Maybe it's because Bill refuses to accept that I dumped him and keeps talking about me in the present tense. Maybe this, maybe that, Mark."

"Mmm. So why did you call this evening?" Mark's mood lightened as the explanation became clearer – for the minute anyway.

"I was calling because I get my kicks playing off one horny dumb buffalo against another."

"Very funny. I'm sorry Nancy, but you must agree that these things sound odd at the end of a telephone three thousand miles away."

"I guess. So you really want to know why I called this evening?" I was calling to say . . . as soon as I've sorted things with CSF I want to take you up on your offer to move to London."

"Say that again slowly."

"I want to live with you."

"I hate all this confusion Nancy." Mark's voice cracked.

By way of perspective Mark had generally been regarded as an imperturbable stoic since his school days. The Original British Cool Customer was how Zack Overwood introduced him before a conference call to a few hundred brokers in Louisiana.

"I'll talk to Shilson and Cosway when the time is right. I'll talk to Bill first so as not to humiliate him in front of his colleagues."

"What are you going to say? Do you expect to keep working with them?"

"We'll see. They want to develop business in Europe through Dublin and it might be useful for them to have an ex-compliance officer on the ground to help set it up."

"You've got me totally confused."

"I'll call once I've spoken to Shilson and the others."

"Good luck."

The jejune, tired and dead apartment of half an hour earlier had mutated into happier colours. Mark kicked off his shoes, dived on the sofa and punched a cushion until feathers burst out of its seams.

Chapter 25

"February's numbers look fantastic." Graham announced with satisfaction as the steaming plate of Risotto with Wild Mushrooms was placed before him. He lifted his glass of Amarone Classico to Mark.

"Let's see . . . " Mark glanced at the report he'd brought to the restaurant. "We're at $1.39 billion. That gives us an annualized fee of . . . "

"North of eight million dollars. I already worked it out."

"It's starting to look interesting, isn't it?" Mark cut into a slice of tomato slathered with balsamic vinegar. He always ordered caprese when they lunched at Tempio's.

"I'm pleased with the way our systems are coping."

"The Fund's four months old and we've established a steady pattern of cash flow through the CSF sales machine. Since December we've averaged twelve million dollars a day coming into the Fund and four million of daily redemptions. The Fund's increasing by forty million dollars a week."

"That's spectacular – CSF are really delivering on their promises. But credit where credit's due, Graham. None of this would be happening without your performance. The Fund's up 7.2% in the first two months of the year, the Index is up 5.8% and our peer group average is 5.6%."

"It's a team effort. Besides, we could always be doing better."

"You're too modest, Graham. Most investment firms would dance on the roof with this kind of performance."

"Our performance comes from the discipline which our systems provide."

Graham's system calculated continuously how much money was available for investment in every market and executed trades automatically. If Toyota stock was 2% of the Fund's value, a daily inflow of $8 million meant that $160,000 was invested automatically into Toyota stock. Share prices sometimes rose above the percentage intended by the portfolio manager. If 2% of the Fund was allocated to Toyota and a strong market increased its percentage to 2.2%, the programme stopped purchasing Toyota stock until it reverted to 2% of the Fund. The system was biased towards buying stocks while they were cheap.

"How's your work going with the model?"

"Never satisfied. I'm always testing new factors to tweak the effectiveness of the model. I'm looking at metals at the moment. Take copper. While the price is crucially important to Chile, it's not so relevant to Singapore. Overall commodity prices, however, are important to every economy, so I've added sensitivity to the Commodity Index as a factor in allocating money to markets."

"Any thoughts on adding politics to the model?"

"I've asked Bob, Clarissa and Alix to keep tabs on politics in their countries to see how they might affect local stock markets. For me to include a factor in the model, it must be quantifiable. Politics can't be quantified but, having said that, we have to look at them. A market may look cheap, but its regime can put off inward investment by foreigners. Look at Venezuela."

"How's everyone getting on in the team?" Mark liked to touch every aspect of Appletree's operations during their weekly lunch.

"Alix behaves as if she's in love. She's mellow, dresses better, smiles, wears makeup. Something happened in America."

"I've noticed a softer edge too. D'you suppose she had a thing going with one of the CSF wholesalers? Randy Marx sounded a likely candidate."

"Can't tell." Graham rarely got drawn into gossip. "What I can say is that her investment performance in the Continental markets is superb at the moment. She's firing on all cylinders in Germany and France, as well as in emerging markets like Poland and Turkey. She's creative and hard working.

"Great. How's Bob doing?"

"It's not as easy to outperform the UK market as you might think. We have the most multinational economy in Europe. To analyse GKN, for instance, Bob has to follow economic conditions, currency forecasts, commodity prices, sales trends and profitability in North America, Asia and Continental Europe. The company's share price is an amalgam of factors around the globe. Then there's the takeover potential of a company. Bob's ahead of the market year to date, but no fireworks."

"Clarissa?"

"Ah, Clarissa ! She may be a newcomer to us but a she's a veteran of the Asian markets. She enjoys working with our systems and watching the new cash come into her portfolio each day."

"She's a handsome woman." Mark forever tried to draw indiscretions out of Graham. "I hear that a besotted Kyoto stock broker once called her Landy Cralissa. The name has stuck in Nipponese brokerage circles."

"Good luck to her. Clarissa's made a major contribution to the Fund's success year to date. She identified depressed Japanese technology stocks, bought them early in December, enjoyed a spectacular January and sold them forty percent later in February. She's having similar success with Singapore shipping companies and some Australian mining companies." Landy Cralissa or not, Graham was clearly impressed by his new hire,

They drained their espressos. Mark requested '*Il conto, per favore*', which failed to impress the waiter.

"Well, my early success in Brazil has gone into reverse." Mark couldn't boast of investment heroics to match his colleagues'. "The market's been clobbered by another of their perennial bloody currency crises, but I reckon we should keep buying as Brazil falls. It's the best time to accumulate."

"I've got no problem with that. Brazil will underpin the portfolio when the rest of the world goes in the tank. Always keep part of the portfolio in unloved parts of the world. That creates tomorrow's performance."

"My Mexican home building stocks are down, but I'm topping up as they fall and am still committed to them."

Graham was unfazed, "They helped our performance before Christmas and they'll help it again."

Mark tapped out his PIN on the machine as the waiter looked away self-consciously. "It's two o'clock. Better return to the grindstone."

Five minutes later Syreta met them in the lobby of Appletree. She looked worried.

"I've been waiting for you both to get back from lunch. We have a problem."

Mark steered her into the conference room. They sat down.

"Remember a short while ago we had that $50 million round trip in the Fund?"

Mark and Graham nodded.

"We've had another three, totalling $162 million. The biggest was $72 million in and $71.6 million out over fourteen days. It came to light this morning."

"One hundred and sixty two million dollars. That's one hell of a turnover. Have you spoken to Cosway in New York?" Mark asked.

"Not yet. I wanted to talk to you first."

"The problem when we get new chunks of money is that the system automatically invests it. We have a zero cash policy, which means there's a hit on the Fund when you get a redemption on this scale." Graham explained.

"Are you sure it wasn't a coincidence?" Mark asked hopefully. "In other words, one broker puts in $72 million and another broker, coincidentally, pulled $71.6 million out of the Fund fourteen days later?"

"No way. There's a New Hampshire-based trader called Bleuestein on both sides of the trade. And even if one was a coincidence there's no way three could be a coincidence." Syreta dismissed his suggestion.

"What's the point of these quick trades? It's a crude way of making money. What about the guy who invested $72 million and pulled out $71.6 million two weeks later? That's a pretty dumb investment strategy."

"Not if the money's being laundered. A criminal wouldn't care less if he dropped $0.4 million if it meant that $71.6 million slipped through the net."

"Aren't they being clobbered by the front end charges of the Fund?" Mark queried.

"CSF has a discretionary exemption from front end charges for amounts over $10 million. I checked the prospectus this morning." Syreta was always on top of the details.

"Whose discretion?"

"CSF's, in New York."

"We need to call Cosway right away. Graham – why don't Syreta and I deal with this? You can get on with your modelling. There's no point all of us wasting time on this."

"I appreciate that. Let me know the outcome."

Apart from their personal ties, the strength of Appletree's partnership was that Mark and Graham had complementary skills and aptitudes. While there was a healthy crossover between their roles, Graham managed the investments and Mark ran the business.

"This is Dick Cosway."

"Hey Dick, this is Mark Telford from Appletree. I'm on the line with Syreta, who's responsible for our Fund accounting among . . . "

"Heaven's sake, Mark. I know who you both are. Why are you Brits so goddam formal all the time?" He tried to be light but couldn't help sounding aggressive. "What can I do for you?"

"We want to draw your attention to some hot trades in and out of the Fund. The sheer size of these trades means that the Fund's performance will be impacted."

"I'm not aware of any trades. Can you give me an example?"

"Three came to light this morning." Syreta took over. "One was a $33 million trade that closed out at $33.3 million after 3 business days; one was for $55 million that closed out at $57.1 million after 8 business days, and the third was for $72 million closing out at $71.6 million after 14 business days."

"These trades sound exceptional. We're not getting trades like these in our other funds." Cosway said vaguely. "Lemme look into it and get back to you."

"Before you go Dick, we know the name of the guys who placed the $33 million bet. The firm is called Bleuestein, in New Hampshire. The record doesn't show who placed the other two."

"OK. Thanks Syreta. I'll call you back later this afternoon."

Two hours later Cosway called Mark,

"Hey Mark. I've got Bill and Nancy on the line. We want to run through those trades that you brought to my attention earlier."

"Hi Dick – Bill, Nancy. How are you?"

This was a novel twist.

"What have you found?"

"Yeah, Mark." Cosway began." We did some digging. As you said, the $33 million trade was out of New Hampshire. Bleuestein's an established market timer. We already deal with him in our other funds. The $55 million trade was by Schleman Weld out of Hamilton, Bermuda and the $72 million trade was a Swiss bank trading account out of Hong Kong."

"Aside from Bleuestein did you know these accounts before they traded in the CSF International Fund?"

"No we didn't, Mark." Bill Tuckwell spoke.

"Can you confirm they're bona fide investors? How do you know the Hong Kong deal was straight?"

"Short answer, Mark, we didn't know it was . . . " Tuckwell was about to apologize when Nancy interrupted,

"Mark, the Hong Kong and Bermuda trades originated from brokers known well by our local reps. So by extension we knew these clients."

I can't believe you're covering for Tuckwell. Mark could have screamed at her.

"So you're satisfied that the 'know your client' rules apply?"

"Yes we are." Nancy replied firmly. "There's no money laundering or compliance issue here."

"That's good to know. I'd appreciate if you put on the record that Appletree questioned the provenance of these trades."

"I will be sure that it's recorded," Nancy confirmed.

"If there's no issue about the clients, how about the legitimacy of market timing trades on this scale? I can't believe that CSF would endorse this kind of activity in its funds. They're extremely damaging."

"How so?" Cosway enquired.

"Well, an investor comes in without paying a front end charge if he invests over $10 million, I understand."

"Correct. We want to encourage institutional clients to invest in our funds."

"That means a big client can swing into the Fund and out again at the NAV price without incurring any transaction costs. At Appletree we always invest money in the market as soon as it arrives. We don't keep cash in the portfolio. If a client puts $33 million into the Fund on Friday morning, it's fully invested in 94 stocks by Friday afternoon. If the client wants his money back the next Tuesday, we have to sell those stocks to meet his request."

"That's what mutual funds are all about, Mark. Money comes in, money goes out. It's your job to finesse the cash flows." Cosway sounded patronizing.

"What worries me is that these traders get their money out expense-free while the remaining investors in the Fund have to pay the transaction costs of selling their stocks. That can't be right."

"Transaction costs on trades of this size are very small, Mark. I think you're stirring up a tempest in a teacup." Cosway trivialized his objection.

"You can net redemptions off against inflows, can't you?" Tuckwell added glibly.

"Yes, but our average net inflow is $12 million a day. There's a big gap between $12 million coming in and $33 million going out."

"You're always gonna get market timing activity in mutual funds. Always." Cosway insisted.

"Is there a penalty if they sell the Fund within a certain time period?"

"In theory, yes. But the cost can be waived." Nancy said.

"Waived by whom?"

"By CSF."

"Yes, but *who* at CSF?" Mark hated being given the runaround.

"My wholesalers are empowered to waive the load on Fund purchases over $10 million, and drop the penalty for early withdrawal." Tuckwell confirmed.

"Do they need to report their decision to waive fees to you or anyone else?"

"Whenever we see an investment over $10 million hitting the wire we assume there was no transaction fee. I trust my wholesalers' judgement.

You gotta delegate in my position, Mark. Otherwise I could never manage this team of wholesalers. They're the best in America and they don't need supervision."

"I know that, Bill, but why would a wholesaler waive fees when that would hit his sales commission?"

"We take care of our wholesalers, my friend." Tuckwell replied conspiratorially. "But I'm sure they'd be real touched by your concern. I will always find a way to pay wholesalers who deliver $10 million into our funds."

"Even if the assets only stay in the Fund for a few days?"

"Sure-the part of the picture you guys don't see from Appletree is that client money has to be in the CSF system before it gets fees waived. So a $10 million investment in your fund that switches out a few days later has to transfer into another CSF fund. The cash has to stay in our system. That's where the wholesaler picks up his slice."

"OK-there's evidently nothing we can do about CSF's culture of market timing , but please warn us when short-term money's about to hit our fund. If we know that money is with us for only a few days then we won't invest it. I'm not thrilled but at least the remaining investors in the Fund won't be hit by the cost of short-term trading."

"We'll try to identify the players and give you warning."

Chapter 26

"Market timers? What the hell are market timers?" Graham's voice rose in exasperation.

"A market timer is someone who has a model that triggers the 'right' time to buy or sell a mutual fund." Mark replied.

"We absolutely don't want investors like that. The whole point of this fund is to make long-term investments in equities around the world. We're in the business of planting oak trees, not harvesting pond weed."

"Good one, Graham. How'd you think that one up?"

"The images come thick and fast when I'm excited." Graham had a charming gift for standing back and seeing how ridiculous he sounded. "Look, Mark, we have $1.3 billion in our fund. Our typical client is a hard-working, long-term saver who dollar-cost averages part of his monthly earnings into the Fund. Then we get these Big Shot financial shysters butting in and swinging out again, skimming profits out of everyone's pocket."

"What bothers me most is the complicity of CSF. Tuckwell completely glossed over the commission question. He said that wholesalers can waive fees on investments over $10 million, and that they would be 'taken care of'. What's in it for CSF?"

"Why don't we call your friend Nancy, off the record? It's lunchtime in New York now." Graham glanced at the time on his computer screen. "Perhaps you could persuade her to take a stroll outside the office with her mobile? If you want a cootchy coo chat, I don't mind not being on the call. Just be sure to ask the right questions." Graham sounded weary.

"I'll let you know."

Mark returned to his office and closed the door. As he passed Syreta he couldn't help noticing the curve of her breasts as she leaned forward to hand papers to a colleague. She'd looked up unexpectedly and smiled. His testosterone was running haywire.

He caught Nancy at her desk. "Hey Mark, how are you?"

"I'm puzzled why you came to Tuckwell's aid when he was thrashing around trying to explain those market timing trades."

"That was a professional intervention, not a personal bail-out. You know, Mark, I can't let personal preferences get in the way of my job.

Not as long as they're paying me to be CSF's Compliance Officer."

"I understand. I don't understand. Anyway-that's not what I'm calling about. I need to have a chat about the mechanics of these trades and the entire bonus structure surrounding them. Is this something you can talk about?"

"That would not be appropriate. Look, I'm heading out to lunch. Can we talk later?"

"No problem." They hung up.

Fifteeen minutes later his phone rang.

"Hey Marko. You do know that every phone conversation at CSF is recorded and archived for seven years, don't you? If I'm abrupt it's because it would be suicidal to talk on the office line."

"I know. I understand the code. Where are you at the moment?"

"In the lobby of the Marriott Hotel. In a comfortable chair with a bagel on my lap. I've got half an hour."

"Have you spoken to anyone about moving to London?"

"Not yet. I've been thinking about how to handle it."

"And . . . ?"

"Here's what I want to do. I need a month to slowly empty my office of stuff that might be useful in my future career. I'll leave obvious things like my art and desk ornaments. They can be packed and sent on when I've gone."

"Don't set yourself up for theft of intellectual property."

"I know exactly what I can take-I just don't want a sudden lock-down from CSF and have them deciding what I can and can't take."

"Fair enough. Then what?"

"Then I go to Tucson Arizona and make the announcement when we're there. I resign after the board meeting."

"Don't you risk pissing off Tuckwell so much that they won't want you in any capacity in London? Remember my conversation with Shilson the other day? Skye's planning an engagement party for you and Tuckers at the Resort. You'd completely throw them."

"First, I don't need to stay working for CSF. There are plenty of jobs for compliance officers in London. Second, my departure is not tied to my relationship with you. I simply tell them I need to take time off."

"So you won't announce that you're dumping Tuckwell for me?"

"I see no reason to do that."

"How will you handle the engagement party?"

Nancy laughed. "I already spoke to Skye. It's off."

"But how will you handle Tuckwell?" Mark was insistent.

"We met in his office this morning. I told him I'm seeing someone else and our relationship is over, over, over. At first he was blustering and all male. Then he kinda deflated into a grey heap. I felt sorry for him."

"He's deluded himself for a long time. Did you tell him about me?"

"I didn't need to. He's been spying on us for a long time."

"Well, your strategy sounds OK. You don't want to leave CSF in the lurch, you don't want to embarrass Tuckwell, you're resigning to take time off and you want to be friends all round. Anything that happens between you and me is coincidental."

"You know, Mark, at the end of this saga Appletree still has to manage its relationship with CSF. There's no point having a dramatic bust-up. You're too much on the line with them."

"Very true, much as I hate to admit it." He agreed.

"Changing the subject, after Arizona, I want to go on vacation. My brother has our family farm in Michigan and says we can use it any time. He works in Chicago and uses it at weekends. It's nice up there in April, real peaceful. We can go on bike rides and walk by the lake, burn hickory logs in the bedroom fireplace. They have nice restaurants along the Lake Michigan shore."

Mark thumbed through his diary for April as she spoke. "Sounds good. There's nothing that week that can't wait. Count me in."

"Crazy about you,Babe." Mark loved the way she reverted the conversation back to *them*.

"I hate to say this, Nancy, but we need to talk about a more mundane subject. I need to know more about these bloody market timing trades. They're beginning to seriously affect the way we run the money. What's going on?"

"You have to be more specific."

"We don't understand what drives them. In our conversation earlier, Cosway and Tuckwell said that they're a fact of life in mutual funds. They said that wholesalers can approve cost-free trades and that they get rewarded from elsewhere in the system when the money comes into our Fund. What does all this mean?"

"Off the record, you're being misled, Baby." Mark was surprised by the gangster talk. "The money does not come from inside the CSF system. We have a unit specializing in institutional market timing. Their job is to get institutions who are not existing clients to place what we call 'sticky' assets in the CSF Funds in exchange for being permitted to market time in the funds."

"Sticky assets?"

"Yes. If a Bermuda-based hedge fund, for example, commits to investing $20 million in our mutual funds for the long term, CSF lets them make market timing calls of up to $40 million in our other funds as long as they keep the $20 million with us. Leaving sticky assets with CSF is the pay-to-play fee for market timers."

"But why would CSF want such short-term capital flowing through the system? It's to nobody's benefit."

"Not true. Shilson, Cosway and Tuckwell's bonuses are calculated on new flows coming into the funds every month. The wholesalers' bonuses are calculated on a similar formula."

"The numbers are not netted? If a timer puts in and takes out $40 million four times in a month, that's $160 million of new money in a fund?"

"Correct, their bonuses are calculated on gross sales into all the funds."

"Where does it stop?"

"It doesn't stop, Honey."

"What do you think, as Compliance Officer?"

"It's not illegal, though it's unethical, in my opinion."

"What would the long-term clients say, if they knew?"

"They'd be horrified, I'm sure."

"Have you said anything to your colleagues?"

"I table it at every Compliance meeting. The board got our Legal Department to rule that it was acceptable, as long as the sticky assets remain with us."

"How many sticky assets are with CSF? What's the potential for market timing in total?"

"I don't have the current figure, but I'd guess $5 to $6 billion."

"On the two to one formula, that means we could have timing activity of $10 to $12 billion at any one time. That's outrageous."

"Not really. Remember we manage over $400 billion of assets at CSF. $12 billion is only 3% of assets. Also, remember that $12 billion is spread over a lot of funds. We've got six funds with assets over $30 billion each. $12 billion makes no overall impact on their performance."

"But what if $12 billion swings in and out of the funds three times in a month? That's $36 billion of timing money, with each trade gouging performance out of the long-term savers in the funds."

"That's pretty hypothetical, Marko. CSF can stop the trades with a phone call if they get too hot. It never happens. It's never needed to happen."

"And each round trip adds to the New Money total for calculating Shilson's bonus each month?"

"Correct. For Cosway and Bill too."

"I'm appalled."

"I promise you, Mark, it's kosher. Everybody does it on the Street. Our lawyers have approved the program, qualified trades are permitted by prospectus, we file copies of every CSF fund prospectus with the SEC, Shilson's deal is on the record. We're not hiding anything."

"Does the sticky asset rule apply on a fund by fund basis? In other words, if someone wants to time the International Fund, do they need to have the requisite sticky assets in the international fund, or is it OK if they have the assets anywhere in the CSF fund system?"

"Anywhere in the CSF Fund system is fine."

"So we could get huge timing activity in the International Fund without the timers' long term sticky assets being affected. The sticky assets could be in a completely different CSF fund?

"Sure. But Mark, you just see the timing from one angle. You need to get used to it. Our other managers handle it just fine. You might want to talk to Chris, who runs the CSF High Alpha Growth Fund. He gets timing trades of hundreds of millions each month. His performance is not affected."

"Does he get a bonus for accepting these trades?"

"I really don't know." She was getting exasperated,

"Mark, sorry I don't have all the answers. I've got to get back to the office. Please don't worry about this stuff. There's no money laundering going on, the terms of our market timing activities are in the prospectus filed with the SEC. Everything is transparent and disclosed. Everybody in the industry does it. Welcome to capitalist America."

"Welcome to one-sided, the rich-take-all, fuck the little guy, capitalist America."

"Oh come on, Honey."

"There's a lot more I need to know but we'll let it shake down for a few days. I'll call Cosway if things get worse. I appreciate your insights into this crazy activity."

"Can't wait to see you in Arizona." Nancy switched from corporate tiger to private pussycat.

Chapter 27

"So here's the deal." Mark interrupted Graham in the midst of some intense number-crunching. He looked up from his papers blearily, keeping his finger on the line he was analysing.

"Hey Romeo, speak to Juliet?"

"I'm afraid it's a really ugly corporate culture we're dealing with." Mark described the Market Timing team, the billions of sticky assets, CSF's executive bonus structure based on gross sales, the revelation that this was apparently an industry norm.

"Well, we have to analyse each trade coming in very carefully. We need to understand what triggers their model to transact in our Fund. What makes me suspicious is the ease and confidence with which they act. It's as if an insider's helping them to pull the trigger. I don't think anyone would gamble with $50 million unless something was tilted in their favour. We need to find out what it is." Graham smiled. He relished the forensic challenge of outwitting the market timers.

"Let's match the price history of the Fund with the trades we've had." Mark suggested. "We can overlay what the markets were doing on the days the trades took place. There may be an obvious factor that triggered the trading."

"That's a good place to start. I've been thinking about ways we can derail the market timers. I want to give them a hell of a fright."

"Just remember, Graham, we're coming up to a quarter-end on 30th March. Our performance on that date will be reported at the Board meeting in Arizona in April. I don't want any clever scheme to destroy market timers that might bugger our performance at the same time."

"Our performance is buggered already, but I can defer my plan until after April 1st" Graham shrugged and smiled.

Syreta came into Mark's office with a spread sheet showing the daily NAV of the Fund since launch the previous October. She put arrows against the dates when market timers purchased or sold shares in the Fund.

"Do you have a record of when the timers actually placed their orders?" Mark scrutinized the spread sheet.

"What do you mean?"

"I mean, the exact time of day when orders were placed for these transactions."

"That would be in CSF's trading records. We're not involved with the client interface over here in London. We just get informed of cash flows each day. I could ask Jessica in Bismarck if they have any information."

"How will you ask without raising their suspicions that we're onto something?"

"Jessica's just clerical. She told me that they permanently archive every email and phone call relating to client trades. I can tell her we need the information for auditing purposes, if she asks. I'm sure she'll oblige." Syreta was looking puzzled, "I'm still not quite sure why we need this information."

"Here's what I think may be going on, Syreta. I was reading the Purchase and Sale rules in the prospectus. They state clearly that orders must be received by one o'clock New York time to transact at the NAV calculated at four o'clock each day. Orders not received by one o'clock have to be transacted at the NAV calculated on the following day."

"Fair enough."

"No exceptions may be made to this rule. It's a legal stipulation."

"So what's your point?"

"My point is that if institutions were allowed to trade in shares of the Fund outside these hours, they broke the law. Or more accurately, CSF broke the law on their behalf."

"Why would they do that?"

"They would do that to give important clients the unfair advantage of trading favourably, to inflate CSF's monthly mutual fund assets and to increase the bonuses of the fat cats at the top of the company."

"I see." Syreta sounded dubious. She was far from the internal politics and front line bullshit and would not naturally comprehend the greed machine at CSF. "I'll get that information from Jessica. Can you give me an hour or so?"

"That's OK, Syreta, take as long as you need. I'm working late tonight."

"Me too. Jay's coming back at the weekend and I'm trying to clear my backlog."

Mark scanned his Bloomberg and studied charts of Latin American markets. They'd been clobbered recently but investment opportunities were opening up in Brazil and Mexico. Chilean stocks looked cheap.

He was glad that Graham's system kept purchasing stocks for the Fund through thick and thin. It meant that he was fully invested in cheap stocks at the bottom of markets. When markets turned upwards, his performance soared.

Syreta forwarded Mark a spread sheet emailed from Bismarck. He studied it intensely. It contained precisely the information he needed. He looked at the first big trade that came through, the $50 million from Schleman Weld in Bermuda. The money was wired on a Thursday and went out again the next Tuesday. The trade made a profit of 1.6%, or $800,000, in three working days. The purchase was marked with a priority asterisk on the CSF sheet. It was accepted at 5.07pm on Thursday 27th February. The sale was also marked with an asterisk, accepted at 5.43pm on Tuesday 4th March. The dealing times were clearly outside CSF's prospectus guidelines.

Mark retrieved market data for those dates. February 27th was a strong day in the US market. The Dow Jones Industrials Average was up 1.3% and NASDAQ 2%. The Asian markets had closed negative in the previous trading session. Tokyo was down 1.9% and the others ranged from negative 0.9% in Sydney to negative 1.4% in Hong Kong. European markets had closed marginally down, with London being the worst performer, negative 0.4% for the day.

New York opened weakly on the morning of the 27th because of poor market sentiment triggered by Asia and bearish sentiment in the press. The S&P 500 index drifted lower until late in the session. At 3.15pm the Fed Chairman made an announcement interpreted as positive for interest rates. The US markets soared. By the closing bell, all US indices were on a roll.

The Shleman Weld order to purchase shares in the CSF International Fund was logged after the markets closed, at 5.07. The purchase was made at the Fund's NAV calculated on that day, which was down 0.8% because closing prices in markets outside the USA had been depressed.

The following morning, Friday 28th February, Tokyo, Hong Kong and Singapore soared in sympathy with Wall Street"s closing level on Thursday. Europe followed suit, with major indices rising from 2% in Paris to 1.3% in London. That day, the NAV of the CSF International Fund rose 1.6%. Shleman Weld's client picked up a cool $800,000.

Mark looked at the market action on the following Monday. There was a small continuation of Friday's euphoria. Markets generally opened up, but drifted most of the day. The Fund's NAV rose 0.2%. On Tuesday

Asia and Europe began to slide and the NAV gave back its gains from Monday. Most interestingly, the US market began a heavy slide in the afternoon of Tuesday 4th March. Shleman Weld put in its order to sell at 5.43pm at that day's Fund NAV. The next morning, all Asian and European markets were in the red. The NAV on 5th March fell to its lowest point for three weeks, but Shleman Weld had already sold at the previous day's price. *Bastards*, Mark muttered.

"Hey Syreta, I've cracked it." he shouted from his office. Everyone else had gone home.

"What have you cracked?" she shouted back from her desk.

"These guys were allowed to purchase out of hours to take advantage of a huge movement in foreign markets in sympathy with the US market. Then they were allowed to sell out of hours to prevent them losing money the next day. You might call it Time Zone Arbitrage – with a twist."

Syreta came into his office. "That sounds pretty serious, if you're right."

"Here, look at the data." Mark walked her through the maze of market activity that took place at the end of February and matched it with trades in the fund. "What do you think?"

"I think it's time for us to go out for a drink."

Syreta had put on fresh lipstick and unbuttoned her blouse one notch. She had loosened her hair and smelled subtly of a light floral perfume. She held out her hand and tugged him from his chair.

"Come on Mark, let's lock up and go. You've got tomorrow to worry about rogue trades."

They drank a chilled bottle of chablis at the Witness Box. It was a mild evening. As they strolled pleasantly through the Victoria Embankment Gardens Syreta slipped her arm through his.

"Mark, I've been thinking a lot. I know about Nancy and you know about Jay. I don't want to mess up your future with her; I think she's a fabulous girl. And I don't want to mess up my future with Jay. He's away a lot, and he's basically a good guy and a great father . . . " She hesitated.

"But . . . ?" Mark was astonished.

" . . . But I think we should be lovers when nothing else is going on in our lives."

Mark stopped dead in his tracks. "That's one hell of a proposition." They turned towards each other and embraced before the statue of the mysterious Henry Fawcett.

"Have you any idea? " he began, mildly drunk, " . . . how much I've fantasized about you over the years?"

"I sometimes see you ogling in a quiet way but I respect that you never made a pass. I rather liked you too but it wasn't easy to do anything about it. Tonight was a perfect opportunity."

"You scheming hussy."

They strolled up the alley towards Charing Cross Station and bought fish and chips. They sat by the statue of General Sir Henry Havelock in Trafalgar Square, giggling like schoolchildren on an outing. At ten o'clock they flagged a cab for Prince of Wales Drive.

"This is what I expected, " Syreta commented as she looked around his subtly-lit flat. "Do you have someone to clean for you?"

"A lady comes in three days a week to tidy up after my riotous parties. Want a drink?"

"What are you offering?"

Mark pulled a bottle of Veuve Clicquot from the fridge and unwired it. "Here's to you, Mrs Mehta."

"And to you, my dear boss."

Syreta went to the window and stared out at the darkened Battersea Park. She sipped her champagne, turned to Mark and whispered, "It's been a long day. I think we should take a shower."

She left his flat at one o'clock in the morning to take a cab home to Clapham.

Mark was up early. The tensions surrounding the deepening mire he felt with CSF had dissipated. He was light hearted and energetic. *God bless Syreta,* he thought. He showered. Oops, she'd left her earrings in the soap dish. He walked across Battersea Park and Chelsea Bridge and took the tube from Sloane Square.

"Graham, we've cracked the methodology behind our market timing trades." Mark explained what he'd discovered the previous evening.

"That's criminal, isn't it?"

"It's certainly out of order, if not criminal. If the prospectus says that trading must be done within certain hours, it's pretty damn bad to let favoured institutions ride roughshod over the Fund. If you offer a deal to a Bermuda hedge fund you've got to offer it to every client."

Syreta came to his office. "I wanted to say thank you. I can't tell you how much I enjoyed last night."

"I feel the same way. I'll have a drink with you after work any time you want."

"Here," she smiled, "I thought you might find these interesting." She handed him three spreadsheets. "They analyse the three trades I brought to your attention last week, totalling $162 million. They all have the same trading characteristics that you identified yesterday."

"Trading out of hours in response to market moves in the USA versus the rest of the world?"

"Yes. And I'm sorry to say that we've had another six big trades into the Fund overnight."

"How much?"

"Totalling $234 million."

"Do we know for sure that it's short term money?"

"We never know for sure, do we? So the model invests it into equities, as it should."

"The problem is, if we don't invest it, that's the day we discover it's long-term money. If we hold cash in a rising market we're buggered. Can you find out the terms of today's trades? In other words, did the investors get a deal on the time they were allowed to trade? If so, chances are that market timers are at work again."

"I'll email Jessica again. She'll get back to me this afternoon."

"Here, I've got something for you." Mark handed her an envelope.

Syreta opened it. A pair of earrings rattled onto Mark's desk.

Chapter 28

Stock markets were buoyant in March. Japan was stirring from its deflationary slumbers, European interest rates were stable – rumoured to be on the decline – and the Bank of England issued a rosy report on the strength of the British economy.

Graham had positioned the CSF International Fund ideally for this scenario: $1.35 billion of assets fully invested in a total of 94 stocks in 13 countries. But performance was starting to drag as the fund received hit after hit from CSF's market timing friends in Bermuda and elsewhere.

The happy mood that Mark and Graham shared a few weeks earlier over lunch at Tempio had dissipated. Syreta scoured the new money coming in each day from CSF for suspect trades. If a round sum like $30 million came in, chances were high that it would be traded out within a few days. If a sum like $8, 673,128 came in, chances were that it was 'real' investment money. Speculators tended to play in whole numbers, often regarding anything under $1million as a rounding error.

Syreta's intuition saved the Fund a great deal of money, but it wasn't flawless. She shunted chunks of rogue money into a cash account, so when it was pulled out a few days later, the Fund did not have to sell shares to meet the redemption. But the profit made by the trader still damaged the performance of other investors in the Fund. A rise in the NAV of 1.6% on $30 million was $480,000. The market timers pocketed that sum, although their money had been on bank deposit and had in fact generated only $18,000 for the Fund over the period.

Trying to identify rogue money was an art more than a science, however, and the Fund was sometimes compromised when Syreta misread the intentions of the investor. On one occasion $50 million invested through nominees of a Vermont bank was not invested, but the investor turned out to be a well-known university endowment fund. During a rising market, holding 3.7% of the Fund in cash was a serious drag on performance.

On the Monday morning of the third week of March, Syreta urgently requested to meet Mark and Graham. They topped up their coffee mugs and closed the door of the conference room.

"I have bad news." she began, "As of today, trading in the Fund this month has exceeded the asset value of the Fund."

"We're being ground into the dirt by speculators." Graham announced. His familiar open face looked drawn and gaunt.

"I've called Tuckwell six times in the past week." Mark said, "but he hasn't called back. I've spoken to Cosway six times and he says I should speak to Tuckwell; he controls the Market Timing operation. I've emailed Shilson – no response – and spoken to Nancy, who's a wreck and convinced that what's going on is, at best, unethical, at worst, downright criminal."

"Should we blow a whistle?" Graham asked.

"You mean, to the regulators?" Syreta was aghast.

"I've wondered about that." Mark replied. "But here's what I want to do before taking radical action. I'm meeting the Trustees of the CSF Funds in Arizona in three weeks. I'll flag the issue, stress our concerns and demonstrate the damaging effect that market timing is inflicting on the Fund's performance." He fell silent.

"Yes?" Graham looked oddly at his old friend.

"I want to flag our concerns in a public, official, fully minuted forum. Point out that the market timing is arguably criminal and ask them to stop it immediately."

"Shilson, Cosway and Tuckwell will be thrilled to be shown up as criminals by a Limey in front of their Board. You'll need to mute your language a bit." Graham cautioned.

"I know . . . " Mark drifted off in another direction "It's a bloody tragedy. It feels like our House of Cards is caving in. Just a month ago we were on a roll. Performance was strong, good money was pouring into the Fund and everyone was thrilled. Now it's in tatters. What happened?"

"Come on, Mark, you're made of stronger stuff. It doesn't become you to feel sorry for yourself. We're looking for leadership here. Appletree's been in difficult situations before and you got us out of them." Syreta spoke like a wife more than a colleague. Graham arched an eyebrow in the way he often did when he was onto something. "We need to address the problem squarely and honestly."

"Thanks for your kind words, Syreta." A surge of affection flowed through Mark. Their eyes met for a moment. Graham looked at Mark, then at her, then at him again. That bloody eyebrow again. He shook his head in a 'no-this can't be happening' way, and changed the subject.

"Syreta, can you find out if there's anything under FSA rules that might cover what's happening here, or is this a uniquely American predicament we're in?"

"I did look earlier into the FSA"s views on market timing. There are obviously rules in the UK that govern insider trading. You could think of this as an inside trading matter, but it doesn't fit neatly into the definition of insider trading. Our market timers are not acting on privileged information, so much as being given privileged trading rights."

"What about the 'know your client' rules? Could we be liable for not knowing who instructs these trades?"

"No. By sub-advising a fund for CSF we've delegated that role to them. Our client is CSF; their clients are the traders. Remember, we checked with Tuckwell and Cosway when the first big trade came in from Bermuda. We asked them about money laundering and were immediately reassured that no laundering was taking place. Mark asked for his concerns to be on the record at CSF. They sent us a written memo."

"We might have covered our tails on money laundering with the SEC, but could the FSA argue that we didn't do our homework thoroughly enough?" Graham persisted.

"We've done everything possible." Mark averred "We immediately flagged our concerns, called CSF and were reassured. I'm doing it again at the board meeting. If things don't improve after Arizona, I'll call the SEC for a chat to clarify the situation. And send copy memos to the FSA. Then nobody can accuse us of failing to contact the regulators. What do you think, Graham?"

"It all sounds jolly worthy, but I'm still faced by a torrent of lousy trades in and out of the Fund. I have to manage this monster every day and deliver performance to our clients. The Fund is being shot to bits. Our performance has fallen into the fourth quartile in March, it's performing nearly 5% under the Index and we only have two weeks to the end of the quarter. What the hell's going on?"

"The reason these trades are accelerating is to increase bonus payments to CSF's top executives. They're paid every quarter-end based on new flows into CSF's mutual funds. 31 March is the last day of the quarter, so we're seeing a transaction frenzy going on. I suspect trades will slow down after 31 March."

" . . . and start up again towards the end of June. Mark, do your best, my friend. I have to return to my office to wrestle our performance back from the brink." Graham bowed to Syreta and Mark and left the room.

"He knows, doesn't he?" Syreta looked accusingly at Mark.

"Intuitively, perhaps. Explicitly, no."

"You haven't said anything to anyone, have you?"

"Some people say I'm the most discreet person they've ever known. My love," his penetrating blue eyes locked with her questioning brown eyes, "the arrangement you proposed is a lonely man's dream. I will do nothing, ever, to betray you."

She frowned.

"We'd better get on with our work or people really will ask questions."

"Yes, OK. We need to start focusing on the April board meeting. I know it's a few weeks away and Graham's right that I shouldn't come out with guns blazing at the directors. But I want to leave the trustees in no doubt why we're underperforming. I need your help."

"I'll put together a draft presentation that you can edit until you have it exactly how you want it."

Back in his office, Mark turned to the Internet and typed *Market timing mutual funds.* There were scores of entries. Surprisingly, many mutual fund groups actively promoted timing as a service.

Graham phoned.

"Mark, I've been reflecting on our conversation about how to handle the board of trustees in Arizona. I think we should be conciliatory, acknowledge there's a problem, be completely open about its impact on our performance, not point any fingers, but come up with a solution. If you go in aggressively they'll clam up and put up a united shield against you. If you present a solution rather than a threat I suspect you'll get much further."

"It's a nice idea. What do you suggest?"

"I was just looking on the internet under *Market Timing Mutual Funds* and found some good ideas."

"That's unbelievably weird, Graham. I just typed in exactly the same words and was starting to read through the entries."

"Great minds . . . OK, if you look at the fourth entry you'll see that the Investment Company Institute has 'three specific measures to help eradicate abusive trading practices.' First, set a fixed 4pm deadline for reporting orders to mutual fund firms. Only orders received by 4pm would receive that day's price. Second, charge a 2 per cent exit fee for all assets leaving within five days of investing in a mutual fund. Third – and this is not a problem with us – control the trading activities of senior executives."

"These are good guidelines, all the more because they come from a credible industry source. We didn't dream them up ourselves."

"One other thing, Mark. I was struck when we met with Syreta just then how beleaguered you feel. You're not alone, you know. We can always get a pile of sandwiches and get everyone in the conference room for a brainstorming lunch. You don't need to show that you're always in control, but you must show that you're always concerned. It's good for staff morale if everyone's brought into the picture. We've got a lot of brainpower in the office – we might come up with ideas we haven't thought of before."

"Thanks Graham." Mark sounded depressed." I'll get Wendy to organize sandwiches and soda pops and go round in person telling everyone to be in the conference room at 12."

"Good lad."

It was the usual scene of excited chatter as Appletree's staff sat around the table eating sandwiches, fruit and bags of crisps.

"The reason I got you together today was to bring you up to speed with the CSF account." Mark began." As you know we've been having a lot of quick fire trades in and out of the Fund that have compromised our ability to run money. Graham, Syreta and I have talked about remedies, but before we debate the matter with CSF I thought it would be good to have your input. Yes, Bob? "

"We're letting the CSF tail wag the Appletree dog, folks." Bob Berwick was his usual demagogic self.

Mark wondered what an Appletree dog might look like. Certainly not a sleek pedigree; a cringing mongrel, perhaps. And the CSF tail? A barbed whip.

"Look, we're under no obligation to manage money for CSF. We're an independent money management firm. It upsets me to see how we're bending backwards to accommodate a client with this outrageously self-serving culture."

"It's backfiring on us horribly." Alix looked haggard "My European performance is in tatters. The model's bought and sold positions in Allianz and Nokia four times in the past three weeks. There's no visibility at all." She'd piled on all the years she'd lost while she was in America six months earlier.

Bob continued, "I know we can go to CSF and implore them to stop this trading, but we have two real choices as independent practitioners. Refuse to take more money into the Fund, or resign the account. As things stand, we're not being asked to invest money, we're just being paid to provide the backdrop for a handful of hedge funds, speculators and God-knows-who else to shaft a group of innocent Fund shareholders."

Graham nodded, "Thanks Bob. The prospectus says that we, as managers, may at our own discretion close the Fund to new money. We could do that tomorrow."

"The problem is, folks, we don't control the Fund. It's CSF's fund. If we refuse to take more money, they can simply fire us and switch the account to another manager. The prospectus gives the comfortable impression that we're in the driving seat, but we're not." Alix tapped a pen on the table as she spoke.

"And with all the overhead we've taken on," Bob added," Appletree's torpedoed if we stop managing the CSF account."

"Not strictly true. We still have our original clients and are doing quite well for them." Mark interceded. "Their assets with us have risen 25% year-to-date."

"Thank goodness nobody here would ever be so nasty as to say, "I told you so." Alix avoided eye contact with her colleagues as she spoke.

After twenty minutes of debate, Mark summarized, "It's clear that everyone's upset with the way the CSF relationship is going. As you know I'm going to the board meeting in Arizona next week. I'll express our concerns and try to bring all market timing to an end. Syreta has given me a spreadsheet of every trade to date and there's enough ammunition to scare CSF out of their wits."

"In the meantime, we must never lose sight of our job – it's to provide superior long-term performance for all our clients." Graham concluded.

When she returned to her desk, Syreta opened her email. The daily afternoon message from Cosway's office was cryptic. In the 'new money' column the printout showed Bleuestein Partners, $67million; Haringey Nominees Grand Turk, $58 million; Lynch and Burnham omnibus account New York $13,323,987; Turbin and Elles omnibus account Detroit $3,345,098. In the 'redemptions' column there were no significant outflows on this day.

After the meeting Mark made his customary call to Bill Tuckwell. Mark was at pains to be on the record for attempting to contact him. If there was ever a court case his numerous attempts to contact the man by email and phone was archived for all to see. Not much of a defence, but it might ease his jail time by a year or two, he imagined sardonically.

As he waited on the phone he opened an email from Shilson's office in New York. It contained a memo, entitled 'Agenda for Board of Trustees Meeting, Saguaro Canyon Resort, Tucson Arizona April 9th to April 12th.'

Mark cast his eye down the agenda.

> April 9th :
>
> 12 noon : Steve and Skye Shilson; Dick and Di Di Cosway; Bill Tuckwell and Nancy Lindstrom arrive Tucson by CSF Gulfstream from Westchester. Great West Limousine Service takes couples to Deluxe Desert Suites at Saguaro Canyon Resort.
>
> 2-5pm : Trustees and Portfolio Managers arrive at Tucson International Airport. Shuttle service provided by Saguaro Canyon Resort. Use courtesy phone on arrival at airport to request transportation to resort.
>
> 7pm : Cocktails in Amaranth Canyon Terrace, hosted by Steve and Skye Shilson to celebrate Bill Tuckwell and Nancy Lindstrom. Trustees, Board members and partners welcome.
>
> 8pm : Dinner in Red Desert Bistro hosted by Bill Tuckwell and Nancy Lindstrom; Trustees, Board members and partners welcome.

On April 10th Appletree had been given exactly 15 minutes, with every other manager, to address the board of trustees. Mark read the Agenda with mounting disbelief. It was surreal. He pressed the Print button. The machine zipped out three pages. He stapled and folded them into his jacket pocket. He strolled casually across the office floor, told Wendy, 'Back in an hour', ran down the stairs to the street and walked briskly towards Blackfriars Bridge.

Light was fading in the drizzly March afternoon. The ugly, powerful, brown current of the Thames sucked against the piers of the bridge as the tide ebbed towards the Channel. Mark leaned on the parapet, mesmerized by the debris bobbing downstream with the tide.

The body of a dog slid underneath. It was black and white, like a Border collie. He wondered what had happened. A young boy had thrown a stick into the river at Kew, perhaps. The family pet jumped after it and never returned. A frantic search and the long, sad trek back to an empty house where the dog had been the heart of the boy's life. Or perhaps a bunch of drugged yobs had beaten up the animal in Battersea Park and chucked it into the water to a merciful end.

A cold, sharp, wet wind sliced down the river from the west, smacking his face, ruffling his hair and soaking his clothes. The Agenda ! Mark hated himself for his vulnerability. He was so stunned he couldn't get his brain around the facts. If it were not for his responsibility to the team at Appletree he would not return to his office. He would grab his passport from his flat, take a taxi to Heathrow and fly to Malawi, where he would vanish to a mountain village and teach schoolchildren for the rest of his life.

What would he teach them? He would teach them how odious the Western world was; that Africa should never aspire to warped Anglo Saxon standards. He would teach them how wonderful their simple lives were. They would teach him, too. He would learn the fathomless joy of children laughing, goats bleating, the smells of rural Africa, the patter of rain on the dusty red earth.

Chapter 29

He bumped into Syreta on the steps of the office as he returned, soaked, just after six. She was dashing out to get the Northern Line to Clapham.

"I didn't think anyone would still be here." Mark said absent mindedly.

"You look an absolute mess. What happened? You look like you fell into the river. You're soaking."

Mark looked despairingly at her. She was so trim, so well-groomed, so *together*. "I . . . I just got caught in the rain. He opened his arms pathetically to demonstrate how wet he was. You're not free tonight by any chance? Perhaps we could meet later chez moi for a drink and a chat."

"I've got to meet my daughter at ballet class in Clapham in an hour. I promised to take her out for an Indian meal afterwards. I could call my mother and ask her to baby sit afterwards. She only lives two streets away from us. I could come round at 9.30."

"What will you tell your mother?"

"Oh, a friend in need. She asks no questions; I tell no lies."

"I'll have my head together by then. I feel better already."

Syreta looked at him quizzically. "Must dash. See you at 9.30."

Mark stood under the shower in the office changing room. The steam roiled over him for twenty minutes. He had no choice but to get back into damp clothes, but at least he was clean. He combed his black hair and managed a weak smile at the pasty white face in the mirror.

The bell rang. When he opened the door of his flat, Syreta entered. They embraced.

He took her hand and led her without a word into the bedroom. Clothes flew off in all directions, random pieces of underwear were festooned on a lamp, a picture, on the back of a chair, the floor.

An hour later they were padding around the drawing room. She wore his dressing gown draped languidly over one shoulder. He had a bath towel around his middle. The Bollinger was nearly empty.

"What do you make of this?" Mark casually handed Syreta the Agenda.

She studied it for a few minutes.

"It's gloves off, isn't it? They're absolute bastards. I can see why you were upset."

"I'm pissed off in so many dimensions that I don't know where to start. They command me to fly 10,000 miles to Arizona and back, and don't include me at dinner on the opening night. I get 15 minutes to review the Fund, in a tight agenda packed with other portfolio managers. They pair up Nancy with the man she says she hates. They exclude me from all serious activities. Their insensitivity is astounding."

Syreta waved the papers at him. "They're trying to limit your time with the trustees. They don't want you spending time with anyone important. They're afraid of you. I would be, if I knew you knew what you know."

The Bollinger was working its magic. Mark looked at her oddly. Her face creased with laughter. "That sounded pretty odd, didn't it?"

"So, what would you do if you were me?"

"I'd give everyone the finger and disappear to the South of France."

That's not far from how I feel. Seriously though, I need to face the music. I need a game plan."

"First of all, my dear darling, Woman to Man, you need to square up over Nancy. Are you sure she's all you think she is?"

"I'm crazy about her. But then, there's you . . . " he eyed a long languid brown leg disappearing into the folds of his dressing gown, revealing a little black fuzz when she shifted on the sofa.

"I'm not available. You know that."

"Yeah, that was our deal. But I can't tell you how wonderful it is to know that you're there, somewhere in the background."

"Thank you. I feel the same way. But our options stop there."

"Nancy? Nancy, Nancy . . . She's bright, well-educated, fun. Physically, she's quite like you, slim, short hair . . . "

"White. I know. I met her when she came to London. I can see the attraction. She's even got the same 'quiet efficiency' you're always on about. But does she love you, and if so, why does she give you the runaround all the time?"

"She's not giving me the runaround."

"If you say so. Let me put it a different way. She does nothing to prevent you finding out hurtful things about her. If I were Nancy, whom I'm not – and if I were in love with you – which I'm *definitely* not, I would go out of my way to ensure you never had doubts about me. I would be far more consistent than she is. How can she tell you one day that she's coming to live with you in London, and the next day allow herself to be publicly paired with a man she says she hates? Either she's weak or she's playing games."

"Or she's got no choice, for some reason."

"Of course she has a choice, Mark. Everyone has a choice. She doesn't have to stay at CSF. She doesn't have to keep seeing that man. She doesn't have to upset you so much . . . "

"What I mean is that perhaps CSF or Tuckwell have got something on her."

"You talk like a thriller writer. The world just isn't like that,"

"Well, maybe the world just *is* like that. You just don't know."

"To quote the Master – "Give me a scenario."

"OK – a scenario. Nancy is the young compliance officer of a powerful money manager in New York. She was hired by two older men who seem pretty awesome to a rookie on Wall Street. They're urbane and bloody rich. In turn they report to an extremely sharp operator – Steve Shilson – who sports the trappings of wealth beyond the dreams of avarice. When the young Nancy joins this team, at first she busies herself on the fringes of Compliance, trawling through personnel files to ensure all the wholesalers have passed their Series 63 and 65 exams, contributing carefully-considered points to CSF's Compliance Manual, attending Compliance Officer conferences in Washington DC and so on. Then she's incredibly flattered to be asked out by Tuckwell, or whatever his name is . . . "

Mark loved the way Syreta laughed.

"As I was saying, she starts dating him. During the afterglow pillow talk he lets it drop how much he makes at CSF. It's a fair bet, because Americans always bang on about how much money they make. Nancy is impressed. Who wouldn't be? Being a woman, she probes around to ascertain the breakdown of his earnings. Nearly 90% is bonuses, related to assets he brings in. She figures out the dishonesty of a formula based purely on gross sales and investigates. She finds out how market timing works at CSF, she finds out about the after-hours trading that allows time zone arbitrage."

"What a clever girl she must be," Syreta tweaked him fondly, sipping Bollinger from the same glass, lying on the same sofa, wearing the same dressing gown, as Nancy a few weeks earlier.

"Yeah. She stumbles on a systemic fraud in the system and has a strong case against Tuckwell. But she's kinda *in love* with him, shall we say. She's intoxicated by his wealth and power and, for all I know, by the size of his . . . "

"Now, now, keep it clean. All right then. She's found out all this stuff. She's done her job as a Compliance Officer. What's bad about that?"

"Yeah, but the crucial thing, the absolutely critical point, is that she does nothing about it. It's understandable to be reluctant to shop a colleague, but if the crime continues, goes on and on, and you still don't report it, then you become complicit in the crime."

"So that makes her a lousy compliance officer."

"If true, yes. Worse than that, a criminal. Worse than *that,* an insider who becomes, by her complicity, a serial offender. That's serious stuff."

"You're getting carried away."

"You asked for a scenario."

"True. Now supposing your hunch is correct, why would you be attracted to a criminal?"

"Why are women attracted to bastards?"

"Seriously, Mark. You go along with her behaviour because you think Tuckwell's got something on her. Why would you want such a weak woman to be the mother of your children?"

"Ouch."

"Either way, it's not a pretty picture. On one hand you have a woman who hurts you by letting herself be publicly used as some kind of trophy. On the other hand, she compromises herself so seriously that she could end up in jail."

"The way you distil it so succinctly, it looks pretty dire."

"Everyone has their weaknesses, Mark. Nancy's not fundamentally a bad person. I think she's very cute, to tell the truth. I can see the attraction. I can understand the obsession that Tuckwell has for her."

"So where do I go from here?"

"Call her and ask what's going on. Don't play the jealous fool. She's already got one on her tail. Be cool and British, courtly. Don't boss her around or manipulate her. Just be yourself, Mark."

"That's a cool thing to say, but easier said than done. I will say, though, you have a great way of boosting a man's ego."

"As we destroy, so we build. Also – remember, she'll know that by now you'll have received this Agenda. She'll be wondering how you felt when you saw it. She'll be wondering how to reassure you. She'll be scared of your reaction."

"OK, so I call her and ask what's going on, I don't put her on the spot. It still makes the Tucson gig bloody complicated. You'd have to be a saint to ignore her shacking up with Tuckwell."

"You don't know that, Mark. It could just be an elaborate cover. For all you know he's engineered the whole thing so he can dump her publicly. His pride is restored. Then nobody will suspect that it was actually Tuckwell who was dumped. If his ego is so big and fragile, it matters enormously who's seen to be dumping who."

"It's all too bloody complicated."

"Put Nancy aside for a moment. What are you going to say in your 15 minutes in front of the Board?"

"I'll spend five minutes describing how the Fund is being invested. Five minutes describing how the Fund is being destroyed. Five minutes Q&A. In the circumstances, all I'm trying to achieve is an on – the – record account of what's happening."

"Who's taking the minutes?"

"I don't know, maybe Nancy."

"You need to have your conversation with her as soon as possible. Depending on the tilt that her minutes take, that could determine who gets the jail sentence."

"Syreta my lovely paramour, you have a way of making a man feel so secure about himself."

"You need a cast-iron fallback position, Mark. Be prepared to tell the board that Appletree will resign the account if ALL market timing doesn't cease immediately. Be prepared to tell them that you will clarify the matter with the SEC if the market timing doesn't end."

"Yea – like I'd get out of the building alive."

"No, no. Say it in that suave accent of yours, with a sweet smile on your face. You know, "I really appreciate your views, but hope you don't mind if I chat to one of the chaps at the SEC – using a hypothetical case, of course. Perhaps one of you would like to come along, so we're all on the same side. Just to clarify, you understand."

"I can already see the incredulity on their faces." Mark laughed. "Even if I delivered the words like Winston Churchill, I'd have the life expectancy of a pig paddling in a pool of piranhas."

"Mark, there's a very serious angle to this. Just as Nancy might have been bullied into silence, so the stakes are extremely high for Appletree, and for you personally. Knowing what you know about late-trading and market-timing at the CSF International Fund, if you don't get satisfactory assurances from the board in Tucson, you *have* to blow the whistle."

"I tell you one thing, Syreta," he eyed the curve of a light brown breast as the gown slipped off her shoulders. "I'm going to blow *your* whistle, right now."

Mark lifted her off the sofa, newly-wed style, carried her across the threshold of his room and threw her on the bed. After some passionate wrestling and a great deal of champagne-fuelled laughter, they drifted to sleep.

The phone rang. Syreta sat up in bed like a spring-loaded dolly. She saw the time on Mark's bedside clock. "It's bloody 2 o'clock. Mum'll kill me."

Mark answered the phone.

"Oh Hello" he answered drowsily. "Can I call you back in a few minutes?"

Syreta crawled on the floor searching for pieces of discarded lingerie. "Nancy?" she asked.

"Nancy."

"I thought so."

"You don't have to go, you know. We have no secrets."

"I'm going to get a right bollocking from my Mum. I told her I'd be back before midnight."

"Blame me for being a friend in great need. You nursed me back to mental health."

Syreta gave him a sweet look, pulled on her cashmere sweater, caught herself briefly in the mirror, tossed her hair and slipped on her shoes. "Oh shit, Mum will know exactly what I've been up to. I look like I've been rodgered in a hayloft. I even smell of you."

Mark put his arm around her shoulder.

"Come on, I'll come down to the street with you to get a taxi. There are plenty of empty ones cruising along Prince of Wales Drive at this time of night."

"You should know."

Ten minutes later, Mark was sitting up in bed, wide awake. He dialled New York.

"Hi. You're not alone, are you?" Nancy sounded timid.

"Actually, I am now. I wasn't when you called."

"I woke you up?"

"You woke *us* up." Mark no longer felt the need to dissemble. This affair was curing him of deviousness.

"I haven't heard from you for a few days so thought I would call."

"Is that it?"

"What do you mean?"

"I mean, you're publicly jetting to Tucson in a few weeks as Tuckwell's squeeze. You guys want me to schlep half way round the world, entertaining yourselves lavishly, excluding me from all but the most banal communal entertainment, and only giving me fifteen minutes to discuss some very serious issues to do with the Fund."

"You're getting the same amount of time as all the other portfolio managers, Mark."

"Have they had the value of their funds traded in and out a hundred per cent since the first of March? Has their performance been driven to 6 per cent below benchmark by the friction costs of market timing? I don't think so."

"I don't know what to say Mark. I know it sounds weak to say this, but I miss you."

"You make me feel like I'm dealing with a schizophrenic. You say sweet nothings on the phone then I read that I'm invited to cocktails in celebration of Bill Tuckwell and Nancy Lindstrom." I'm tired of this bullshit, kiddo."

"I'm trapped by CSF."

"Oh yea? How so?"

"You wouldn't understand. Not in your current mood."

There was silence on the line. Despite Syreta's advice to act like a gentleman with Nancy, Mark hoped she was squirming at the far end of the line in New York, not knowing what to say or how to say it. She restarted the conversation,

"You had someone in bed with you when I called, didn't you?"

"Yes ma'am. A lovely lass she was too."

"Why? " he heard sobbing.

"What a stupid question, Nancy. Why does anyone ever have someone in bed with them? Ask Tuckwell."

"Will you still come on vacation with me after Tucson?"

"I'm seriously considering giving Tucson a miss. Why travel 9,000 miles to be ignored and insulted? I can accomplish that perfectly well on a conference call from my desk in London."

"That's not true, Mark. I told you what's going on between Bill and me. Nothing, absolutely nothing. He's on a power kick. He wrote the Agenda. His ego's so tied up with me being his date that he's blind to reality."

"Here's the test, my friend – if I come to Tucson will you stay in my suite?"
"Yes," she said quietly.
"Will you take your name off the Agenda as Tuckwell's partner?"
"Yes, I will."
"Will you travel by scheduled airline instead of the corporate Gulfstream?"
"Yes."
"Will you arrange to have me invited to the Trustee and Board Member-only functions and attend as my date?"
"I'll try."
"Will you arrange to get me an open-ended session with the Board instead of the pathetic 15 minute slot that gives me time to say precisely nothing?"
"I'll try, Marko," she was exasperated.
"Will you show me the minutes of the board meeting before they're finalized?"
"Yes."
"Confirm these things in writing to me tomorrow, and I'll let you know if I'm coming."
"You know, Mark," she warned "your demands could have deadly consequences."
"Come on, it's late at night. Let's not be dramatic. Who could it be deadly for?
"For me, for you, for them. We're playing with fire, Mark."
"I'll call you tomorrow at home at 6 pm your time. You can tell me how your day went and we can get to the root of your terror for your weird organization."
"OK."
"Bye."

Chapter 30

On 2nd April Syreta prepared a schedule of cash flows for the International Fund in March. She presented it after lunch to Mark and Graham.

"On 1st March the Fund's assets stood at $1.39 billion. On 1st April the Fund's assets were $1.41 billion."

"Sounds promising." Mark commented. Graham remained tight-lipped.

"In March, the Fund had inflows of $3.68 billion. It had outflows of $3.663 billion, giving us net new assets of $17 million."

"I'm certain that 90% of inflows were market timing trades, because nearly every inflow had a matching outflow a few days later."

"Can you give an example?" Graham asked.

Syreta clicked the Powerpoint three slides forward.

"Here's the schedule of trades for March. The first inflow of $33 million on 1st March was matched with an outflow of $34.1 million on 6th March. That corresponds exactly with the 3.3% rise in the Net Asset Value of the Fund that took place between 1st March and 6th March. Do you want me to highlight other trades?"

"No thanks Syreta. What was our overall performance for the month?" Graham knew precisely what the answer was.

She turned to the Performance slide.

"The Fund fell 0.82% in March, despite many short-term upticks that the market timers exploited during the month. The Index was up 5.79%. The peer group average was up 5.81%. We were 6.61% behind the index and 6.63% behind our peer group. Our Fund's year-to-date performance to the end of March was up 6.38%. The index was up 11.59% and our peer group average was up 11.41%. Do you want any more statistics?"

"No thanks . . . The bright side is that our peer group average also failed to beat the index in the Quarter . . . "

"There is no bright side, Mark. I do wish you'd stop trying to put a cheery gloss on everything. This is disastrous." Graham snapped.

"He's right, Mark. The CSF International Fund ranks 181 out of 193 funds in its peer group for the quarter. That's terrible."

"Sorry if I sound as if I'm trivializing this, but I can assure you I'm as pissed off as you are."

"We have to call Tuckwell and Cosway today and warn them that the numbers are dire. More to the point we need to tell them – command them – unequivocally to get all market timers off our backs. I simply can't manage money this way. It's a travesty."

"We have to exit the CSF relationship before it destroys us." Mark heard himself say.

Graham was utterly exasperated, "What a fucking waste of time these people are. Their loyalty span is zero. It's all about short-term greed. Money, greed, me, me, me."

"I'll leave it to you, gentlemen." Syreta saw the temperature rising and gathered up her papers. "I've a lot to get on with. Mark, will you let me know what you want in your presentation materials? Remember, we need to get the final draft to Bill Tuckwell's office by the 5th."

"Thanks Syreta," Mark smiled after her as she closed the door.

"You're not having a . . . a thing with her, are you?" Graham waved his hand towards the door in a French kind of way.

"What an odd suggestion, Graham."

"Just wondered. Strange vibes around you both."

"D'you want to come to Tucson with me? It might help for you to meet the trustees. You're seen as the practitioner. I'm seen as the politician."

"No thanks. I don't fit with that crowd. I don't mind joining on a conference call from London, though, if that takes the heat off you."

"I'll think about that. Now, we need to run through the draft presentation for Tucson."

"Sure. Fire ahead."

"We've got fifteen minutes in front of the trustees. I've asked Nancy to pull strings to get us longer, but I've designed the presentation to last for fifteen minutes."

Graham nodded wearily.

"I'll take five minutes to describe our process. I'll give them our flow chart showing a million dollars coming in, filtering through the country allocation model, the stock analysis process and how it ends up invested in ninety four stocks in thirteen countries. I'll describe our trading system, the currency overlay and the daily NAV price creation process."

"You're doing all that in five minutes?"

"Yup. Then I'll give a history of the Fund, showing our performance in the run up to 31st December – first decile against all comers – and the first two months of this year. I'll show the orderly cash flows entering the Fund during these periods, then I'll show Syreta's spread sheet of flows and redemptions in March. I can easily demonstrate that our performance was torpedoed by market timers in March. Finally, I'll be open to questions. What do you think?

"I think we need to call Tuckwell and Cosway right now. We really need to talk." Graham snapped.

"Go ahead." Mark pushed the conference phone across the table towards him. The number's 001 212 34 . . . "

"It's ringing."

"Mr Tuckwell's office." A pleasant female voice came on.

"Is he there, please?"

"Who may I say is calling?"

"It's Graham Birch from Appletree in London."

They were treated to the usual recording of CSF mutual fund prices for a few moments.

"Hey Graham. How are you, my friend?"

"I've got Mark on the line. We need to talk about market timing. It destroyed our performance in March. It has to stop, Bill."

"Whoa, Graham. One thing at a time. First things first; hi Mark. How you doin'?" *Unctuous bastard.*

"I'm doin' fine thanks Bill." Mark mimicked Tuckwell's accent.

"Graham, I'm real glad you called. We're being driven crazy by these market timers. You close them down in Bermuda, they show up in BVI. You close them down in BVI they show up in Cayman, if you clo . . . "

"That's fine Bill. Why don't you just refuse to take market timers on board, plain and simple?"

"Because it ain't plain and simple, Graham. D'ya really think a guy who wants to trade $40 million will call and say , "Hey, I want to rip off your mutual fund over the next week."? No Sir, we get a call from a reputable New York Bank's nominee department, who represent kosher institutional money, and they say they're looking at a few international mutual funds to put the money in. The cash comes in, we bed it down and, shee-it, the bastards pull the money out after three business days."

"To be blunt, Bill, your explanation doesn't hold water. We had 23 matched trades in March, totalling $3.68 billion in and $3.665 billion out." Graham fiddled with a paper clip as he spoke. "There are many ways to kill market timing. Like slapping a 5% exit fee on any investor who leaves within thirty days of investing in the fund. That would stop this kind of trading, stone dead. This fund is unmanageable Bill." The paper clip snapped in Graham's fingers. He tossed its mangled remains to the floor.

"I wish you guys could see us in board meetings arguing how to stop this market timing. I agree with you absolutely that we gotta stop this trading. I'm a hundred and ten per cent on your side, fellas."

"We appreciate your efforts on our behalf, Bill." Mark lied. "Given your support I would really appreciate more than fifteen minutes to talk to the trustees in Tucson in April.

"Sure, fellas, I'll do what I can to stretch your time at the meeting. In the meantime I'm gonna put my personal cojones on the line to stop any further trading in and out of the CSF International Fund."

"Well, thanks Bill. Will you let me know as soon as possible how much time I have in Tucson? I need to tailor the presentation."

"Sure, Mark. I'll email you later today."

"Thanks."

Graham slammed the phone down and shouted. "The guy's a fucking joke. Power's rotted the man's brain. Does he think we're imbeciles?"

"You know what the motto of the City of London is?"

"Everyone knows that. Meum verbum pactum est – My word is my bond. What's that got to do with anything?"

"Everything. It dawned on me as Tuckwell was talking that we're dealing with ethical aliens here. We speak and treat them as our own, but they're not. New York's all about maxing out at the other guy's expense. The closest I can think of a Wall Street motto is 'meum verbum coitus es' – My word and you're fucked."

"Dubious Latin. That would be funny if it weren't true."

"Don't worry, Graham. After Tucson we must be ready to pull the plug on this relationship. The more I deal with CSF, the sicker I feel."

"If Appletree's to survive we have no choice. Best if it were done quickly."

"Changing the subject, I'm going to cross the Atlantic a few days early. I'm going to stay with Frank Blazerman in New York. He's good therapy."

"He should have an interesting perspective on what's going on. Will Nancy be with you?"

"I hope so. We've recently had a few spats. I won't bore you with the details."

That evening after work Mark took his normal route through the Victoria Embankment gardens. Daffodils, hyacinths and crocuses were blooming in profusion. He mentally cut out the relentless traffic noise from the Embankment by imagining that he was hiking in the Fells. The light was fading and a vernal sunset streaked the western sky.

In the midst of his reverie he didn't pay attention to the young man weaving towards him on the path. Few people were in the vicinity and there was plenty of passing room. The fellow looked harmless enough. Mark assumed he was drunk and steered to the edge of the path to allow him to lurch past. But the further Mark stepped aside the more the man homed in on him.

They collided.

"Oh, I'm so sorry." Mark said in his very British way. The man smelled of spiced food and alcohol.

"You will be, mate, if you don't keep your hands off her, you're goddam dead meat."

Before Mark could react the man had lurched towards the park's gate, turned the corner and disappeared from view. Mark stood dumbfounded, patting his pockets instinctively to check that his wallet and watch were still with him. They were. He shrugged and picked up the pace towards Westminster.

Over the next hours he couldn't get the incident out of his mind, mulling over what the man had said, and trying to recall what he looked like.

He had a curious, almost fake, accent. It sounded colonial, but didn't ring true. The 'mate' could have been Australian, as in Chiz Mite. Or it might have been cockney. 'Goddam dead meat' was pure Hollywood C movie. The man was stocky, wore jeans, a white open-necked shirt and a lightweight black linen jacket. Italian? He wore black loafers; the heels were unworn. They were either brand new or the guy didn't walk much. His hair was black, mid-length. He had a wiry body with the look of a street fighter.

Was it a warning? There was no way Tuckwell's machine could track him in London, was there? Obsessives will stop at nothing. Look how the paranoid Soviets tracked their enemies overseas. Poisoned umbrellas . . . *Crikey – did he spike me? Is the poison ticking away slowly in my veins, ready to invade my organs and kill me?*

Was Mark reading too much into a non-event? Most probably. His febrile imagination was stoked by fatigue and a long day. By the time he'd flicked through an entire imaginary street map of possibilities he'd crossed Chelsea Bridge, traversed Battersea Park and was unlocking the door to his refuge in Prince of Wales Drive.

Chapter 31

Mark arrived at JFK in the early afternoon. He was deliberately free of appointments in New York and not expected until six o'clock that evening. He took a leisurely cab ride to Frank's apartment on Park Avenue, left his bag with the concierge and wandered westwards along 65th towards Fifth Avenue.

It was a cool April afternoon, but there was warmth in the sunshine when he was out of the wind in the woody folds of Central Park. New York's spring was a few weeks behind London's. The air was sharper and clearer. Mark headed towards the Metropolitan Museum.

He strolled through the Egyptian collection, pausing to study small bronze and granite artefacts retrieved from excavations over the years. He studied the Metternich Stele, an Egyptian stone talisman carved intricately with spells to ward off scorpions, crocodiles and snakes. Ancient Egyptians were terrified of reptiles and often displayed talismans in their houses to protect against these creatures. This stele dated from about 370 BC and described the legend of Isis and Horus. It was found in the grounds of a Franciscan monastery in Alexandria in 1828. The symbols were so crisp it might have been carved that morning.

He spent half an hour afterwards on a sweep through the European Art section of the museum, noting one iconic painting after another. He was jolted when he caught sight of a young man walking away from the sculpture of a cat by Giacometti. He didn't catch the man's face, but he wore the same clothes, had the same gait, the same *presence*, as the fellow who had knocked him in the Victoria Embankment Gardens in London. Damn, he was getting edgy.

He steadied himself by staring at a painting of a startlingly beautiful child by Bougoureau, then mingled with the crowd as it filtered out of the museum at closing time.

Mark checked his email outside the museum. A note from Syreta:

> *Month to date, no market timers. You and Graham did a good job of persuading Mr Tuckwell. Have a great trip.*

This put a spring in Mark's step. At last, some of the stress he had endured seemed to be bearing fruit. He arrived at the Blazerman residence in good spirits.

Frank was his usual welcoming, loud and blunt self, hugging Mark as he walked off the elevator directly into the Blazerman palazzo in the sky.

"Mark, I can't tell ya how great it is to see ya again. This CSF deal's not all bad, buddy, if it gets you over here this often."

"No it's not all bad, but I'm going to need your advice."

"Can't wait." He yelled along the black and white-tiled corridor, "Laura – Mark's here. Come say hi."

"Get him a drink, Darlin'. I'm on the phone. I'll be ten minutes." Laura's powerful Texan accent shouted back from an adjoining room.

"We're eating here tonight. Just me, you and Laura. We thought you'd appreciate an easy night instead of dinner on the town. Frank handed Mark a flute of champagne. "Here, siddown."

"Thanks. It's midnight already in London. I appreciate the break. I'll take you out tomorrow. I'll see if I can persuade Nancy to join us."

"Still seein' her? She can stay here, you know. We won't tell."

"Thanks." Mark was abstracted. "Now, Frank, I need to run through what's happening before Laura shows up. I don't want to bore her with business talk. As you know I'm in New York for a couple of days on my way to Tucson. At the end of this week CSF are having their quarterly trustee board meeting at the Saguaro Canyon Resort."

"Nice place, buddy. How's your golf? "

"Lousy. Now, they're giving me 15 minutes to cover the entire Appletree proposition in front of the board. If we'd been running a fund successfully for six years, 15 minutes would be fine. But this is the first time I've met the trustees, and we've got a problem which could take a while to explain."

"No sweat, go ahead." Frank opened his arms in his generous manner.

"We started running the fund last October. We raised about six hundred and fifty million in the underwriting. Graham's model is tried and true, and the money was immediately put to work in equities around the globe. Our performance from October to December 31 was strong. Appletree was in the top decile of comparable managers over the period."

"I know. I put some of the Blazerman fortune into the Fund at the time of the underwriting. I watch you guys closely."

"Well, the broking community was pleased with our performance and we got cash flow, day after day. This year started strongly. In January and February, performance was well ahead of the index and our peer group average. Graham and I celebrated with a well-lubricated lunch in early March. We counted our annualized fee revenues and I was about to order my yacht catalogue . . . "

"When . . . ?"

"Syreta, our head of investment administration, was waiting for us in the lobby when we returned to the office after lunch. There had been an odd trade of about $50 million into the Fund a few weeks earlier. It picked up 1.6% and was sold out the following week. You'll appreciate that when we receive a chunk of money that size it's imperative to get it in the market. If we keep cash on the sidelines in a rising market, our performance is buggered."

"I can see what's coming." Frank leaned over to top up Mark's champagne.

"Well, Syreta was there to tell us that three more trades, totalling about $160 million, had just hit the Fund. We ended by selling millions of dollars worth of stock to meet the redemptions. In early March we were then bombarded with new money that traded out a few days later. Chunks of $40 million, $60 million, some even over $200 million. It was chaotic. In the month of March alone the Fund received $3.71 billion of new money."

"$3.71 billion? That must be the best cash flow of any international fund in the business."

"That's the good news, but $3.68 billion was traded out. Every business day, slabs of money came in, stayed a few days then were traded out. Some client money traded in and out of the Fund three times in the month."

"Did these guys make a profit on their trades?"

"Some did, others didn't. But the effect on us was that the Fund's performance was absolutely creamed in March. As markets were rising we had to keep a cash reserve to meet redemptions, averaging about 12% of the fund. As you know, keeping cash in a portfolio kills performance in a rising market."

"Do other mutual funds at CSF have the same problem of market timers?"

"No – and here's why. If Wall Street closes up strongly today, chances are that Tokyo and London will rise strongly tomorrow. Very often, events that power Wall Street have a lagged effect overseas. For example if the Fed lowers the discount rate, Wall Street rallies and the rest of the world follows the next day. They call it Time Zone Arbitrage. The international Fund is the only way to play these lags at CSF."

"That makes sense, but I don't understand the problem here. People are allowed to trade mutual funds, aren't they?"

"Yes, but for one thing. CSF lets people with assets over $10 million purchase shares in the Fund tomorrow at today's price. The prospectus states clearly that all orders must be made by 4pm New York time into the CSF International Fund. Remember, the Fund's daily price comes from stock markets that close hours before Wall Street."

Frank nodded, "Go on."

"Well, if Wall Street has a bang-up day and it looks like foreign markets are going to be strong the next day, CSF lets timers into the Fund after 4 pm – sometimes, long after 4pm – at today's price, knowing that the price of the Fund is going to rise the next day. They benefit from a trading perk that isn't available to other investors who came into the Fund earlier in the day."

"Sounds naughty, my friend." Blazerman's expression clouded as he realized what might be happening to his own investment in Mark's fund. "What are you doing about it?"

"In March we became increasingly strident with Tuckwell and Cosway. On 2nd April, after we saw the impact on our March and year-to-date performance, we called Tuckwell and essentially ordered him not to let in any more market timers."

"How did he react?"

"He played innocent, promising to put his cojones on the line to stop all timing trades."

"He would. What's happened in April so far?"

"To give Tuckwell his due, trading has stopped. So far."

Frank emptied the remaining champagne into Mark's glass, saying, "You know what's going on here, don't you?"

Mark began to fuzz from the effects of champagne and jet lag.

"Surprise me."

"It's an old ruse. I thought it went out with the last gang of securities shysters on Wall Street. I'll wager that the bonuses of the top cats at CSF are calculated on gross sales. They're paid each quarter based on new money coming into CSF's mutual funds. It's the sales team's job to pull the money aboard, not to keep it there. That's the client service team's job. So your fat cats get their bonus on the $3.71 billion that entered the fund in March. The $3.68 billion that *left* the Fund wasn't their concern."

"That explains the same capital entering and leaving the Fund two or three times in the month."

"Exactly. The more they get their hedge fund friends in Bermuda or the British Virgin Islands to trade, the bigger the bonus that Shilson and his boys will swing for themselves."

"At least they stopped trading this week."

"Sure they stopped. They got three months until the end of the new quarter. They don't need to let in the timers until it's clear what current quarter sales look like. If sales into the Fund look slow by mid-quarter they'll call their pals in Hamilton and the BVI and say, "Let it rip, Charlie." Trades will pick up in May and overwhelm the Fund again in June. Exactly like in the March quarter."

"You see my problem, then."

"The bastards haven't changed. This is exactly the kinda abuse that cratered CSF two years ago. Before Shilson took over. As fast as you get rid of them, those slugs keep sliming up the Street."

"If you hire an asshole, everyone he trains will be an asshole." Mark added absently.

"Yeah. You got three choices, my friend. First, you can keep quiet and enjoy the legendary money-raising power of CSF. Second, you resign the account honourably, citing 'the desire to concentrate on other market segments'. Third, you blow the whistle to the SEC, FSA, FBI and the New York Securities Commissioner."

"Which would you do?"

"Ethically and tactically you should do option 2, followed by option 3 once you're clear of the bastards. Financially you could probably get away with Option 1 – doing nothing – for a few years. Then everything hits the fan. The longer you say nothing, the bigger the wrinkle you push down the rug, and the bigger the scandal at the far end. My advice, pal, is to break ties with these folks. Or they'll take everything, destroy you and spit you out. I'd hate to see you go through that, buddy. I really would."

"I went to the Metropolitan Museum this afternoon." Mark went off at a tangent.

"Apropos of what?" Even the intellectually-agile Blazerman couldn't connect the two propositions.

"Apropos of clearing my head."

"Well, la di da."

"Frank, I think I'm being followed." Mark described the incident in London and his sighting of a man beside Giacometti's Cat.

"Buddy, you need a real long break. Giacomeddi's Cat, my ass. Nobody's after you."

"Hey, Mark, great to see you again." Laura strode into the room and smooshed him on both cheeks. "So sorry I was stuck on that phone for so long. Crazy regional editor in San Francisco. All's well now." Laura wore a casual $5000 black dress from an Italian designer. It flattered her Rubenesque curves. She was jolly, looked great and was *all there*. He couldn't imagine a dark side to Laura.

"Now – give me some champagne, Honey – when d'you want to eat, Mark? We're having flaming yarns and a salad for dinner. We can be ready any time. You must be tarrd. It's way past midnight in London. Perhaps you want to freshen up and we can eat in half an hour? How does that sound?"

"That sounds great, Laura. It gives me time to call Nancy."

"Invite her over if she's free. Totally casual."

Laura and Frank launched into a domestic discussion. Mark sloped off to his suite. He kicked off his shoes and lay on the bed. He dialled her number.

"Mark! Where have you been? I've tried to call again and again. Your office number's on answer, your home number doesn't pick up and your cell's always turned off. And you know I can't use email between us."

"Sorry." Mark said unconvincingly. It excited him to know that she'd been trying so hard. "I was calling to get the scoop on Tucson."

"You're driving me crazy, Mark. We don't talk for days, we've had a troubled few weeks. You finally call and you want to talk about business."

"I've been preoccupied with Appletree. Sorry, Nancy, but Tuckwell's memo turned me off. I haven't really felt like making my daily cootchy-coo calls to you."

"Mark. I need your help." She ignored his last comment. "I asked Bill and Dick Cosway to a meeting the day after we last spoke."

"Together?"

"Yes. I wanted them both to hear what I had to say. I told them I needed to distance myself from Bill and that I wouldn't travel in the Gulfstream, stay in his suite or co – host any events with him. Bill put on his big-hearted act. "Sure. I had no idea you wanted time to yourself, Honey. I completely understand. Do whatever you're comfortable with." He was almost likeable.

Dick thought it was funny to be involved in Bill"s personal life. He was about to leave when I said, "Dick. There's something else. Our friends at Appletree need more time at the Trustee meeting in Arizona to talk through their concerns about market timers."

Bill went ballistic. "I was just on the goddam phone with Birch and Telford. Told them I'd stop the market timers. There has not been a single timing trade since we spoke. What more do these goddam people want?"

I said, "What they want is enough time to explain to the Trustees how much damage has been done to the CSF International Fund by market timers."

His reply was, "You're the goddam Compliance Officer. You figure it out."

"Sounds like a positive interchange of views."

"My problem, Mark, is that I've known about rogue trades in the system for a long time but I've let myself be overrun by Bill and Dick. I've warned them at board meetings – my concerns have never appeared in the Minutes – and sent memos to Bill, Dick and Shilson. At first, the way they talked, I believed them. They said there certainly wasn't a legal issue. These guys had twenty years professional experience on me. They hired me. If they told me something, I believed it."

"So where did you leave it?"

"It got worse. I said that you were flying 10,000 miles round trip to Tucson and they should at least invite you to their social functions."

"That goddam pushy Limey. Why should he get privileges the other portfolio managers don't get?" It went on like that."

"I appreciate you trying."

"I had no idea how ugly the place was until you showed up. You got caught up in Bill's insane jealousy, in the greed of the board, in blowing the illegal market timing. Why did I fall for you?"

Mark softened. His hunch had been more or less right. Nancy had got so embroiled in corruption at the top of CSF that she'd lost her compass. Her relationship with him-Mark- had inadvertently highlighted the whole rotten edifice of CSF to her.

"It would have been a lot easier if you'd fallen for the guy who ran the New York Tax Free Fund."

"That's a thought. Ricky's quite sweet." Nancy lightened up.

"Stepping back, we still have a couple of hurdles to jump. You need to prepare your exit discussion with Tuckwell and Cosway and I need to discuss an exit strategy from CSF with Graham."

"I've already got a script for my resignation. It's about wanting a change of pace and time to pursue my own interests. There's nothing negative in there. I'm not resigning from something so much as going to something."

"What are you doing tonight?"

"Going crazy in my apartment."

"Dinner at Frank's place. Right now. Come on over."

Chapter 32

As soon as the elevator doors opened Mark could not believe he'd been so obtuse with this lovely woman. Nancy wore a pale green silk blouse and black slacks, her bare feet slipped into soft leather moccasins. Her hair was tied into a pony tail. For a person who wielded so much corporate power, Mark was always surprised how delicate she looked.

"I'm so happy to see you. You've lost weight." she said, taking his hand.

"All this Appletree stuff gets to me."

"Appletree, schmappletree, zappletree . . . There's so much more to life than Appletree you know, Marko."

"I know. We just need to resolve it and leave everything in good order."

"Hey lovebirds, come in for a drink. Great to see ya Nancy."

Frank strode towards the elevator wearing a striped French chef's apron, carrying a sharp implement in one hand and a full glass of champagne in the other.

"Here-take this."

"Thanks Frank, I appreciate it."

He enveloped Nancy in a bear hug.

"How d'ya like your flaming yarn?"

"Flaming yarn?"

"F-e-e-l-a-y M-e-e-n-y-a-n-n-e." Frank mouthed it out.

"Oh- Medium rare".

It was a congenial evening. Nancy laughed with Frank and quizzed Laura about life in her world. "Honey, if you ever wanna come over for a chat about journalism, I'd love to give you the scoop. I'll introduce you around some of my friends."

It was obvious to Laura, if not to her blustering man, that Mark and Nancy needed to be alone. As soon as practicably after the meal, she announced, "Guys, I hate to poop the party but I gotta make more calls to the Coast before it gets too late. Mark, Nancy, make yourselves comfortable. Frank – don't you have something to do in your office?"

"Do I? er, yea. I guess I've got that prospectus to work through. I hope you don't mind, guys. Please finish the champagne and" – Laura tugged his arm – "Er, I guess we'll see ya in the morning." They tumbled out of the kitchen.

Mark smiled at Nancy, sincerely appreciating Laura's intuition. "I guess our hosts are telling us something." He kissed her on the lips. "Come on, bring your glass. We also have some business to discuss." He put his arm around her waist and they walked unsteadily along the passage to the guest suite.

They faced each other by the window of their darkened room overlooking Park Avenue. A line of taxis waited at the lights thirty floors below. Nancy deftly unbuttoned Mark's shirt; he lifted her blouse over her head. They kicked off their shoes. He unzipped her slacks; she wriggled and her clothes slipped to the floor.

They held each other on the bed, vaguely listening to the street sounds far below. "I can't wait for Tucson to be over." Nancy spoke sleepily, "I'm still scared of what might happen."

They were booked to travel separately to Tucson three days later and stay in different rooms, although their suites would be adjoining. They didn't want to inflame Tuckwell's obsessive jealousy.

"Everything'll be all right," Mark soothed her. "Remember, this is the last time we need to be secretive. We'll play it out in Arizona, then fly to Chicago at the end of the meeting. You'll have resigned as an employee of CSF. Depending how the board meeting goes, Appletree may have resigned the International Fund account. We'll then both be clear of this weird organization."

"I'm still worried about everything they have hanging over me. As Compliance Officer I should have prevented all those market timing trades."

"Maybe-but they exerted undue influence over you. You simply must tell them you want a clean break. After you resign you have to go to the SEC and blow the whistle as part of a plea bargain."

"Plea bargain? That makes me sound like a criminal." Nancy sat up.

"That's why you have to speak to them before Tuckwell and Cosway concoct a story that you approved their activities. They can go to the SEC too, remember. They could say they always had doubts about market timing, but you repeatedly told them it was OK. They could come up with dates when the three of you met and tell the SEC, in the absence of minutes, that Market Timing was the subject of discussion. They could say that you told them, at each meeting, that their activities were kosher. And that you always 'forgot' to record a memo to that effect. They could tell the SEC that it was only after you left CSF that the illegality of the trading became clear.

"So it's a race to the SEC . . . ?"

"It's a race to the SEC. The clock has to be ticking on their side too."

Mark reflected, "They'll be watching you very closely."

"Like I have to watch you very closely." She kissed his neck, "Who were you in bed with the other night when I called?"

"I closed my eyes and pretended it was you."

"I'm sure of it. Her name?" Nancy dug a finger nail hard into his buttock.

"Undisclosed, but she loves her husband and doesn't want to leave him."

"Yeah, right."

"After reading Tuckwell's agenda, I couldn't imagine that you and I could still be an item. So I had a fling."

"Then I called. What's her name?"

"No names. I'll taunt you with one titillating possibility though."

Nancy lay behind him, cupped into his body. "Oh yes?"

"She's seen you from afar and finds you very cute."

"You're dangerous, Marko." She nuzzled into his body.

"Nothing wrong with a bit of fantasy, is there?"

Chapter 33

Mark's plane left La Guardia airport at 9am. After a layover in Dallas he caught the flight to Tucson, where he arrived at 2pm. The air was dry, fragrant and warm. He hired a car and, after a few erroneous turns in the desert, found the drive leading to Saguaro Canyon.

The resort consisted of an imposing Spanish colonial hacienda set prettily among cactus and bougainvillea, with numerous *ranchettas* tucked into the landscape out of sight of each other. It was a perfect location for discreet liaisons or off-site business meetings. Transport between the main building and the far-flung ranchettas was either by foot along a groomed desert trail, or by golf-buggy.

Mark was booked into a suite south of the main building. Nancy was booked into the adjoining room. Their suites shared a veranda separated by a low wall. Fifteen yards away, tucked into the base of a vast peeling ochre sandstone boulder, was a hot tub accessible only from their two suites. Mark threw his kit on the bed and took the short path to the hot tub. It wasn't fizzing, but the water was the same temperature as the air, 88 degrees, according to the built-in thermometer. He looked back at the neighbouring room. Nancy had not checked in yet.

A folder had been delivered to his suite outlining the timetable which Tuckwell had planned for the next three days. It contained vouchers for unlimited free enjoyment of the resort and its facilities. Golf, food, horse rides, drinks, falconry, spas and therapies were all on the house. CSF would pay for every activity described in the blue folder.

In his earlier banter with the receptionist, she'd told him that trustees were given gold folders bestowing even more 'fabulous privileges'. They included one hour flights in CSF's corporate Gulfstream over the desert with a partner, unlimited expense allowances and cute female or male Mexican escorts for their evening entertainment. Mark couldn't resist asking,

"Have any trustees booked to join the Mile High club?"

The receptionist smiled knowingly, answering cryptically, "All facilities will be fully utilized."

"Spouses or partners?"

"I couldn't possibly disclose," she smiled again.

"I guess that's how Mr Shilson keeps everyone voting the right way."
"Tut tut, Mr Telford." The receptionist concluded.

There were omissions from the original agenda. Mark saw immediately that Nancy's name was missing from the roster of attendees at Saguaro Canyon.

He also noticed the slot on the following day from 2 to 2.45 pm at the Turnberry Lounge. It was described as *Presentation by London Associates to Trustees*. That was the time he should have been spending with the trustees. Why was it being given to a competing firm from London?

Heavy hearted, Mark was unpacking his suits when he heard the sound of activity next door. He ran out to the veranda, stepped over the partition and peered into the neighbouring window, ready to welcome Nancy to their haven in the desert.

The elderly couple who had just checked in seemed surprised to see a man with his face pressed to their veranda window. They slid back the screened door. "Can we help you?"

"Oh, I'm so sorry to disturb you. I thought someone else was checking into this room."

"No problem, son." A chipmunk skittered along the veranda, ran down the steps, hightailed across the garden, around the hot tub and under the ochre sandstone boulder, where it disappeared. The scent of wild sage permeated the air as the temperature cooled and the dusk released the desert's fragrances.

Mark checked his mobile phone. First message 1pm EST :

Hi Honey. There's been a change. I won't be coming to Tucson.

Her voice echoed, like she was in a bathroom. Second message 1.30 pm EST :

Hi Honey. Be real careful. I don't know exactly what's happening but something's up. They want you out of the way.

Her voice faded out. He could hear background voices. Was she in an airport? A hotel lobby? Third message 2.01pm :

Call as soon as you get this message. Thinking of you only.

It cut off abruptly.

Nancy's home number rang eight times before being picked up by her recorded voice. He left a message. He tried her mobile. It rang four times and defaulted to the answering service. He left another message.

Where is she? They last spoke when he was in La Guardia that morning and she was at the Chicago gate at Newark airport. There was no hint of a problem. What did she mean, *'They want you out of the way'*?

He emailed her. She always picked up emails on the road :

> *Where are you? Place? Address? Phone number? Leave message on my mobile, home number, office number, hotel, email, anywhere. I'll find you.*
>
> *Mark xxx*

No CSF events were open to him that night. Cocktails were hosted by Steve and Skye Shilson at 7pm but only available to Trustees, Board Members and their escorts. Investment advisers who made the mere 10,000 mile round trip from London were not invited.

He was not required until 9.45 the next morning for Appletree's Presentation and Review. He had to think clearly – jetlag was clouding his brain. He had to act fast. First, book a flight to Chicago leaving straight after his presentation. CSF were obsessed about keeping on time, so he could count on his presentation finishing by 10am. It would take 90 minutes to drive to the airport, dump the rental car, check through security and board the aircraft. The earliest flight he could hope to catch was early afternoon. The website showed a flight to Chicago at 12.25. Availability? One rear middle seat. He booked and paid.

What would he do when he got to Chicago? Nancy's brother's farm was across the Indiana state line in south west Michigan. She'd talked about the township but he couldn't recall its name.

Mark found a roadmap on a Michigan website. He scoured the Bottom Left of the State, as she described it, for townships. There were five in a row along Lake Michigan: Michiana, Grand Beach, New Buffalo, Union Pier and Lakeside. None sounded familiar.

She said her brother's place was an old family farmhouse, left to him by their Norwegian great aunt. He owned land. That suggested somewhere away from the Lake. Three Oaks? Galien? New Troy? Eauborne? Yes – he thought she said Auburn. It had to be Eauborne . He would head there tomorrow and ask around for the Lindstrom farm. Someone would be bound to know.

To prevent raising suspicions, Mark did not contact the CSF event organizers to book any of the recommended activities at the resort. If he failed to arrive for a company-sponsored activity, they might search for him and discover he'd left Tucson. He would call the Saguaro Canyon Resort from Chicago later in the week to check out of his room. It was being paid by CSF, so it didn't matter to him. He smiled as he plotted to tell the Resort he was calling from Miami, to put Tuckwell off the scent.

Mark ordered room service. While waiting for delivery he poured a heavily iced rum and Coke, stripped and lay out in the hot tub. A brilliantly clear single star shone in the darkening cobalt sky between two branched saguaro cactuses; the scents of the desert were intoxicating.

Why is everything so bloody complicated? he mused to the churn of the pump in the hot tub and the foaming bubbles. *Blazerman warned me about CSF, even though it seemed like a great idea. But nothing prepared me for this; market timers destroying our performance? Tuckwell destroying my private life? What could be more natural than going out with a beautiful woman and aspiring to financial success?*

He smiled when he realized how pathetic he must have appeared. Self pity was not a Telford trait. He sipped his drink and closed his eyes.

After a light supper of flame-roasted desert quail, sweet potatoes, South West salad, lemon sorbet and a glass of dry Chardonnay from Sonoma Valley, Mark locked his doors, closed the blinds and crashed out.

He dreamed violently in the night. Someone was trying to slide open his patio door and force the lock. The blinds rattled. A dark presence tried to force the main door of his suite. He'd chained it. The phone rang, he couldn't reach it. He ran and ran across the desert as he hadn't run since he was a teenage athlete. His feet were light, springing off the hot rocks like a gazelle. He found her house. She was cooking. Red-checked table cloths and sunshine poured into the kitchen. It got dark. The doors were being battered, they rattled the windows. There was a frightful groaning in the basement. THEY were now inside the house . . .

He woke at seven o'clock. A text message flashed on his phone. 11.44 pm EST :

Hi Honey, it's me. I'm OK. Call my mobile ASAP. I'm at the farm. Join me as soon as you can. You MUST get out of Tucson. Love you. N

It was nine o'clock in Michigan. She answered immediately. "Hi. Thank God you're OK. Where are you?"

"Tucson. What's the panic? You make all this sound like high drama. I'm only here to give a fifteen minute presentation today, then I'm free. I'll come to Chicago after then."

"Mark, They're going to kill you."

"You're kidding. How?"

"They have a professional in Tucson who'll find the best way. It will be an accident."

"Good, so I won't be shot or stabbed. That's a relief. Should I leave now, or wait until my presentation?"

"Don't be facetious, Marko. Every hour you stay in Tucson puts you more at risk. If you stay for your presentation, leave straight afterwards. Change in the men's room. Drive quietly down the road. Don't let anyone see you."

"You make this sound like a 1960s spy thriller."

"But this is absolutely real. Just be careful, Marko."

"How do I know you're not part of the plot? You might be the bait."

Silence.

"Nancy? "

"Yeah, I heard you." She sounded exhausted. "That's a horrible thought but it's a risk you have to take. Call me when you get to Chicago. I'll give you instructions where to come."

Fear tapped lightly on Mark's shoulder. He once got stuck on his prep school chapel roof as the result of a prank. It was at night and frosty. One slip and he would have fallen sixty feet onto the cobbles below. That was *terror*. The Fire Brigade got him off; he was nearly expelled from school but was thrilled to survive and merely be gated for six weeks.

The chapel roof incident was the only time Mark had ever felt real fear in his life. The fear he felt now was more abstract, less immediate. His best chance now was to behave normally, as if he suspected nothing. He always travelled lightly, so nobody would notice if he left his room with a tote bag and threw it on the back seat of his rental car. The car . . . *They must be staking out the damn thing*. Later in the day he'd call the rental company from Chicago to say it broke down and would they please go to the Saguaro Canyon to recover it. Mark called the concierge,

"Could you arrange a limo for ten fifteen sharp, picking me up outside the West Conference Wing? My name is Mark Telford. It's for down town Tucson. I'll bring a bag to Reception at 9 o'clock for loading on the limo."

"Certainly, Mr Telford."

Nancy said it would be an accident. He'd just eliminated the rental car as one obvious way to contrive the event. He opened his window blinds, startling two quails on the gravel a few feet away. They flew off with a whirr. It was such a lovely day. Why him, for heaven sake? He was just an innocent Brit trying to do his best. He was enmeshed in a web of corruption, refused to play ball and happened to be the unlucky dope to draw it to the board's attention.

He pulled on his swimming trunks, threw a towel over his shoulder, slid open the patio door and wandered down to the sandstone boulder. As he approached the hot tub he heard a sputtering sound. Sparks fizzed intermittently from a broken wire half-buried beside the deck. In the hot tub two dead animals floated limply on the surface, face down. A *javelina* wild pig and a chipmunk, electrocuted as they'd taken a drink in the night.

Bad idea. Mark returned to his room, locking the patio door behind him. He shaved more deliberately than usual, studying himself in the mirror.

THEY want to kill YOU, the easygoing financial guy who got lucky with CSF. Condemned for being caught up in their scam. If you blow it open, Shilson, Tuckwell and Cosway will lose their huge bonuses, pay fines, disgorge their profits and go to jail. They have weighed the odds and judged that YOUR demise stacks up favourably against THEIR day of reckoning. He smiled as he shaved the foam methodically off his face.

Mark showered, dressed and packed his bag. His laptop, wallet, tickets and essential papers were in a briefcase that he would bring to the trustee meeting at 9.45. He walked along the groomed desert trail, past beds of bougainvillea, venerable cactuses, flowering mimosa and sage brush, to the main building of the hotel. His lungs filled with the sweet, still desert air. Chipmunks and brown lizards skittered about the rocks.

He found it hard to believe that such an idyllic place could possibly be the setting for a contrived accident of his own death. He walked up to the Receptionist. "Hi, my name's Mark Telford. I ordered a limo for down town. Could you load this bag on it? Please make it 10.15 sharp outside the West Conference wing."

"No problem at all, Mr Telford." His presentation was in the East Conference Wing. He would stroll back and forth between the East and West Wings after his presentation, feigning a phone call. He would affect the self-important strolling act that businessmen always performed while talking on their cell phones.

After the second round trip, there would be no *back*. Anyone observing him would take a while to realize he wasn't returning. They would run out of the door and might be lucky to see a random limo with darkened windows gliding towards the Resort exit. With relief Mark's pursuer would spot his rental car sitting in the car park and assume that he was still on the property somewhere.

Mark walked past Reception towards the East Conference Wing. A line of sofas was occupied by various important-looking people. He was too distracted to pay attention to their occupants. One came to life.

"Hey Mark. How you doin'?"

" Good Lord. Vern. How nice to see you. This is a pleasant surprise." He lied.

"I want you to meet Wilfred Gibson, Chief Executive of London International Associates."

"Hell-A-Oh, delighted to meet you. Do I detect a fellow Englishman?" Mark was struck by Wilfred's clammy handshake.

"Mark Telford. We run the CSF International Fund and I'm meeting the Board of Trustees in a few minutes."

Wilfred Gibson looked quizzically at Vern, who explained,

"London International Associates are presenting to the Board this afternoon about managing a pool of international equities for CSF."

"That's right. If we get the business Vern's going to join us and work as our rep in the USA, aren't you Vern?" he patted the boy on the back.

"I certainly am, sir." Vern looked at Mark triumphantly.

A third man rose out of the sofa and extended a hand to Mark,

"Jack Bolt. Good to meet you." He, too, had an unexpectedly weak handshake.

"I've heard all about you," Mark couldn't help saying. Bolt was different from what he'd visualized. He'd expected the former US Marine to ass-kick his way around a room; a bully and an enforcer. The real Jack Bolt wore a tailored dark blue suit, white shirt and tie, black wing-tip shoes. He was in his fifties; brown hair receding severely. He was overweight with a round, paunchy face. His pale blue eyes were the giveaway: they were utterly cold, devoid of any trace of humour or kindness. There was something of the SS officer about the man.

"Well, I need to get to my meeting. Good to meet you. Good luck with your presentation this afternoon." Mark shook Wilfred Gibson's flaccid hand again.

"You wouldn't say that if you knew which fund he's pitching for." Jack Bolt swiped at Mark.

Chapter 34

Mark was detained in a stuffy anteroom as the previous CSF manager wrapped up her presentation on Municipal Bonds. She was shown out of the back door of the conference room as Mark was ushered in through the front.

The room was darkened and heavily air conditioned. Mark was invited to sit at the end of the table. The chair was still warm from the heat of the previous speaker's clenched sphincter. The long table was littered with the universal debris of dreary board meetings: empty coffee cups, plates of half-eaten muffins, scrunched up sheets of paper, bottled water, plastic cups and partially-read files that the trustees should have studied before arrival in Tucson.

Mark connected his laptop to the room's audiovisual hardware. A slide appeared on the screen with Appletree's logo. It was an apple tree set in the middle of a globe. Each apple was a round flag representing a different country. Corny, but Mark was often complimented on the design.

Steve Shilson chaired the meeting. He sat at the head of the table; Tuckwell sat on his left and Cosway to his right. Four trustees sat along each side, hunched like vultures on a wall. They were a mixed collection of grey suits and eccentrics. Their jackets were off, cast over the back of chairs. Mark tried to match Shilson's description of the trustees with the worthies who sat before him. The Woman Lawyer and The Black Guy were obvious. The Jewish Woman was in her late thirties, he guessed. Very attractive, she looked fun – had it been in different circumstances.

The Well-Known Entrepreneur had to be the scruffy guy in the open-neck golf shirt. He looked young, bored and disturbed, too preoccupied to be wasting his time at a mutual fund trustee meeting. His fingernails were chewed to a stub. The Accountant, The Actuary and The Professor were like cloned reptiles. In youth each must surely have had his jolly personality, a bit of charm and a full head of hair. Life had moulded them into impotent ciphers converging obediently towards non-executive boardrooms. They were grey, grizzled, thin and stooped, with gimlet stares through thick glasses.

"We appreciate you making the trip from London, Mark." Shilson began. Neither Cosway nor Tuckwell caught his eye. "In the interests of time, we'd like you to launch straight into your presentation. Please pace yourself and be sure to say what you want in the time allocated. You've got fifteen minutes for the CSF International Fund."

"Thank you Chairman." Mark nodded at Shilson. He paused, during which he deliberately made eye contact with every trustee.

"I have two missions today. First, to run you through the Appletree Investment Process to remind you of the rigour with which we manage assets for our clients around the world." The trustees were attentive.

"Second, to explain our investment performance since we started managing the Fund last October."

He flicked the slide from Appletree Logo to Appletree Investment Process.

"Appletree has a proprietary model designed by my partner Graham Birch. It starts by analysing the key macroeconomic factors which determine whether countries are worth investing in or not. We score twenty-five factors that we believe are critical to a stock market's well-being.

For example, take interest rates. Are they going up? Flat? Down? Where are they today relative to their history? What are a country's trading partners doing? We look at each factor that determines interest rates and come up with a score. Our interest rate score for Japan today is seven out of ten. That means that Japan has a benign interest-rate environment.

We reach an overall score of every factor in each country, then rank countries according to their scores and make our country allocation based on their rank."

"That's all very well, Mr.Telford." Professor Grey-Reptile interrupted Mark's flow. "But what if Belgium scores 100 in your model, and Japan scores 20? Would you have five times more in Belgium than you would have in Japan?"

"Good question." *Smug little shit.* "We make an adjustment. The Tokyo stock market is approximately thirty times the size of the Brussels Bourse. We would underweight Tokyo and overweight Brussels relative to the size of each market. We might end up with a 200% weight in Brussels, relative to the Index, and a 60% weight in Tokyo."

"Thank you."

"Once we've decided how much to invest in each country, further analysis determines how much we allocate to each sector. For example, there are times when you want to overweight mining stocks and underweight financials. And times when you want the exact reverse."

He flicked to the next slide.

"Finally we decide which stocks to invest in. Appletree has four investment professionals who pick stocks in the key world markets outside the USA. Alix Newlin covers Europe; Bob Berwick covers the UK and some emerging markets, Clarissa covers Asia and I cover Latin America. We never have more than 100 stocks in a portfolio. At the moment we have 94 in the CSF International Fund.

"Our aim is to be in the right countries, the right sectors and the right stocks at the right times. We believe that by constantly honing the model, we will deliver superior performance for the foreseeable future. Any questions?" Mark looked directly at each vulture.

"No? Very well, I'd now like to address the performance of the CSF International Fund."

He clicked up a page showing performance from the Fund's start date in October until December 31st. It was excellent, beating the Index and 95% of its peers.

He then clicked to a page showing monthly and cumulative performance from 1 January to 28 February, year-to-date and since inception.

"As you can see our performance was stellar. The model was working beautifully and stock selection was strong."

He focused on a page showing March performance. Without comment he ran through the numbers.

"The Fund fell 0.82% in March. The Index rose 5.79% and our peer group average rose 5.81%. The Fund's performance was far below the Index and behind our peer group.

Year to date to the end of March, the Fund was up 6.38%. The Index was up 11.59% and our peer group average was up 11.41%.

You might wonder what happened, what caused the Fund's excellent performance to crater in the course of just one month?"

Mark flicked to the next page.

"As you can see from this page, there were 23 matched trades in March. What's a matched trade? Here, for instance." Mark pointed to the first of the month. "On March 1st, $33 million came into the Fund. We invested it immediately in 94 stocks in 13 countries. On March 6th we had a redemption of $34.1 million. The difference corresponded exactly to the 3.3% rise in the Fund's share price between March 1st and March 6th.

"This was not an isolated event. By mid-month the amounts flowing through the Fund rose to over $200 million a day. In March alone, we had total new inflows of $3.68 billion, and outflows of $3.663 billion. For all that massive activity, the Fund only added $17 million of new money in the month. All the rest was hot flows."

"What was the average size of the Fund during March?" Lovely Jewish Trustee asked.

"It averaged around $1.4 billion."

"So you're telling us that the Fund had combined inflows and outflows over five times the asset value of the Fund, in one month? I find it hard to credit."

"That's correct. It played havoc with our performance on two fronts. First, once we got wise to the matching trades we began to keep the cash inflows in cash until they switched back out again. Then at least we didn't need to sell equities to meet the ensuing redemptions. But the problem was that holding cash in a rising market – like it was in March – was very expensive. Our model required us to be100% invested in equities. Instead we had an average of 88% invested during the month. Holding all that cash hurt our performance.

"Second . . . "

"I'm sorry to interrupt you, Mark." Shilson silenced him with a deadpan smile, "You're gonna have to wrap up your fascinating presentation. Your fifteen minutes are up."

"I'd just like to conclude, ladies and gentlemen, that we believe there is evidence of irregularity in these trades, and that you, as Trustees, would be well-advised to . . . "

A stentorian voice came from behind Mark's chair at the head of the table.

"I would be inclined to recommend the trustees to vote to terminate Appletree on this account." Mark turned, to see Jack Bolt. *What the hell's he doing here?*

"The fact is, they suffered a loss of nerve in a crucial month. Thinking markets were going to soften in March they kept high cash levels. It's all too convenient to blame market timers for underperformance. Appletree has always had full discretion to do what they like on this account. It doesn't sit well with me, and I hope you, too, when a manager starts throwing blame around when their performance slips."

"Thanks, Jack. We need to let Mark go. I'm sure he's a busy man. Thanks Mark. We appreciate your presentation."

Shilson waved Mark off with a cold smile.

Mark was fuming as he unplugged his laptop. He looked helplessly along the row of Trustees. Lovely Jewish Woman caught his eye and gave a sympathetic shrug. The other vultures merely turned the tab in their folders, ready to interview the next manager on the agenda.

He left the room with a thunderous expression, noting that Tuckwell and Cosway lightened up considerably as the trustees considered Jack Bolt's comments. They leaned across Shilson to share a private joke as Mark exited.

He meandered in shock along the East Wing corridor towards the reception area of the main resort building. This part of the building was designed like an 18th Century Spanish Mission. The corridors were cloistered, with potted palms spaced in each archway and bougainvillea running rampant up stone pillars towards the sunlight. The contrast between such lovely surroundings and his experience in the meeting was grotesque.

His rendezvous with the limo was at the far end of the West Wing. He passed the concierge desk – "Good morning, Mr Telford" – and kept walking west. Apart from the usual cluster of porters, taxi hailers and valet parkers in the entrance there was nobody to be seen. He'd obviously been ridiculously cautious earlier, falling for the paranoia engendered by CSF wherever their tentacles stretched.

He didn't pay attention to the purposeful steps catching up with him on the tiled floor. Stunned by his humiliation at the trustee meeting, he was lost in thought. He was a few yards from the glass doors of the West Wing into the car park where his limo waited. It was 10.10. He still had a few minutes so ducked into the Hombres' Restroom. There were five cubicles in a row. No sooner had he sat down than someone entered the restroom and took the cubicle next to his. No sound emanated from his neighbour. Usually there was the sound of a belt being unclipped, a zipper opening and the whole shebang dropping to the ankles. Dead silence.

Mark prickled with fear. He'd been cavalier earlier, in front of the shaving mirror, but could this be IT? He would not have imagined in a million years that he might end his days in a toilet in Arizona. What was the guy doing next door? The top of his cubicle wall ran to the ceiling, so he couldn't be hit from that angle. The gap underneath was only two inches high, so he was unlikely to be attacked from there.

He whistled and started making noises in the toilet that suggested he was preoccupied. He carefully stretched to the floor to see what his neighbour was up to. At ground level he saw a pair of cowboy boots standing motionless, pointing towards the door. They were brand new, with no wear on the heels.

He's going to burst out of the toilet door as soon as I leave my cubicle. Hell's bells. What if he has a gun or a knife? My survival depends on how fast I leave the loo and get out of range. But this guy's a professional. Nancy said they had a pro on the job to kill me. This is ridiculous. Appletree's only a job, dammit. Why does everyone have to take it so seriously?"

Mark spotted the long-handled toilet brush in a plastic bowl in the corner behind the pan. *So I'm reduced to defending myself with a toilet brush!*

"He put up a valiant fight, inflicting serious brush wounds on his assailant before succumbing to a hail of UZI fire… We recommend that Mr Telford should be awarded the George Cross posthumously for conspicuous gallantry." He mouthed his obituary citation and smiled grimly.

Mark sat and thought very hard, trying to remember in detail what the toilet doors looked like from the outside. They opened inwards. That would buy him a split second. They had chrome handles on the outside. Yes; his cubicle and the adjacent one had looped chrome handles. He looked at the toilet brush. Its shaft was made of thick, stiff plastic. He racked his memory to recall if it would fit into a looped handle. He would have two to three seconds, at the very most, to find out.

He made straining noises at the toilet as he dressed silently and prepared to make his exit. His neighbour shuffled and obviously figured that he had a few minutes before his quarry got off the porcelain. Mark heard him unbuckling his belt and sit down with a sigh.

"This is my moment!" he muttered to himself, while making other, more explicit, toilet noises.

Mark silently teased open the lock, swung out of the cubicle and jammed the plastic brush into the stainless steel loops attached to the adjoining doors. It was a perfect fit. As he ran out of the men's restroom, he heard the frantic sound of a man cursing and hauling up his trousers. The brush might hold for two minutes. Mark ran out of the building, flagged the limo and disappeared into the darkened rear compartment. The chauffeur slid down the connecting window.

"Señor Telford?"

"Si, si. Downtown Tucson please. I'll tell you the address when we get there."

The limo glided out of the car park and turned left out of the Resort. Mark kept looking nervously out of the rear window. No sign of anyone in pursuit. They barrelled along the highway towards downtown Tucson.

Mark called Graham in London. He was on his way home from the office. "Well, my friend. You ain't gonna like what I'm about to tell you." Mark explained his exact 15 minutes, the trustees' complete indifference towards the market timing issue, meeting Vern Badore, Wilfred Gibson and Jack Bolt.

"How did Jack Bolt behave?"

"Well, he looked unexceptional, like a pudgy middle-aged lawyer. You're right about your hunch – listen to this, Graham. At the end of my session he slunk into the room behind my chair and announced in front of the entire board that 'he would be inclined to recommend that the trustees terminate this manager', or words to that effect.

"Any more light on his position at CSF?"

"Not really. He's obviously close to the seat of power but he doesn't seem to have a formal executive role, except to do Shilson's bidding. He's a kind of eminence grise, a quiet, behind-the-scenes, corporate assassin . . . "

"Charming. So the bottom line, Mark, is that I should tell the troops to ready themselves for losing this account to Wilf Gibson's shop. Strange choice. We've outperformed them for years."

"That would be smart. I suspect it'll happen very soon, although they've got to give thirty days notice. The more we spin this out the longer we earn a fee. I wonder what deal Gibson'll get with CSF?"

"What pisses me off is that we worked so hard to get the business in the first place. Think of all the due diligence speeches, the travel, the conference calls at unholy hours. We bust ourselves on this project."

"Yes Graham, but it's unworkable. These guys are evil."

"Any news from Nancy?"

"She didn't show up in Tucson. She's with her brother in Michigan. I'm on my way to Chicago to meet her today. If anyone calls to ask where I am, you don't know. She left several messages saying that I'm in great personal danger. She probably heard man-talk about eliminating Appletree and assumed it was a death threat."

"It does sound pretty far-fetched." Graham tried to reassure Mark. "Enough said, sport. I'll get the ball rolling over here. Sorry you had to fight through all that shit."

"Comes with the territory. Bye."

Mark called Syreta's number. It was late in the afternoon in London, but worth a try.

"Syreta Mehta speaking."

"Mark Telford."

"Mark! How did it go?"

"Bad, I'm afraid."

"Never mind. We're well shot of them. It's a complicated and corrupt structure that caused more pain than it's worth. They always acted like they owned us. On the bright side, Mark, we were notified today that the Mid-West Teachers Superannuation Fund have appointed us to manage $200million in Emerging Markets at a fee rate of 0.85%."

"That's $1.7 million of fees a year."

"Correct. You win some . . . are you still thinking of me?"

"That's an indiscreet question to ask on an archived office line."

"There's nobody left in the office and I know how to de-archive calls so I can say what I like."

"OK then. I've been preoccupied so you haven't been in the front of my mind, to be honest. But when I think of you I get very excited."

"Jay's back for three weeks so I haven't thought much about you either. Are you going to marry Nancy?"

"Maybe, although I have a premonition. I can't explain it."

"Probably something to do with giving up 42 years of bachelorhood."

"Maybe. Gotta go, Syreta. Take care."

As the limo drove under an overhead gantry with a sign pointing towards the airport, Mark leaned forward and shouted at the driver,

"The Airport. Please go to the Airport."

"No down-town?"

"No, the Airport please."

The chauffeur swung to the right with a squeal of tyres, just catching the off-ramp towards Tucson International Airport.

As he bade farewell to the driver Mark passed him a $100 bill with instructions:

"If anyone asks where you took Mr Telford, tell them you left him downtown on the corner of Alameda and Granada – by the Museum of Art."

"Thank you sir, Mr Telford. Corner of Alameda and Granada." he tipped his cap and smiled, "I tell them if they ask."

As soon as he was ensconced in his rear middle seat on the flight to Chicago, Mark closed his eyes. What if his neighbour in the toilet had been a perfectly innocent gentleman? But he couldn't help smiling at the possibility that he'd locked a CSF vulture into the crapper.

The flight landed on time at O'Hare. It didn't take Mark long to find the car rental desk, plough through the paperwork and hop on a shuttle that took him to the rental lot on the eastern fringe of the airport. He was given a nondescript white Chevy with Illinois plates. The Kennedy Expressway was moving well. Sixty minutes after landing he was cruising anonymously along the Chicago Skyway into northern Indiana.

Chapter 35

Mark drove off Interstate 94 and headed north. Michigan City, Indiana seemed like a vast discount shopping mall. Massive parking lots fed into a central zone of flat-roofed warehouses teeming with shoppers. They converged from Chicago and the Tri-state area like fat insects in the warm weather, consuming, munching and licking. He made his way through the complex, turned right by the NIPSCO power plant and headed east towards Michigan on Route 12. A screen of dunes, woods and second home developments blocked his sight of the lake. After about fifteen miles the view opened up in the pretty town of New Buffalo.

He parked his Chevy on the main street. He needed to stretch his legs and orient himself. On the map, Eauborne was quite close to New Buffalo, but he'd fallen foul of American maps before. He once set out to drive around Wyoming one weekend. Fifteen hundred miles later, he returned to Salt Lake City a day late for his flight home. Colourful boutiques and restaurants lined the road to the beach. Tubs of tulips and hyacinths were displayed along the sidewalks outside the shops. Seagulls wheeled around the garbage bins by the dunes. *Welcome to the Hamptons of Chicago*, announced a poster in the window of a liquor store. New Buffalo was bustling and jolly. People were out enjoying the spring weather.

He stood in the lobby of a café and dialled Nancy again.

"There you are. Where are you?"

"A pretty town on Lake Michigan called New Buffalo."

"You're not far at all. Got a pen? I'll give you instructions how to find the farm."

"Shoot."

"Take the Red Arrow Highway east from New Buffalo, through Union Pier to Harbert. Turn right to Sawyer and New Troy. Go left on West Krieger. You'll see a huge old red Dutch barn . . . "

"Are you alone?"

"Bruno's here."

"Bruno?"

"My brother's dog."
"Otherwise alone?"
"Only for another twenty minutes."

He turned right into the driveway of 8672 West Krieger, to the crisp sound of tyres on fresh gravel. He crunched past the Huge Old Red Dutch Barn to his right and parked at the front door of the white farmhouse. The light was fading but a warm southerly wind blew across the fields, nodding the daffodils and lilac bushes in the garden. The climate was much milder than the brisk wind slicing across Lake Michigan a few miles away. The house was surrounded by farmland and woods. No neighbours were in view.

The two storey farmhouse was clad in white clapboard; the doors and windows trimmed in dark green. The front garden was neat and private. A tall rambling hedge interspersed with Colorado blue spruce trees screened the property from the road. The Dutch barn was old and lovingly kept. Its paintwork was fresh and the roof recently restored with wooden shingles. The property spoke of hard work, love of the land and sturdy values.

Mark stood up out of the car and stretched. A muscular brown Labrador appeared around the corner of the house and barked furiously. Mark knew the breed well; he beckoned to the dog, reached down and scratched his ears. Instant friends. Nancy followed Bruno from behind the house.

"Marko!" she ran to embrace him. "I see you've met Bruno."

"You look so . . . so . . . *rustique*. Quite the lady from Country Life."He stepped back to admire Nancy in her white cotton summer dress, straw hat and gardening gloves. "Quite enchanting. Are we alone?"

"Yes, absolutely. Totally alone for a whole week."

"Except for Bruno."

"Except for Bruno. Bring in your stuff and I'll show you our room."

Nancy led him into the house. The storm doors banged shut behind them. The hallway was lit warmly by Tiffany-style table lamps. Recent architectural and design magazines lay on the hall table. Fresh flowers cascaded out of a vase at the base of the stairs. The wooden floors, brass fittings and furniture were well-polished.

"This place is wonderful, Nancy. What's its story?"

"Brad inherited it from our Norwegian great aunt Eva Olsen. Her grandfather homesteaded in this part of Michigan in the 1870s.It's been in the family for five generations." They walked upstairs, led by Bruno.

"My Mom used to spend summers here when she was a girl. She remembers milking the cows early in the morning and last thing at night. Neighbouring farm children came round to play. They swam in the creek and slept in the hayloft in the Dutch barn. There are no cows here any more."

"Tomorrow morning, I want to see everything, the entire property."

"Brad just added six hundred acres to the farm. We now have over two thousand acres of Michigan countryside, including virgin hickory and oak stands, a small vineyard, peach, plum, apple and pear orchards, a thousand acres of soybeans, corn and clover. See over there?" Nancy pointed at an immense field tinted with the light green fuzz of millions of small corn plants in the first flush of growth. The field ended in a hazy blue, dense line of trees about half a mile away. Mark leaned over her for a better look out of the window.

"What are we looking at?"

"This entire view belongs to the farm. The field, the trees, everything."

"We've known each other for eight months and you've never talked about your brother. What does he do?"

"Brad? He trades financial futures on the Chicago Mercantile Exchange. He earns great bucks and he's real canny. He invests heavily in the farm, he saves over 50% of his income. He's got a duplex in Chicago on Dearborn and Astor. If you met him you'd never know he was a multi millionaire."

"That kind of frugality is so un-American."

"You hate Americans, don't you?" she looked at him in a revelatory way.

"I don't hate anyone, but I'm a bit leery of certain Americans at the moment."

"I'm American, you know."

"Nothing personal. Just that I can't imagine having a contract put on my life in England for speaking up at a board meeting."

"I'm so sorry." She slipped her hand into his. "Honey, I've got a surprise for you." Nancy led him to their bedroom. Everything was white or off white. The floors, the duvet, the walls, even the vase of white lilies on a white make-up table. Cream curtains billowed in the breeze as she opened the door. A sweet scent filled the room from a lilac tree below the window. The room was spare and minimal, redolent of New England.

"This is like coming home. It reminds me of my godmother's house in Dorset when I was a boy. We always used to stay there at Easter time. Ever since then I've loved spring flowers and the fragrance of the season."

Nancy pushed open the door to an adjoining room. The bathroom contained a Jacuzzi, full and steaming. The water circulated slowly, creating a pattern with jasmine flowers turning on the surface.

"You think of everything."

Late afternoon sunshine slanted into the bathroom as she slipped off her cotton dress. She unbuttoned his shirt and unbuckled his belt. Mark lay back in the foam and closed his eyes.

At breakfast Nancy percolated coffee and heated the croissants.

She sat down at the table opposite Mark, cupped her hands over his, "I feel scared, Marko."

"How so?"

"We've both been through hell in the past weeks. Do you think we have the strength to pull through?"

"I think we're here together precisely because we have the strength to pull through."

"I think there's more to come, Honey."

"What do you mean?"

"After we spoke about the race to blow the whistle to the SEC I decided to leave CSF immediately and take whatever consequences I had to take. I resigned two days ago. I wrote a simple, businesslike letter to Steve Shilson, copied to Bill and Dick, saying that for personal and family reasons I needed a change and was tendering my resignation as Compliance Officer of CSF with immediate effect."

"So *you* skipped Tucson? You were the proactive one? Didn't you need to give six months' notice? Why didn't you tell me?"

"I didn't discuss it with you because it had to be my decision, and mine alone. I didn't want to trouble you, or to weigh up more advice. New York's an employment-at-will state. You can get up and leave – or they can fire you – at will. No ifs, buts or rights.

"It wasn't a crime to resign from CSF. Why are you so concerned?"

"Dick Cosway came into my office after receiving my note. He was understanding and sweet. Nothing was said about compliance complications. He asked if I could stay for a month to help the transition. I said I preferred to leave immediately but would be available on the phone if needed.

"Then Bill came in, ranting about how I was letting him down, how I'd been 'perverted and influenced by that Fucking Limey, that ungrateful bastard'. He screamed that nobody at Fucking Appletree knew how to play the Wall Street game. He said you were naïve and 'That SOB wouldn't recognize an opportunity if it came up and bit him on the ass'."

"How did you react to Bill's tirade?"

"I said quietly, "can I go now?"

"He screamed, "Go? Yea, get the fuck out of this building." I was prepared for this kind of extreme behaviour. There was nothing of value left in my office. I didn't say a word, packed my office photos into my briefcase, put on my coat, gave Dick my office I/D card and left the building. I haven't been back or spoken to anyone there since."

"So that's why you were air-brushed out of all events at Tucson?"

"I guess so. They really had balls to pair me off with Bill in the first place. He can't take no for an answer."

"That's why he's in marketing. He's one of those guys who smile at rejection, who invent weird little sayings stuck on their office boards like 'Every No takes you one step nearer to Yes.' 'Every kick in the nuts takes you one step nearer to not being kicked in the nuts'."

Nancy laughed. "That's Bill all right."

"So why has the whole thing become so bloody complicated? I want to be left alone to run Appletree and have a quiet life. We want to live together peacefully in London. What could be simpler?"

"I reckon I could have left without a problem but you were tied into the picture. Even though I split with him before you were on the scene, he became consumed with jealousy. You're so different. He's the all-successful, all-singing, all-dancing sales guy who runs a fiefdom at CSF. You're the free spirit who set up his own company, you measure success by a different metric, you always ask the one simple question that you're not supposed to ask. He can't handle that kind of honesty coming out of left field."

"Then he should be thrilled you've gone and that Appletree are shortly going to resign their account."

"That's the point – he's scared that he's got no more hold on us. He can't believe we won't do something to destroy him from the outside." She held Mark's hand tightly, adding, "There's one other thing you should know. I wrote an open letter to the Wall Street Courant. When that's published all hell will break loose at CSF."

"You did what? What the hell did you write?" Mark was aghast.

"I'd rather not discuss that now."

"Fair enough, but we need to spell out the issues at stake. First is your role as Compliance Officer. You were bullied and influenced to turn a blind eye to corrupt practices around market timing. What started as an innocent oversight became fully-fledged complicity once you understood what was going on. That's why you need to tell the SEC before CSF does. Get your plea bargain on the table first."

"That sounds so chilling."

"We need to be completely level-headed. Second, the International Fund was set up with Appletree because we're in London. Remember at the beginning, Shilson said he liked us because we had no other business in America? He thought we would be seduced by the big bucks – which we were, I have to admit – and so tied into the CSF Fund that we couldn't extricate ourselves. If the market timing trades were fewer and smaller we would probably have ignored them. To keep the peace Graham might have settled for a 1 to 2 per cent haircut on performance. But once it got to 6 percent, we had to ring the bell."

"You Appletree guys are implicated too, you know. That's like saying a little bit of crime is all right, but not beyond a certain point. The NASD and SEC will say that no crime is tolerable."

"I agree, but remember that the first trade we became aware of was only in early March – just over a month ago. The trades escalated wildly during the month, and it was always our intention to table it for discussion at the Arizona trustee meeting in April."

"That's what got Bill so rattled. He's not a stable guy, you know. He's facing the end of his lucrative scam to ramp up sales and bonuses for himself and Dick and Shilson."

"Does anyone know we're here in Michigan?"

"Just Brad. He might come visit at the weekend, if the markets calm down."

"Did you ever bring Bill here?"

"You're kidding. His idea of wilderness is a bunker on the golf course. I don't think he ever went to the country in his life. He grew up in Queens. I would never bring him here. Why do you ask?"

"I'm not sure if I was being followed but I think I lost them in Tucson. The question is, did they just want me away from the trustees in Tucson, or did they want me dead? It wouldn't be hard to pick up the trail if they knew I was coming to see you."

"Marko, I don't want you to get so worked up about all this."

"But you're the one who warned me. I didn't exactly have an accident at the resort, but an odd thing happened. I sat in the outdoor hot tub for a while the evening I arrived. Yesterday morning I went down with my towel for another soak and found a wild pig and a chipmunk dead in the water. They were electrocuted. An electric wire was uprooted nearby. If the animals hadn't been killed I would have been zapped in the tub."

"It was probably the animals which uprooted the power line."

"Maybe."

"Here's what I think, Marko. We need to put this stuff away. Now you're here I feel safe . We need to relax and play." Mark didn't comment, but he was confused. Only five minutes earlier Nancy had begun the conversation by announcing that she felt scared.

"Relax and play?" he put his arm around her. "All right. Why don't you start by showing me around the house?"

"Sure, follow me." Nancy opened a door at the back of the kitchen. A steep stairway disappeared into the gloom below. "This . . . " she found the light switch, " . . . is the den. Brad's not cleared it out yet, but they say it's quite fun if you're a man."

The stair opened into a basement area as large as the house, panelled in dark baronial style. An oak banqueting table with matching chairs dominated the room. Suits of armour, armorial shields, swords, halberds and pikes – all fake – were arrayed along the walls. Without any sense of architectural irony, a young man's dream bar dominated the far end of the room. It sported taps of Michelob, Pabst and Budweiser beers. Bottles of spirits were lined up on mirrored shelves behind the bar, beside rows of glasses and beer mugs. A sign hung above the bar: 'Prohibition is better than no whisky at all.'

"Well I'll be damned." Mark had seen similar set ups at friends' flats at university, but never expected to see anything like this in rural Michigan.

"This was my great uncle's secret place. He built it in the 1920s to entertain his friends during Prohibition. They didn't have TV in those days, so they occupied the long winter nights partying, gambling, joking. They were farmers. He lost interest after the war. It was never the same after his brother was killed in the Pacific."

"So this place has been untouched since the 1930s?"

"Pretty much. Come look at this."

Nancy pushed an invisible door that was flush with the panelling. The bulb had long since blown in the small room, but Mark peered inside. He dimly made out cabinet after cabinet of guns. Revolvers, over-and-under and side-by-side shotguns, twelve bores, twenty bores, target rifles, rifles with silencers.

"Jeez, there's a bloody arsenal down here."

"In the 1930s during the Depression, folks wandered around farms to steal food, kill livestock and sometimes worse. There were many desperate people in those days. Hobos jumped off the railroad cars in rural areas to see what they could find. Farmers sometimes had to shoot to kill."

"And your great uncle?"

"He was a devout Lutheran and would never shoot anybody, but he put rumours about in the township that he would shoot to kill anyone foraging on his land."

"Deterrence obviously did the trick." Mark picked up a box of 50 Winchester 22LR hollow point cartridges. "Are these 1930s vintage too?"

"I guess so. Brad never hunts and my great aunt didn't hunt. Family legend goes that she killed a bear with a rifle when she was a girl, but I don't know."

"Mind if I take a look?"

"Go ahead."

Mark lifted a gun off the rack. He cracked open the side-by-side twenty bore and peered through the barrels. "Francotte. Beautiful condition. Have you any idea how valuable this is?"

"Five hundred bucks? I don't know."

"Closer to thirty thousand bucks. Look at the engraving of ducks around the trigger guard. True craftsmanship. What's this?" Mark replaced the shotgun in its rack and picked up a slender rifle. "Bohemia 1928 .22 calibre. Karl Zeiss telescopic lens, neat little silencer." He slid the bolt, "Dry but still workable. A sniper's gun, accurate to about four hundred yards."

"How do you know so much about guns?"

"I spent many summers as a child on my uncle's Scottish estate. We had to shoot deer to keep the numbers down. It's called deer stalking over there. We shot pheasants, grouse and vermin such as rabbits and crows. You get to know a lot about guns and what weapon suits the situation."

"Let's go outside. It's a beautiful day."

Chapter 36

"I'd like to check my mail before we go out and play."

"That's fine Marko, but remember we're on vacation."

"Just in case there's a fire that has to be put out."

"See you downstairs in fifteen."

Mark sat on the bed and scrolled through his emails. He ignored most, like the Daily Asset Reports, bank circulars on currency analysis, the French housing market, the Yen carry trade and interoffice memos on Health and Safety. He opened the first email from Graham :

> *Hi Mark. Bad news – the Bastards got us first! I'm forwarding this email from CSF for your interest. It might appeal to your sense of irony. You don't need to do anything just now. I've acknowledged it and Syreta will liaise with Jessica in Bismarck to ascertain the procedures for handing over the Mutual Fund. Call if you have questions but it can wait until you get back next week.*

Mark read the text :

> *From : Dick Cosway*
> *To : Graham Birch; Mark Telford*
> *Date : April 12, 3.15pm*
> *Re : Change of Manager*
>
> *Bill Tuckwell is not available but he wanted me to advise you of the following :*
>
> *As you know, for some time, our Trustees have been concerned with the performance of the CSF International Fund and have been pressing CSF to take action to improve the situation. Now, because some definitive action will be required by the Board and probably by the shareholders as a result of your poor performance, we think it is likely that*

our Board at its next meeting may either (i) confirm the replacement of Appletree by London International Associates; (ii) recommend merging the International Fund into one of London International's existing funds; or (iii) both. I will keep you advised of developments.

Mark glanced out of the window. Nancy was in the garden filling a flat wicker basket with lilacs and spring flowers. Newly-arrived swallows screeched in the eaves of the farmhouse, building their nests with clean Michigan mud. He was numb.

He scrolled disconsolately through the remaining emails. He enjoyed Graham's response to Cosway. It was defiant, even though there was no hope of changing the outcome :

Dick, as we approach closure on this fund, it is important that Appletree is not misrepresented to the Trustees, the public, or indeed the press, if CSF chooses to go that route.

We only became aware of the 'Trustees' long standing concerns about performance' a few days ago, when Mark went to the meeting in Tucson Arizona. Frankly we are baffled that one month's underperformance should translate into a 'long standing concern', particularly since our 'long term performance' from October through February was consistently in the top decile since inception. It is obvious that the Trustees have failed to appreciate – or chosen to ignore – the phenomenal drag created by CSF-sponsored market timing on the fund's performance . . . You are well aware of the numbers – Syreta, Mark and I have brought them to your attention many times in the past month.

I have personally been involved in the management of 9 international equity mutual funds over the years. This one has been radically different in its cash flows and resulting underperformance.

If other managers at CSF have outperformed with similar cash flow patterns, they should be heartily congratulated, and we evidently do not know how to play the game. The trustees need to be aware of the particular handicap faced by Appletree in managing this fund. I am bringing this to your attention to ensure that the wording of Appletree's termination is mutually agreeable. Graham

Dick's reply was cryptic :

I am not aware of any plans to make any judgmental statements to the press or to shareholders. The Trustees have already requested that we find a replacement, and no negative statements will be made. Dick

Syreta copied him on her exchange of emails :

From : Jessica Schwarz, CSF Bismarck
To : Syreta Mehta, Appletree
Date : April 8, 9.48am
Re : CSF International Fund

I have a quick question. The Trustees have requested that every fund manager provide a list of peer funds to which it compares its performance (in other words, funds that are managed most similarly to their own fund). Do you have a few peer funds to which you compare the performance of the CSF International Fund? The Trustees would greatly appreciate it. Thanks, J

Syreta, God bless her, didn't pull her punches :

Jessica, this is difficult because I am not aware of any other international fund that has experienced the massive cash flow in both directions that this fund experiences. In March alone, the Fund had aggregate two-way cash flows of $7.34 billion on an asset base of $1.4 billion. That's equivalent to $88.1 billion of cash flow through the fund per annum, which is sixty three times the value of the fund. I am challenged to find a relevant peer group for the trustees. Best regards, Syreta

It wasn't too late to call Graham.

"Hey Mark. I take it you've been reading your emails. In less than a year we've gone from the euphoria of unlimited riches to being the boring little investment house we started as. It hurts a lot. We've been badly misjudged.

"Graham, cheer up. At least you didn't have to go through the ritual humiliation in front of Shilson's Trustees. As soon as I started to discuss the market timing I was shut out. Meeting over. Cosway and Tuckwell sniggered together as I gathered up my papers and left the room. But, putting pride to one side, this is the best outcome for us. Remember, we decided on a separation a while ago. There's no point hashing through what went wrong, or why. Shit happens."

"I know. We need to put this behind us as fast as possible and get on with our lives. I just hate being manipulated, used and spat out. All on the pretext of poor performance. What do you think old Wilf Gibson has that we don't? We've out-performed London International for years. In every index, every peer group, every sub-set. Right down to our Japanese small-cap equity portfolios."

"We can only assume that Wilf knows how to play the game. That's probably what he has over us, pure and simple. He'll never get anywhere through performance, as you say, but he gets there through politics, good old fashioned guile and corruption."

"Isn't he going to come a cropper like we did when they approach the end of the current quarter? Shilson and his buddies will want to spice up mutual fund sales to get their bonuses, won't they?"

"Possibly. But for all I know they renegotiated terms at the trustee meeting after I left. Maybe they decided they were flying too close to the sun with their structure of bonuses based on gross sales. It's a licence to fraud. They might just quietly pocket their March 30 bonuses then generously offer to decline future bonuses 'for the benefit of the shareholders'. You can just see the spin they'd put on it."

"Then why did they fire us?"

"We know too much. They want us out of the way, as far as possible from the Fund, from CSF, from America. They'll portray us as a dumb little English investment firm terminated for lousy performance. Supposing the market timing is now going to stop, and only happened for a brief time to leverage their bonuses, they would bury this incident forever by firing us. Then they could section off the fund's lousy performance to coincide with the time we were running it. Easy."

"I suppose there's no point in speculating what happened. You know the old gambling adage; if you look around the card table and can't spot the sucker, the sucker is probably you. Changing the subject, you should be aware that Tuckwell's gone AWOL."

"What d'you mean?"

"I called his mobile after getting this email. It defaulted to messaging. I then called his office and spoke to his secretary. She was in a real state. She said, highly indiscreetly, "Mr Tuckwell's gone missing." I said, "What do you mean, missing?" she replied, "He was due to host an event in Tucson and left the resort without leaving a message or explanation. We can't find him."

"What's the word?"

"He could be anywhere."

"Not that I really give a damn, but I hope they find him where he belongs – under a subway track in a million shreds."

"Charming."

"Anything else to report?"

"Only that the markets are cooperating and our funds are up strongly month-to-date. We're beating the Index by 4% and our peer group by 3.6%. It's good to know that as soon as the market timing stops, our performance races ahead. There's life in the old model yet. Oh – and the Mid Western Teachers are funding us next week."

"I heard that. There's a lot to be cheerful about, isn't there? Not least, I'm about to go on a bike ride with my lady friend. She's absolutely gorgeous. We're staying at her brother's farmhouse in rural Michigan. It's a pretty clapboard house similar to those you see around Kent."

"Sounds like home from home. Give her my regards, will you?"

"Sure."

"Hey, Mister Mark," Nancy called from downstairs. "Your fifteen minutes are up."

"I know, Nancy Lindstrom. One more quick call and I'll be down in your arms."

He called the Hamptons store in New Buffalo and ordered a case of champagne to be delivered later in the day 'From an admirer', and bounded downstairs to find Nancy. She was arranging an armful of spring flowers on the kitchen counter. Vases of daffodils, hyacinths, lilac and tulips were deployed around the house in a sweet cloud of fragrance.

"I adore flowers. A house without flowers is a sad place. What do you think, Marko?"

"What do I think? I think we should go on our bike ride." He kissed her.

"Not before you tell me who you called and what emails you were reading?"

"I called Graham and my emails were the usual boring crop of stuff that I deleted straight away."

"How about your little London lovebird?"

"She's history."

Chapter 37

Arm in arm, they strolled across to the barn.

Heaving and giggling like children they managed to slide back the colossal creaking red door on its rusted runners. The cavernous space inside was a trove of obsolete agricultural equipment. A row of parked tractors dating from the 1920s to the 1960s, spring harrows, rollers, a horse-drawn plough with its harnesses, pit saws, wooden hay rakes, hoes, chick incubation boxes, corn-huskers, seed drilling machines, chains and pulleys attached to a gargantuan oak rafter strong enough to take the weight of an engine block from a combine harvester.

Lines of tools were arrayed above a mechanic's work bench, each carefully labelled and numbered to correspond with the equipment it was designed to fit. Then the bikes. At least twenty bicycles in various sizes and states of decrepitude hung off pegs behind the bench.

"There you go, Darling." Nancy pointed to the collection, "Take your pick. There's that old Schwinn with three gears. Or you can go high tech." She pointed at a contraption with a wooden frame and spokes. "I'm going to take this one." She said, selecting a Huffy ladies' bike.

"I'll take this. The male version of your Huffy. It's a modern one; younger than I am, at any rate."

They laughed as they dusted the frames, squirted oil on the chains, pumped tyres and sorted the saddle heights. Nancy's was too low; Mark's too high. They found a set of wrenches and made the adjustments, but couldn't get them tight again. The bolt threads had been stripped over the years.

"That's as tight as they'll get. Prepared to risk it?" Mark enquired.

"Sure. Let's go."

"This feels like a mediaeval castration device. Oh well. Where shall we go?" Mark shouted as they freewheeled down the drive.

"Down Krieger Road. It's long and straight for a mile, then it gets twisty through the woods. It's a beautiful day for cycling. Ready?"

The open prairie-like countryside around the farm began to close in as they cycled along the narrow road. It became wooded, with small undulating fields and hedgerows reminiscent of Sussex or Somerset. The scenery shifted from large scale arable fields to tidy fruit farms. They passed vineyards in the first flush of spring growth, majestic hickory and oak woods, neat farmhouses and ramshackle red barns.

"Take a look at that, Marko." They came to a curve with a view of the surrounding fields. On both sides of the road, acres of fruit trees were in full blossom. A light, heady scent floated on the breeze.

"It's unbelievable. It's so quiet here. Can you hear the insects buzzing?" Mark marvelled at the ranks of pink-blossomed trees.

"Billions of bees are enjoying their first outing of the season. Let's hide our bikes behind that gate so nobody can see them. I want to show you something." They dismounted and Nancy took Mark's hand.

They walked along the edge of the field for a short distance and into a nearby wood. There was a faint path through a magical carpet of white flowers.

"Milliums of trilliums, as Dad used to say. They've been here since the Ice Age. And so has this . . . "

Nancy brushed a branch aside to reveal a pond about thirty yards wide and sixty long.

"This is our little spring-fed pond. The water's always the same temperature whatever the time of year." Nancy pushed branches aside until they reached a rickety wooden jetty. The water was turquoise and brilliantly clear. "We used to come and swim here when we were kids. So did my Mom, my Grandmother and our ancestors back to the 1870s."

They sat on the jetty, their feet dangling in the water.

"I know it's April, but the water feels pleasant enough." Mark slipped a hand under her tee shirt and kissed her mouth. "I think we should continue the family tradition and take a swim."

"Me too". She put her arms around his neck and held him.

They stripped and leaped into the pond. Mark was surprised that he couldn't stand in the water. There was no bordering marshland, no shelf. The pond just went straight down. It reminded him of a Mayan sink hole he'd encountered in the Yucatan. They swam the length a few times and hauled themselves back onto the jetty. Nancy lay on her side, water drops glistening on her skin as she dried in the sunshine. Her eyes were closed. Mark watched her, propping his head on one elbow.

"You know how gorgeous you are? I don't know where to start. You're my dream girl."

"You Brits always talk fancy about everything but never move on anything. You can start by kissing me and getting me excited, real slow."

Together they played on the jetty in the sunshine. Afterwards they lay peacefully, staring up at the pale green aspen leaves dappling their bodies.

"For the first time in my life," Mark kissed her neck. "I'm completely content. I know I've found the right person. I'm crazy about you."

"I forgot to say, Marko, but I'm coming back to London with you next week."

"Yes?"

"Yeah. We need to stop futzing around and get down to business."

"Will you marry me, Nancy?"

"I need time to think about that."

She paused for a moment.

"OK."

"You will?"

"Absolutely."

They dressed and returned to the bikes. The ride back up Krieger Road was long and slow by comparison to the open-hearted free-wheel they'd enjoyed coming down. Mark led the way uphill.

Vehicles on the road were sparse. They were overtaken by two old pickups and a muddy John Deere hauling a trailer, driving about 40 mph. It was a surprise, therefore, to see a sleek black limousine barrelling down the hill towards them at high speed. A Lincoln with Illinois plates and darkened windows shot past at 90 mph.

"Wow, you could easily get sucked into the slipstream of that thing. I wonder what the President's doing in such a hurry around here?" Mark looked back at Nancy. She wasn't there. "Nancy?" he shouted, "Nancy? Where are you?" He rode his bike back downhill to the spot where the Lincoln had roared past her. No sign of her. The roadside verge was scrubby, flanked by a narrow ditch with a few inches of stagnant water at the bottom. On the far side of the ditch was a marshy wood with aspens, birch and sassafras saplings. The undergrowth was dense.

He caught a glint in the woods and blundered his way through. It was a bike, mangled, its front wheel bent at a right angle. "Dear God, where are you, Nancy? This is serious. Please don't play games if you can hear me."

He searched around the bike. No Nancy. He snapped small branches with his hands in desperation to create space in the woods, when he saw the white among the trees. It was her tee shirt. She lay motionless, her head bent grotesquely to one side, eyes open, blood dripping from the corner of her mouth onto the whiteness of a trillium flower. The pretty blue ribbon still held back her pony tail. "Oh God, please tell me this is a horrible dream." Mark felt her pulse. Nothing. He put his ear to her mouth. No breathing.

"NO!" he screamed and fell on his knees. He pressed her hand to his lips. Her slim, feminine, practical hand.

He heard a car approaching on the road. He stumbled back through the undergrowth and blindly waved at the driver. "Help, please help."

The Lincoln braked and a window hummed open. The driver was alone in the front ; he wore dark glasses.

"Good God, it's you." Mark instantly recognized the man who had collided with him in London and stalked him in the Metropolitan Museum.

He was like a caricature of a Mafia getaway driver. Looking over his shoulder, he spoke to someone on the back seat. "We got the wrong one. You got me to bang my goddam limo for the wrong fucking guy." Mark heard raucous laughter from the back seat. The man had lost his pseudo-Cockney accent and reverted to neighbourhood Chicagoan.

He turned to Mark , "You goddam lucky I gotta make this look like an accident, Buster, or I'd pop you right now. I'll be back to finish the job." He spat a ball of gum out the window. The Lincoln fishtailed off the edge of the road, showering gravel over Mark. All that remained was the smell of exhaust fumes in the spring air. And the desperate, devastating silence of the crushed pile of broken rags on the forest floor.

Chapter 38

Mark made a detailed statement to the Eauborne Deputy Sheriff. He played naïve, portraying it as a freak accident, saying that 'the Mercedes probably didn't even know it hit her.' He didn't report that the car was a Lincoln with Illinois plates. He knew they would be back to get him, one way or the other, and soon. He knew that if he were to make a truthful statement to the police, it would take a long time for the driver to be brought to justice, if ever. It would boil down to one man's word against another.

He decided to handle this situation privately. If he got killed in the process, so what? He'd already lost everything. If he killed and was apprehended, he would plead self-defence. In his febrile state the odds seemed in his favour. It was between him and them, and they had no idea that he might have an offensive strategy.

Nancy lay in the township funeral home. Mark sat beside her until dusk. He desperately wanted to be with her, stay all night and talk, tell her how crazy he was about her. But even funeral homes have visiting hours; even spirits needed to settle down.

Bruno barked furiously when Mark entered the kitchen, his hackles rising. Mark kneeled to pat his head. "Don't worry old chap, it's only me. I'm on my own now." The Labrador had been cooped inside the house for fourteen hours. Mark let him out. The soft fragrance of Nancy's vases of lilac and hyacinths filled the hall and the kitchen. A note was stuck in the back door :

"You were out so we left the box of champagne in the woodshed. We appreciate your order."

He sat moping in the kitchen, emptying the remains of a bottle of bourbon and opening a fresh quart of The Glenlivet. Bruno knew something was up as he lay quietly at Mark's feet. The joy of seeing his new friend was dampened by the weight of events.

Mark reflected about Nancy's happy summers around the farm as a child with her Great Aunt Eva. The frayed rope of the swing tied to the branch of the walnut tree was still there. It was the same swing that heard Nancy's girlish laughter twenty years ago. He thought about the pond where generations of Olsens swam.

He was shattered and dazed. His face was a mess of tears. He stood up shakily and took the oval kitchen mirror from the wall beside the door. He returned to his seat, and began a disjointed conversation with his grim face. "I asked her to marry me as we lay on the jetty. She said , "I'm gonna have to think about that". She waited five seconds then said 'OK.' in such a cute way."

"Yeah?

"Yeah."

Mark sobbed; over-lubricated with bourbon and Highland spirits.

"Nancy took me into the den, downstairs. She showed me the guns."

"The guns? No kidding?"

"Yeah. She said, they're old and too dangerous to keep lying about. She said they'd been lying there for generations."

"Are they registered?

"I doubt it. They've been lying in there for seventy years. Nobody knows they exist."

"What are the rules in Michigan about guns and self-defence?"

"Got me there, Marko. I guess if someone prowls around your place with intent you're allowed to shoot them. Why'd ya ask?"

"In Britain if someone breaks into your house, steals everything, beats you up, kills your children, rapes your wife and burns your house down, and you injure them in the mêlée, the criminal can take you to court."

"What kinda goddam cockamammy legal system is that?"

"Good question." Mark replied to himself in the haze, rising unsteadily off the kitchen chair. "Very good question . . . I'm going to bed. I pray to wake up in the morning and find that this has all been a horrible dream."

His eyes were red with whisky and tears. He leaned on the table and squinted hard at himself in the dim light.

"What's up, sport?"

"What's up is that your face is so bloody rough that Nancy wouldn't have given you a second look. Get a grip."

It was many years since Mark last experienced Pillow Vortex. He had not drunk on this scale since his early student days. His head spun vertiginously the instant he lay down. Seismic convulsions rose through his gut like magma in a volcano. He staggered off the bed and discharged a bilious cocktail of whiskies out of the window into the lilacs below. He retched and retched; he retched until he spat the last squeeze of bitter fluid out of his body.

He fell to his knees, leaned on the open sill and wept into the warm night.

It was still dark when he groped his way to the bathroom and stood under a cold shower for twenty minutes, washing, scrubbing and swallowing the shower water. A cracking headache pulsed behind his eyes. He fought to regain focus.

"If . . . I were them and wanted to arrange an accident, what would I do here in Michigan? It's the middle of bloody nowhere . . . Farm equipment – unlikely. Car accident? Still an option. Electrocution? Tried in Tucson. Failed. A fall? Where from? The barn, of course. Sheriff looks at the crumpled body and says, "Poor bastard fell off the ladder. No suspicious circumstances". They would have a double funeral in the Eauborne Township Cemetery. Nancy and the guy she had up for the weekend. Some fancy Brit laid to rest in the plot beside her in the Michigan soil.

"A fire . . . ? I might try a fire. How to be sure the fire would work? At 4 am, long after the lights went out, I'd sprinkle petrol or some other kind of accelerant along the clapboard and light it. Flames would lick up into the eaves and the property's an inferno in minutes.

I'd have a couple of fellows on picket outside the house. If someone staggered out in flames their job would be to throw him back in the fire. Skeletal cinders in minutes. The local newspaper would report on the Terrible Double Tragedy hitting the Olsen family. Young Nancy killed in the afternoon, the Olsen Homestead in flames the same night. Boyfriend dead in the conflagration. A terrible, frightful coincidence. Everybody loved Nancy. There would not be the slightest hint of a motive for all these awful things to befall the family.

Mark crept downstairs into the kitchen. Bruno's tail swept the floor lazily when he appeared. His ears went back. Mark reached down to hug the dog for a moment. "Dear old Bruno. You have no idea how much Nancy meant to me." He opened the den door. It creaked loudly, as did the stairs leading downstairs. Funny, he hadn't noticed the creaking earlier. He stumbled across the baronial basement and pushed the secret panel to open the gun room door.

He didn't have time to match up stray bits of ammunition with the guns on display, so he grabbed what he knew would work. He took the

Bohemia .22 with telescopic lens and a box of fifty hollow point cartridges. He closed the door, retreated through the den and returned upstairs into the kitchen.

The gun was light and lethal. He liked the feel of the stock, the telescopic lens and the silencer. It was decades old and the bolt was stiff. He lubricated it with olive oil from the kitchen and slid the bolt in and out of the breech until its movement was smooth and slick. The motion was almost silent after the oil had worked its way through the gun's parts. It reminded him of a well-oiled engine piston.

Mark inserted ten bullets with his right thumb into the spring-loaded magazine and fitted it into the chamber slot until it clicked. He adjusted the range finder to 70 yards. Far enough for them not to hear the bullet exploding from the silencer; near enough to blow a man's brains out. He'd heard of people being killed a mile away with stray .22 bullets.

Mark was in shock from the day's events. He was going to protect Nancy's heritage to the last bullet. He had nothing more to lose. He expected that Telford's Last Stand would probably kill him. And he knew he didn't care.

In his drunken anger he was determined to keep the bastards away from her family house. He saw her flowers bursting out of the vases. It was all too precious. He would take the fight to them long before they reached the front step, and before they even realized they were in a fight.

Mark slipped out of the back door into the night. It was warm for a Michigan April, dry and cloudless. A half moon provided enough light to create shadows. It hung to the north of the farm.

"Good," he whispered, "they'll be silhouetted if they come up the drive".

Mark took a tarp and a horse blanket from the barn. He tried various locations, finally deciding to lie behind a low tree stump on the edge of the lawn. *If I were them and someone attacked me in the darkness I would assume that fire was coming from a barn window, or the corner of a building. Nobody would expect it to come from a small mound on the flat lawn.*

He was too mad and muddled to care about planning an escape route. He controlled the element of surprise. He should be able to shoot a couple of them before they realized they were under attack in the darkness. Chances are any survivors would then get the hell out of the place. In fact, he mustn't kill too many because survivors were needed to take away the bodies. They would need to be dumped in Lake Michigan or on a conveyor belt, tipping scrap steel into a smelter at the US Steel plant in Gary Indiana. So reasoned his addled brain.

Mark wrapped himself in the horse blanket and lay on the tarp. He locked a bullet into the chamber, checked the safety catch and waited. He played with fields of fire from his tree stump. Nancy called him for lunch. "Hey Honey, I've got the best ham in Michigan. Want a sandwich and a bottle of beer?" "Sure" "You know what I want to do in London?" "No, what do you want to do in London?" "Have your baby." "That's heavy stuff." "No it won't be heavy. She'll be a beautiful baby. Absolutely the most beautiful baby in the world." "I can't wait for you to have my baby. We'll have a lot of babies." "A lot of babies?" "Sure, Honey, un homme et une femme. That's what it's all about." The delicious tape played continuously in Mark's whiskied underworld.

He woke to the familiar crunch of tyres on gravel. It was still dark; he could faintly make out the time on his scratched Omega. Four o'clock. He felt nauseous. A car had entered the drive, turned on the front lawn and stopped by the gate, facing back out towards Krieger Road. Its engine stopped and the lights clicked off. Mark strained in the darkness to recognize the car. It might be a lovers' tryst. He'd hate to blow away a pair of innocent kids out for a romp in the back seat of a car. He stared into the telescopic lens looking for an identification opportunity. The lights of the car momentarily went on and off again. He heard two words from the open window, 'Goddam Jackass.' and spotted the Illinois plates on the Lincoln in that split-second.

Mark was cold, cramped, drunk and exhausted. He wanted to sleep, more than anything in the world. He wasn't in the mood to kill a man. On the other hand, he wasn't much in the mood to be killed either.

"Homicide doesn't look too good on a CV. Why not just lie low and slip away? But the bastards are here to destroy sweet Nancy's house. More to the point, they're here to destroy *me*. If they don't get me now they'll keep trying until they do. If I sought cop protection they wouldn't believe me so I may as well slug this one out myself. They won't let me leave Michigan alive."

He tensed behind the scope. A breeze shimmered along the front hedge, shaking the leaves. The trees sighed. Wind chimes tinkled faintly from the back door in the distance. A flashlight went on in the car. Mark watched the men pass a sheet of paper between themselves. They gesticulated and seemed to be tapping the paper aggressively. Three guys. He slipped the safety catch. How he'd love to talk through their differences rather than kill anyone.

The front passenger door opened. A man's voice said, "See you in ten." The door clicked shut. Mark squeezed the trigger. *Pffft.*

The shot was almost soundless. The man dropped like a sack a few yards behind the car. It was so clinical that the others were probably not even aware of their friend's demise. The sack was silent. No moans, no movement.

Strike one for Nancy.

Mark slid the bolt back to load a second bullet into the chamber. He pocketed the spent cartridge case. It was a habit he'd been taught by the family gamekeeper in Scotland. Never leave a trace.

"I'm in really, really deep now. This is totally surreal. What's the CEO of a London investment firm doing in the grass, killing people with a sniper's gun on a farm in Michigan? I'm just a money manager. How did I get here? This has to be the weirdest predicament on the planet at this precise moment. Who did I kill? Does he have a family? Naa – He was probably an irritating little shit; no loss to humanity. Could Tuckwell be in the car? Surely not? Who else was there? A couple of low-life killers from Chicago, probably.

Activity was picking up in the car. The torch flicked on and off. They looked agitated, looking back towards the house, apparently arguing who should go and find their accomplice. The rear left passenger door opened. Mark heard talking in low tones but couldn't make out what was being said.

A figure got out and closed the door with a click. Mark squeezed the trigger. Not so clean this time. His victim gave a single sharp yelp and staggered against the rear end of the car, propped himself for a moment and slid to the ground with a thud.

Strike two for Nancy.

Mark slid the bolt back to load a third bullet into the chamber. He kept the second spent cartridge case.

"There's no way the other guy couldn't have heard that." he muttered. "He'll be shitting himself, big time. One pal hasn't returned, the other was shot. What if he realizes he's alone in hostile territory?" Mark's adrenalin was up. He had already decided to shoot them all if the occasion arose. This was easier than stalking a stag in the Highlands. Many were the times he'd spent the daylight hours of an autumn day in Sutherland scrambling on his hands and knees through tundra, heather, rocks and ice, yet failed to catch his quarry.

Mark peered through the telescopic lens. A faint streak of dawn began to spread across the eastern sky. Two lumps lay motionless by the car. "What's the other guy going to do? Shall I wound him? Shoot his legs so he has to check into a trauma ward in Michigan City? He looked through the scope and studied the back of the car. Clouds scudded past the moon, obscuring his vision. He waited for a moment, got a fix on the left rear tyre and squeezed the trigger. *Pfffftt.*

Mark slid the bolt back to load a fourth bullet in the chamber. He kept the third spent cartridge case.

He looked through the scope and studied the back of the car again. He got another fix and squeezed the trigger. *Pfffftt.* "That's both rear tyres shot out. I wonder if the guy has any idea what's going on?"

Mark slid the bolt back to load the fifth bullet in the chamber, pocketing the fourth spent cartridge case.

The engine started. Mark had a fix on the driver's head as soon as he switched on the lights. He squeezed the trigger. The back and front windscreens shattered into crazy opaque pieces. The car accelerated out of the driveway and headed west on Krieger Road. The driver was very much alive. Mark heard the car picking up speed through the automatic gears as it raced down Krieger Road. It sounded like it was driving as fast as when it hit Nancy.

Mark slid the bolt back to load the sixth bullet in the chamber.

The car was almost out of earshot when an explosion ripped through the darkness. Mark ran out onto Krieger Road. At the end of the long downhill straight an orange fireball hung over the woods. The car had failed to take the corner with its burst tyres.

Strike three for Nancy.

Mark cleared the bullet chamber. He walked over to inspect his victims. They lay face down on the driveway. He turned the first body face upwards. It rolled over, limp arms flopping over on the gravel. A wavy-bladed combat knife fell out of his right hand.

"Holy hell!" Mark staggered backwards. The man had a small hole drilled neatly in his forehead. The back of his head was a mess of wet hair and matted blood. His eyes stared vacantly into the sky; his mouth smiled grotesquely in the thickening stubble of his face. "I shot Jack Bolt."

He tugged the arm of the second corpse. It wore a back to front baseball cap. An automatic pistol lay on the gravel nearby. Mark recognized the driver of the limo from the previous day, the man who vowed to come after him. The bullet had smashed through his throat and severed his spinal column.

"I wonder who the hell the third guy was in the car. What's going on?" Mark was past endurance. He hauled the corpses behind the hedge, picked up their weapons with his sleeve, threw them beside their owners and covered everything neatly with the tarp. "I'll deal with this stuff later. Got to sleep."

Chapter 39

Mark was dragged from the mire of dead sleep by the sound of persistent barking. At first, he was a boy playing with the family terrier in his childhood garden. He threw a boomerang; it made an arc around the trees, turned back and whacked him in the eye. A path in the back of the garden led up to a mountain in Switzerland where he was hiking with his father. They were set upon by an ugly mongrel, part sheepdog, part wolf, snarling at their ankles. His father clouted the dog's balls with a walking stick. Instead of scaring the beast, it became demented and leaped at their faces.

His caked eyes opened. The curtains wafted back and forth at the open window. It was a flawless day, sunshine dappling into the room. He was alone, fully clothed, filthy. Bruno barked furiously downstairs. The bedside clock told him it was 2.17pm. His head, neck and shoulders crackled; his entire skeleton ached. A door slammed. Bruno fell silent.

He heard footsteps on the staircase; a man's voice called, "Mark? Are you there?" It sounded urgent, but pleasant enough, oddly familiar.

He managed to swing his feet onto the floor when the door opened. A tall, slim, brown-haired young man entered.

"Are you Mark?"

Mark groaned. He braced himself for the shot. His face was creased and stubbly. "Go on. Do what you have to do."

"Sorry?"

Surprised to be alive, Mark looked up. "Who are you?"

"I'm Brad, Nancy's brother. I've just been to the township morgue. What the hell's going on here?"

"You're Brad?"

"Yes. I'm Brad. You're in my house and my sister's dead. What in God's name is going on?"

"*You're* Brad?" Mark repeated.

"Look, you're a real mess, man. Take a shower, shave yourself, get into clean clothes. I'll wait for you downstairs with a coffee. Be quick."

Mark shuffled through to the bathroom. He stared at the mirror. He sported two days of stubble. His eyes were puffy and bloodshot. His black hair was greasy and matted. He had aged ten years in one night.

He shaved in the cold, high pressure shower, bizarrely whistling the leitmotif of a Handel Organ Concerto. The music was like a prayer. It helped to focus his splintered brain. He dried, pulled on his jeans and a clean shirt, slipped into his shoes and padded downstairs. Bruno welcomed him in the kitchen; ears back, tail swinging. Brad sat motionless facing the door, his hands flat on the kitchen table. He made no effort to hide that he had been crying.

"Brad?"

"Yes, Mark, I'm Brad." He spoke quietly. "Now will you tell me what in God's name is going on? Why didn't I hear about this until today? I was on a flight to Nassau this morning. We were taxiing towards takeoff. The pilot announced we were returning to the gate. The door was disarmed; the flight attendant announced, *Would Mr Bradley Lindstrom please identify himself?* I was escorted off the plane and met by a Chicago cop. The Chicago Police Department had been requested urgently by the Eauborne Township Sheriff's Department to track me down. The cop told me my sister Nancy was killed in a road accident in Michigan yesterday. Why wasn't I told yesterday?" Brad had the same intonations as his sister, the same hands, the same eyes.

"I killed three guys last night." Mark said flatly.

"Excuse me?"

"I killed three guys."

"What the hell's going on?"

"I killed them because they killed Nancy. They were prowling around the property last night."

"The Sheriff said Nancy was knocked off her bike in an accident. You're saying she was killed?"

"It was murder, Brad. I saw the guys. As soon as they knocked her off the bike they drove back along Krieger Road and said they would come back for me. After spending a few hours at the funeral home I returned here. I sat drinking for a while at the kitchen table, trying to make sense of things. Then I went upstairs. I was too sick to sleep. I took a long shower. I had a hunch that they would be coming to find me. I went to your gunroom, took a .22 and a box of ammunition and went outside to wait for them."

"How did you know about the gunroom?"

"Nancy showed me. She gave me a tour of the house." Mark paused, adding, "Yesterday morning."

"OK – So you thought they were coming to get you while you were asleep in the house, so you went outside?"

"Correct. I was too wired to sleep and too drunk to think. I hid in the garden with the gun, waiting for them."

"How did you know 'they' would show up?"

"I didn't. It was just a hunch. I bundled myself up in a rug on the lawn. I woke up when a car hit the gravel driveway about four o'clock. I was lying behind the tree stump down there." Mark gestured with his thumb. "The car turned on the lawn and parked, facing back down Krieger Road. I saw three guys in the car. One got out. I shot him behind the car. The shot was silenced; it was so quiet the others didn't know he was hit. Some time later another guy got out. I shot him too, but he made a noise going down. The last guy stayed in the car for a while. I shot out his rear tyres while he sat waiting."

During Mark's description of the mayhem, Brad looked incredulous. "So – run that by me again. You were lying on the front lawn and killed two guys with that old .22 in the basement?"

"Yup. That's not all. After a while the guy in the car got spooked. He switched on the ignition and roared off down Krieger Road. I tried to shoot him as he turned but I missed. I blew out his windscreen. He didn't know his tyres were shot. He didn't make the corner at the end of the long straight and banged into the trees at 80 miles an hour. The car blew up."

"So you were responsible for last night? The Sheriff said a guy was fried in a car, didn't know who he was. It had out-of-state plates."

"Illinois."

"So who were these guys who killed my sister?"

"Colleagues from CSF, as far as I can tell."

"But why? Nancy was a great kid. She wouldn't harm a mouse."

"I know. But Nancy had some inside knowledge at CSF that they had to suppress. She'd just resigned. She was mixed up with one of the senior guys who used to date her. She dumped him. I became a target because of that."

"So they killed her?"

"So they killed her."

Mark looked at his hands. After a few minutes he said quietly, "She took me to your family pond yesterday. We went swimming."

Brad studied his face. "She used to say when she was a little girl that she'd only ever take one man there, and that she would marry him."

Mark looked at his hands clasped on the table and smiled sadly.

Brad smiled for the first time since they met. He leaned across the table and put his hand on Mark's shoulder,

"I'm real, real sorry, Buddy."

They sat in silence for a few minutes.

"What about the guys you shot? Where are they?"

"Under the tarp by the front hedge."

The Sheriff rolled up, followed by an unmarked police ambulance. He handcuffed Mark and bundled him into the back of his car. A colleague put on a pair of surgical gloves and lifted the knife and pistol carefully into forensic plastic bags. The corpses were loaded into the ambulance. "This sounds like a case of trespass with intent to commit a crime. In the State of Michigan you can defend your property with firearms if you can prove the intruder intended to commit a violent act. Of course it's a rebuttable presumption, but the law is on the side of self-defence." The Sheriff was almost apologetic. "This looks like a case of justifiable homicide, sir, but we need to follow the usual procedures."

After a surprisingly short stay in the county Sheriff's office, Mark was released on a bail bond of $50,000. "Please do not leave the area until we finish our enquiries."

"How long will that be?"

"Up to two weeks, sir."

Nancy's funeral service was held in the white clapboard Lutheran church on the main street of Eauborne. Her parents, cousins, aunts and uncles drove in from Muscatine, Iowa. They were dignified, kindly, god-fearing folks. The pastor had known Nancy as a little girl visiting the church over the years. She was buried in an open prairie cemetery beside her Great Aunt Eva.

On the evening after the funeral Mark returned alone to Nancy's grave. The light was fading and it was quiet but for a pair of cardinals singing and courting together in the hanging branches of a gnarled hemlock in the cemetery. He kneeled by the fresh mound of earth and read the condolence notes attached to the wreaths and bouquets. Graham had sent a bouquet of lilies, with a note, "from all your friends at Appletree in London". There were no flowers from anyone at CSF.

A softly scented wreath of tightly interlaced white carnations, red roses and blue hyacinths caught Mark's eye. The attached note read: "As with these three colours, we were bound together in ways that you never knew. Another time, another space, your admirer and friend, Syreta Mehta."

He heard the Sheriff's car arrive on the gravel driveway. He rose from the kitchen table and opened the front door. Bruno ran out and barked at the intruder. The Sheriff threw the dog half a donut. Silence.

"Mr Telford, the State Prosecutor has determined that your role in the events of last week was not criminal." The Sheriff pulled out a notebook from his hip pocket.

"It was determined that you killed two armed men, intruding on this farm with clear intent to harm you and the property. A notebook was found on one of the bodies containing a detailed plan of this property, indicating the best places to set fire. Forensic tests show the weapons originated with the intruders and were not planted by you. More weapons and fire accelerants were found in the remains of the car that crashed along Krieger Road. The guns were loaded so it is presumed that the intruders harboured ill-intent as they entered the Olsen farm property. Our forensic examiners found two fired .22 slugs on the road.

"Krieger Road?"

"Yes sir. The spent slugs were determined to come from the rifle you used. They correspond to the spent cartridge cases you gave to the police department. Your story lines up with the evidence. You may be required at a later date to appear as a State witness, but you are free to return to your country."

"Do you have any positive identification of the people who died?"

"Yes sir." The Sheriff flicked through the pages of his notebook. "The two gentlemen deceased on this property from gunshot wounds were a Mr Tony Veronese, from Chicago Illinois and a Mr Jack Bolt, from Hoboken New Jersey. The gentleman deceased in the car on Krieger Road has been identified as a Mr William Tuckwell from New York City."

"Thank you."

"Their remains will be held for further forensic examination prior to being released to relatives for disposal as they see fit."

Mark's cell phone rang, "Telford speaking".

"Blazerman here. They blew the lid off CSF, man. Did ya see the *Wall Street Courant* this morning?"

"No – what's the scoop?"

"Front page shows Shilson, Cosway and six other guys chained together and paraded outside the CSF building in Lower Manhattan like a Georgia chain gang. They were arrested on multiple charges of fraud, theft, front-running, insider trading, racketeering, deception and breaching the securities code of New York State. Prosecutor's getting them under RICO."

"RICO?"

"Yeah, RICO – the Racketeering Influenced and Corrupt Organizations Act. It's legislation aimed to catch the financial turds they can't catch any other way."

"What triggered the arrest?"

"Your sweetheart, Buddy. Didn't you see? Nancy sent an open letter to the Wall Street Courant detailing the market timing trades, the CSF bonus structure, Shilson's personal use of the executive jet, how your International Fund was shafted, how the trustees were in Shilson's pocket.

Nancy fessed up totally about her complicity in the CSF deal. Let me read what she said, here, "As Compliance Officer of CSF I accept full responsibility for my inability to enforce strict ethical and legal guidelines among my superiors. I accept the legal sanctions that may come my way as a result of this failure. I apologize sincerely to all the clients of CSF who trusted us to be guardians of their savings, and whom we let down." She goes on further – you can get the paper for yourself.

"Shareholder interest groups have already filed suits against CSF. I hear a sum of $50 billion in reparations is being sought. She's one classy, courageous broad, Buddy. You should be real proud of her integrity."

"Frank, she's dead."

"Pardon me?"

"Nancy's dead, Frank. She was killed in a road accident here in Michigan."

"Sorry?"

"DEAD, Frank. She's dead."

"Holy excrement. I'm so goddam sorry. What happened?"

"I was with her. We were biking along a quiet road a few days ago. A car with Illinois plates hit and killed her deliberately."

"Who were they, Mark?" The wind was out of Frank Blazerman's voice.
"Guys from CSF."
"I can't credit this stuff you're telling me, Buddy."
"It's totally true."
"It says in the Courant that the one key guy they couldn't find at CSF was Bill Tuckwell."
"He's dead, Frank."
"Pardon me?"
"DEAD. His car exploded."
"Jeez man, what the hell happened? Was it you?"
"No, Frank. Just a chain of weird coincidences. I'm not implicated."
"So what's gonna happen with you?"
"I'm going to finish my vacation in Michigan, then go back to London."
"If I can help in any way, Buddy, you know who to call."
"I appreciate that, Frank. I don't think I'll be looking for another joint venture any time soon, but I'll let you know."
"Any time, Buddy. Just keep away from those financial shysters."

Chapter 40

Mark was invited by Brad to stay in Michigan 'for as long as it takes, buddy.' Brad returned to Chicago the day after Nancy's funeral, leaving Mark with the run of the property. For three weeks he biked and walked over the farm with Bruno, restlessly exploring every field, every track, every barn, every hickory ravine. In the afternoons he finished his ramblings by detouring to the pond. He would sit on the jetty for a while and slip into the water. He lay naked on the old planks to dry out, staring through the aspen leaves at the dappled sunshine. The place was electric. She whispered to him, "Stay and keep me warm, Marko, please stay." Defeated, at dusk he cycled slowly back up the road to the farmhouse.

He bought a gold ring at a jeweller near the campus of Notre Dame University in South Bend and had it engraved with the initials NL – MT. At dawn on his final day in Michigan he cycled to the pond. He stood on the jetty, intoned a short prayer and threw the ring into the deep. He never looked back.

Brad's car was parked in the driveway when Mark returned to the farmhouse with Bruno. They met in the kitchen. "Hey buddy, thought I'd come down to see you before you headed off today."

"How nice to see you. I really appreciate your hospitality and you giving me the run of the farm for these few weeks."

"It's the least I could do, buddy. I can see that Bruno's had fun."

"Perhaps you could come and stay in London one of these days?. There's plenty of space."

"That would be a good trip."

That evening Mark drove to O'Hare Airport and flew to London. It was time to return to his world.

"Hey, Mark's here" Wendy shouted from Reception as he walked into the office. He was immediately surrounded by his Appletree colleagues, chattering and welcoming him with spontaneous comradeship.

"Great to see you again. I'm so very sorry about everything that happened." Graham gave his partner an affectionate pat on the shoulder.

"I appreciate you saying that."

"I've got some interesting news. I'm in the middle of a trade but come in when you've finished reacquainting yourself with everybody."

Mark was relieved that nobody pitied him. He was treated with genuine warmth. Syreta hugged him; Alix, Bob and Clarissa shook his hand heartily. He eventually made his way to Graham's office, feeling quite robust.

"So what's the scoop?"

"The scoop is that we are still managing the CSF International Fund. An interim board of trustees was appointed by the SEC and they determined that we are the best managers for the job. Your whistle-blowing at the trustee meeting in Arizona and dear Nancy's open letter to the Wall Street Courant convinced them that we're squeaky clean. Shilson and Cosway are on bail. They've publicly accused Bill Tuckwell of engineering the market timing programme and Nancy of covering it up."

"What an incredibly cheap shot." Mark's hackles rose at the thought of Shilson shifting the blame onto his dead colleagues. And accusing Nancy, for pity's sake.

"They both claim they knew nothing about the market timing. Tuckwell was Director of Sales & Marketing and was a well-known control freak so it's been easy to make him look responsible. I should warn you that their lawyers have been quick to portray Nancy as Bill's malleable piece of fluff. Cosway and Shilson are being defended vigorously as innocent bystanders, victims of their colleagues' greed, deceit and dishonesty."

"I'm speechless"

"I understand – but it's their only viable defence strategy. If it makes you feel better, and if recent cases are anything to go by, it looks like they'll get hefty penalties. Because of their position at CSF they'll be held liable. They'll have to disgorge their bonuses to compensate shareholders of the fund. Plus there will be a huge fine for CSF. And did you hear about Vern?"

"No – what's his story?"

"Vern was arrested with the others for his part in promoting the market timing scam. He claimed he was under orders from Cosway, Tuckwell and Shilson and had no choice. At first he played the dumb southern kid, but this act was blown apart by Shilson's defence team. Then he approached the prosecutor and on a plea bargain offered to give all the evidence they needed to incriminate Cosway and Shilson."

"Nasty little shit." Mark reflected, "Well I suppose there is some justice in the world."

"We're beginning to hear about indictments at other mutual fund groups. If you look on the Internet, some very big names are being fined for their part in market timing scams."

"I'll take a look. I'll search for Mutual Fund Market Timing Scams and see what comes up."

"On a brighter note our performance is righting itself. Since April 1 we're in the first quartile again. Cash flow is steady. It looks like Appletree is going through calmer waters."

"That's a relief. Look, why don't we catch up with a drink after work? I'll go back to my office and wade through my backlog of mail and emails."

"Great idea. Five o'clock?" Graham shook Mark's hand," And welcome back."

"Five o'clock. Thanks. It's great to be back among friends."

Wendy had sorted his papers into various stacks. Research materials, annual reports from dozens of Latin American companies in one heap, back copies of Euromoney, The Economist, The Bank Credit Analyst and dozens of investment newsletters and the Financial Times in another. Business and personal correspondence were laid out on his desk in two neat piles. The message light on his phone was flashing. There were one hundred and eighty two unread messages on his email. He'd ignored his laptop since Nancy's death.

Mark walked to the rear door of the office and pulled over a large empty wheelie bin marked *Recycling.* He placed it beside his desk and, with a practised eye, rapidly triaged the piles of paper into *must read, look again* and *junk.* In fifteen minutes he'd filled the bin and reduced the materials by ninety per cent. He then cleared his electronic in-tray by deleting scores of messages, mainly daily research updates from brokers, price feeds from banks and obsolete administrative memos from CSF and Appletree.

One email message caught his eye. It was two days old :

> *Mark, On a golfing tour of Europe and wonder if you would care to join our party at the Hotel Eugenie in Biarritz for the weekend of June 2nd. Yours ever, Skye Shilson*

"Holy cow," he whistled, "here's a turn of events if ever I saw one." He studied the screen again. He had so many unanswered questions for Shilson. Was he out on bail? A barge churned under Greyfriars Bridge, gunwales awash in the ebbing tide. He tapped out his reply :

Skye, sorry so slow to get back to you. I'm not a golfer. How's Steve?
Mark

Shortly afterwards he received the following response :

Steve and I have separated but if you can make it to Biarritz I would be pleased to welcome you as my guest. Golf not necessary. Yours ever, Skye Shilson

Skye, most unfortunately I am occupied that weekend.
Mark

That's fine. Just let me know when you're free. I'll send over the Gulfstream. Perhaps you can join me for lunch in Paris sometime.
Skye

How did you get to keep the Gulfstream?

Mark was in no hurry for an answer.